DECOY 17

ROBERT VALLIER

Robert Vallier comes from one of the world's most distinguished musical families and spent much of his life in music and theatre production, and publishing. For his close friend the late Sir Patrick Moore, he created the *Into Space!* series of theatre lectures and books, which he published. He was responsible for collecting and sending via sponsors British Airways over 5½ tons of catalogued books as working libraries to underprivileged schools in South Africa.

Robert Vallier raised his three children as a single parent, juggling tour dates around kids' play dates, sports events and birthday parties. After his children were grown, Robert Vallier committed himself to realising a lifelong ambition of becoming an author. His first book *Spider 2-3* became an Amazon #1 Best Seller.

Robert Vallier holds a Private Pilot's Licence and for many years has flown aircraft in the UK, USA, around South Africa and in Europe. When he isn't working on a book, or enveloped in music, he can be found up in the air flying, or at the home ranch thinking about the next Big Adventure.

www.robertvallier.com

ROBERT VALLIER

DECOY 17

Jaguar Publishing Inc

Jaguar Publishing Inc
3103 Hulmeville Road, Suite 200
Bensalem, PA 19020
USA

ISBN: 978-0-9908811-5-5

www.RobertVallier.com

This Edition first published by Jaguar Publishing Inc *Publishers* 2021.

Cover Design: Damonza

For Becky and Tatsy

CONTENTS

ACKNOWLEDGEMENTS

Many have suffered helping me along the journey.

My thanks to Diana, Becky, Tatiana, James Crabbe, Ian Hoare, Nick Gambino, Brian Eagles, James Cherry, Pam Tabor, Gavin Ashdown, Mark and Mai Richardson, Sue Constantino and last but certainly not least Mike Hollister.

Each has given kindly and generously of their own time and thought, and to each I am once again most grateful.

Robert Vallier

www.robertvallier.com

PART ONE

THE FIRST DAY

1

CHALK AND CHELSEA

IT WAS TIME. The old lady pushed herself up unsteadily from her favourite armchair and walked across the room. She unhooked the dog lead from the back of the door and smiled at the little Scottie that was already wagging its tail. She nodded.

"Come on then."

The evening air was crisp following the setting of the sun but the sky was not yet dark, and the few low clouds glowed a dull deep red. The old lady crossed the road and set out up the hill, like she had a thousand times before, enjoying the greenery of the gentle slope and the roughness of the sea to her right. Her grey hair blew in the wind and she pulled her coat tighter. Her feet always hurt nowadays, but the doctor had said it was better to keep walking than not, even if there was discomfort.

The path ahead was deserted. As the old lady reached the lamppost about halfway up the hill she glanced at a house on the left. A man was sitting in his bay window looking out and he spotted her, like he often did. She raised her hand in greeting and he waved back. It was a pleasant, caring neighbourhood.

A few minutes more and she reached the top of the hill. She sat on the bench, tied the dog to one of its arms and looked out over the water. There were two big tankers on the horizon. The old lady wondered where they were going. She missed the excitement of travel, her journeys around the world, the challenge of her work. As the years had gone by she had embraced a happy family life; but she had never quite given up the old ways.

The Scottie looked up adoringly, tail wagging, her friend for twelve years. She stroked his head and he licked her hand, making her smile.

"Be a good boy," she said, and stood.

The old lady walked ahead a few feet. She raised her arms and held them level like a cross, enjoying the breeze again, gazing once more at the ships. Then she took a deep breath, closed her eyes and leant forwards. She toppled off the edge and fell silently five hundred feet onto the rocks below.

The chalk cliffs of Beachy Head had claimed another victim.

The frantic barking of the little Scottie shattered the stillness of the dusk.

≈

Fifty miles north, a man stepped out of a taxi, opened the door to an apartment block and took the elevator to his flat. London was enjoying a typical Saturday night but he was glad to be home. It was 1am. He chucked the keys down onto the plate by the front door, shrugged off his coat and walked into the kitchen. He poured himself a whisky, dropped in some ice and went through into the lounge. The city lights bounced off the Thames and gently lit the room. He stood by the desk and looked out.

If they only knew, he said to himself, sipping at the whisky.

He didn't hear the intruder; it was the smell. A different scent, food on the breath; suddenly he knew he wasn't alone. He put the drink down nonchalantly, then spun round, reaching for the gun under his armpit. But he was too late. The intruder fired his weapon. The force of the shot flung the man backwards as the bullet hit, breaking a rib, then puncturing his right lung and severing his spine. He rolled along the top of the desk and collapsed face down onto the parquet floor.

The intruder knelt by the man. He felt his neck. There was no pulse. The lifeless eyes stared ahead. The intruder gave a little smirk and put the gun away. He rummaged through his victim's pockets, pulled something out, then quietly left the dead man's apartment.

The man on the floor was still, but suddenly his body jerked. His heart auto-resuscitated[1] and pumped again. He gasped and choked violently, his eyes blinked and he regained consciousness. He was in agony, he couldn't move his legs and his breathing faltered, spluttering through the blood in his mouth.

But he remembered what had happened. He raised his eyes to glance across the floor. The smashed glass, the streak of whisky, the broken table lamp; the light bulb that had popped out and rolled a few feet.

One last effort… He slid his right arm across and reached for a fallen pen. His fingers pulled at an envelope.

Twenty seconds later the man died. The pen was still in his hand.

He had scrawled: *'DECOY 17'*.

---

[1] *Known as Lazarus Syndrome. There have been forty-one recorded occurrences since 1982.*

2

INCOMING NEWS

JIM PEREGRINE HAD been enjoying dinner with his two companions at the start of what was to be a wonderful month on St Lucia in the Caribbean. His uncle, Sir William Barton-Banes, the British High Commissioner to the Island, had loaned his favourite nephew the official residence, a rather imposing traditional mansion with five suites built on a private beach, and JP was now happily ensconced there with Stephanie Raughton and Anna Kepling. It was time for a well-earned and much-needed rest.

Stephanie and Anna had played vital roles with him in the last three months. The terrorist mastermind, Barakah Malekka, an Iranian with immense wealth and an unpleasant personal agenda against the West, had been planning a massive attack in a plot codenamed Spider 2-3. Fortunately the deadly conspiracy had been defeated. It had been close-run though, with success achieved only after JP's clever planning, much international action and considerable sacrifice and courage from the three of them. They now shared a unique camaraderie.

The SAS raid, codenamed Operation Waterhole, on Malekka's private residence and headquarters at Cuttle Cove to neutralise his forces had been decisive, and the collaboration of the governments of six countries that followed brought the terrorist plot to a close in the public eye. Everyone at the complex had been rounded up; interrogation of personnel was ongoing, as was MI6's clinical examination of the files, papers, electronic items and computers that had, much to their professional delight, been left intact and seized.

Details of the raid and the reasons for it, and the huge

explosion at the premises, were highly confidential and had to be restricted; a different story was given to the world's media - that a terrorist cell had been trying to implement a major attack against the West but had accidentally blown themselves up in the process.

In fact, they had been trying to kill three million people.

There were two remaining problems, though, for which the cover story wasn't satisfactory. First, somehow it had come out that an Englishman had been heavily involved. His name wasn't known; only a nickname: *The Falcon.* The story had gone viral in the media around the world and was only now beginning to die down. It couldn't go away soon enough for JP, who preferred the safety of anonymity. The second problem - and this had not been made public - was that Malekka had been able to flee the complex just as the net was being thrown over it, using an escape route built into Cuttle Cove's design. Everyone knew that could be a problem in the future.

Jim Peregrine didn't think it was a matter for immediate concern. Yet, when the dinner was interrupted by a phone call from his old friend and boss at the SAS, and now Deputy Head of MI6, Charlie Melton, he felt a sense of foreboding as he excused himself from his guests and went to take the call.

The Falcon reached the drawing room. He sat down, and picked up the telephone. "Hello, Charlie?"

"JP. I'm sorry to interrupt your evening," said Melton on the scrambled line.

"No, not at all, we've almost finished the dinner, just on to desserts. What's up?"

"I'm afraid I have some bad news. Dave Tilsen's been killed. Murdered."

"What?" replied JP, "oh God, not Dave."

"I'm afraid so."

JP sighed heavily, squeezing the leather arm of the

Chesterfield. "What happened?"

"He'd just got home. Apparently someone was waiting for him in the flat. Jenny came back from her mother's around 2am and found him sprawled on the floor in the living room." Charlie Melton's voice, five thousand miles away in London, was grim and tense. "Terrible thing for a wife to see. Blood everywhere."

"I thought he was at Cuttle Cove."

"He was. He was heading up our analysis team."

"So what was he doing in London?"

"He found something, JP. It looks like Spider 2-3 wasn't the only game in town. There's a second scheme, running alongside it, or planned as a sequel. We don't know how advanced it is or even what sort of thing it is. Dave was about to leave to follow up a lead."

"Do we know *anything* about it?"

"We have a name. A title. 'Stingray'."

"'Stingray'? That sounds ominous. Which means it's probably deadly. And if it's half as well planned as Spider it'll be another nightmare."

"Yes, that's why I'm calling." Melton paused. "JP, I think you should come back. It would appear it's not over."

"Shit," he said quietly. "So much for the holiday."

"I know. There'll be others. The Yanks have sent an F-15 to St Lucia. It should be landing in about an hour. By the time you get here, the CSEs[2] will be heavily into it and you can see the place for yourself. And the note."

"The note? He left a note?"

"Yes." Melton paused. "And… be careful, JP. You're probably a target now, and the girls. It won't be like in Cape Town. This time they'll be aiming to kill. I'll fill you in on it

---

[2] *Crime Scene Examiners.*

all when you're here."

They spoke for another minute, before JP replaced the phone onto its pad and sat back, thinking. He crossed his legs, pulled at the black bow tie and undid the top button of his evening shirt. Christ, here we go again, he thought. Well, the break would have to wait. The stack of items, files and papers found at Cuttle Cove were apparently light on specifics - much had been in a shorthand code known only to Malekka, and the computer files were heavily encrypted - but had revealed enough to convince MI6 that there was another threat, either already in or nearing action.

That was something neither he nor anyone else had foreseen.

A second scheme by Malekka would doubtless be as intricately planned and as finely woven in detail as the first, and have been years in the making with global consequences if successful. And this one might work where the other didn't.

Especially as we know nothing about it, thought JP.

He saw the butler pass in the hallway and called out. "Nawson?"

"Yes, sir?"

"We'll be skipping the dessert. I have to leave. Thirty minutes. And the two ladies will be going tomorrow."

"Very good, sir."

"I want you to take me to the airport - my flight should be there shortly. Then I'd like you to stay with the ladies and help all you can until they're safely on board a plane. My two guys will be around as well, and they'll travel back to London with them as security."

"Yes, sir."

"Could you serve some coffee first please. Straight away."

"Yes, sir."

Nothing ruffled Nawson, thought JP. He could have said he was leaving for the moon and the response would have been the same. JP walked back into the dining room. The women each had an open envelope on the table in front of them that contained a substantial cheque, donated from his clandestine gains from Spider 2-3. The gesture had hit them with so much astonishment and surprise a few minutes ago while JP went to take the call from London that their eyes were still filled with amazement and delight. But the celebratory mood abated swiftly as they saw the look on his face.

"What is it, Jimmy?" said Stephanie. "What did Charlie want?"

"We need to talk. Forget the envelopes, we have to put all that aside for now."

"Forget that amount of money?!" said Stephanie, still with a little humour, "I'm not sure we can!"

"You have to. Seriously," said JP. The coldness of his reply shocked them both. "We'll come back to the other stuff. But for now, you have to listen to this."

"Why, what's up?" asked Anna.

He sat at the table once more. Their humour and excitement had all but vanished.

"Charlie says that the team at Cuttle Cove has discovered that Spider 2-3 wasn't the only plot."

"What?" said Stephanie, pushing her long blonde hair out of the way behind her shoulders.

"You mean there was something else?" said Anna incredulously.

"Yes," said the Falcon. "There is something else."

"Oh, no," said Anna, just as Stephanie came out with a more colourful "Shit," followed by, "What?"

"We don't know yet," said JP, "but it seems that Malekka had another plot running parallel, a backup, I suppose, maybe, or perhaps Spider was half of his plan, and this is the other half. In his hurry to escape while trying to kill everyone else around him he left some details buried in papers and files that

Charlie and his team found and identified, both from Malekka's rooms and the plane that was getting ready to leave. They clearly relate to another operation. And - brace yourself Stephie - Charlie called because Dave Tilsen has been found on the floor of his flat with a bullet in him."

The women let out a gasp. *"Dave Tilsen?"* said Stephanie, horrified. "Not *Dave*, oh no." She put her hand to her mouth. She had known him for as long as she had been at MI6.

"I'm afraid so," JP continued. "Apparently Jenny found him two hours ago. Charlie has put the team back on high alert. He reckons that Malekka has regrouped and is active again. And, as he's probably out for revenge, we all have to be careful, as we'll certainly be targets."

Nawson brought in and served the coffee.

"Thank you, Nawson," said JP, and waited until the butler had left. "So - the holiday is cancelled. Or, mine is anyway; I have to go back."

"Well, I'm coming too," said Stephanie.

"And me," said Anna.

JP smiled. "I was going to talk to you about my plan - what I wanted to do after Spider 2-3 now that it's ended, or so I thought, and I was going to ask if you'd like to join me. But it seems that events have taken over..." He sipped at the coffee. The two women glanced at each other silently, then looked back at JP, waiting. "Clearly, the job's not finished," he continued. "However, you're on three month's leave, Stephie; and," turning to Anna, "you're not even part of MI6 so you don't have to get involved at all either."

JP wasn't sure how the women would react. Spider 2-3 had ended just days ago. When he had first brought his counter-terrorism plan to Charlie Melton at MI6, their agent, Stephanie Raughton, had at once stepped on board. She was twenty-six, smart, had no qualms about using her considerable beauty as a weapon, was an expert with a handgun and skilled in hand to hand fighting. Yet she still seemed to be the epitome of the girl next door; she was a gentle caring person, her cheeks blushed when she laughed and long eyelashes danced over sparkling emerald eyes. JP had been drawn to her at a Christmas party and they had been dating ever since. She knew his plan had been conceived with her as an integral part. She had put herself into harm's way to trap Malekka, had endured much, and after Spider's successful conclusion was now meant to be having three months' vacation.

Then there was Anna Kepling. She was a little younger than Stephanie; Russian, the daughter of JP's close friend and former tutor at Cambridge, who had first alerted JP to the danger and who had lost his life in the process. She was a former soldier in the Russian forces, highly intelligent, multilingual and had a deep knowledge of the Bolshoi and Tchaikovsky as much as ABBA and western democracy. The two girls had bonded within hours of their first meeting. Her figure was slim with a rounded face of light pale skin and wild blonde hair, but in spite of an enchanting smile that played constantly around full lips, the deep sadness in her blue eyes betrayed her. For Anna carried a heart shattered not only by the death of her beloved father but also the assassination of her fiancé, both by Malekka's cronies. Her part in Spider 2-3 in Moscow had been essential, but highly dangerous.

The Falcon needn't have worried. He had chosen his future business partners well.

"I'm already involved, JP," said Anna, "and if you're going to hit at this madman again, then I'm coming too. We Russian girls don't quit easily." The other two smiled briefly. "Anyway, I owe it to my father. And," she added quietly, "to one other person."

"Yes," said Stephanie, "to hell with the holiday, we can do that later, and everything else. If Malekka's on the loose again we must stop him. Count me in, JP." She put her hand on his across the table and smiled. How I love that smile, thought the Falcon fleetingly. And the sparkling emerald eyes…

"Thank you. Ok. So, put the envelopes away. We'll pick up where we left off later. For now, well, we must get a move on."

The SAS hadn't christened him The Falcon because of his surname. JP's speed of execution in covert activities had earned him the title, and it was matched with a ruthlessness that was often shocking. When the danger of Spider 2-3 had first arisen, he had seen how to defeat it and hadn't hesitated in putting his girlfriend into harm's way. What sort of man am I to do that, JP had asked himself repeatedly. Part of him loathed it; yet it had been the only option. He was six foot three, had black hair above a toughened tanned face with a square jaw and a powerful physique. The ruggedness was softened by laughing hazel eyes, and a charismatic smile carried a hint of danger. He had declined Melton's invitation to work with him at MI6 but JP's abilities and integrity made him a natural bearer of the Fifth Rubric[3] for MI6 and the British Government. He was freer outside the Firm, and was a more dangerous, unofficial operative because of it.

"When do we leave," said Anna.

"I go in about thirty minutes. There's an F-15 arriving for me soon. You two can get the next flight off the Island, which won't be until tomorrow now. Nawson will be here and stay with you to help all he can, then get you to the airport. The

---

[3] *The Fifth Rubric is an international covenant allowing specified personnel covert operational ability with unrestricted use of firearms at home and in signatory countries abroad, providing maximum security clearance, full co-operation of all internal policing and military forces and immunity from any prosecution for the bearer of the Rubric. It is rarely invoked outside a state of war or extreme national tension. The archaic meaning of rubric is 'red ochre', or 'written in red'. The colour of blood.*

lads will be on hand too, and they'll travel back with you."

"Ok. Do you have a plan?"

"Of course he's got a plan," said Stephie to Anna, before JP could open his mouth to answer. She turned to look at him. "The Falcon's always got a plan."

JP breathed in deeply. "Well, actually, yes, as it happens, I do have the makings of a plan." The women smiled. "Ok, so this is what I think we should do…"

≈

Thirty minutes later, JP was ready. He had swapped the dinner jacket for a black T-shirt, chino trousers with dark trainers and a leather jacket. He would be travelling light. Nawson was at the wheel of the Rolls-Royce and was driving at speed; Sean Mullen, one of the two men that JP had hired as security, both a friend and formerly SAS, sat in the front with him.

The arrival at Hewanorra International of one of the most advanced military jets in America's armed forces was unusual nowadays, although the airport had seen plenty of USAF aircraft over the years as Beane Army Airfield, until its conversion to a civil aviation facility.

Hewanorra's Assistant Manager, Beverly Matthews, was standing at the terminal entrance waiting. JP said his goodbyes - a quick handshake with Nawson and Mullen, a peck on the cheek to the girls. He turned to be escorted into the terminal but Stephanie pulled him back, and said, "You take care of yourself, ok?", then kissed him passionately on the lips, holding him tight and pressing into him. As they separated, the Falcon said, "Mmmm, does this mean I should go away more often?!" Stephanie responded with an "Oh…," bashing his chest with the base of her clenched fist. He smiled; and then he was gone.

He met the pilot, suited up and they walked out to the F-

15E. The pilot helped JP buckle up in the rear seat, which was usually the domain of the Weapon Systems Officer, and then climbed into the front. He started the engines, obtained clearance from ATC at the Terminal, taxied along Runway 28 to the end, and turned round ready for departure on what had now become Runway 10. The engines screamed, the fighter surged down the tarmac, took off, then suddenly tilted up and climbed almost vertically into the sky, watched by JP's companions from outside the terminal.

At fifty thousand feet the aircraft carrying the Falcon back to London went supersonic, tearing through the air at over eighteen hundred miles an hour, leaving a sonic boom fifty miles wide chasing along the Atlantic Ocean far below.

≈

In Eastbourne, England, two policemen gained access to the small detached house using a bunch of universal skeleton keys. They stood in the hallway for a few seconds, then walked into the lounge. They looked at each other in amazed silence, and turned their heads to stare again.

The hallway and lounge had been totally ransacked.

As they were about to discover, so had the entire premises.

≈

On the way back to the house in the Rolls, the two women sat silently, separated from the men in front by the soundproofed glass partition. Then Anna spoke.

"So what was that all about?" she said nonchalantly.

"What do you mean?" said Stephie.

"What you went through during Spider - I know it made you pretty neutral. And, well, you've been very cool with him. That didn't look like you were neutral any more…"

Stephie shrugged her shoulders and stared out of the window. "I guess it's the thought of that crazy Malekka on the rampage again, it seems to have woken things up inside me all at once."

Anna nodded, then looked away. "Yes, well I would say it's definitely done that," she said teasingly.

The lush greenery of tropical ferns and tall palm trees permeated by intermittent sidewalks sped by in the darkness of the night.

Anna couldn't see the little smile and slight reddening of her friend's cheeks.

3
THE FIRST ACTION

BARAKAH MALEKKA HAD been almost deranged in his fury when he made his escape just over a week ago. He had been thwarted in Spider 2-3 in the final few minutes. He didn't know how, or by whom; but the sudden new circumstances - gunfire and helicopters arriving - were enough for him to execute his escape plan, which he had built into his original design of Cuttle Cove. The elevator dropped him a hundred feet; then the high speed monorail took him at ninety miles an hour due north and five hundred feet beneath the sea in the tunnel to the man-made subaquatic cave. He boarded the enhanced powered-up Aurora-5 submarine, joining the two men already aboard who had been on readiness watch, Ghazi and Zaim, and who had sprung into action the moment the automated klaxon, tripped immediately the elevator started its descent, warned of the imminent emergency departure. Twenty seconds later they were submerged and passed through the cave's dual underwater gates, emerging in the open sea some eighty fathoms down and one and a half miles away from Cuttle Cove.

They continued north at three knots, following the contour of the seabed, reaching a maximum depth of four thousand feet. In eight hours the submarine surfaced twenty-nine miles from its base and rendezvoused with the luxury yacht *Free Spirit*. They were quickly aboard and moved at once to the readied helicopter. Ghazi dismissed the duty pilot, powered up the aircraft himself and within five minutes the Bell 429 was airborne, for a ten-minute flight to a small airstrip on the Turkish mainland. The three men stepped into the waiting Gulfstream G650, which departed immediately. The pilot amended the flight plan in the air and in another forty-five minutes the G650 crossed into the safety of Iranian airspace.

The Gulfstream touched down comfortably on the private airstrip at Barakah Malekka's principal home, a sumptuous palace thirty miles southwest of Tehran. He was welcomed by staff and several women. He bathed luxuriously, relaxed, ate, enjoyed the pleasures of some of the girls and then retired to his private bedroom suite.

He had not smiled once since leaving Cuttle Cove.

Although the extreme stress of the last twenty-four hours began to abate, and he was able to sit and begin to think calmly, his eyes were heavy, and his thin lips continued to convey his fury with no words. He sat back on the couch.

What had happened? How had he been tracked? How had he been discovered? Had he been betrayed? If so, by whom? They would pay, and pay dearly, he vowed. Years of planning, years of effort, plus a small fortune, all for nothing.

Still, I have the other one, he said to himself.

Then, his heart skipped a beat… and Malekka cursed…

In his frantic panic to escape he had left the codes behind. The phone. *And the micro SD card.*

He stood. He ran his hands through his jet black hair, pacing back and forth. He looked up at the ceiling, filled his lungs and stretched out his arms, shaking his clenched fists.

He let out a deep frustrated roar…

≈

The F-15E refuelled mid-air twice on its way to London, touching down in less than three hours, at 7am at RAF Northolt on the outskirts of West London. A car was waiting, and forty minutes later the Falcon was outside Dave Tilsen's flat. JP showed his ID to the policemen at the entrance, took the elevator to the top floor and presented his ID again to the two officers by the front door.

"If you're looking for Major Melton, sir, he's in the apartment next door," said the taller one, a burly young man with alert eyes that darted everywhere and missed nothing.

"Yes, I am," said JP.

"This way, sir," and the officer walked him a few feet down the hallway to the door of the adjoining flat, and rang the bell. A woman answered.

"Hello, my name is Peregrine, I'm looking for..." and the door opened wider and Melton was standing there.

"Hi, JP. This is Mrs Tina Wenton. Tina - a friend of mine, Jim Peregrine."

"How do you do, Mrs Wenton."

"Mr Peregrine." The woman was about fifty. She was still in her pink dressing gown, her hair was a little bedraggled but her eyes were soft and sympathetic, and slightly red, JP noticed. "Come in, please. Major, you take him through for me."

The men greeted each other in a quick bear hug as the Falcon stepped into the flat, then Melton led the way into the drawing room. It was small, comfortable, the walls were papered, a TV and small table and chairs were on one side, a large couch on the other. The lighting was low. Lieutenant Jane Chapman, Melton's senior assistant, was sitting with Jenny, trying to console her. Jenny looked up as JP walked over; he crouched onto his knees in front of her, and they hugged.

"Oh Jimmy," she cried, the tears streaming down her face. "What did he do to deserve this?" She had a small frame that now seemed brittle as JP hugged her, its life energy tragically depleted, the side strands of the brown hair that fell around her face wet from heartbreak.

"Jenny, I'm so, so sorry," he replied. "He was a good man. And a good friend." He hugged her close again. "I promise you, we're going to find out who did this."

"We were so happy. He loved his work with Charlie at the Firm, he was such a decent, kind person. It doesn't make any sense."

Still embracing her, the Falcon gave a grim smile at Jane who nodded back, adding a quiet, "Hey, JP."

JP shook his head in disbelief, anger in his eyes. After the action the three men had seen, the years together; for Dave to be murdered in his own home was a bad way to go.

"Jenny," said Melton kindly, "just sit with Jane again for a while, let me talk with JP and fill him in."

They left the distraught woman, excused themselves from their kind hostess and stepped into the hallway. They walked back to the other flat, donned some full covering suits, masks, gloves and overshoes then stepped through the doorway into Tilsen's apartment. The forensic team had locked the place down and were examining each room in detail. They were walked along some carefully-placed surface cover into the lounge, in which the twisted figure of a man lay on the floor in a wide pool of blood.

"Luckily Jenny was sensible enough to know not to touch anything," said Melton. "There was no fight. It was murder, pure and simple. There was only one shot, fired from against the wall by the door, and the killer left. It may be there was a lot of noise in the fall and he, or she, wanted to make a quick getaway. Dave didn't even get his gun out. And look at this."

Charlie Melton squatted down and JP followed. They stared at the messy lettering on the envelope.

"DECOY 17," said JP. "What the devil is that?"

"We haven't the slightest idea."

JP put his hand on Dave's shoulder. They had been comrades in Afghanistan - the Falcon in the SAS, Tilsen in Intelligence - and were good friends. He had been an outstanding spook; a brilliant mind, excelling in data and electronics analysis, always calm, and could adopt other guises so completely and convincingly it was bordering on pathological schizophrenia. The men in his unit often wondered which person went home to Jenny, and if it was the same one she had married. JP smiled, and gave a final squeeze.

Then they stood, thanked the lead CSE and when at the front door, removed their protective clothing, which was placed into a plastic bag for later analysis in case anything had inadvertently been picked up. They returned to the other apartment. Mrs Wenton let them in, then left the men to talk on their own by the door. They spoke quietly.

"You know he was overseeing the analysis work at Cuttle Cove, trying to piece the fragments together," said Melton. "He was on to something. He had discovered an activity that carried the name 'Setingerai'[4] - the best English translation came out as 'Stingray', as I told you on the phone. Twenty-four hours ago at Cuttle Cove, he came across someone that had a contact… a person he should meet. Yesterday evening he arrived back in London. As soon as we learned of his killing we were round here fast but also started the usual internal searches. Dave wrote very little down; but there was an entry in his Firm calendar. Here's a printout."

Melton brought out an envelope from his inside jacket pocket and handed it to JP.

"It's a plane ticket. To Panama City. Not Florida; Central America, leaving later today, 2pm. It's all we have, together with the memo - a scheduled meeting with a man, and the company name and address. Whatever else Tilsen knew, he didn't have time to tell us."

JP looked at the contents. "It was enough to get him

---

4 *The Arabic word is:* يارغنيتس.

killed."

"Yes."

"Had he been to Panama for you before?"

"No. The first we knew about it was when Jane checked his credit card and saw the purchase, and then we looked at his internal calendar. So far that's all we have. No notes; nothing."

The two men looked at each other in silence.

"You want it?" asked Melton.

JP nodded grimly. "You bet I do."

"Ok good. I thought you would. Whoever killed Dave did so because they didn't want him to make that rendezvous. And so someone should keep it for him."

"Not as Jim Peregrine though."

Melton nodded in agreement.

"Can you get the papers ready in time?"

"Er, well I thought you'd be up for it. So we've already put it in motion," said his friend. "I reckon it will be in on time."

JP smiled. "Good, Charlie." Then he continued, "I don't know if I'm meant to be the seventeenth decoy, or who the other sixteen were, or what the decoy was for anyway. But the trail starts there, and I'll follow it. I'll see what I can find."

The two men went next door to talk with Jenny and the Lieutenant. They outlined their intentions. Jane Chapman excused herself and left at once, to chase up the Home Office and make other arrangements.

"Charlie… JP… I don't care how you do it," said Jenny, "but you have to find out who did… this… thing, who killed Dave. You have to." Her eyes were red and puffed, her hands shaking. "And, get them. Please, just get them."

"We're on to it," said Melton. "I promise you, we want the same."

"I have to go, if I'm going to make that flight," said JP. "Jenny, I'm really sorry to rush."

"It's ok, I'll be fine." She put her arms first around JP; he hugged her hard, and then Charlie followed suit. The newly widowed Mrs Tilsen was joined by a policewoman for comfort. And her mother was already on her way.

Once in the elevator going down Melton said to JP, "Can you be in at around ten, or maybe a bit after, for whatever we can get together on this for you?"

"Ok. Charlie, what is Malekka up to this time? The other one was bad enough, and if this plot is anything like that you can bet it'll be just as deadly and as well planned. It's not going to be easy, this time we're starting with nothing. What is he trying to destroy now?"

"God only knows. But it's clear he was running Stingray alongside Spider. And it's either active already or about to be." They exited the building.

"Christ, the man's a nightmare. It's a shame we didn't get him the first time."

"Isn't that the truth. We were close though." Melton got into the back seat of his car and lowered the window. "I'll see you later." He turned to the driver. "Ok George, let's go." The car sped off heading for the Albert Embankment.

JP walked over to his own transport. The sun was already well in the sky as the Falcon's car drove him to Claridge's in Brook Street. The low grey morning clouds reflected the sombre mood of the day.

Along the way, the driver said, "Sir, while I was outside the flat waiting, a car passed by three times. It pulled up for a while a few streets behind, but went by one more time as you came out."

"Really," said JP, more concerned than he was letting on. "That's interesting."

"Yes, sir. I'm not sure, sir, but I would say you've been photographed. I've already messaged in to Mr Melton."

"Good work, thank you, Ben." Shit, he thought. Score one

to Malekka.

"You're welcome, sir. And, we're being followed. The silver Lexus behind. Darkened windows. It's sitting five blocks back. I reckon when you get out it'll go by with a camera clicking."

"Thank you, again."

"All part of the service, sir. We'll pick them up in a few minutes."

When they arrived at Claridge's JP opened the door to get out. Sure enough, the Lexus drove by as JP stood up outside. He bent down and put his head inside the car. He looked at Ben, and nodded discreetly.

"So - just how many pairs of eyes do you have?"

The driver smiled at the compliment. JP closed the door.

4

IN IRAN

MALEKKA'S FURY HAD lasted a full twenty-four hours. Servants had rushed into his room after they had heard the roar, which had been followed with the sound of several items' being thrown around the room and crashing against walls. He had yelled at them to get out and leave him alone. He was inconsolable and word quickly spread among the staff on the estate to stay clear of their master.

Finally he resorted to some pills and - most unusual for him - some other substance that together calmed him down, sent him to sleep and indulged his body's and his mind's need for a separation from the elements of stress that had so possessed him.

He remained semi-comatose for two days.

On the third day following his return to Iran, Malekka rose in the morning and decided he wanted no more pills and no more hashish. He dismissed the two females who had entertained him the previous night, bathed on his own, ate lightly, drank lots of water, slept on and off, and by the evening he was able to think clearly again.

At 6pm Malekka was seated in his huge luxurious lounge, its soft furnishings a plush red, and gold for ornaments, picture frames, table rims and even light switches. He rose and crossed to a small table, and pressed a button protruding from the top of a box. Within ten seconds there was a knock on the door.

"Come," said Malekka.

A maid in a plain black burka entered.

"Yes, sir?" she asked.

"I want some coffee. And, I want you to find Latif Yameen and ask him to come to see me immediately."

"Yes, sir, right away."

The maid scurried off.

Fifteen minutes later, as Malekka was sipping his coffee, there was another knock on the door and this time it was Yameen.

"Come in, Latif, sit, and have some coffee."

"Yes, sir, thank you." Yameen was around thirty years of age, a good six foot tall with a powerful athletic frame, yet he moved with grace and style, and was full of authority and competence. His dark brown eyes, sharp and alert, were set in a rugged face below wavy black hair parted on the right. He was a soldier, and a leader of men. He walked to his master and sat on the sofa opposite, reached forward for the coffee and filled a cup. "How are you now, sir?"

Malekka smiled. "I am feeling better, thank you. Something went wrong, something terrible. Everything was in place, it was all going to plan, and then there was gunfire, and some helicopters, and everything collapsed."

"Yes, sir, I had heard something of the sort from Ghazi, about the emergency escape, but no details, as he and Zaim were with you in the submarine."

Malekka paused, then spoke again. "Latif, I want first to congratulate you on the execution of your part of the plan." Yameen beamed. "You carried out your duties magnificently, and your team, and I want to thank you."

"You're very kind sir. It was an honour. It went like clockwork, and the boys behaved very well. We had no problems at all. And after the drop we made our way back here with no difficulties."

Malekka nodded. "Yes, you did well. But there was no success of the project. I don't know what happened yet, and I have to find out. And there is Stingray, which must be initiated. Unfortunately in my surprise and ensuing confusion, and my effort to escape, there have been some things left behind which Stingray needs."

He sipped some more coffee. Yameen sat quietly and waited for his master to continue.

"I have to assume that all personnel left behind have been neutralised. They are either dead, or detained. I have to consider this is so also for Haddad and Raboud. And therefore I want you to take over from Raboud and return to being my First Assistant. You trained the other two anyway, and were their immediate superior officer. Now I need your strength and wisdom close to me once more."

"Yes, sir," said Yameen, who could not hide the pride in his voice. "It will be a pleasure to do as you ask, sir."

"Thank you, Latif. I want you to pick one other from your team, who can replace Haddad."

"Duha," said Yameen without hesitation. "He is strong, loyal, intelligent, and his English is perfect, which might be helpful. He is also fluent in French and Spanish."

"Good," said Malekka. "Very well then. Tell him, and get him prepared."

"Yes, sir."

"Now, next, is a little dangerous. I need to get information from Cuttle Cove. So, I want you to send Zaim and Ghazi. They will have to improvise and find a way to infiltrate the area, and discover what they can about what happened, how and who was responsible. I am not so worried about what the infidels will find about Stingray on my computer, it's heavily encrypted, it will be meaningless to them or at least take them weeks to decipher, and I believe our obtaining that back would be impossible. I would *like* to have the phone if it can be obtained. But, as the computers are lost, I *need* the phone's micro SD card, I cannot initiate Stingray without it. Unless I have all of the data collected again, but that would be difficult to do and will take time; an inconvenience, though not impossible. However, and perhaps more importantly, there is some narrative information on the card which, if deciphered, would enable our enemies to understand what our project is and so possibly intercept our efforts. We must get the card back; or find it and destroy it."

They discussed the outline of a plan. Then Yameen was dismissed, to meet with Zaim and Ghazi. The planning went on through dinner and into the night, but at the end they had the details worked out.

Since 1974, when Turkey invaded Cyprus, the island had been split in two. The southern and west part, the Republic of Cyprus, had close ties with Greece; the Turkish Republic of Northern Cyprus was in the north and east. The Republic of Cyprus was Christian; Northern Cyprus, Muslim. Malekka had many friends in Turkey, which had been happy to accommodate the establishing of his estate, Cuttle Cove, in Northern Cyprus.

Following the action of Operation Waterhole in Spider 2-3, MI6 commenced its investigation of seized material, and began to send items on to London. The interrogation of captured personnel was deemed best conducted within the confines of Cuttle Cove itself, as Cyprus was a small island and the estate had been well confined by the large security force. However, the collaboration of governments had meant that, while the investigation of Malekka's base was headed up by MI6 and military services sent from the British headquarters in the Republic of Cyprus to the south, fifty percent of the security forces had by agreement been drawn from Kerýneia in Northern Cyprus, where Turkey maintained close to thirty thousand military personnel. In fact, Malekka had several contacts within those. Two, unbeknown to MI6, had managed to become part of the combined security forces at Cuttle Cove.

Zaim and Ghazi had left for Northern Cyprus in the Mediterranean first thing the following morning. By 3pm the next day they had met up with the resident operative, who was still free and mobile. Coded contact was made by text message with the friends in the Turkish army within the security forces. By 5pm they were close to the Cuttle Cove facility and began casual talking to the locals, as they looked for a way to infiltrate across the heavily-protected cordon swung around the property.

Zaim and Ghazi decided the best method into the estate was from the sea. The next afternoon they took a fishing boat out and Zaim quietly slipped over the side in scuba gear. As the sun set, he was on the shores of Cuttle Cove.

It didn't take him long. Disguised as an officer of the Turkish army Zaim met with the contacts and explained what was required. Loyalty to Malekka still existed, or at least to his money, of which a considerable amount was made available. The information discreetly materialised. In another twenty-four hours Zaim slipped back into the water and rejoined Ghazi. They combined the information they had each gathered, judged it to be sufficient and departed on the earliest flight they could, routing via two other countries back to Malekka in Iran and arriving the next day.

Malekka had listened to their report intently. At the end, he knew much of what had transpired at Cuttle Cove, although he still didn't know how his enterprise had been discovered or how he had been betrayed, or by whom. He knew that a man called David Tilsen was heading up the intelligence debrief and analysis of the computers, files and other materials found at the centre. He discovered that Tilsen had come across a cell phone with a micro SD card, and had separated them as standard procedure. He knew the phone had already been sent to London, as had the computers earlier. And, more importantly, he knew some critical information, that Tilsen was returning to London and was bringing the card with him. And they knew when.

He also learned that Stella, the girl whom they had kidnapped and forced to reveal vital information needed to enable Spider 2-3 to go live, had survived - she had been rescued and taken to safety away from Cuttle Cove. During the gun battle she had been seen on top of the big rocket transporter at its control panel, with what looked like a screwdriver in her hand.

That didn't make any sense to Malekka. Not yet, anyway.

So, there was a chance to get the SD card back, but they would have to move quickly. It would have to be done covertly, carefully; when Tilsen was alone they could get at him. At the moment, Tilsen didn't know of its significance. And it was imperative not to make a move in public and risk letting the enemy know of the importance to them of what Tilsen was carrying, in case the snatch for some reason was not successful.

Once it was in their hands, it didn't matter what anyone knew.

Malekka discussed a plan with Yameen. They would get into Tilsen's flat, search it and silence Tilsen as soon as he returned, retrieving the card. They would have the flat watched, so that they could see who was involved and heading up the forces against them, which, Malekka reasoned, would lead them to discover who had foiled their efforts in Spider 2-3. And the people watching would take pictures and send them, so they could see the faces of the infidel enemy.

Malekka had instructed Yameen to select three more men and send them out from Iran, this time to London. He chose Fadil, Anwar and Mulayl. Carrying pictures of Tilsen, and details of his private address that Malekka's international web of contacts had been able to obtain, they had arrived in good time at Gatwick Airport and were there when Tilsen's flight landed. They easily spotted him as he came through the arrivals hall.

The three men discreetly followed him, first on the train down to Eastbourne, where he visited someone in a small house. It was decided Mulayl and Anwar would stay in Eastbourne, go into the house and find out its importance, if any. Fadil boarded the train and followed Tilsen to London. As the train departed Eastbourne station, Malekka's resident London agent, a man named Riad Al Solh, a particularly unpleasant individual with varied skills embracing torture, murder, housebreaking, theft and blackmail, broke into Tilsen's flat, searched it and lay in wait for Tilsen to return. Although she had had no way of knowing, it had been lucky for Jenny she had been out that evening herself.

≈

The occupant of the car that happened to pass Claridge's as JP was exiting his, and who had photographed him a few minutes earlier as he had left Tilsen's flat, again clicked his camera. Instantly it beamed the pictures to the internet.

Two thousand seven hundred miles southeast, a short distance outside Tehran, Malekka looked at the pictures of the Falcon on his computer.

"Well now," he said to himself. "Just who is this?"

5
PREPARING

JIM PEREGRINE WAS back in his suite at Claridge's again far earlier than he had expected. As a result of his gains from the previous enterprise, which some might consider ill-gotten but which the Falcon felt he had acquired justifiably, he had intended to buy a large house in central London as his international headquarters. All he had wanted to do was take a month off first.

While he showered, he counted the days they had had away. One day travelling. One night on St Lucia. The next day the meet-up with Anna; the dinner; then the phone call from Charlie. The flight back to the UK the same night; and now here I am again, he thought, back in England.

One night's holiday. Not much of a vacation. But what was more to the point, there had been a few days of debriefing and preparation since Spider ended. Today was 2nd May. *Eight days total*. That meant that Malekka had a considerable start on them. Plus all the time beforehand preparing Stingray. A month, a year. Longer.

JP had breakfast sent up, devoured it, then he set out for the meeting with Melton. He decided he would follow the same route he had used before. A taxi to the Grosvenor Hotel at Victoria, walk through the lobby and out using the Hotel's second exit into the busy station complex beyond to mix with hundreds of people. He walked briskly to the escalators, went up to the upper level, through the shopping mall and out into Belgrave Road. He took a cab from there and headed to Regent Street, got out at New Burlington Street and continued up Regent Street by foot. He turned left into Hanover Street. He stopped frequently to make sure he wasn't being followed.

Halfway down Hanover Street he entered a little souvenir and card shop called *Cards Galore*.

It was empty of customers. However, given that the time was 10am and the sign hanging on the door declared the opening hour to be 10.30am, reinforced by a 'Closed' sign underneath, that wasn't surprising. The elderly man behind the counter looked up and smiled.

"I didn't think I'd be seeing you again quite so soon, sir."

"Me neither, Beefie," said JP. "Are they in there?"

"Yes, sir, go right on through."

The Falcon passed behind the curtains into the back of the shop, the reinforced steel door at the end of the small recess opened for him and he walked into the safe house. He strolled down a slight ramp to what was a comfortable lounge and meeting room with high tech support. Jane Chapman, in uniform now, and Charlie Melton were seated at the big conference table, Melton at its head. He stood to greet him. They shook hands sombrely for the second time that morning and then JP sat opposite the Lieutenant.

"Charlie, before you start, I've had a thought," said JP.

"Ok, go ahead."

"Well I was counting the days since the end of Operation Waterhole at Cuttle Cove. Eight days in all. Nine including today."

Melton and the Lieutenant waited.

"So… why hasn't something happened?" continued JP. "If Malekka has this other thing, Stingray, running as a parallel or second terrorist plot, why hasn't it occurred?"

"Yes, I know what you mean." Melton looked at Jane, raising his eyebrows.

"We had the same thought," she said. Her auburn hair was loose this time, shoulder length, but pinned back in place with two long brown clips. She was crisp, elegant efficiency. "We have come to two possible conclusions. One, Malekka was not far advanced enough with Stingray to start it; or, two, he can't start it without something that he left behind at Cuttle Cove. Now it may well be," she continued, "that he's not ready; but we think it's more likely the second of the two. He would have had to leave Cuttle Cove rapidly. He may not have had the time to collect everything necessary to initiate Stingray."

"You know, JP, Malekka had an intricate escape system," said Melton. "Two minutes. A lift that dropped him a hundred feet and then a monorail train that whisked him along and down farther in a tunnel under water and out to a cave with a waiting submarine. We've timed the system; it's one minute and forty-five seconds to the cave and another fifteen seconds to be out in the water, five hundred feet down. If the gunfire was the trigger for him to escape, which it probably was, he may not have thought about anything other than getting out safely. It would make sense."

"Around thirty-six hours ago," said Jane, "Dave Tilsen sent back another batch of items and materials from Cuttle Cove that included a cell phone. It was the third to be found in Malekka's suite of rooms. Together with computers, papers and other electronic items that we'd received earlier. They're still being dissected by the boys and girls in the lab but they can already tell from the directory pointers on the phone memory that it should have a micro SD card. It's missing. We know Tilsen separated it from the phone for reasons of security or safety - no possibility of interaction nor that they could both get lost in the same transit package."

"So where's the card?" asked JP.

"We don't know," said Melton. "Maybe Tilsen planned to bring it in to me today before leaving but he would have known that this morning is the usual weekly brief that Sir Alastair and I give to the Prime Minister, which I was doing on my own today as Sir Alastair's away, so he may have decided to wait and store it safely pending his return. Obviously, that meeting's now been put back[5]. Or, maybe the card's on its way to us by another package or method. We presume he didn't try to make a copy before getting it back to the lab, in case there was auto-destruct software on the card, and that therefore only the original exists. Frankly we don't know. However, it's possible that the phone - or any phone - and the card are an initiator of some kind. We're still trying to find the card. Our bet is, Malekka hasn't got the initiator for Stingray… whatever it is."

"Thank the Lord for that."

"Well, that was before Tilsen's killing of course. We now think that's why Malekka went for Tilsen, to try to get the card back, and to silence him and make sure he couldn't tell anyone else what he had learned, or follow up at any meetings. Hence the scrawled note that Dave left." The lines of worry on Melton's forehead seemed deeper than a week ago, although his brown eyes somehow still smiled.

"If it's the SD card that Malekka needs to start the other plan and if he hasn't been able to recover it," said JP, "then he's going to get another one with the same information on it, or collect or compile the information again somehow. Either in person, or it's going to be sent to him. Maybe even encrypted codes by email. But… it could take time. If he hasn't got it already." He shook his head. "If he has, then the world, or our world anyway, could blow up literally any second. This is tougher than Spider."

"I'm afraid that's the situation, JP," said Melton. "There's nothing we can do about it, other than to follow the lead to Panama we have. And hope that somehow it can be unravelled before Malekka can initiate Stingray."

"You know, sir," said the Lieutenant, "I wonder if there's

---

[5] *Sir Alastair Crewe, Head of MI6 - see Spider 2-3.*

something we could do to hinder Malekka."

"What do you mean?"

"Malekka must be feeling pretty angry. Weeks, years, of planning all gone for nothing. He's managed to escape capture and getting thrown into prison, or killed, by the skin of his teeth. If I were he I'm not sure I'd want to venture out so freely and risk my security just now."

"You're right, Jane," said JP, "So - where is he? My guess is he headed back to the safety of Iran. He's probably holed up in some palace somewhere, protected, secure... but possibly thinking he doesn't want to cross the border again yet, until things have died down."

"Yes, I agree," said Melton. "And if he is thinking like that, it will hinder his efforts to get the replacement information or phone or card needed to start his other plot." Melton reached for the coffee, and poured some for the others as well.

Jane added cream to hers and sipped thoughtfully at the hot brew. "So, let's make him stay there. We could come up with a media leak that would let the world know we were looking for a wealthy Iranian… but didn't reveal any classified details. And perhaps a picture?"

"We have a picture of him, right?" asked JP. "I presume he's on his own CCTV cameras somewhere."

"Yes," said Jane. She reached for the remote to work the screens on the wall, and pressed a couple of buttons. Two pictures of Malekka appeared side by side, one a facial close-up, the other full length.

"So, this is Malekka," said the Falcon thoughtfully. "How decidedly *un*pleasant to see you at last..."

≈

At the same time in Iran, Malekka was staring at the picture of the Falcon on his computer screen. He didn't know who the man was. However, he was going to find out. It was only a matter of time. And the strange thing is, he thought, I'm sure I've seen you somewhere before. I just can't place where…

And then it came to him.

Of course. He's the boyfriend…

≈

JP, Charlie Melton and Lieutenant Jane Chapman studied the two black and white pictures of Malekka displayed on the screens in the conference room. Around forty, stylishly short black hair, dark deep-set eyes, heavy eyebrows, straight nose, rather thin lips, set on a slightly elongated face. Tall slim frame, maybe six feet or just over.

"He must know we have pictures of him now," said Melton.

"Yes, and probably furious that they have come from his own security system," said JP, with a dry laugh. "I bet he never thought that little lot would fall into someone else's hands."

"That will be another reason," said Melton, "why he may not want to venture out from Iran just now. Jane, the more I think of it, the more I think that's a good idea. Put together a story that can go out to the media, so that it reaches all the news outlets. Not the pictures though, hold them back; there's no need to let him know we have them. Keep him guessing."

"Yes, sir," said the Lieutenant.

"Now, to Panama, JP," continued Melton. "You are going to see the President of International Shipping Transport Services, or ISTRAS, a Mr Jon Lano. This is the contact name that Dave Tilsen came back with from Cuttle Cove in such a hurry. I guess he was going to tell me where he had got it from, but I doubt we will ever know now. The commercial section of our embassy in Panama was apparently asked by Dave through channels to arrange the meeting and it's set for tomorrow noon, which you'll now take as Mr David Tilsen. Your passport as Tilsen and documents have come through." He paused. "Jane?"

"Lano's pretty high powered, as one would expect." The Lieutenant handed a series of papers to JP as she spoke. "Hong Kong origin as far as we know, quite a global mover, believed to be fairly ruthless and highly successful. Lano speaks English fluently, as he does several other languages. Incidentally, and you might know this anyway, English is widely spoken in Panama too, as a second language. The company, as the name suggests, acts as a shipping agent and books and ensures the smooth transit of Panamax ships through the Canal and more recently of the larger Neopanamax ships for the new wider lane of the Canal. Your credentials are as Chairman and principal shareholder in Globaldex Ltd, an international privately-held conglomerate specialising in commodities trading, with interests in acquiring and developing its own shipping line, and you would like a relationship with a top agent at the Canal. Companies House have put in place paperwork going back four years, you also have a corporate presence on the Virgin Islands, and the Isle of Man to a lesser extent. Coutts Bank will vouch for your financial standing." She looked at her boss.

"Tilsen had been putting this in place for himself," said Melton. "You'll pick up from where he was. Other than that, we have nothing more to go on. You'll be on your own and will have to see where it leads."

"Ok, Charlie, that seems fine," said JP, looking at the papers. "And the passport?"

"Oh yes, here," said Jane, handing it over from another file. "Sorry. Literally hot off the press. You as Dave Tilsen."

JP smiled. "Thank you, Lieutenant."

"The location is in the Bicsa Financial Center," continued Melton. "Sixtieth Floor, Bicsa Building, Avenida Balboa,

Panama. Cross street is Avenida Aquilino De La Guardia. It's one of the newest and most prestigious buildings in Panama City. You'll be staying at the Intercontinental, also on Avenida Balboa, about three hundred yards on the other side of the street closer to the Ocean."

Melton paused, and looked hard at his friend.

"Of course, if Tilsen had the card on him when he was killed, then they will have it now. But if he was going to hand it to me in person, which would be very like him - you know how he played his cards close to his chest - and he waited then it could be stored safely elsewhere. He's not going to mail it, that would be too risky; and it hasn't turned up in any bags from Cuttle Cove. But what is clear, what is crystal clear, is that time is of the essence. You have to move fast, Falcon."

JP smiled, and nodded.

"Ok, that's it. Except to say, you still hold the Fifth Rubric for this Firm and the Government of Great Britain. And, of course, good luck."

The Falcon departed from the MI6 safe house as he had done before, using the exit that put him close to Brook Street. Within five minutes he was at Claridge's. He packed quickly. At 11.45am he was collected by the same driver from the Firm, Ben Alton, and taken out to Heathrow Airport.

The flight to Miami took nine and a half hours. The cabin crew was efficient and friendly, the food good and the film selection overwhelming, but JP grabbed the opportunity to catch up on some sleep. The Boeing 777 landed on time at Miami International. One and a half hours later the American Airlines flight took off for Panama City. It routed due south over Cuba, above which crossings with a correct flight plan and paid fee had been permitted for well over twenty years.

It was dark when the 737 crossed into Panama airspace, and the lights of the City twinkled appealingly as the aircraft made its decent. JP was greeted by two British Embassy staff, who helped clear him quickly through customs. He stepped outside the terminal alone.

The Panama air was a warm twenty-three degrees, even at that time in the evening, and thick with the smell of seaweed, salt, car exhaust and aviation fumes. He feigned an internet search on his phone while waiting for the first two taxis in the queue to be taken by somebody else, then nonchalantly took the next cab.

They raced along the South Corridor, with the driver taking advantage of the highway's three lanes all of which she apparently considered fast ones. They passed across the Panama Bay along the two kilometres of viaduct, and the darkness of the sea to the south was broken by the lights of huge tankers awaiting their turn to traverse the Canal. The cab swung into the Avenida Balboa, and was quickly amidst the high rises of plush hotels and well-to-do apartments that make up Panama City's relatively new and ever-developing skyline. He was delivered safely to the Intercontinental Hotel.

The Falcon's suite on the top floor was comfortable and provided stunning views over Panama Bay. He showered, dined in his room and slipped under the sheets for the night. However, he couldn't sleep. The jet lag was troubling him and his mind was racing, with the thoughts not only of the meeting tomorrow but of what Malekka could possibly have running alongside Spider. What is he up to now, he asked himself for the hundredth time? It was difficult to imagine the sheer hatred that Malekka must have for the West, its institutions, its way of life, freedom, democracy… what had happened to the man to make him so poisoned?

En route to Heathrow JP had learned that the drivers of both cars that had followed him, and presumably taken photographs, had been picked up and were being "sweated", as Ben liked to call it. Good, thought JP. It was a smart move from Malekka. Not only did he have Tilsen murdered, but he had some of his people hang around to find out the response of his opponents, and who those opponents were. He should have seen it coming, he thought; he may have been distressed over Dave, but he couldn't afford any more such personal luxuries. It might get him killed. And, probably, a great number of other people on the planet too.

His mind switched to Cape Town and his friend Kuhle, the head of South Africa's Anti-Terrorist and Serious Crime squad known as the Scorpions, who had nearly lost his life helping JP destroy Malekka's vicious Cape Town terrorist cell... "Go. Just get the fuckers, Jimmy," he had said, as JP held his head and the man spluttered the words through the blood in his mouth from the gunshot wound. He thought of the car chase that followed... Suddenly he was amidst the battle of Operation Waterhole at Cuttle Cove... he felt the pain of the three bullets that hit him in the back and threw him forwards...

Finally, the Falcon drifted off into a troubled sleep, tossing and turning through the night.

≈

As JP was being driven along Avenida Balboa to the Intercontinental, thirteen hundred miles northeast Stephanie and Anna took off from St Lucia, heading back to London's Gatwick Airport. They would have only eight hours the next day to gather what they needed, before they too would be outbound on a plane once more.

PART TWO

THE SECOND DAY

6

IN PANAMA

THE KILLER RIAD Al Solh had watched Dave Tilsen roll over the desk and onto the parquet. It had been an easy shot, but his target had made a considerable amount of noise knocking things as he twisted then crashed to the uncarpeted floor. There were flats above and below, and on either side of the apartment on the same level, and sounds carry farther and more easily at night. He needed to get out fast in case a neighbour had heard something and came knocking on the door, even at that late hour.

Solh knelt at the man's side and checked for a pulse. Nothing. He replaced the gun with its attached suppressor into his shoulder holster. He started to rummage through the pockets in the man's jacket, taking care to avoid any direct contact with the growing pool of blood on the floor and to minimise its disturbance. He checked the inside ones first; he found a train ticket and a wallet but ignored them; then he found a phone. He pulled it out, looked at it, popped open the space where a micro SD card should be, saw there wasn't one and pushed the slide closed. He would have liked to have taken the phone away to be examined, but was under strict instructions not to do so; he knew cell phones could be used as trackers, and he was to take no risks. He carefully replaced the phone. He turned his attention to the flap pockets, and in the left one found what he'd been looking for - a small plastic container. He prised it open, and inside was a micro SD card. Its dimensions were fifteen millimetres, by eleven, by one. The killer smiled to himself, snapped the slim box shut and put it into his own pocket. He stood to have one more look round. He had worn gloves all the time and maintained a high degree of sanitisation throughout his search of the flat, so there were no fingerprints or DNA residue, nor would there be on the items he had touched in Tilsen's pockets.

Solh buttoned up his coat, took out a cap from an inside pocket and pulled it down low over his face. He moved through the hallway back to the entrance door to the flat and put his ear up close to the door; he could hear nothing. He opened the door quietly, peered outside and stepped through. He closed the door gently and walked over to the elevator, but thought instead it would be safer if he took the stairs. He pushed through the heavy fire doors and made his way down the steps to the ground floor. He turned the collar of his coat up, had a quick look outside to the street, then exited through the main door to the building. He was at the end of the bordering pavement in thirty paces, went round the corner and disappeared into the night.

Two blocks away, Solh reached his car. He started the engine and slipped it into gear. The streets and sidewalks were still busy. He drove away slowly heading north, and in a couple of minutes turned into Fulham Road. Opposite the cinema on the corner of Drayton Gardens he took a left into Beaufort Street, found a parking space, then walked briskly back to Fulham Road. In a hundred metres or so he was at VQ Chelsea, one of more well-established all night eateries. He found Jafri Fadil at the end of the long row of tables. He was finishing what appeared to be a dish of smoked salmon tagliatelle and looked up as Solh approached.

"Hello!" he said more for the others in the restaurant than for any reasons of friendship, "glad you could make it!"

"Hello, my friend," replied Solh, undoing his light coat, and taking off his cap. "So nice to see you."

"Come, sit down. Would you like to eat, what will you have?"

"No, nothing to eat. But I'll join you for coffee, please."

The waiter appeared, Fadil's plate was cleared and the coffee ordered.

Fadil was a soldier and had fought in battles, he had killed and had seen comrades close to him die. Fighting was his profession, and he was good at it. But he had not known an assassin and torturer before. Now he could glance across the table and look at one. The trait that struck him most was the coldness of Solh's face. A deep knife scar trickled down from his left eye across his cheek to the corner of his mouth. His head was more square than round, with a flat-topped haircut that emphasised the lack of soft contours. The eyebrows were long but thin, and the eyes piercing and dark, in fact almost black. He was a cold-blooded killer for sure, who thought nothing of slitting a man's throat any more than eating a sandwich. Which, thought Fadil, was exactly the reason why his master, Barakah Malekka, retained him. They exchanged a few more pleasantries until the coffee arrived. Then Fadil leant forward to speak.

"So how did it go?" he asked quietly.

"Fine," replied Solh. His voice was low and guttural, with an acquired Sloane Square accent. "Job done. No problems."

"Did you find it?"

"Yes." He brought out the small plastic box and, cued by Fadil who first scanned the restaurant and close tables using only eye movement before nodding imperceptibly, slid it across the table top. Fadil picked it up, glanced inside, then placed it in his own pocket.

"Well done."

"Thank you. Tell the boss any time, glad to be of service."

Fadil nodded and smiled.

"I will."

The men left the restaurant together apparently as friends having enjoyed each other's company over a dinner, and then parted once they had moved away from the immediate vicinity.

Solh headed for his car and retreated back into his own cold world. Fadil hailed a taxi and travelled to Gloucester Square station, walked a few minutes, then took another taxi to Heathrow Airport. He checked into a hotel for a few hours' sleep and was on the first British Airways flight to Paris in the morning.

Once there, he bought a ticket to Zurich. Upon arrival he walked out through customs and over to Departures where he bought another ticket, this time to Istanbul, and repeated the process there, routing direct to Tehran. He arrived a little before 11am local time, just as JP was at last falling asleep for the night in his suite at the Intercontinental Hotel in Panama City.

One of Malekka's helicopters was waiting for Fadil, and he was ferried quickly to Malekka's Palace. At 12 noon he was making his report to his master.

"So, Jafri," said Malekka excitedly as he led the way into the large sumptuous room that for convenience was both lounge and office. Fadil walked over and took Malekka's outstretched hand, bowing slightly. "I want to hear everything."

"Yes, sir," he replied. "First I must apologise for my appearance, sir, I have been travelling for almost twenty-four hours and before freshening I came as instructed straight to you."

"Yes and in another half hour you can go and take a well-earned rest and have some sleep. My present rule of non-communication from outside the homeland is sensible but at the same time is very frustrating. They can hear and read everything, and we must be safe. We were discovered or betrayed, possibly both. But now you are here, and I want to know everything." Malekka waved the younger man to a chair, and sat down opposite.

The room was rectangular, around fifteen metres long and

perhaps ten wide. Enormous windows ran along the lengths of the two external walls, their borders clipped by luxurious maroon and gold tapestries that hung almost from the very top of the high ceiling. Despite the fact that the palace was set deep within Iran, many of the rooms, including this one, were modelled more on traditional western style than Arabic. Two great crystal chandeliers hung from the ceiling, the air conditioning hummed almost imperceptibly and sofas and deep armchairs, with heavily-patterned styles of gentle red and gold braiding based on a Pugin 1850 design complementing the drapes, were dispersed comfortably around the room, and paired with elegant brightly-polished mahogany tables that bore gold leaf trims along the edges of the top and down the full length of the legs. A selection of original paintings hung in ornate frames on the walls that were themselves papered with a gentle gold damask design. A huge desk rested towards one of the walls, and on it set to one side was a computer and large display screen.

Fadil quickly gave his report in direct sentences, and answered his master's questions. In ten minutes, Malekka had heard everything.

"...and this is what Mr Solh took from Tilsen." Fadil pulled out the plastic box from his pocket, and rose to walk over to Malekka, who stood excitedly.

"This is wonderful, Jafri, I thought we had lost this and it would have to be compiled again. And the target date is fast approaching, we must be on time."

"Yes, sir," said Fadil. He handed the box over. Malekka opened it gently and looked at the SD card, then walked towards his desk, adding, "Come, come," to his young servant.

Malekka put the card into an adaptor and pushed it slowly into the slot on his PC, his heart racing and a smile playing on his lips. He sat, and worked the mouse.

As the screen opened the contents of the SD card, the smile

vanished from Malekka's face to be replaced by an expression of fury. His cheeks reddened, he let out a snarl as he raised his hand and slammed it down onto the desk with such a loud force that it made Fadil jump.

"This isn't the card! This is not it. *That cursed infidel has switched it.*"

≈

JP slept late, but by 11.30am - as Malekka was having a solitary dinner after his furious day of disappointment with Fadil, that necessitated revised plans for action pending the return from the UK of his two other operatives - the Falcon was in a dark blue pinstripe suit walking in the corridor outside his room over to the elevator, carrying a briefcase. His dark hair was brushed back, a red tie sat neatly against his white shirt and complemented the silk handkerchief dangling from his breast pocket, and his black brogues shone. He appeared to be a determined young businessman who had clearly already learned to enjoy the trappings of financial success. He entered the taxi waiting for him.

The one-way system took him round the hotel complex close to the bay, and back up along the Cinta Costera, past the harbour. The private yachts gleamed in their multitude of shapes and sizes and bobbed gently on the water waiting for their next excursion into the Pacific Ocean. The taxi rejoined the Avenida Balboa, moved over perilously to the right lane accompanied by the sounds of numerous angry car horns and turned into the Avenida Aquilino de la Guardia, where the driver pulled up on the corner. Directly opposite was the Bicsa Financial Center building, towering sixty-eight storeys high. The Falcon crossed the road, announced himself at the main reception desk set midway in the large shopping precinct and was escorted to the express elevator. It took him nonstop to the sixtieth floor. He exited, and was met by a girl who had just left the large mahogany desk opposite.

"Mr Tilsen?" she smiled as she walked over.

"Yes," said JP, taking in her bright face, shoulder length auburn hair and slim figure.

She shook hands firmly. "Would you please come this way. Mr Lano is waiting to see you."

They walked through some heavy glass doors bordered with gold trim that stretched all the way to the high ceiling, and passed down a wide corridor, exchanging simple chatter as they went. The girl took him through another pair of doors into what was an anteroom for a bigger office beyond.

"This is Mr Tilsen, Emily," she said, and smiled her goodbyes to JP.

"Hello," said Emily, and quickly escorted JP to Lano's office. She knocked and went in. "Mr Lano, this is Mr Tilsen."

"Ah, Mr Tilsen," said Jon Lano, in an accent that was a mixture of American and Chinese. He emerged from behind a huge desk set in front of a glass window that comprised one wall of the office, overlooking the Bay. He was a short man of about fifty, with thin dark hair greying at the fringes and combed over his small head from left to right. If the wind blew in the wrong direction, he would be bald. They shook hands. "Won't you sit down?"

"Thank you," said JP.

"Have you had a good journey?" asked Lano as he walked back to his desk. "Where have you come from, London?"

"Yes, to both," replied JP. "I arrived last night."

"Your first time in Panama?"

"Actually, no, I have been here before but a good few years ago."

Lano smiled as he lifted his open spectacles frame up from the desk and put them on again. He looked at the screen and touched the mouse sitting close to the computer on his desk.

"I have had the opportunity this morning to study your company, Mr Tilsen. Most inspiring."

"Thank you." JP paused, then added, "And, I would like to say the same also of yours."

Lano smiled again. "And so, Mr Tilsen, what can I do for you? We like to accommodate our British friends wherever we can."

"In your research on Globaldex, you may have seen a recent Board Report in which I mention my plans to acquire an international shipping line." Lano nodded. He's quite impressive thought JP. "This will be achieved through direct commissioning of an entirely new fleet to be built over a period of years, and first by the acquisition of an existing one."

Lano moved the mouse and clicked it again.

JP continued. "We have need of a shipping agent that is influential at Panama and specialises in Panamax and of course Neopanamax designs and that, furthermore, should the need arise, can guarantee a priority for my vessels in the transit process. You have come highly recommended."

"Who has recommended me?"

"Frankly, Mr Lano, the British Government."

"Thank you, Mr Tilsen, I am flattered at such an introduction." He played with his keyboard a little more, and didn't twitch a muscle as the picture of JP emerging from Tilsen's flat in London appeared on his screen. "We would be delighted to act as agent for you."

"Thank you," said JP.

"We will get some draft contract papers over to you. At your hotel?"

"Yes, very good. The Intercontinental."

"You might also benefit from seeing our handling office, located close to the Canal. Would you care to visit while you are here?"

“I would indeed,” said JP, with a nod of his head.

“Very well, Mr Tilsen.” Lano put his glasses down onto the desk and stood, signalling the end of the meeting. “I will have my colleagues call you later today and arrange an appointment.”

“That would be most kind.”

“I look forward to doing business with you.” Lano extended his hand. “Goodbye, Mr Tilsen.”

“Thank you, Mr Lano,” said JP, shaking hands, “you’ve been most kind. Good afternoon.”

Lano waited for JP to make his way to the hallway, then pressed a button on his desk. His assistant appeared, and with his index finger he beckoned her close. “Yes, Mr Lano?”

“Kill him.”

7
A GOOD SHOT

JP WALKED ALONG Avenida Balboa heading to his hotel. It had been a fairly simple and uneventful meeting. Lano was obviously successful, or well financed, or both, and the number of people that JP had seen in the office was substantial. The plushness of the business rooms and obvious affluence were, he knew, in strict contrast to a large proportion of the Panamanian people. It was the same story all over Latin-America; a small number of people own most of the country and its wealth, and the rest have next to nothing; a five minute car ride would take him into areas of extreme poverty, where there were children who wouldn't even get a plate of food a day. Yet the opening of the expanded Canal produced enormous profits for the Treasury, and the country looked set to continue its growth at twice the rate of others in the region in recent years. Add the financial and tax sectors and popular duty-free zone services to the income from the Canal operations and the country's economy would continue to boom.

Jon Lano didn't strike JP as the kind of man who would care in the slightest about the poor. What was his game? Why had Tilsen been killed to prevent him from having a meeting with Lano? There's only one way to find out, said JP to himself. Somehow, I have to get back into that office when no-one else is around.

He reached his room and flung the case down onto the large and luxuriously-covered bed when the telephone rang. JP picked it up.

"Mr Tilsen?" said the voice on the other end of the line.

"Yes."

"My name is Max Schroeder at ISTRAS, I run the handling office of the Corporation out at the Canal area. Mr Lano asked that I give you a call?"

"Oh, Mr Schroeder, yes, how nice to hear from you," said JP.

"Mr Lano has said that you might care to see our operation at the Canal and look at the work we do here. I'd be delighted to welcome you if you have some time?"

"Thank you, I'd like that very much."

"Excellent," said Schroeder. JP was trying to place the accent; German but with what sounded like Italian influence. "We tend to keep rather odd hours by the nature of the work we do, but may I suggest this evening at say 8pm? Our Canal traffic for the day which always takes much attention will have completed by then so it's an easier time for us, but also I can show you what is in line for the morning. Would that be convenient?"

"Yes, that would be perfect. Where do I come?"

"I'll give you the address, do you have a pen and paper handy?"

"Yes, go ahead."

"We're at the Panamá Pacífico Airport, which is the old Howard Air Force Base, on the other side of the Canal entrance. You go across the Puente de las Americas, or Bridge of the Americas, take a left down Boulevard Panamá Pacífico and we're on the right at the International Business Park. The ISTRAS block is a big building set back on its own. Any cab will know us."

"Ok, got it. I'll see you at eight this evening."

JP hung up the phone.

A few hairs bristled on the back of his neck. Somehow the Falcon could always sense danger.

≈

Stephanie and Anna had landed in London at 8am that same morning and promptly set about buying all of the things they needed. They only had a few hours. They already had their holiday clothes, from the aborted vacation on St Lucia; however, finding the right shop that could provide the wigs off the shelf had proved a little difficult. Both women were natural blondes and had decided against dyeing their hair, and although they had visited a couple of suppliers the problem had been the need for an instant fit. Finally Mandeville in Fulham had come through with exceptional ability and provided a perfect solution. Stephanie had ended up with shoulder length brown hair; Anna's hairpiece was darker, and longer.

The coloured contact lenses changed Stephanie's eyes from their emerald to brown; Anna was no longer blue-eyed but hazel. Subtle changes to makeup, and less of it, aged them and removed the natural soft texture of their skin. In a further effort to avoid the holiday-tourist look they would also buy some clothes at their destination, to help them mix in with the locals.

In the late afternoon, as JP was walking back to his hotel following the meeting with Lano in Panama, they grabbed a taxi and headed for London's Heathrow Airport. At 8.10pm their flight departed.

≈

Not long after the phone call from Schroeder, JP checked in with Charlie Melton in London on a secure line.

"...and so I'm going to try to get back into Lano's office tonight," said JP.

"Ok, good," said Melton. "I don't need to tell you to be careful. But, be careful."

JP smiled. "Don't worry, I'll be fine."

"There is one little bit of news here," continued Melton. "Those two people following you in the cars. We've checked them out and grilled them pretty well. They're private investigators, both registered, one for over five years and the other seven. They were hired at short notice by someone over the telephone who spoke perfect English and they were paid very well, in advance, for two days' work. They were to take pictures of everyone going in and out of Tilsen's flat and upload the pictures to the internet, which they did direct and immediately from the cameras, and from 6am one of them was to follow anyone they thought they should, or could. The web address has since been deleted as have the pictures, and the memory cards wiped by reformatting after each upload as per their instructions."

"That probably means that they saw Tilsen's killer. And even had pictures of him. Or her."

"Yes. The lab techies are seeing if they can recover anything from the cards; it might be possible, as it's unlikely low level formatting was used by the cameras. Actually, the two men were keen to co-operate once they realised there had been a murder and, if they didn't, they could be implicated. One of them does remember someone going into the building at around midnight and coming out again an hour or so later, but there is no description; they just worked the cameras."

"Have you let them go?"

"No. We're going to hold them for another forty-eight hours, just in case."

"Good. I'm sure they're unwitting accomplices, the sort of people that Malekka likes to hire; no loose ends, no links, no leads."

"Yes, but we'll play safe and keep them for a bit longer yet. We're searching their offices and homes anyway."

JP took a light lunch around 3pm, undressed and lay down

on the bed to try to get some rest. He still felt tired from his poor sleep the previous night and now the jet lag was kicking in.

Two hours later JP woke courtesy of his cell phone alarm ready for the evening's excursion. He showered, dressed again in a suit and by 7.30pm was downstairs in the hotel lobby, walking through to the waiting taxi.

Night had arrived quickly with little twilight at Panama's low equatorial latitude. The driver of the cab listened to the radio and moved his shoulders to the rhythm of the tamborito and cumbia dance music as he drove, every now and again singing along, magnificently out of tune. They went over the Puente de las Americas and the night skyline of Panama behind grew smaller, soon replaced by low steel and aluminium constructions of the sort found all over the world in dull but practical industrial estates. Some brick buildings three or four stories high stood along the way. In another few minutes they came to one that was set back from the road on a grand double driveway with a front placard on poles carrying the name ISTRAS. The Falcon paid the driver and walked up to the large heavy front door. A sign read simply *Por Favor Escribe*. He pushed open the door and stepped inside, and called out, "Hello?"

The desk inside was vacant and the large hall dark but at the other end was an office with lights shining through the open doorway. A man at a desk looked up and smiled.

"Ah, Mr Tilsen?" he enquired, standing. He started to walk over.

"Yes. Mr Schroeder?"

"Yes, how nice to meet you." Schroeder reached JP; the two men shook hands. Schroeder was short with a large waistline, in a jacket that had no chance of buttoning. His hair was dark and greasy, and the bushy moustache in need of a trim.

"Do come in." He led the way back into his office. "Found us ok then…"

Schroeder was heading to his desk, and JP a few feet inside the room. If it hadn't been for the picture on the wall opposite, the Falcon wouldn't have had a chance but the glass reflected the movement. JP managed to dodge the downward blow of the cosh from behind. He caught the man's arm, leant left carrying the momentum and hurled the torso forwards, crashing him onto Schroeder's desk. A second man approached, knife gleaming. JP kicked him viciously to the groin, the man let out a scream and doubled up in agony. JP punched the face, the knife flew away and the man went to the floor senseless. The first one was up already and landed a blow to the back of JP's head that nearly took him to darkness and he stumbled almost to the ground, but found the arms of a chair in front of the desk. He slid the chair across and up through the air at the man, hitting him backwards. One of the legs cut both his lips and gouged an eye. He screamed obscenities, then lunged again, two arms locking around JP's chest, taking him to the floor as both men crashed downwards. This wasn't going according to Schroeder's plan at all and he pulled open the middle drawer of his desk. The man on top of JP tried to get two hands around his neck. JP pushed one away and with his other hand punched hard at the man's throat, causing him to choke and relax his grip, and he followed with a punch to the left eye that sent the man unconscious. From the floor JP saw the gun in Schroeder's hand being levelled at him. He rolled his opponent back across for protection and reached under his armpit for his own gun.

A suppressed shot rang out with a 'phut'. JP saw the red ring on the shirt appear as Schroeder was thrown backwards and his gun bounced with the recoil from the pull of its own trigger. The bullet went past JP's head, as Schroeder went down dead. Panting, JP turned towards the shooter.

A woman stood in the doorway.

JP stared amazedly for a couple of seconds, then recovered his composure.

"Exceptionally fine shot," he wheezed, pushing his former opponent, still unconscious, off him and bringing his Sauer round to bear at the woman. He was propped up on one elbow.

"I thought so too," said the female. JP recognised her immediately. It was the receptionist from Jon Lano's office, who had greeted him as he stepped out of the elevator. "Come, Mr Peregrine, we should not stay." She opened her handbag and popped the gun neatly back inside.

JP was quickly on his feet and over at the person who had quite possibly saved him from a nasty injury. "Thank you," he said with a smile, holstering his gun, and added, "and just who the hell are you?"

She smiled back. "My name is Coco Chavarez. I work for SENAN, the Servicio Nacional Aeronaval, part of the security forces for Panama. For the last six months I have been undercover at International Shipping Transport Services and have been watching Jon Lano and his operation closely. We heard you were coming. And we thought you might need a little help."

"I'm glad you did," said JP, and then said abruptly, "Just a minute." He walked out of Schroeder's office and quickly across the reception hallway to the street door. He made sure it was closed, and firmly turned the key in the deadlock. He went back into the office.

"There may be some others here. I haven't been able to check…"

"Don't worry," said Coco, "there aren't. We know how they do this. When Lano wants someone new out of the way quickly, they are sent innocently to meet with Schroeder and see the 'operational' side of ISTRAS. Then Schroeder's men take the person, force what information they can out of them and kill them. They disappear, without trace. They sometimes surface in the Bay a couple of weeks later, or part of them anyway, what's left over from the sharks after the bodies have been dumped farther out in the water. So there's nobody else here, nothing is recorded, no surveillance; only Schroeder and his two 'helpers'." She almost spat out the last word. "And you seem to have taken care of those."

"Yes. What a nice corporation," said JP.

"But we should go anyway," said Coco, "and I'll get my friends at the Police to come over and clean up."

"I'm going to have a little look round first."

"Ok. But not too long, please."

She picked up a telephone and punched some numbers, spoke for thirty seconds or so and hung up. Then she went to the entrance and carefully looked out through the window. The streets and walkways were empty; there were no cars to be seen.

The Falcon went over to one of the men on the floor. He was still breathing, but out cold. JP rummaged quickly in the desk drawers and found some string, and used it to bind the man's hands and feet securely, then took the tape from the dispenser and wound it round the man's mouth, to stop all but the quietest moans should he regain consciousness before Coco's colleagues arrived. The second attacker received the same treatment.

The Falcon returned to the drawers and methodically went through Schroeder's desk, examining papers, shipping documents, invoices. The computer was still on and its screen open. JP took out a high capacity data stick from his jacket pocket and plugged it into one of the USB drives. He waited a few seconds and then the LCD screen on the drive lit up. It indicated seven minutes to copy the entire hard drive. He moved to the lifeless body on the floor, the jacket pockets first. He took out the cell phone but it was protected with a password; that would have to be looked at later. In one of the trouser pockets, he found a key.

It didn't take long to locate the safe, under a shelf by the window and concealed by a simple drop curtain. The safe was an old heavy iron one worked by the single, but complex, key. JP had it quickly open. He rummaged through more invoices, found fifty thousand US dollars in notes, some pro forma documents and uninteresting correspondence. There was one other item, in a bubble-wrap envelope. He opened the flap, and pulled out what looked like a Printed Circuit Board, that was about twenty by twelve centimetres and maybe three centimetres thick at one end, from the centre of which the board and circuitry protruded, just a little larger than a PCB card that would fit into any desktop computer. It could even be some kind of motherboard. He put it back into the envelope and pocketed it. He locked the safe, and placed the key back in Schroeder's pocket.

The Falcon retrieved the USB stick, then with Coco's help carefully wiped the room down to remove their fingerprints.

They left the building through the front door, closing it firmly and ensuring it locked behind them, using a handkerchief so as not to leave any traces. The Police would break in. They walked quickly round to the back to an exit alley, where Coco's car was parked.

"How did you know what time I was going to be there?" asked JP, glancing over at the girl driving. He noticed the long pink nails as she worked the gearstick easily. About twenty-eight, simple blouse, skirt just above her knees, maybe three inch heels. Feminine, competent, fearless. And thankfully a bloody good shot, he thought.

"We have someone in the hotel on the switchboard. She listened in when Schroeder called you."

"Lucky for me I'm staying at that hotel."

"Not really," she replied, "we have someone at all the big

hotels, and most of the little ones."

"Ah."

"And anyway, Charlie Melton asked us to keep an eye on you," she added nonchalantly. "In case you needed anything."

"Nice of him to let me know," murmured JP, smiling to himself.

As they crossed over the Puente de las Americas heading back into the City, five Police cars with lights flashing screamed past them in the opposite direction.

"Friends of yours?" asked JP.

"Yes."

"So why are you interested in Lano and ISTRAS. How long have you been watching them?"

"Jon Lano arrived in Panama around six years ago, although he had had interests here prior to that. He came from Hong Kong where he'd built up a substantial international trading company as well as specialising in shipping movements around the globe. The authorities there were never entirely happy with his operations but nothing could ever be brought as hard evidence of any wrongdoing. Then things got hot for him when the son of the Consulate General of South Korea disappeared and later was found dead in a waste bin at the waterfront. His last known activity was meeting with Lano; they had started doing some business together about three months earlier, and the word is that Lano was somehow double-crossed in a deal. The authorities brought some major pressure on him, although once again no charges; but it was enough for him to leave. Especially when he got wind that the South Koreans said they were going to deal with him direct and unofficially. So, he came here. And it's been the same sort of thing. There are vast sums of money known to be flowing through his bank accounts yet it cannot possibly all be related to the kinds of activities that ISTRAS does which, although substantial, can't justify the cash flow. I was placed inside to monitor him and find out what I can."

"And have you?"

"No. Well not much anyway. We know about how people he doesn't like disappear. I have also seen some impressive names come in and visit him on more than one occasion. Tonight is the first time that we have been able to witness any direct criminal activity from anyone connected with Lano's little empire."

They drove in silence for a minute or two. Then JP spoke again.

"My hotel's that way." They had turned off the Highway and joined Avenida A, heading east.

"Yes, I know. We're not going back to your hotel, Mr Peregrine."

"Ah." The Falcon looked across at his female companion. He wasn't sure he liked this sudden and unexpected diversion. "Where are we going then?"

"Relax, Mr Peregrine."

"JP, please, or Jim."

"Ok. Relax, JP. Or, should I say, relax, Falcon."

JP smiled.

"We're not going back to your hotel. Not yet. We're going to meet my boss. I mean, my real boss."

JP turned away, and looked ahead through the front windscreen. It would seem that the evening was nowhere near over yet.

≈

Seven thousand miles to the east and slightly north, Stephanie Raughton and Anna Kepling checked into the Meridien Hotel in Limassol, on the Mediterranean Island of Cyprus. They entered their adjoining rooms and each went quickly to bed and slept.

8
THE SOUTH COAST

WHEN FADIL, ANWAR and Mulayl had first arrived at London's Gatwick Airport in good time before Dave Tilsen's flight landed, they were faced with several problems. First, how would they follow him? If he headed to London by train, that would be fairly simple, they could all board the same train. If he went home to his flat then that was covered already by Solh who would be there lying in wait. If he went to London but didn't go straight home and instead headed to another venue first, they would follow until he reached his home. But supposing he didn't go to London and instead headed for another destination? Or, supposing he was met by someone who gave him a lift to somewhere in a car? Or, he hired a car himself?

The obvious solution to all of these problems was a tracker. The difficulty would be getting a tracker onto Tilsen's person. Malekka's research and development team, who had previously been headed up by a brilliant female scientist named Aisha but of whom nothing had been heard since the raid on Cuttle Cove and the collapse of Spider 2-3, had a vast array of electronic devices at its disposal, many of which formed an integral part of the arsenal of Iran's own subversive intelligence and terrorist forces, and those others it supported, stationed in other countries around the world. They decided to take two items with them for the purpose.

They also had thought it wise to have a car for themselves on standby, and so it had fallen to Mulayl to go to one of the hire companies and rent one. He parked it at the MacDonald's carpark at the South Terminal, waiting, and was a mere few minutes' drive from the arrivals terminal. He could quickly collect his colleagues if the transport method Tilsen used was road, or drive to rendezvous with them later should they need to board a train.

Anwar who was five foot ten and thirty-five was wearing jeans, an open-necked blue shirt, light brown zip-up jacket and a navy blue baseball cap. He was pulling a small cabin bag on wheels behind him. Fadil was two years younger, a little taller with a slim frame, and also wore jeans with a T-shirt beneath a double-breasted half coat. He carried a light backpack that was thrown over one shoulder. His hair was dark and curly, his face tanned and eyes sharp and friendly. The two men fitted into the melting pot of arriving and departing holiday and business travellers at the airport with consummate ease.

As he walked into the arrivals hall Fadil nonchalantly exchanged glances with their contact, another of Malekka's resident operatives. The two walked separately into the men's toilets. It was easy enough, when they had taken care of business and reached the sinks, for them to place their identical backpacks on the tiled floor side by side as they washed their hands, and then for Fadil to pick up the other one instead so making the switch before exiting to rejoin Anwar. The contact lifted Fadil's backpack, threw it over his shoulder, headed for one of the short term car parks and left the airport.

As they spotted Tilsen coming through from customs into the arrivals hall, Anwar knelt to tie a shoelace and before standing pulled a protective strip off from the tiny black tracker that was two millimetres by two and less than a tenth thick pushed into the tip of his right shoe. It exposed the highly adhesive glue on the front side of the transmitter that would set instantly on contact. He had noticed that Tilsen was wearing dark coloured slip-on shoes; the tracker on Anwar's left shoe was white, that one would not be needed. Fadil made a phone call to Mulayl and told him to stand by.

It was easy for Fadil and Anwar separately to keep pace

with Dave Tilsen, who walked across the terminal towards the exit walkways but then split off to the entrance to the train station. Anwar moved forwards quickly as people headed for the tickets area and skilfully positioned himself behind Tilsen as they joined the heavy, slow-moving queue. Just before they all inched ahead yet again Anwar nudged his right foot forwards apparently too early, catching the heel of Tilsen's shoe. The glue hardened instantly, the tiny tracker was yanked away from Anwar's toecap and transferred to the back of the heel of Tilsen's shoe as Anwar pulled his foot back. Tilsen half turned his head, Anwar gave a harmless "Sorry" and everyone shuffled ahead a little more, getting closer to the ticket counters.

Tilsen reached the glass panel and Anwar was able to hear him say to the person on the other side, "Single to Eastbourne please". Anwar bought a ticket for Eastbourne, then called Fadil on his cell phone and gave him the destination. Fadil at once called Mulayl and told him to drive as fast as he could to a town called Eastbourne, then bought his own ticket and followed Tilsen and Anwar down to the platform. As luck would have it, a train for Eastbourne had just left, and the next would be in half an hour.

They waited for the train. Anwar and Fadil looked at their phones, as so many others on the platform were doing, and studied the display map of the local area and station showing clearly on their screens. In the centre a small red dot was flashing. The tracker on Tilsen was working perfectly.

They sat separately, in different carriages from Tilsen. The train was a slow one and made several stops. By the time it rattled into Eastbourne, and with the half hour start, Mulayl was at the station waiting. Tilsen took a taxi, and the two men walked over to Mulayl's vehicle, opened the doors and got in. Mulayl drove off and followed Tilsen's taxi, staying well back and glancing frequently at his phone propped on the dashboard which also displayed the tracker's position on a GPS basemap.

They drove through the town and then out heading towards the south and the sea. In ten minutes' time the taxi reached its destination, a small detached house set in a row of similar ones on the left of the road overlooking the sea off to the right. They pulled up some fifty feet back and were able to see the front door of the house open and Tilsen embracing an elderly lady. He went inside and the door closed.

Anwar put his phone on speaker and switched the software over to 'audio'. The tracker on Tilsen's heel had a dual purpose; its primary function was to provide the tracking signal, which it did very well over a distance of up to two miles. But it also had a listening and transmission capability, which was of course useless when the subject was walking since the jolt and street sounds were too loud to be of any use. But once the subject was in quiet surroundings, and especially if seated and still, the sensitivity level could be adjusted and a reasonable amount of any conversation close by could be picked up and relayed over to the receivers with clarity, in this case to the phones on each of the three men, played through attached earpieces.

They heard the bang of the door closing, a dog barking excitedly, a strange scraping sound, more greetings and then voices fading away, one saying, "Would you like a nice cup of tea, darling?" followed by an almost inaudible fading response from Tilsen, "Oh, that would be so lovely, they can never serve that properly on the planes…" and then a door clicked and there was no more.

Anwar cursed. "He's taken his shoes off."

The three men continued to listen, but deemed it best to get out of the car and walk away lest they be spotted. There was little else for them to do presently, and when Tilsen was ready to leave, or if anyone else arrived, they would be able to hear it instantly and could get back to the car quick enough. Anwar wandered down the hill a little way as if off for an evening's walk, reversing his direction every so often; Fadil found a small square of joined benches set in an open-roofed shelter typical of English coastal towns, and tucked himself away on the hardwood surface of one facing the sea so as to be out of sight of anyone who happened to peer from the houses; Mulayl walked down the road on the pavement by the houses and turned a corner, finding a small pub a little further on. He went in and sat quietly on his own sipping at a Coke.

As the evening passed, the three men heard only a few sounds from the tracker on Tilsen's shoe, once when the occupants of the house moved to the sitting room at the front of the house and again when another cup of tea was made, but all that came over were garbled sentences between what appeared to be two people, Tilsen and the elderly woman. The sun headed downwards in the sky and the temperature started to drop. Suddenly there were voices, quickly getting louder and clearer.

"Well thanks, Mum, it was a lovely dinner. And lovely chat."

The three men headed for the car.

"That's ok, darling," came the reply, the voice light and gentle, but wavering a little, as though she didn't want the man to go. "You take care of yourself."

"I will, don't worry." There was the sound of a door opening. "The cab's out there now, I'd better go or I'll miss the train."

"Yes ok. Be careful. And give my love to Jenny."

"I will. You be careful too. I'll see you in three or four days."

"Alright, darling, have a good trip."

The heavy banging of footsteps crashed through the earpieces of the three men and they reverted to tracking mode. As the cab drove off, Fadil and Mulayl drove off following.

Anwar stepped into the darkness under a tree and smoked a cigarette, keeping a watchful eye on the front door of the house.

Dave Tilsen paid the cab and got out at Eastbourne Station, glancing up at the clock on the tower, then passed through onto the small concourse set beneath the vaulted canopy of the old Victorian building. He bought a ticket to London. Fadil had already exited the car and spotted Tilsen heading to the platform for the London trains. He bought his own ticket for London. Ten minutes later the two men boarded the train, Tilsen in the front and Fadil one carriage behind. As they were getting closer to London, Fadil sent a text message to Solh. Once at Victoria Station, Tilsen grabbed a cab and went home to his flat, to his fate at the hands of the waiting assassin. Fadil followed in the next cab and checked that Tilsen did indeed get out at his flat and go into the building, then went to find somewhere to eat and pass the time.

After dropping Fadil, Mulayl drove back to the house and found the same parking spot as before, unoccupied. He met up with Anwar. They spoke quietly together.

"Are you sure about this, sir?" asked Mulayl. "It can't be anything important surely, she's his mother."

"I know. I don't want to. But we have our instructions, anyone he makes contact with, we have to cover. He may have left something. We have to check."

"Yes, sir."

The two men approached the house and Anwar rang the front door bell. As the old lady opened the door they forced their way in, easily snapping the simple safety chain as Anwar leant heavily against it. She stepped back in horror, the men grabbed an arm each, ignoring the fierce yapping of the little dog that was going berserk.

"What do you want," the elderly lady said, still being held in each arm by the men, "who are you?"

The hall was small, neat, tidy with a light coloured carpet, and wallpapered with a simple pattern of light flowery green and white stripes. A low chair set beside a half-moon table holding a key plate rested a few feet from the door, there was a silver-framed mirror conveniently placed near the front door and a few pictures hung on the walls, mainly reproductions of the Great Masters - The Hay Wain marked the entrance to the little dining room at the back located close to the kitchen. They took her in and sat her on a chair.

She looked up at the men with fear in her eyes, her light frame almost brittle in their hands. She wore a white cotton blouse with lace fringes beneath a pink cardigan buttoned from half way down, and a long tartan skirt. Her shoes were brown leather with a gold buckle. Her grey hair was neatly permed, though shaken now and a little out of place, and her face soft and gentle, with lines around her blue eyes. She had some light makeup on including a soft pink for lipstick. She was smart and elegant, but now suddenly shocked by having been pushed into a dangerous situation. However, she had known dangerous situations before. It might have been long ago; but it all came flooding back.

"Lady, we have no wish to hurt you," said Anwar in good English, although the Arabic accent was unmistakable.

"What do you want," she said again, "I don't have much money, or anything valuable, but you can have it all, please just take it and go."

"We are not thieves, Lady," continued Anwar. Then turning to Mulayl said, "Go and pull the curtains, everywhere."

Mulayl started to move but the dog was now standing by the door and still growling and barking, and showing its teeth in a worrying snarl. Unfortunately it was a rather high-pitched sound, as it was a small dog, but it was making a lot of noise and could doubtless deliver some nasty bites.

"Madam, you have to get your dog under control,"

continued Anwar, "Or I'm going to shut it up for you," he added, pulling a handgun with a silencer on it out of his jacket. Dismayed, the woman hastily called to the dog, and he ran and jumped onto her lap as she slapped the top of her thighs. She put her arms around him protectively, and spoke quietly to calm him down.

"Good, that's better," said Anwar, still holding the gun threateningly. "Now listen carefully, Lady. We have your son, Mr David Tilsen." The old lady drew in her breath, almost imperceptibly. "We saw him arrive here and we took him after he left. He is being held in a house not far from here in an area of countryside," lied Anwar. "He is our prisoner and we are going to kill him unless you do exactly what we want. Do you understand?"

The lady nodded, her eyes wide.

"We want the little item that he gave you when he was here."

The woman frowned and looked up confusedly at the man. "What are you talking about," she said, "I've no idea what you mean."

"Yes, you have, you know exactly what I mean. The card."

"Card? You want the card? What on earth do you want that for?"

Anwar looked at Mulayl, who had returned, and they raised their eyebrows at each other with a slight smile.

"Never mind that, Madam, you get it for us, show us where it is."

"Well, yes, if you want, of course, then be careful and don't hurt us."

Mulayl held open the door as the lady stood and Anwar marched her out. She steered over to the adjoining sitting room carrying the dog and they all walked in. It was comfortable and homely, with a blue crushed velvet-covered three piece suite, a bureau, television, fireplace with a mantelpiece surround and a couple more paintings on the light-coloured wall. There were two lights dangling from the ceiling with matching 1970s lampshades, and a dark blue carpet covered the floor. She walked over to the mantelpiece.

"Here it is," she said, taking a card from amongst several others, and handing it over to him.

"What is this," said Anwar, looking down at the birthday card in confusion and then staring over at the woman. "This isn't what I wanted."

"I don't understand," said the woman, "you said you wanted the card. Well, there's the card. It was my birthday two days ago and my son came to see me and he gave me the card."

Anwar went slightly red in the cheeks and looked as though he was going to burst. He didn't know if the stupid woman was being serious or trying to be funny or was senile or was just being honest.

"Sit down, there," he said agitatedly, pointing to the chair. She did as she was told, still clutching the dog. "Now listen," Anwar continued. "I want the micro SD card, not a birthday card. The small little card that fits into a phone or a computer, that we know your son gave you. That's the card we want. And if you don't give it to us we are going to have our colleagues put a bullet in your son's head!"

"No, no, please," she said, "don't do anything to hurt him." Tears started to appear and she pulled a tissue from her pocket and wiped her eyes and nose. She covered her mouth trying to calm herself, then stroked her eyes again and looked up at the men, shaking her head. "No, please, no, don't hurt him."

"Then tell us where it is."

"But I don't have anything else, he gave me a card and a box of chocolates and we had tea and some supper, that's all, I promise you, I have nothing else."

"Where are the chocolates?"

"There, on the table," and she nodded across to the other side of the room. Mulayl walked over, examined the box, tipped everything onto the floor and pulled it apart. He shook his head at Anwar.

Anwar stared at the woman, who looked back with fear still in her eyes. He wasn't sure whether he could see a steely resolve in her eyes too. No, he must be imagining; this is just an old woman who had had a birthday. But they needed to be sure. Before they killed her.

"I don't know whether you are telling me the truth or whether you are lying. We want that card."

"I'm sorry, I have no idea what you're talking about, the only card I have from my son is the one I've given you."

"Ok. We'll do it the hard way."

Anwar raised his hand, ready to strike the woman around the face. Mulayl called out, "No, Sir!" as the woman turned away to shield herself. He started the downward stroke, but stopped half way.

"It's ok," he said, lowering his arm, "I wasn't going to."

The old lady looked up at Anwar, with disgust in her eyes. Now he knew he was seeing a steely resolve in them.

"I am eighty-six years old," she said quietly but proudly, raising her chin a little. "If that is how you treat an elderly woman, then you get on with it. But to me you are scum. Just scum."

Anwar stared back. Then shook his head.

"Don't worry, Lady. We have another way."

Anwar took out two of the three small metal detectors that their contact had provided at the airport along with the guns. The units were fifteen centimetres tall by ten and about three centimetres thick, with two protruding nodules on the top. He chucked one to Mulayl and switched the other one on. It bleeped, whined, then fell silent. Mulayl's did the same.

"We'll search your house. You sit still and no harm will

come to you. You give us any trouble, and your son dies. Do you understand?"

"Yes," she said, sombrely, "I understand. Perfectly."

"We'll start with you first. Where is your cell phone?"

"It's in my handbag. It's there, on the sideboard."

Mulayl went over to it, took out the phone and searched for a card. There was none in it. He threw the phone onto the floor and stamped on it, crushing it. Anwar ran the detector over the woman's handbag; nothing.

"Hold the dog still."

The lady did as she was told. Anwar grabbed the dog's collar from behind its head, twisting it round the animal's neck and scanning the unit over it; it soon bleeped. The dog was growling fiercely and struggling to get free as Anwar examined the collar. He read the metal dog tag and released the collar. Then he ran the machine over the woman's hair, down her neck, over her shoulders, and the machine went off again at her brooch, a butterfly design in blue amethyst set in gold. He took it off her, looked at it, twisted it to make sure it was solid, then threw it on the floor.

"Stand up please." He prodded the old lady with the machine as he ran it up and down; it bleeped at one of her cardigan pockets. They took out a small gold-plated pill box, opened it, saw a couple of pills, threw them and the box onto the floor. The detector bleeped at her belt and at the buckles on her shoes; they pulled at them and examined them; nothing. They moved on to other things in the house, and the woman sat down again. She looked on as they started to tear her sitting room apart; they opened the television, found nothing, then smashed it; they opened the Sky box, found nothing, smashed it.

"Do you have to make such a mess," she said, as they pulled open the bureau drawers and tossed everything onto the floor.

"Be quiet and sit still," said Anwar as they continued.

The old lady did as she was told.

They took the landline telephone, opened it, found nothing, smashed it and yanked the cable from the box on the wall then broke it. They asked if there was an extension; she replied honestly, that there wasn't. The dog had calmed down a little so she put him on the floor. He sat, growling under his breath from time to time, and stayed by the chair. She was thinking calmly as the two men went about their unpleasant work thoroughly but quickly. She was convinced that they were going to kill her. They wore no masks or disguises of any kind, they could be recognised, she could give a description, they had committed any number of crimes already and they had kidnapped David and threatened his life. After a few more minutes, she knew what she must do. She swallowed and then gave a quiet sigh.

"Excuse me."

"Yes," said Anwar, "what do you want."

"If you don't want any trouble from the police, then you have to let me go out."

"What are you talking about, Lady? The police?"

"Yes, look I don't want any harm to come to my son, so I have to tell you this. You see, we have a very close-knit community here, people look after the elderly. I have to walk my dog every evening, and Mr Higgins further up the hill looks out for me and if he sees me each evening then he knows I'm alright. If he doesn't - if the weather is bad, or if I just don't go - he'll telephone me on my mobile phone to check I'm ok. That isn't going to happen now as you've destroyed it. If he can't get me he'll call me on my landline number, and that isn't going to ring either for the same reason. If he can't reach me he'll assume something is wrong and he'll call the police. They'll come here as an emergency to find out and make sure I'm ok or if I've had an accident or fall or whatever, or worse."

Anwar glanced at Mulayl, then back to the woman, who continued.

"So if you don't want the police here, then let me do the walk. One of you can follow easily enough. The dog needs to walk anyway. I don't want anything to happen to my son, I don't want any trouble, and so I'm telling you about the routine here."

The two men spoke in Arabic, then nodded.

"Ok, you go out. My friend Mulayl here will be following you, he has a gun, he can kill you at any time and anyone else that gets in the way. If you don't want your son or anyone else hurt you go and walk the dog, wave at your friend, then come back afterwards."

There can be no harm in that, thought Anwar, and the woman is co-operating. He was beginning to think this was all a waste of time anyway, she was just a mother and had nothing and was hiding nothing. He would go through the rest of the house quickly while she was out with Mulayl.

It was time. The old lady pushed herself up unsteadily from her favourite armchair and walked across the room. She unhooked the dog lead from the back of the door and smiled down at the little Scottie that was already wagging its tail again, in spite of these unwelcome visitors. She nodded.

"Come on then."

Mulayl hung a good two hundred metres behind the old lady as she walked her dog. He took out another cigarette and lit up, another person out for an evening's stroll, yet he kept a careful eye on the woman ahead. He saw her sway as she struggled over a small mound of grass; he saw her look over and wave at someone in one of the other houses half way up the hill and saw a figure wave back. That must be the Mr Higgins she had told them about. He paused as he saw the woman sit on the bench and tie the dog up, waiting as she glanced out to sea. He looked out at the water himself, and took another drag on the tobacco. Then he saw her stand, thinking she was about to turn round, and looked on first in puzzlement as she took a few steps ahead, then in astonishment with his mouth falling open as he saw the old lady raise her hands and topple forwards off the cliff.

He threw the stub of the cigarette away and turned to walk back briskly and get away from the area, then he broke into a run and didn't stop until he reached the house. He knocked on the door, Anwar let him in and he quickly relayed what had happened. In amazement, they gathered up their equipment, left the house, got into the car and drove off.

They had no way of knowing that Dame Mary Tilsen, GCB, CBE, eighty-six years of age, formerly a senior operative of MI6, having worked with great courage and success as a spy in East Germany in the 1970s and 1980s through the deadliest time of the cold war and as Head of Section until her eventual retirement, though now riddled with cancer and having not long to live, would take one more positive action for Queen and Country, confuse the two men in her house and their superiors and do what she could to help her son, even though she feared he might already be dead.

9
PANAMA SECRETS

COCO FOLLOWED AVENIDA A to the end and almost at the sea turned left into Central then right into Calle 2a Este. She joined Avenida B and drove west past the National Theatre and the Plaza Simón Bolívar, watching for anyone that looked as though they didn't belong there at that time of night. The cafés were colourful and busy, the older people sat and spoke quietly and the young lovers laughed carelessly, the girls in their heels and short skirts, most with long dark hair swirling around bare shoulders, the men in close-fitting trousers and open shirts, their wide smiles enticing and seducing as best they could. Every now and then a couple would stand and dance in the street, not bothering to go inside to the small wooden dance floors.

They went round the block once more. JP read the sign Plaza Simón Bolívar for the second time, fleetingly recognising the name more from the famous Symphony Orchestra and its former conductor, the charismatic Dudamel, than the history lessons at school, from which he could only vaguely recall that Bolívar was responsible for a number of Latin-American countries' gaining their independence from Spain including Panama and Venezuela, and that Bolivia was named after him. They passed the Theatre again. Its doors and ground floor windows were boarded up and its status of being closed was firmly announced by the large angled signs that declared 'CERRADA' all around the building. It was rather a sad sight, thought JP briefly, as Coco pulled the car up away from the cafés in an alley that ran the length of the Theatre. They quickly exited and made their way to the stage door which, although appearing to be similarly boarded, in fact on close inspection was still accessible. She knocked quietly, and they were let inside.

"Were you followed?" asked the man at the door, nodding to JP.

"No, we're clear," said Coco.

The man locked the stage door and led the way through a myriad of corridors and out onto the bare stage. A man sat at a table reading some papers, and stood as they approached.

"So, Coco, you had some action I hear? I'm glad you're ok."

"*We're* fine, thank you," said JP to the speaker as they drew close, feigning indignation at the lack of interest in his own wellbeing.

"Colonel Hector Alessandro… Jim Peregrine," said Coco taking care of the introductions. The men shook hands. "… and," turning to the man who had let them in, "Alberto Mendes, Communications and Electronics Security. The Colonel is the Head of Panama Intelligence."

"Mr Peregrine. The Falcon. I'm very pleased to meet you," said the Colonel in perfect English and with a smile that lit up his heavy-set face. The bushy eyebrows bounced up and down cordially. He was a short man but seemed to be built like an ox, judging from the strength of the handshake. "She's a good shot, eh?"

"With good timing," said JP. "I was given a very warm welcome by Schroeder."

"I don't think that man is going to be missed by anyone," said Alessandro. "Except of course by Jon Lano."

"So, Colonel, why are we here? I mean here exactly, in this rather unusual setting."

"MI6 has its own safe houses in London, away from your Headquarters on the Albert Embankment, does it not? We have ours. This is one of them. Do you like music and the plays, Mr Peregrine?"

"JP, please. Yes, of course. This is a lovely theatre."

"Five point four billion US dollars and counting for the new Canal Extension. And our Government can't find a measly one point two million for this beautiful place. It's crumbling and in need of restoration, we are told. Maybe they will get around to saving this important cultural building before it collapses into the sea. In the meantime, while it's officially closed, we use it as a safe house for our meetings from time to time, and I get to show it off to our visitors as we talk." The Colonel stepped forward and held out his hand towards the empty auditorium. "Italian operetta architecture, beautiful ceiling frescos, four rows of balconies with boxes, and wonderful acoustics. It breaks my heart."

"I am sorry, Colonel Alessandro," said JP. "Sometimes our governments don't deal with the things we would like them to."

The Colonel paused and looked over at JP, then smiled. "Thank you, young man, for indulging me for a few seconds."

JP waited patiently for his host to move on to the business at hand.

"I like to see how people react to my little passion. Everyone is different. It tells me something about them."

"Did I pass?" asked JP raising his shoulders slightly.

"You did, young man. Enough now of my digression. Come."

He led the way off Stage Right into the large number one dressing room, which contained an array of electronic listening and recording devices and computer terminals that seemed strangely at odds with the quintessential makeup mirrors with bare light bulbs around the borders. He turned to Mendes. "Alberto, we are secure?"

"Entirely, sir." Mendes was around thirty with straggly dark hair parted in the middle falling down over a rather slim face with sharp features and matching thin rectangular spectacles. He looked at JP and nodded confidently to him.

"Please, sit and be comfortable." They did as directed. "JP, I spoke with Charlie Melton earlier today. He called this morning to explain why you are here and what is at stake. There are a number of, shall we say, shady people in Panama and Jon Lano is by far the worst. I am not surprised that your fallen colleague Mr Tilsen was pointed towards him, and I would say that you are probably on the right track. This is surely confirmed by the fact that he tried to have you killed this evening."

"Probably first captured, tortured for all the information they could get and then killed," added Alberto.

"Thank you for that pleasant clarification," said JP.

"You're welcome," smiled Mendes.

"Lano will have a few questions to answer now about his operation at the Canal building at the airport," continued the Colonel, "but he will probably say that Schroeder was doing something independently and it got him killed. There is not much more that we can legally do at the moment. Coco will be back at work there tomorrow morning as usual and can report back on any developments though I doubt there will be any. There is only one question, really, and that is what do you want to do now?"

Coco had taken a chair in the corner and was sitting with her legs crossed and leaning back at ease, quietly listening. She looked from her boss to JP, expectantly.

"Colonel Alessandro, first, may I ask, does the term Decoy 17 mean anything to you? They were the last words to come from Dave Tilsen, written by him on the floor of his apartment on an envelope as he died. It's obviously a message of some kind. Are there couriers that you know of that pass through Panama on errands for Lano? Any regular routes or personnel that you could consider to be couriers, or decoys to throw the police off the passage of the real messenger? Anything?"

"No, JP, nothing," replied Alessandro thoughtfully. "There is nothing that I know of. What about you two?" Coco and Alberto shook their heads.

"Ok. And, does the term Stingray mean anything? Other than the obvious one of a fish. It's the codename that Malekka has used for his second plot. Major Melton probably mentioned it to you?"

"Yes, he did, and, as I told him, we have not come across that either. Nothing new at Lano's offices, Coco?"

"No, sir, nothing. I've never heard anyone use that term."

"Ok, thank you, all of you." JP sat silently and thought, then continued. "The meeting with Lano itself was pretty low key. Nothing extraordinary, nothing that I would consider unusual, in the circumstances. Just a typical uneventful but I suppose successful business meeting. However if Lano is indeed the key to Stingray then I have to get back into his office and see what I can find."

"What, you mean you want to get in out of office hours, when nobody's there?" asked Coco.

"Yes. Does he have a safe? And of course his computer - he was fiddling with that all through our chat. I'd like to know what's on it. The next lead may be resting on his hard drive, information that explains more about why Tilsen had this meeting set up. I think I should go in and steal it, get it back to you and then you folks can rip it to shreds and see what's on it. I could see the cabling when I was there, it seems to be an independent desktop, not linked to a mainframe for the company. Better for him that way, of course. Obviously if I steal the computer, it will give the game away to Lano, but we can't do anything about that."

"Why do you have to steal it," said Coco.

"I won't be able to get into it, there will obviously be a password."

"I know the password."

The three men looked at the young woman incredulously.

"How do you know the password?" asked Alberto with admiration and, JP thought he noticed, some affection.

"I was in his office one morning, just last week, it was early and he had called me in for something as Emily, his Personal Secretary, was off for the morning. I was standing by the chair in front of his desk which is quite close. There is a television screen off to his right and behind. It was not turned on, and I had a full view of the reflected keyboard. The angle happened to be perfect. The view was reversed of course, but I got it." Coco gave a smile to the men, and said to JP, "We may be a small country, Falcon, but we're well trained."

"So I see," said JP. "Ok, as long as Lano hasn't changed his password then I won't steal the computer."

"The best way for you to get in is for me to help. I have a pass card that will open the doors into the building and the office. We'll need to erase the CCTV systems of the main hall and the one in the office, and wipe out the record of my swiping the access points with my card, otherwise my cover will be blown; but I know where those are kept and I can do that."

"Very well, then it is settled," said Colonel Alessandro. "When do you want to go in?"

"Now. Tonight," said JP. "We haven't any time to waste." He turned to Coco. "What time do the cleaners go in?"

"At 6am. Why?"

"In case we need his fingerprints. For a safe."

"Ah, ok. We'll be fine."

They stood, making ready to leave, then JP remembered the envelope in his pocket. "Colonel, could you have this looked at please, I'd like to know what it is." He handed the envelope across. "I took it earlier from Schroeder's safe. Oh, and this," he added, pulling the data stick out as well. "It contains the files from his computer, that was still turned on when I was there. It might be helpful to you and your own work against Lano and of course I'd like to know what you find. Can you upload the data to London as well please?"

"Yes," said the Colonel. He looked at the PCB and handed it and the stick to Mendes. "What do you think, Alberto?"

He took the board and the stick. "The stick we can upload at once, and I can keep a copy and go through everything with ease. The board, well as much as I would like to play around with it our resources for this sort of analysis is limited. If speed is important, which I know it is, I think you would do better to send it to London, señor, or the CIA in Washington."

"Can you copy the stick now? I'm going to need it later."

"Sure," said Alberto, and sat at one of the keyboards.

"Do you have these kinds of data sticks?" continued JP. "Flick the slider over or it'll copy everything from your machine."

"Don't worry, Mr Peregrine. These, we have."

JP thought for a moment.

"Colonel, will you arrange for the board to get to London as quickly as possible."

The Colonel nodded. "Yes, of course."

Alberto was back in a few minutes and handed the data stick to JP.

"Data copied and uploaded to MI6. And the stick is clean."

"Thanks," said JP. He looked at Coco. "Ok, we'd better go."

"I'll call Charlie Melton," said Colonel Alessandro, "and tell him what is happening and what he can expect to receive shortly. Good luck. We will wait here until you return. And be careful, Falcon."

"*We* will," said Coco. They all laughed.

The two made their way out of the dressing room and headed towards the stage door.

≈

Anwar and Mulayl had received different instructions from Malekka for their departure from the UK. The general security surveillance at the two main London airports was extremely sophisticated and there was a real possibility that, had Fadil, Anwar or Mulayl been caught on camera elsewhere around the time of Tilsen's demise, they might be picked up and linked by computerised facial recognition software during what would undoubtedly be a review by the British intelligence forces of Tilsen's whereabouts and movements following his return to England. They would be tracked, possibly traced to Iran and to Malekka. Fadil was at Gatwick, and left the country from Heathrow on a different passport; that was enough. The arrangements for Anwar and Mulayl were to be different, and they would first have to disappear.

The two men drove from Eastbourne to Gatwick Airport, where Mulayl dropped Anwar at the South Terminal, but not for a flight. He went at once to the train station and bought a ticket to London. Mulayl dropped the hire car off, took the company bus back to the airport and also headed for the train station inside the South Terminal, where he too bought a ticket to London.

Even at that late hour there were fast trains running to the capital. Anwar caught the last one to Victoria, walked out into Buckingham Palace Road and took a right into Victoria Street. He strolled along for a few minutes, hailed a cab and went to Bayswater Road to a small hotel for the night. Mulayl was able to catch the next train thirty minutes later which took him to St Pancras International. He exited onto York Road and signed into the Premier Inn.

The following morning the two men made their way to Euston Station and took a train to Manchester Airport, Anwar at 9am and Mulayl at 10am, both with a journey time of two and a half hours. Anwar, also armed with a substitute passport as was Mulayl, took the 2pm flight to Berlin arriving 5pm local and checked into a hotel for the night. The next morning he took the 10am flight to Vienna, had a lazy lunch in the city, returned to the airport and took the 5pm flight to Istanbul. Mulayl took a similarly scenic route, first to Zurich where he spent an overnight, and the next day he flew to Rome and then on to Istanbul. The two men met up in the evening, stayed at a local airport hotel and took the early morning flight to Tehran.

They arrived at Imam Khomeini International Airport a little later than scheduled at 10.12am, just as in Panama City, some eight thousand miles west, JP and Coco Chavarez began to head back to Jon Lano's offices for their covert night activity.

PART THREE

THE THIRD DAY

10
BACK INTO ISTRAS

COCO CHAVAREZ DROVE swiftly and they were soon back on the Cinta Costera heading northeast into the city centre. The main roads were still busy but most of the business section had closed down and its occupants were enjoying home life or the numerous all-night bars, restaurants and clubs deeper in the older parts of the town. She steered off the one-way system and onto the northern set of three lanes of Avenida Balboa which flowed west in the reverse direction they had just travelled, and then turned right, into the Avenida Aquilino De La Guardia. The Bicsa building was on the corner. She drove past their destination, the traffic promptly disappeared. The night was still. It was just after midnight, at the start of a new day.

Coco parked the car in a side street. She took JP's arm and they strolled nonchalantly back along the streets, talking quietly and smiling, as though a couple out on a date. But there was nobody around to see them.

Only the large Bicsa nametag was still lit up at the building, several floors above the ground. Coco guided them to a door to the side of the main large revolving entrance doors, pulled a card from her purse and swiped it down the entry system, entering a code on the panel as well. The door clicked and she and JP entered.

"I'll get the CCTV," said Coco, and disappeared down a corridor. JP walked to the elevators that he had used a few hours before, and waited for her to return. He looked up as he heard her footsteps.

"Ok, I've erased the hard drive and have the backup disc," she said quietly. "I've reset it to start in four hours, so that should give us ample time."

"With a new backup disc?"

"Yes, but no-one will know anything unless they view the discs or go through the HD time codes, and there should be no reason for that."

"Ok."

She pressed the button for the elevator. They were taken rapidly to the sixtieth floor. The doors opened with a gentle 'ping', and they stepped slowly into the entrance hall. It was in darkness save for the city light drifting in from the windows. Coco disappeared again, to deal with the internal security cameras, and reappeared with another disc.

"Done?" said JP in a low voice.

"Done. The internal surveillance system is bleached and off. We have four hours here too."

She led them down the wide corridor, through the two pairs of double doors and into the anteroom at the entrance to Lano's office. They both slipped on some nitrile gloves. She worked the keypad.

"How do you know the code?"

"Because I'm good," replied Coco with a smile. "I picked it up over many visitors, a glance at a time."

They were in.

The window behind Lano's desk had its blinds down from the ceiling, to take away the glare from the hot afternoon sun. JP worked a switch to tilt them shut. He pulled out his cell phone and used its light to look around.

"Where's the safe?" asked JP. Coco walked to the wall to the right of the desk. "Behind the Picasso." She pulled at the side and the frame swung away on the hinges on the left. JP stared at it.

"Well this one is going to need more than just a key." He pulled out a small envelope from his jacket pocket, and removed a circular metal disk four centimetres across with two tapes a centimetre wide protruding from opposite ends. He placed the disc over the silver combination dial lock proudly printed up with Sargent and Greenleaf and uncovered the two adhesive-coated ends of the tapes, which he put onto the surface of the safe. On top of the disc was a little LCD screen. He pressed a small concave recess button, and the screen lit up and began its work.

"I've heard about those," said Coco looking on with interest, "but never seen one in action, we don't have them."

"The latest safe cracker. These used to be x-ray, but this is gamma-ray based, from Cobalt-60, and can even see through lead. It was developed from the same technology that our friends in the US use in their Container Security Initiative to see inside ship containers. It will pop up the combination in a minute." He looked at the scanner below by the unlocking spindle. "But this is going to need a fingerprint to open." He slid the screens across on his phone, the light changed colour and various filters flicked in front of the soft beam. He chose a blue light and orange filter. They walked to the desk.

The surface was awash with fingerprints, as was the computer keyboard and mouse. JP removed some covered cellophane strips from the same envelope, and held the light as Coco pressed a strip on what was an index finger and thumbprint, lifting the strips off carefully.

Just then the LCD screen on the disc started to flash. They walked over to it. JP read off the screen.

"Ten, thirty-seven, seventy-five."

He removed the safe cracker and returned it to the envelope, and put it back carefully in his pocket. He spun the dial a few times counter clockwise and came to rest on the first number, ten. Then he went clockwise to thirty-seven, and rotated twice more to the right coming to rest again on thirty-seven. Left to seventy-five and round counter clockwise once more ending carefully on seventy-five. Finally, he turned the dial clockwise again, felt the resistance and continued to turn a little harder. The safe clicked, unlocking the mechanism.

The LCD scanner by the spindle handle lit up.

"What do you think? Thumbprint?" he said to Coco.

"Let's try it."

She took the cellophane that carried the lifted thumbprint and placed it onto the scanner screen. They heard a small hum and the screen displayed a green tick. JP turned the handle carefully. The safe opened and he pulled the door ajar.

"Ok, I'll have a look. Will you do the computer?" He handed her the data stick.

Coco switched on the PC and waited. She entered the code.

"I'm in."

She plugged the data stick into a USB port and saw the strip light begin to glow green, indicating the copying was taking place. She waited patiently.

There was little in the safe. Except a bubble wrap jiffy bag, which JP removed.

"Well, well, look at this," he exclaimed as he pulled out the contents. "Another PCB board. The same as Schroeder's."

Coco came over. "So it is. Obviously it means something important to them and Lano's work."

He popped the board into his pocket. "See if you can find some blank paper that won't be missed, I'll fill the envelope out with them."

While Coco tackled a small printer by the wall opposite, JP continued his search of documents from the safe. He photographed five sheets, that seemed to be invoices or receipts for large sums of money, four of them in seven digits.

"He's got some big turnover here."

"Good, maybe we can use it to get him on something at last," said Coco, who was back with several sheets of blank paper. JP folded them up and wedged them into the jiffy bag, swelling it up to the right proportions. He went through the final couple of papers from the safe. The last was a handwritten note, with a name and address. He took a picture of that too. He placed all of the sheets back into the safe, and the jiffy bag. He closed the safe, spun the spindle and rotated the dial lock a few times, carefully placing it back on the same digit on which he had found it resting - eighty-eight. JP pulled the picture frame shut over the safe.

They walked to the desk and looked at the disk. The green bar was almost full. “Maybe another five minutes,” said Coco.

JP nodded, and leant against the edge of the desk thoughtfully.

“That’s two electronic boards we’ve found this evening,” he said quietly, “and I would wager that the Decoy 17 Tilsen had found out about refers somehow to the boards and their movement. Perhaps there are seventeen boards that have been stolen and replaced with something else as decoys, and the stolen ones are transported a different way, covertly. Seventeen decoys for seventeen stolen boards.”

“Yes!” said Coco excitedly. “That could be it! It makes sense.”

“We need to find out what those boards are.” Then he sighed. “No, that can’t be it.”

“Why not?”

“Because if the boards were of any value or significance, they could easily be replicated from the first stolen one. There would be no need to steal seventeen of them.”

Coco nodded, rather dejectedly. “I see what you mean,” she said. “How disappointing, I thought you had something there.”

“Unless they were all different boards…” he continued, more to himself than Coco. “Still, it could be something along those lines. The boards are tied in for sure.”

The stick started to blink. The copy was complete.

Coco removed the stick and handed it to JP, who pocketed

it. She logged out of the computer, and turned it off. They placed everything back in its original place on the desk, and looked around the office one more time. JP had a quick rummage through the drawers of the desk, which revealed nothing untoward. In fact, it was notable how tidy and organised Jon Lano appeared to be.

JP returned the blinds to the open position. They retraced their steps back through the anteroom and the corridors, to the elevators. Coco pressed the button to open the elevator doors. JP followed Coco in. They turned to face the hallway, and JP pressed the button labelled 'L' for Lobby.

≈

As the elevator doors began to close on the headquarters of International Shipping Transport Services, the tiny camera at the top of the mirror hanging on the wall opposite behind Coco's desk silently recorded its final images, linking in to those taken by the micro camera in Lano's office, that formed the secret secondary monitoring system that only Mr Jon Lano knew anything about.

11
THE NEXT FLIGHT

THEY WERE QUICKLY back at the car and within fifteen minutes were once again inside the safe house with Alberto and Colonel Alessandro.

"It's another circuit board," said Alberto in curious surprise. "Apparently identical to the other."

"Can you get them both sent to London as quickly as possible please," asked JP. "The sooner we can find out what those are, the better."

"Of course," said the Colonel.

"And here's the data stick.," he added, handing it over.

"You were able to get it all?"

"Yes. The password worked like a charm." They looked over at Coco, who smiled.

Alberto left to copy over the data on the stick. JP pulled out his cell phone and showed an image to the Colonel.

"Does this name and address mean anything? It was on a notepad in Lano's safe."

Alessandro looked at the screen, then read out loud.

"'Mr Jorge Monterroso, 425 Rua Souza Lima, Rio de Janeiro, RJ, 22081-010, Brazil.'" He shook his head. "No, I'm afraid not."

JP was silent for a moment. Then he decided.

"If it was just a random name and address, why would Lano have put it in his safe? It must mean something, and I reckon it's the next lead. I don't think I can do much more here. We have the boards to send to London, and you have all the material from the computers to be digesting. I'm going to go to Rio on the next available flight. And find out who this Monterroso is and how he's involved."

"Very well, Falcon," said the Colonel.

They waited for Alberto. Coco moved over to the Colonel and spoke quietly in Spanish. JP sat and waited, thinking. He would call Melton as soon as he was back at the hotel.

Alberto returned and handed the stick to JP.

"Copied, and uploaded to London. And cleared."

"Thank you." JP looked over at Alessandro. "Colonel, if you find anything interesting from Lano's computer…"

"Don't worry, you'll hear it as soon as we do."

JP smiled. "And, do you have a couple of pictures of Lano, for London and me?"

"Sure, we'll send them. Alberto?

"Yes, will do."

"So, if we're done," said JP to Coco, "can I have a lift?"

Coco drove the Falcon to his hotel. It was just after 3am. The sky was still dark and the sun a couple of hours away from rising. JP looked across at her as the hotel came into sight.

"Are you planning on going back to work at Lano's place?"

"Of course. Why wouldn't I?"

"It's a dangerous game, Coco. What more can you achieve there? You have the details from his computer and the safe, you'll be able to dissect Schroeder's place, and you probably have all the sensitive information there is to be had about him. If you can't get him now, you probably never will."

"If I don't go in it will alert them that something is wrong, if not today then tomorrow, or the next day. I can't just not show up again. It might make him suspicious, and then he might run."

"Why don't you go and hold him for forty-eight or seventy-two hours, pending your investigation into what we have found."

"We can't do that. Lano may be a crook and a murderer, but he also has many friends here, placed high in the Government. If we don't play this straight and be sure of our facts before we make a move, it will weaken the Section and compound the problem we have in bringing Lano down. I have discussed this with the Colonel, and he agrees."

She pulled the car up outside the foyer entrance. JP put his arm around the back of her seat and leant over towards her. She looked at him.

"You know, if this was a slightly different time, I'd ask you up for a drink."

She smiled.

"You know, if this was a slightly different time, I'd accept."

He kissed her lightly on the lips.

"You be careful partner, ok?"

"You too, Falcon."

JP exited the car and crossed into the foyer, then watched as she drove off.

JP took the elevator and unlocked the door to his suite. He pulled out his cell phone, placed it in search mode, and looked at the display as he walked briskly around the rooms. There were no microphones, no transmitters; the suite was still clean. He poured himself a whisky from the extensive selection of spirits and wines in the drinks cabinet, and sat on the deep couch that faced towards the wide window overlooking the Bay. He put the call through to Charlie Melton. It was almost 10am in London. He gave his report on the scrambled line to his friend.

"… By the time I get to Rio, you should have the boards. I'm sure they're tied in somehow. I thought it was those things that were being carried as decoys or something. Perhaps they are, I don't know. In any event, for both Schroeder and Lano to have one must mean something."

"Yes so it would seem," said Charlie Melton. "We're looking at the stuff from the computers, as soon as we have anything we'll pass it on of course. It's probably just as well you're leaving later today. Lano expects Mr Dave Tilsen to be dead by now or at least being persuaded to talk, and when he realises neither has happened, you can probably expect another hit or snatch attempt. You'd better get out of there."

"Don't worry, I'm keen to go."

"The thing I don't understand is why Lano would want you - Tilsen rather - dead. What could you possibly have said or done in the meeting with him that triggered that?"

"I haven't the slightest idea. And if it hadn't been for Chavarez I might be talking to you from the hospital now, or worse." He paused, then added, "They're a good team here, Charlie."

"Yes."

"Anything on the Rio name?"

"Nothing. Hang on, JP." Melton picked up the phone that had just buzzed on his desk, listened, gave an instruction and replaced the receiver. "JP, Transport tell me that the flights to Rio from Panama seem to be in the afternoon, so we'll lay on a Gulfstream. They'll see what they can organise. Don't go to bed, just pack and be ready. We'll let you know."

JP showered and packed, and ordered a large breakfast to be brought to his room. He hadn't eaten for a while and was hungry, and consumed it with relish. The coffee was strong and invigorating. At a quarter past eight his cell phone rang and Melton passed the details of the travel - the G650 aircraft would be ready for him at 10am, they just needed Colonel Alessandro to allocate the pilot and crew from his own people, to ensure his safety and that Lano had not somehow infiltrated the plan and flight personnel. Melton had arranged for the local Consulate personnel in Rio to meet him, and sent JP some ID pictures.

A little before 8.30am, Coco Chavarez was getting ready to leave for work at the International Shipping Transport Services at the BISTRO building. As the Falcon left the foyer of the Intercontinental Hotel at the same time to head to the airport he thought briefly of a few hours ago, when he had watched the young woman drive off into the night. *Competent, fearless. And a bloody good shot.*

He didn't know, then, that he would never see Coco Chavarez alive again.

12

REPORTING TO MALEKKA

THE SAME DAY at 2pm Iran local time, some nine and a half hours ahead of Panama, Anwar and Mulayl were waiting at Malekka's residence for their master to return from a private lunch with the President of Iran, to make their report. They had been collected by helicopter within an hour of their arrival, they had had an opportunity to shower or bathe, change clothes and eat, but they were nervous about the forthcoming discussion. They had learned from Fadil that the micro SD card recovered from Tilsen's person by the assassin Solh was not the right one, that Malekka had been furious, the operation in London had not been successful and he was hoping for positive news from the two of them. They knew he wasn't going to get it.

One of the servants came up to the men and asked them to accompany her to Mr Malekka and a few minutes later they walked smartly into his sumptuous lounge. His newly-appointed prime bodyguard and personal assistant, Latif Yameen, was there together with Duha. Ghazi and Zaim, who had gone back to the Mediterranean and Cuttle Cove and returned, completed the group. They exchanged greetings, then at Malekka's direction took seats in the matching deep luxurious chairs placed around a huge low oval table on which had been placed some light refreshments of fruits, dates and nuts, coffee and soft drinks. Malekka sat at its head and the report and discussion began. A few minutes in and Malekka had his first question.

"Why didn't you just execute the woman?" he asked coldly, with slight frustration in his voice. "Now there will be attention from the police because of a suicide, they will have gone into her house and learned that it was apparently burgled, and the security forces will be alerted much earlier than was necessary."

"Well, sir, we were going to, of course," said a rather unnerved Anwar, "but she was worried about her son, she knew we had Tilsen, or believed we did, and she was keen to co-operate and help us. That's why she told us about the routine, she always has to walk her dog last thing and around a certain hour each evening. They have a community help system or neighbourhood care group. A man watches out for her; provided he sees her on her walk then he knows she's well and ok each evening, but if she doesn't appear he assumes something must be wrong and he calls her on her cell phone or landline. We'd already destroyed or disabled both of those in the search. If he can't reach her, he calls the police, raises the alarm and gets them out to her, in case she's had a fall or been taken ill or something. And of course we did not want to risk having the police arrive at the house while we were there."

"Yes, sir, that's true," added Mulayl, "And I saw her wave to someone in another house half way along the route, and the man waved back. He recognised her and it was like she had said."

"We had carefully checked everything," said Anwar. "She didn't have the card on her anywhere, or in the house, we searched it thoroughly. If Tilsen didn't have the card in the flat or on him when he was terminated, and if the old woman didn't have it, then he didn't bring the card with him when he left Cuttle Cove."

"Well that is most definitely not what I was told when I went back there," said Zaim. "It was for sure going to be taken to the UK by the man in person. And that would seem to be the case as Fadil says Solh gave him the little box with the SD card in it that he had found in Tilsen's pocket. So that does support the thinking that Tilsen had the card but then switched it."

"If that is so and Tilsen had it with him," said Malekka, "then where is it? And why did this old woman throw herself off the cliff? What was the point of that?"

"Excuse me, sir," said Ghazi, "but I have an idea about that."

They all looked at him. "Yes?" asked Malekka expectantly.

"Well, it seems to me, sir, I mean, let's assume Tilsen left Cuttle Cove with the card. That is what Zaim is certain of. But we know he didn't have it on him when he reached his home in London - that is what Solh and Fadil learned - and so he must have switched it. So, obviously it's somewhere else. He was followed all the time. He didn't post an envelope; he didn't meet with anyone else. Therefore it seems to me that he must have had it when he entered the house to see his mother and must have left it with the old woman at the house before he went."

"That's impossible, my friend," said Anwar, with a slightly raised voice, "it wasn't there."

"We know for sure it wasn't," said Mulayl, getting a little agitated. "We searched it. It wasn't there."

"Hang on, please," smiled Ghazi, so that he could finish. "And then we have the fact that the woman threw herself off the cliff. If she didn't have the card, why would she do that?"

There was a pause.

"I know why she did it," continued Ghazi. "It was because she *did* have the card. She had it all the time. But she managed to hide it. She put it where you couldn't get it and where it couldn't be picked up by the metal detectors."

He looked over at his master.

"Of course," said Malekka slowly as realisation dawned, staring back at Ghazi, then emphasising the words. "She *swallowed* it," he said.

"She swallowed it," repeated Ghazi.

The words sank into the others and they nodded and murmured amazed acknowledgement. They had the explanation.

"Yes, let's think about this," said Anwar. "There were a few occasions when she put her hand to her face. She was scared - terrified - it looked as though she was protecting herself, catching her breath." Then to Mulayl, "Remember, when she did that, a couple of times?"

"Yes. Once in the kitchen as we started talking to her, and then again when you pulled out the gun and threatened to shut the animal up. She was frightened for the dog, raised her hand to her mouth and breathed in shaking her head. And then she bent down to call the animal over."

"There was a third time," said Anwar firmly. "She started to cry when we told her we had Tilsen?"

"Yes," replied Mulayl, with eyes that widened slightly. "She pulled out a handkerchief."

"Yes. She pulled out a tissue from her pocket, wiped her eyes and nose, held it over her mouth catching her breath - or so it looked - then wiped her eyes again. All innocent, all natural. Just a distressed, terrified woman."

"Was that before you searched her and started the search of the house?" asked Malekka.

Anwar nodded ruefully. "I'm afraid it was, sir. I didn't spot anything, she did it all very well. I regret to say I saw nothing."

Mulayl agreed. "It's true. It's possible she put something into her mouth and swallowed it." He shook his head in astonishment. "She looked like a tired elderly woman that was nervous and scared. Instead she was a clever conniving crafty old bitch. I didn't spot anything either."

"I am very sorry, sir, to have let you down," said Anwar to Malekka.

"Me too, sir, I'm very sorry," added Mulayl.

"She said she was eighty-six years old," added Anwar. "Yet she outsmarted us both."

Malekka looked at the two men, first at Anwar and then Mulayl. He shrugged his shoulders.

"Never mind, my friends," he said with resignation in his voice. "Although we don't have the SD card, the fact is the enemy doesn't have it either. And they're not going to be able to get it. It will take them days to recover the body. I know that stretch of the English Channel, there have been hundreds of shipwrecks at Beachy Head over the years, the waters are dangerous and the currents unpredictable and often fierce." He sat back and crossed his legs, comfortable in the knowledge that his secrets were still safe.

"When they do recover the body," said Ghazi, "it won't do them much good. The stomach acids will have done their work on the SD card, unless it was in some kind of pre-prepared coating to protect it, which seems unlikely as she didn't know in advance she was going to have to swallow it. There might have been a small case and she somehow popped it out of it, probably it was in her pocket with the handkerchief."

"Oh," groaned Anwar, "there was a case. A small pillbox, in her pocket."

"So, this is looking as though it is correct. And if she swallowed the card unprotected, the card will more than likely be damaged. Or even crushed in the fall."

"And would they even look for anything," asked Zaim rhetorically. "Why would they look inside a dead old woman's stomach?"

"Autopsy?" asked Duha, who had otherwise sat silent for most of the discussion.

"Maybe," said Yameen. "Their law might require a standard postmortem on a suicide jumper. But they'd be looking for the cause of death - which obviously will be multiple injuries sustained from the impact as a result of the fall, not a little bit of metal in the stomach - if they get that far."

"Gentlemen," said Malekka, "I think these deductions are correct. It will take them time to find the body; time to recover it; time to organise and undertake an autopsy and a coroner's hearing. A good few days at least; perhaps two or three weeks. If they find anything in her they won't know what it is for, it will be meaningless; and the chances are they won't be able to recover anything from the card anyway even if they do locate and retrieve it and try to in the first place. In any event everything is encrypted and that will be difficult for them, and would take even longer." He sipped at a fruit juice thoughtfully. "No, it will be of no use to them, and I doubt they'll find it. And, the time involved will make it of no consequence to us either way."

The others around the table looked at Malekka, waiting for their leader to give the next direction.

"The point is, though," continued Malekka, "that *we* don't have the SD card and its data either. However, the difference is, *we can get the information back again.* It is an inconvenience, a serious inconvenience. But we can recover it. Fortunately we have the time - just - before our primary date and target. It was right to have tried to recover the original card. That would have made things so much easier, safer and quicker. But, so be it. We'll have to take the tougher route and gather the data again. Unfortunately I do not believe I shall be leaving the confines of our Motherland for some time, it is not safe for me. As a result of the collapse and failure of Spider the infidels will have information on me. I shall not be travelling to recover the data. That I shall have our colleague do. Sadly, it means I will not be able to instigate Stingray; that, our colleague will also have the privilege of doing." He gave a slight sigh. "But, it doesn't matter. That Stingray *is* instigated, and on time, is what matters."

They nodded at his words, Anwar and Mulayl particularly glad that their master was not displeased with them to any serious degree. They knew they would have to work hard to make up for their shortcomings and the disappointment they had caused him.

"We must move quickly," continued Malekka, "now that the course of action is clear. We have a few days to the start of Stingray. We have time. I will give the instructions, today, in a few minutes. This is now our priority and it must be completed as fast as possible." He paused, then continued with a slight smile. "That - what did you call the woman Mulayl?"

"A clever conniving crafty old bitch, sir," said Mulayl, regretting again how Anwar and he had been outsmarted.

"Oh yes. That clever conniving crafty old... lady," corrected the ever-polite albeit genocidal Malekka, "will not be able to stop or hinder the international implementation and operation of Stingray in any way whatsoever. This time, we will succeed."

The men smiled broadly and stood as Malekka rose, signalling that the meeting was at an end.

They would not have smiled quite so much had they known how clever, conniving and crafty Dame Mary Tilsen had actually been.

13
GAUNCHON

THAT SAME MORNING, a little over a thousand miles west and one and a half hours behind Iran time, Stephanie Raughton and Anna Kepling had made good use of the 'Do Not Disturb' signs they had each placed on their doors. They had decided that as there was little they could do in the morning they would take the opportunity to sleep and rest; as with most people, the change in time zones was playing havoc with their body clocks, and the next couple of days could see their working well into the night. They rose at around 11am, had lunch at 12.30pm - just as Malekka's group of men in Iran were beginning their meeting - and by 2pm were walking through the foyer of the Meridien Hotel out to the waiting car. Not long after, they were in the offices of Air Vice-Marshall Sir Donald Gaunchon, Commander British Forces Cyprus at the RAF base of Akrotiri.

"Forgive my apparent staring, Ms Raughton, but you are so different from when we met a couple of weeks ago that I have to check you are actually the same woman! It's an extraordinary change."

"I'm glad you're having that difficulty, Sir Donald," said Stephanie, smiling as they shook hands, "to be different is the intention."

"Didn't you have green eyes before… how have you done that? They're dark now."

"Contact lenses," said Stephanie, now with a broad grin. "That's actually quite an easy one." She turned towards her companion.

"Anna, this is Sir Donald Gaunchon, who runs things here. Sir Donald, meet Anna Tchepikova, now Kepling."

Gaunchon extended a hand, and as they shook he said, "And I suppose you don't look anything like I'm seeing you now, do you?!"

"Actually, no, at least I hope not," she replied, giving him a smile back.

He gestured to the women to sit, and resumed his own seat on the other side of the desk.

"I didn't expect to see you back so soon, Ms Raughton, and I'm sorry there is more work to be done. Charlie Melton tells me there is something else going on. It's shocking… terrifying. What kind of people are these devils."

"Alien to the lifestyle we believe in."

"That's for sure."

"And it's Stephanie, or Stephie, please."

Gaunchon smiled and nodded. "I was sorry to hear about Dave Tilsen," he continued, "I didn't know him well, in fact only since he arrived here after Operation Waterhole. He was obviously highly intelligent and a charming man, and I liked him."

"Yes, Dave was all of that."

"And, Ms Kepling, or Anna, if I may…" Anna nodded courteously… "I know of your part in Spider, and I would like to offer my sincere condolences for what you have endured, as well as my admiration for your own role, played out with great bravery if I may say so."

"Thank you, Sir Donald," said Anna, still having difficulty stopping the tears from welling up.

"So, ladies, to business. I am at your disposal. First, as requested by Charles Melton, here are the passes through the Demilitarised Zone into Northern Cyprus. As you can imagine, the passage of any personnel north or south is now jointly being carefully monitored, and you would not be able to get through without these. They are multiple entry and exit, as you will see."

He handed over two passport-sized certificates, each carrying their new-look ID photographs that were hastily emailed ahead from London prior to their recent departure.

"And we have a car ready and available for you. It's not a particularly modern car, but that was the request from London and so that's what you have."

"No, that's perfect," said Stephie.

"I understand the plan. Posing as reporters who are sniffing for a story, you are to infiltrate into the northern community in an effort to discover the individual who originally gave Tilsen the information about Decoy 17, and the contacts."

"Yes, that's it," said Stephanie. "JP is in Panama and following up on the only lead we have, taking the meeting that Dave Tilsen had prearranged. Obviously Dave received that information as a tip-off from someone here on Cyprus. We need to find the same person, or persons, and see what else we can uncover, if anything. When Tilsen was killed he had written down *'DECOY 17'* but we have no idea what that means or refers to. We need to find out. And fast."

"And how are you going to do that? We have about fifty persons within the Cuttle Cove estate still. The rest - around two hundred people - have been deemed to be safe and have been released and come and go, although none has been permitted to leave the Island or cross into the South, and that policy will continue. It was extraordinary to discover just how little Malekka had told his people about what was happening at the place, and what his plan was. A few at the top knew; but most he considered expendable and couldn't care less if they lived or died."

"And maybe that's the reason why someone spoke up," said Anna. "But they did it quietly, in case there were recriminations against them."

"I imagine many people are still loyal to Malekka," said Stephanie, "and whoever it was who spoke might have to be careful. You will obviously have the personnel at Cuttle Cove re-question the fifty then?"

Sir Donald nodded.

"And in answer to your question, our plan is to visit the bars and bistros and restaurants and start asking around, to see what we can find, under the cover of being reporters. Obviously I could be recognised, hence my appearance change, and Anna and I felt she too should be disguised, as a safety precaution. Especially as it makes us both look some years older."

"I understand," said Gaunchon. "I don't have to say this, but I will anyway - be careful, both of you. The North is a Muslim country, even though this is the Island of Cyprus in the Mediterranean, and women are treated differently from that in the western world. Your very presence in some of the places you are thinking of going to might cause trouble."

"Yes," said Stephanie. "That's why we're reporters. Everyone knows they don't care about anything except a good story."

14
BENEATH THE CORCOVADA

BRAZILIANS SAY THAT in the Beginning, God didn't spend six days creating the world and the universe before He rested on the seventh; He spent five days on everything else and then one entire day on Rio de Janeiro. That's why it's so beautiful.

The G650 aircraft descended in evening sunlight that bounced off the calm waters of the southern Atlantic Ocean, with the white sands of Copacabana Beach and Ipanema glinting off the wingtip. The great statue of Christ the Redeemer on the top of the Corcovado Mountain towered above them, arms outstretched, offering peace to all, welcoming and protecting.

At Galeão International Airport the Falcon was met on the tarmac a few steps from the aircraft. "Mr Tilsen?" said an English voice, the man recognising JP from the image sent him securely from London by MI6. It had come with a written brief, after the call from Charles Melton to the Rio Consul General.

"Yes," replied JP.

"I'm Paul Towsing, from the British Consulate."

"How do you do," said JP. "How kind of you to meet me."

"I was asked to come down and greet you at the aircraft, and help you through the customs here."

"I suppose the customs can be a bit trying at times."

"Yes, all the more so after a long flight."

"And I'm ready for my hotel right now."

Good, thought JP, that was the coding cleared. He had recognised Towsing from the pictures sent from MI6 earlier in the day, but one could never be too careful. Towsing was twenty-eight, tall, slim, and his light flannel suit was so baggy it seemed the trousers might fall down at any minute. His blond hair hung over his glasses and needed frequent pushing away. He arranged the discreet clearance of JP's firearms case and his other luggage. They were soon out of the terminal.

"I'm glad your Portuguese is good," said JP as they got into the waiting car, "because mine isn't."

"I understand, sir," said Towsing, "my instructions are to assist you in any way I can, and that includes translation. English isn't so widely spoken in Brazil. I think most families are happy if they can get their children a good education in Portuguese, never mind learning a foreign language."

They quickly reached Avenida Atlântica, and at 9pm pulled up outside the Rio Othon Palace Hotel. JP checked in as Dave Tilsen and the two men were shown to his suite on the twenty-first floor, which had a corner balcony overlooking Copacabana Beach. JP put his bags onto one of the large beds, took out his cell phone and used the surveillance sweeper to check the suite was clean of bugging and transmitters. He had just finished when there was a knock at the door. Paul Towsing opened it.

"Ah, Major Savedra, come in."

"Olá, Paul," said the Major's gruff voice. His body matched the voice. The Major was thick set, with dark wavy hair, bushy eyebrows, full moustache and heavily mottled skin. If he were to enter a china shop, thought JP, he would have been the archetypal bull.

"Mr Peregrine, may I present Brazil's Police Commissioner and Head of the Anti-Terrorist Squad, Major Ernesto Fabiao Savedra. Major, this is Jim Peregrine."

"How do you do, Major," said JP, shaking hands.

"Ah, so, you are the one they call the Falcon, yes?!" said Savedra. "I have read about you, about your operation in the Mediterranean. Thankfully we share terrorist reports on activities around the world these days. Fantastic, what you did to prevent disaster. And those two women… such bravery. Fantastic work, young man."

"Thank you, Major, that's most kind," said JP. "It's unfortunate that there are so many reports on terrorism for us to have to share around the world in the first place."

"That is true," said the Major. "So do you know our lovely city Mr Peregrine, have you been here before?"

"JP, please, or Jim. Yes, I've been a couple of times before. And Rio becomes more beautiful every time I see her. Do sit, Major. Would you like coffee, or a cold drink?"

"No, thank you, nothing."

"Paul?"

Towsing shook his head. They sat around the dining table.

"So," continued the Major, "you've vacationed, and danced the samba a little… But this time I think there will be no dancing, am I correct?"

"You are correct, Major," said JP. "No samba this time."

"And I have never met a bearer of the Fifth Rubric before." The two men sat opposite each other, hands on the table, summing each other up. "If you are here with that title, and as I have had a call from the President, there is something more serious going on than samba and the beauty of our beaches."

Their eyes were locked, both suddenly cold. JP smiled.

"So, Falcon," continued Savedra, "what can I do to help?"

"Major, a little over forty-eight hours ago an operative of MI6, and a good friend of mine, who had participated in the Operation Waterhole aftermath, was murdered in London. His name was Dave Tilsen. He was working under Charles Melton, the Deputy Director, heading up the debriefing of all personnel captured."

"I know Charlie Melton," said Savedra. "A good man."

"Yes. Dave was also tasked to go through the masses of papers and computer data found at Cuttle Cove after the mastermind of the terrorist operation, Barakah Malekka, had managed to elude capture and escape. We believe Dave found something, a second terrorist plot from Malekka, either running parallel with or to be implemented after the Spider 2-3 action. From what we can find out, the name of the plot is Stingray."

"Stingray?" said the Major.

"Yes," said JP. "Does it mean anything to you?"

"No, nothing."

"Ok. We believe that the only reason Stingray hasn't happened yet is because of the action at Cuttle Cove and the fact that his first attack, Spider 2-3, which we know had been planned for years, was thwarted at the last minute. He avoided capture by using an emergency escape system, but he had to leave in a hurry and left many items behind. Now he has had to regroup, and reorganise. We don't know anything about the plot; we don't know which country is the target, or countries, nor do we know the nature of the attack. We do know there is a micro SD card that perhaps is essential to Stingray, and that it is missing; we're trying to track it down. We do not believe the plot nuclear in nature, since his former Russian partner is now dead and the Russian Government has confirmed to us that only one weapon was taken. That's now been returned by the way. And, they are anxious to assist us in any way we require. It would therefore seem that this second plot has to be something else, perhaps chemical or biological. Or even something that we haven't thought of. However, we can be certain that, as Malekka is behind it, this threat must be taken very seriously, that it will be large-scale and that it will be catastrophic."

Neither Savedra or Towsing spoke; they waited for JP to continue.

"It is possible, Major, that Brazil is Malekka's next target. Dave returned home at 1am, and was shot, but he did not die immediately. He managed to scrawl one word and two numbers onto some paper: *'DECOY 17'*. Does that mean anything to you?"

"I'm sorry, my friend, that means nothing."

"In Tilsen's electronic diary at MI6 were a plane ticket to Panama City and a man's name and address with a time for a meeting, in Panama. Charlie Melton and I decided that I should take that meeting and see what I could find out and where it led, if anywhere. I met with a Jon Lano, the head of ISTRAS, a shipping company in Panama. A few hours later, an attempt was made to kill me."

Savedra raised his eyebrows.

"What nice people."

"Yes. Fortunately that attempt failed. I, and an agent from Panama's special security forces, re-entered Lano's office in the evening to see what else we could find. We raided his safe. Inside, we found the name and address of someone here in Rio. I want to meet this person tomorrow morning and see where it takes us."

"Who is this person," asked the Major.

JP took out a piece of paper from his wallet and handed it to Major Savedra. "My Portuguese is not good, so Paul will come too," said JP. "And frankly we could do with as much assistance as you and your department can provide."

The Major stared at the paper, and looked at Paul Towsing, and then JP. He shook his head.

"What is it, Major?" asked JP.

"I'm sorry. But this man is dead."

"What?" said JP.

"This man is already dead, JP," said the Major again. "He was on what we call the X-Sheet today, that lists suspicious deaths in the city. At around noon this afternoon he either jumped, or was thrown, from the balcony of his apartment on the fifteenth floor."

15
SNATCHED

THE MORNING IN Panama City had arrived bright and sunny and bode well for another beautiful day. Coco Chavarez hadn't had enough sleep after the night's excursions with the Falcon back at her place of work, but she didn't want to draw attention to herself by being late - she was never late - so she pulled herself out of bed and headed for the shower.

In a few minutes the sleep had vanished and she was wide awake. She dressed, put on her makeup, gathered her purse, keys and light jacket and opened the front door to her apartment. A man stood facing her with a gun in his hand. Another was behind.

Before she had time to recover herself and slam the door shut, the man fired. The dart hit her in the middle of the chest, and within five seconds she collapsed. The two men moved forwards into the apartment and caught her as she fell, pulled the laundry basket in and closed the door. They searched the apartment, putting any papers of interest into a pile, together with her laptop, PC and phone, then bundled them all into the laundry basket. They placed the girl on top, covered her with some sheets and moved out of the flat along the hall to the small service elevator. The block of flats was tall, with about thirty floors, and the elevator went straight to the basement to the carpark below ground. They wheeled the basket out and onto the waiting white transit van, which carried the sign, *'Blue Bay Laundry'*.

The van drove out of the carpark and turned onto the Puente de las Americas. Some minutes later, they went past the ISTRAS building where Jim Peregrine had had his interaction with Max Schroeder and in another fifteen minutes they were in dense jungle terrain. They arrived at an isolated ramshackle old house and drove into its small garage. The men got out and unloaded the basket, wheeling it over an uneven pathway of paving slabs and brick into a side entrance of the house. Coco was lifted from the basket and placed in what was one of two main rooms of the house, onto a dentists-like chair set in the middle of a small room. White tiles were on all walls from base to ceiling, with larger light brown tiles on the floor. White worktops stretched the length of two walls, with some cupboards above and an array of drawers below. There was one large central light, directly above the chair. The appearance was clinical, cold and threatening.

Coco's legs and arms were strapped down securely. One of the men made a phone call, and within an hour, Jon Lano arrived, as Coco began to stir. He waited for her to regain consciousness, and stood calmly before her.

Coco felt sick at first and almost vomited from the effects of the drug that had been shot into her. It passed quickly, and now she was able to see the precariousness of her position. She was entirely helpless, and knew there was no assistance at hand. She was on her own.

"Good morning, Ms Chavarez," said Jon Lano quietly, in an almost soothing tone.

"Mr Lano?" Coco replied, in apparent disbelief and astonishment, "what have you done, why am I here?"

"You made a mistake, my friend," said Lano, with a satisfied smile playing on his lips. "Do you know what it was?"

"What are you talking about, Mr Lano, I don't know what you mean. Let me up out of here please."

He walked over to his briefcase that was lying on a small table, and picked it up. He pulled out an iPad.

"You were very clever. And very slick and efficient. You

disabled the CCTV security system like an old pro. But you made a mistake."

"What are you talking about," said Coco, who was now really scared. "Mr Lano, I don't know anything, why are you doing this, what's the matter?"

"And the mistake was," continued Lano, ignoring Coco's remarks, "that you didn't realise there was a secondary surveillance system. My private one."

Her eyes widened in astonishment as Lano turned on the iPad and held it up for her to watch. She saw the pictures of her and JP exiting the elevator and entering the offices of ISTRAS. The images followed them into Lano's private office, and showed the search for the safe and the accessing of the computer.

She knew she was blown. She fell silent.

"So now, as there is no need for any more silly denials from you, I want some information. I want to know who you really are, whom you're working for. And I want to know who that man is that came in with you."

"Ok," said Coco. "Ok, I'll tell you." She took a deep breath.

"Good," said Lano. "I'm waiting."

Coco looked at the three men in front of her, and at her bound hands and legs. She raised her head again.

"Look Mr Lano, I don't want any trouble. But Mr Tilsen offered me a large amount of money if I could get him into your office out of work hours. He said he would give me $50,000. He wanted to get some information about you that he and his company Globaldex could use against you so that he could gain some control of your organisation and the shipping system here in Panama. He said it was worth $2m a year to him, maybe more. He wanted to use that information to blackmail you to cut him in. That's what he said, and that's all I know. I'm really sorry, Mr Lano, I just wanted the money."

Lano looked seriously at Coco, as though he were genuinely considering her story, and with sympathy. Then he burst out laughing.

"That's really good, Ms Chavarez. Given that you haven't had much time to come up with a story, that's really good."

"What do you mean, Mr Lano, it's true, I swear it. I can even prove..."

He cut her off.

"Enough nonsense, now, ok?"

"It's not nonsense, sir, it's the truth."

"Of course it's nonsense. That man is no more Dave Tilsen than I am. How do I know this? I know it because," - he shouted the next sentence - "Dave Tilsen was killed in London *two days* ago. And this man..." Lano touched the screen on his iPad a couple of times, until it showed the picture of JP, "... was photographed outside as he left Tilsen's flat when the police were investigating his sad demise."

Coco's mouth fell open.

"Well he said his name was Tilsen, Mr Lano, I swear it, and I believed it."

Lano looked at one of the men.

"Get ready."

The man moved to one of the walls with the work surface along it, pulled open one of the top drawers and took out two trays of stainless steel instruments - an array of sharp knives, scissors, spikes and pliers. From a large drawer he pulled out an assortment of whips and sticks.

Coco was horrified.

"Look, I don't know anything, Mr Lano, that's the truth I've told you, I swear it."

Lano looked at Coco, and ran his eyes down along her body to her feet, and back up again. He shook his head.

"Have you any idea what a mess these men are going to leave your pretty body in when they've finished with you?"

She started to cry. She looked down at her bonds once more, twisting her hands and wrists, and moving her legs to pull at the straps on her ankles. The shackles didn't give one millimetre.

"For your own sake, why don't you tell us the truth now? Tell us the information that we want before you put us to the inconvenience of having to persuade you. I promise you, you will go free, unharmed, you can leave the company, and nothing further will happen to you." He looked at her kindly, or as kindly as it was possible for Jon Lano to look at anyone, and smiled. "Tell us what we want to know. It will be for the best. Think about it."

Coco was terrified and felt sick with fear; she knew what was coming. But she wasn't going to let him see it.

He moved a little closer. "So I ask one more time. Who are you, whom do you work for, and who is that man?"

Coco Chavarez knew there would be no escape. Her crying stopped, and she raised her head. She looked up at Lano defiantly.

"Fuck you," was all she said.

Lano looked over at the men and nodded. He left the room, closing the heavy soundproofed door behind him.

He would expect a phone call back at the office.

≈

Five hours later, Jon Lano got the phone call he had been waiting for.

"What do you mean," he said angrily down the receiver, "what did you do?"

"Nothing, sir. It's what she did," said the man on the other end of the phone. "She had a pill somewhere in her mouth, under a tooth. She took as much as she could for as long as she could. Then she took the pill. We got nothing from her."

Lano thought for a while, then spoke again. "Very well. Clean it up. Get rid of the body." He put down the phone.

16

THINKING OF YOU

STEPHANIE AND ANNA left Sir Donald and departed in the Daihatsu Charade that had definitely seen better days. They drove past the outskirts of Limassol eastwards along the coast then turned northeast inland, routing close to Kokkinotrimithia and reaching the border crossing at Astromeritis on schedule.

Their passage across the Demilitarised Zone was significantly more scrutinised than JP's had been a few days before. Papers were checked thoroughly by customs and border control officers both as they departed the Republic of Cyprus and entered the Demilitarised Zone, and then again on the other side crossing into the Turkish Republic of Northern Cyprus. However their papers were of course in order and despite the more intense inspections they were through in just over half an hour.

After releasing the original media story about the event at Cuttle Cove, the government authorities, both of North and South Cyprus who were now working closely together, had ensured that entry and travel permits were strictly controlled for reasons of 'national and international security' and access was generally tightened. Nevertheless half the world's journalists seemed to have descended on the area immediately after the explosion at Cuttle Cove and the news had flashed around the globe. There had been a certain amount of investigative journalism in the local towns, but the intrusion especially of television crews was not welcome by the locals; a few tougher reporters sniffed about for a while longer but didn't gel with the community and achieved a nil result. The machine that was the media circus quickly moved on to the

next current event or tragedy, political scandal
things died down after three or four days and then p
Stephanie and Anna felt they had a good chance of su
that, if there was anything to be found, they would fin

They drove as far north as Livera, the small village that was the last grouping of civilisation before the road steered away to Cuttle Cove on the tip of Cape Kormakitis. There was a café in Livera, and that was their starting point.

Over the next few hours they visited one café and bar after another, routing systematically south and taking in each town and village in a comprehensive sweep. Playing their part well as journalists, they made it clear they were out for a story: only limited details were known of the head of the terrorist organisation - what kind of man was he, why did he hate the West, what did they know of Cuttle Cove, what was the explosion, who worked with him, how involved was the leader in ISIS, or, as that group was in demise, was this ISIS or was it a new terrorist group, what other kind of work was he up to…

However, the afternoon and evening of that day produced very little - except one interesting and unusual fact that almost all the locals seemed to know. Four people had disappeared suddenly over the past week. One body had been found at sea, returned to the coastline by the currents of the Mediterranean. The other three had vanished.

Tired, hot and sticky, the women decided to call it quits for the day at around 11pm. They stayed overnight in Kerýneia, or Girne as the locals call it, at the modest Palace Hotel. In addition to locking and bolting the doors to their rooms, each of them wedged a chair under the door handle as an extra precaution to ensure that no unwanted entry was possible.

Anna Kepling, wearing a simple short nightdress, snuggled down under the light duvet. She lay still for a few minutes, then reached over and grabbed one of the other pillows on the bed, pulling it towards her and wrapping her arms around it, holding it tightly as her usual bedtime thinking began. Each night she had tried to get past it; each night she had failed. It was still too soon. She closed her eyes, and thought of her beloved father, his brilliance, his bravery, the childhood she had so enjoyed, the close retained companionship she had shared with him as she had matured; and the sudden loss and emptiness when he had been murdered and had gone forever. She thought of the man she had planned to marry, had loved so much, of the life they were to have together, the children that would have followed, of motherhood; then of his demise, when he had been taken so viciously from her, and in such a violent and shocking way. She scrunched her eyes up a little more, but it was no good. A tear pushed out from under an eyelid, trickled part of the way down her cheek and dropped onto the pillow. Another, and then another, followed. But the tiredness was stronger and, luckily, this night it soon took hold, removing her mind from the coldness of reality and transporting it into the depths of a warm and comforting dream world.

After showering, Stephanie Raughton checked the curtains again and the door. She rummaged in the suitcase resting on the adjacent double bed and pulled out a light blue shirt. It was one of JP's, that she had taken from his room on St Lucia unbeknown (or so she thought anyway) to him. She let the towel wrapped around her fall off and slipped into the shirt, fastening all the buttons bar the top two or three. It was too big for her, and hung loosely, but it reminded her of him. She crept under the covers, turned off the lights and nestled down comfortably. She, too, lay still for a couple of minutes, before stretching over to the side table for her phone and opening the protective cover. The phone lit up, she pressed her thumb against the reader and entered a four-digit code for the security; the image changed and then she could see the man she loved, in the cover picture, a snap she had taken after they had been splashing in the water and he had grabbed her and lifted her out as she giggled and screamed and laughed. He had carried her up the beach to the house and put her on one of the steps of the porch, then walked to the water's edge to retrieve his sandals, the sun hot in a dazzling clear blue sky; her phone had been left there, she had picked it up and snapped JP in his swimming shorts as he walked back. In spite of all that had happened, she loved him more now than ever before. She smiled, closed the phone, pulled it against her breasts and held it there, thinking of him, of how they had been together, of how they would be together again. She drifted off to sleep almost immediately, a smile still resting on her lips, the love of her life close by, still with her in her bed.

≈

JP slid open the balcony window and stepped outside with the coffee tray, placing it onto the table and sitting slowly on the cushioned sundeck chair. He poured in some cream, stirred the sugar and sipped at it thoughtfully. The fun sounds of the Rio evening rose from the streets twenty-one stories below, the tooting of car horns continued to hail the national win at the football friendly and the salt smell and sounds of bursting beach waves mixed invitingly with the lights and gentle curve of Avenida Atlântica, set against the backdrop of Sugar Loaf Mountain in the distance.

The Falcon had not expected the man he was planning to meet in the morning to be dead. The news had brought the meeting to an abrupt end; he had politely excused himself from Major Savedra and Paul Towsing for the evening, since there was nothing more to be done, and he was tired, hungry and wanted to think. He ordered a meal from room service, and then had hot coffee brought up. Savedra would try to find out all he could about the dead man and return at 8am in the morning. The only other link they could turn to now was the man's wife, who apparently was under heavy sedation at home, with her daughter who had come in from the north of the city to share the distress and provide care and comfort for her mother as best she could. The Major placed two guards at the door of their residence, and the crime scene investigators would continue their work into the night, focusing on the living room that opened onto the balcony from which Jorge Monterroso had fallen.

There was one nagging question playing on JP's mind. What does it mean that both men had been killed? To stop the meeting in Panama, kill Dave Tilsen, which they had done in London. Obviously he had been discovered by the people running Stingray and they wanted to end the possibility of any more information going to the UK authorities, including the SD card, which presumably they had taken if Tilsen had had it on him. Once that had been done, why would they also remove Jorge Monterroso? Presumably because he had been discovered too, as a traitor to the Stingray plan or as an unknowing witness. Had the two killings been ordered by the same person? If they had, then his own position had suddenly become more dangerous, since the Brazil segment would know that Dave Tilsen had been executed and so anyone turning up claiming to be Tilsen must be a fraud. Which presumably was what had happened in Panama. He would have to be careful. It was time to revert from being Dave Tilsen with others to Jim Peregrine.

He moved back inside. He locked the balcony doors securely, drew the thick curtains, took a chair and wedged its back under the handle of the entrance door. Then he undressed and slipped naked under the duvet. He twisted round and flicked the switches in the headboard to turn off the main lights of the suite, leaving just the sidelight, which he dimmed to its lowest setting. With a sigh he settled down on his back, put his hands behind his head and stared up at the ceiling.

Despite the reasons for his being in Rio, in a strange kind of way he was delighted to be back in the city and Brazil again. He spoke little or no Portuguese, but that had never been a problem for him before; he had always found that English was all one needed on holiday, together with a happy disposition and smile. He knew there was trouble and violence in Rio, in fact generally in many of the Brazilian towns, and the disparity between the rich and the poor was greater here than in Panama. One could leave the hotel, turn away from the sea and walk for half a block, and find people including young children sleeping in doorways, while the favelas - like the shantytowns of South Africa - were a horrendous overcrowding of the poorest families into the tiniest of spaces, with little or no sanitation and services.

Somehow the wonderful spirit of Brazil's people still shone through and her men and women perhaps more than those from other countries seemed always to find the happiness and goodness in life, particularly those who were penniless; from the volleyball games on the beach - played with no hands but with feet, knees and chest imitating a footballer - to the exciting samba dance and their famous carnival each February or March, to the wonders of their music and the famous bossa nova. It was a lesson that others around the world could learn, thought JP as his mind began to relax at last. He had been saddened by the passing of João Gilberto some time back, one of the originators of the bossa nova style, whose recording of *The Girl From Ipanema* had made such an impact around the world. The song, by Antônio Carlos Jobim and Vinicius de Moraes, two other great exponents of bossa nova, written about a beautiful girl that walked past them each day as they sat in a café on her way to Ipanema Beach, was still the second most recorded song on the planet. How do I know that, said JP to himself, drifting… He must bring Stephie here one day, so they can dance the samba and enjoy life in the way the Brazilians know so well.

How were Stephie and Anna doing, he wondered. He smiled as he reflected on how they'd had no compunction about getting back on the wagon to ride off into the unknown and deal with Malekka. No hesitation, in spite of what they had both been through. Brave women. Lovely women.

He put his arms down and turned onto his side.

Lovely Stephanie. He missed her. They'd hardly spent any time together after Spider, before they had had to return to tackle this new plot. God, he hoped they would be ok.

The Falcon was asleep in ten minutes, his last thoughts about Stephie and Anna still drifting in his mind. God, I hope they'll be ok…

He wouldn't have slept at all if he had known.

Sadly… unfortunately… one of them wouldn't be.

PART FOUR

THE FOURTH DAY

17

SEARCHING

THE TWO GIRLS set out early the following morning. Each of them was dressed simply: Stephanie wore flat black shoes, trousers, a tank top and a covering light jacket; Anna was in trainers, a long brown and rather baggy skirt, a blouse and leather jacket. Breakfasts, coffees, lunch visits, more coffee, some bars in the early evening… Nobody was talking. If anyone knew anything, nobody wanted to say it. By 11pm they were in a quiet bar in Morfou in the west of the island, trying again to find a source that might speak a little of Cuttle Cove and Malekka. The word had travelled fast; when Anna passed some money to the barman in an effort to get some names or get directed to someone among his present clientele it was clear he knew of the women, and had been expecting them. He leant over the bar top towards them.

"Stylianos. The man at the back table," he whispered in Turkish, tilting his head almost imperceptibly in the direction of the darkest-lit part of the bar where one man sat alone at a table in the corner.

Stephanie and Anna looked fleetingly at each other. At last. Anna smiled at the barman and said quietly, "Thank you," adding in Turkish and in a slightly louder voice, "two raki and water please."

The girls tipped the chilled water into the small tumbler that contained a generous measure of raki. The clear liquids mixed and instantly turned milky. They walked over. A few people stared as they went by, then were quickly back into their own conversations. The bar was full of smoke from heavy cigarettes and a few cigars that mixed with the smell of coffee, beers and wines together with fish and overcooked kebabs, all encased in a strong dose of unpleasant body odour.

The man looked up as the two women stopped beside him.

"Mr Stylianos?" said Stephanie quietly.

The man had been drinking heavily. His eyes were red and glazed, thick smoke rose from the Turkish cigarette in his left hand, and the half-emptied glass of zivania whisky rested in the other, ready to be steered towards a mouth that was almost hidden beneath a heavy moustache in dire need of a comb. He was about forty. He raised his head in an enquiring nod and grunted.

"Could we join you for a minute," said Anna, again in Turkish, and before the man could answer the women had seated themselves in the two other chairs.

"Teşekkür ederim[6]," said Stephanie. The man looked over, then raised his glass. The women sipped at their own drink.

"Mr Stylianos," said Anna, in Turkish, "we're…"

He cut her off.

"You can speak English, I understand. I know who you are. You are the journalists." His English was fluent but heavily accented. "Or, at least, you are the women who say they are journalists. Word travels quickly here."

The girls nodded and smiled.

"I am Stylianos Agne. And you…?"

"My name is Clara Johnson," said Stephanie. "And this is my friend, Nicky Elsonberg. We're from the UK. We'd like to ask some questions. About… what happened."

"What do you know about me?" He stared from one girl to the other.

"Just that you are Mr Stylianos Agne," said Anna.

"Well I can tell you about me," he said, slurping again at the whisky. "I can tell you lots. I am…" he paused for a moment,

---

[6] *Thank you.*

and sighed. “I am a man who no longer has a wife. Blown up. Dead. Killed. My lovely woman.” He poured more zivania from the bottle and drank again.

“In the explosion?” said Stephanie.

“Yes. In the explosion.” Stylianos sighed again, looked at his glass, then raised his eyes to meet the women’s.

“She was 33, full of life, beautiful.”

“I’m so sorry, Stylianos,” said Stephanie. She saw his eyes well up with tears. She looked across at Anna, then back again.

“So… will you help us?”

Stylianos looked away, behind the girls at the other people, who were mainly men, in the bar. They were busy talking amongst themselves, some laughing, some already overly drunk, but all apparently indulged in their own lives and oblivious to his corner of the world. When he spoke again it was in a much-lowered level.

“Not here. Outside.” He lifted his glass to his lips again. “Leave after me. Travel west on a road called Evagorou. At the first fork stay left, and at the second. Three and a half kilometres from town there are some big farm buildings. The road splits. Stay on the road and drive past, do not turn left. Another half a kilometre or so there is a small house on the left, set back from the road. I’ll meet you outside there, in one hour.”

Stylianos emptied his glass and stood, pushing his chair back noisily. In Turkish he grumbled, “Leave me alone, I have nothing to say to you,” and staggered off towards the door. A few heads turned but turned away again soon enough.

“What do you make of that,” said Stephanie, sipping at her own glass.

“I think we may have found someone interesting at last.”

“Unless we’re being set up.”

“It’s possible of course,” said Anna. “But I don’t think so.

Did you see his eyes? Those weren't fake tears."

The women continued chatting quietly, laughing every now and again, as though two friends out for the evening. They were hit on twice, by two separate men who came to try their luck but who were sent away with smiles and charm, and reference by Stephanie and Anna to their respective rings on their fourth fingers, a ploy which they had decided to adopt in London as a useful defence. Forty-five minutes later, the girls left. They reached the car parked fifty yards down the road and, with Anna at the wheel, drove away. Checking frequently behind that they weren't being followed, they found Evagorou and headed west.

≈

Standing in a dark alley opposite, one of the men who had hit on the girls watched them go. He quickly walked to his own car metres away in a small side street, opened the trunk and took out a light structure with four helicopter-like blades. He placed it on his car roof, switched it on, took up the remote control and hit 'lift'. The drone rose vertically and quickly disappeared into the blackness, its high-pitched whine lost to the ear in seconds.

18
MONTERROSO

AT FIVE TO eight the next morning the phone rang, announcing that Major Savedra was in the lobby waiting. The Falcon left his room and strolled to the elevator. He had slept well, showered and devoured a light breakfast. The white business suit, blue shirt and red tie contrasted with his tanned skin and black hair, brushed back cavalierly. The jacket comfortably concealed his shoulder holster and Sig Sauer P226. His six foot three frame had both attractive charm and a hint of danger as he crossed the lobby towards the Major, who had exchanged the uniform for a smart suit and looked more like a stock broker than the Police Commissioner.

"Good morning, Falcon," said the Major, "I hope you managed to get some sleep?"

"Yes, thanks," replied JP, shaking Savedra's hand once more. "I'm sorry we had such a short chat last night, but there seemed little else we could do, it was a bit of a surprise about Monterroso."

"I understand, of course. But today we will get more details."

"What do you know so far?"

"Actually not very much," said the Major as they moved out through the main glass doors into the bright sunlight of the Rio morning. The air was brisk and fresh, and full of salt and the smell of eggs and bacon from the local open-air restaurants. "I need more time, but so far I can tell you that the man was a true Carioca - he was born in Rio - he lived here all his life, he was forty-five and was married with three children." They reached the car and got in. "He paid his taxes.

He was schooled here and went to the *Universidade Federal do Rio de Janeiro* - the Federal University of Rio de Janeiro which we call the UFRJ. He was an engineer and computer programming specialist, and apparently was one of those quiet but extremely clever types. Other than that I don't know much else."

Savedra took the car south along Avenida Atlântica. The traffic was heavy but flowed smoothly.

"Is Rua Souza Lima far?"

"No," said the Major, "it's just a few blocks down. It's in one of the better areas of Rio, so this man was well placed in society and standing. You have to have money to live there."

"That's interesting," said JP. "So does his income cover his living costs, or were they somehow topped up?"

"No, it seems he was a hard worker all of his life, and he saved, raised his family and climbed the ladder like most decent folks do as the years go by."

JP considered this. Then said, "I think I should be Jim Peregrine for this meeting, Major. Any possible reason for being Dave Tilsen has evaporated since Monterroso is now dead. And I get the feeling that, if the family is decent and enduring a bereavement, I don't want to go in with a lie or deceit. Any objection?"

The Major had none. After five blocks the car turned away from the beach into Rua Souza Lima, which was a small tight street with traffic that flowed one way. Trees began to line the kerb edges after the second block, the traffic tailed off and the street became a well-to-do residential area. They pulled up outside number four eight five, a plush tower block twenty stories high with a gated communal entrance that was open but which had two police security guards very much in evidence, who saluted the Major as he and his guest passed by swiftly into the lobby. They took the lift to the fifteenth floor. Another two-policeman guard, rotated overnight, had moved into the hall outside the flat when the forensic team had left, at around 4am. They both stood quickly as the elevator opened and Savedra stepped out. The Major received a quick update, which contained nothing of interest, then rang the bell to the flat.

The door opened slowly and was held on its chain by a young woman in her dressing gown and nightdress. The Major showed his identification, and the two men were admitted. Savedra spoke in Portuguese and then switched to English. "And this is Jim Peregrine, who is from the United Kingdom. JP, this is Senhorita Carla Monterroso."

"How do you do, Senhorita Carla," said JP shaking her hand gently. "I am so terribly sorry to learn of the tragedy that you have endured here."

Savedra began to translate but was interrupted.

"We can speak in English," said Carla Monterroso, as she moved to the couch in the living room and gestured to the men to sit. "My mother will be out shortly, she is just showering." She let out a sigh. "Things are going slowly today." She crossed her legs and one side of her dressing gown fell away, exposing the soft skin of a tanned thigh. The woman was beautiful. Her dark long hair curled around a face with brown eyes, small straight nose and full lips still pink with the makeup of the day before. The eyes were puffy, and the whites reddened from tears. The two men sat in comfortable arm chairs opposite.

JP was about to speak but was cut off by the woman.

"So, Major. You, I know. But you," she said to the Falcon with slow emphasis, smiling with cold charm yet no humour, "you I do not know. And before I let you anywhere near my mother I would like you to tell me what your interest in my father is, and why you are here."

JP looked at Savedra, and back to the woman.

"Why do you say that, Senhorita Carla?"

"My father did not commit suicide, Mr Peregrine. That means there is only one other thing that could have happened to him. He was murdered. There is something dangerous and worrying here obviously. And so, I would like to know, as I have said, what your interest is in my father, and, why you are here."

The Falcon decided to trust her.

"Very well, Senhorita Carla. You are correct. There is indeed something dangerous going on here. Forty-eight hours ago in London, a man called Dave Tilsen, a close friend of mine, was murdered." The woman let out a slight gasp. "He and I were in the British armed services together; and more recently he worked for our security forces, called MI6. I do not work directly for MI6 but I work with their full authority and collaboration as well as that of the British Government. I am trying to find out who killed him, and why. Just over ten days ago, we defeated a major effort by terrorists who were trying to detonate a nuclear bomb and kill a large number of people. The person who planned that attack, a man called Malekka, has - we learned thanks largely to the efforts of Dave Tilsen - another plot to attack the West. Dave was to meet a man in Panama City; I took Dave Tilsen's place and had that meeting for him, as Dave Tilsen. That same evening an attempt was made to kill me."

"I am glad that they failed, Mr Peregrine."

"Me too. And, it's JP or Jim, please. Anyway, I discovered with the help of the security forces in Panama City that your father's name appeared amongst papers kept in a safe of these murderers. I have come to find out why and see what I could discover. The fact that your father is now tragically dead makes me think that he was - forgive me, Carla - either involved, or, more likely, that he discovered something, and paid for it with his life."

There was a silence. Carla lowered her eyes to her knees

and her shoulders sank a little as she exhaled slowly. She looked at the fallen side of her gown as though for the first time, and pulled it up to cover her leg.

"I am sorry for the directness, Carla," said JP softly. "But you asked me directly, and so I have given you straight answers." She nodded in agreement. "And there are a great number of people including the media who would pay a lot of money to know some of the details that I have just given you. I am trusting you with the truth. I hope you can trust me too. We are dealing with murder here. I have to take whatever steps I can to find out who did this. The murder of my friend and, now, of your father. I don't think he threw himself from the balcony any more than you do."

She raised her eyes again and shook her head.

"No, he certainly did not. And, I can tell you with absolute certainty that my father had no association with anything illegal or bad. It is simply…" She stopped herself, sighed, then restarted. "…it *was* simply not in his nature. Therefore as he was murdered, for sure, it can only mean one thing, and that is that he discovered something, as you put it."

"Carla, can I ask you," said Major Savedra, "did you notice your father acting strangely or differently in the last few days, did he say or do anything that was out of the usual at all?"

"No, nothing. But I was not here a great deal the last week or two. The one you should ask is my mother. If you will excuse me gentlemen, I will go and talk with her and see if she is willing to come in and speak with you."

She stood to leave the room, and the men rose as she did, then sat again. They waited in silence. JP looked around the room. It was comfortably furnished, and was of a generous size; there were some bright-coloured rugs resting on the parquet flooring, some large paintings on the walls that appeared to be original oil, although he didn't recognise the artists, and two large chandeliers each with fans below, that rotated virtually in silence, giving a gentle movement of air in the apartment. Two closed windows overlooked the street below, each with an air conditioner attached at their base.

The door opened and Carla returned with her mother. She again spoke in English. The men were on their feet again. Senhora Monterroso was early forties, and walked to the men with an elegant dignified step, her shoulders back and head slightly raised. Her short dark hair was tinged with grey and her face soft and round, but her wide dark eyes betrayed the great sorrow that was searing through her.

"Mama, this is Major Ernesto Savedra, who is Police Commissioner and the Head of our Anti-Terrorist Squad."

Senhora Monterroso held out her hand. The Major took it and bowed slightly.

"Senhora Monterroso, my department and I are so very sorry for this terrible tragedy. We extend our deepest sympathy."

"Thank you, Major."

"And this is Mr Jim Peregrine, the one I mentioned that is from the UK," continued Carla. "He is investigating the murder of a friend in the UK and it seems it might be linked to Papa's killing."

"Then you have endured a loss yourself, Mr Peregrine, and we are sharing a similar kind of pain" said Senhora Monterroso.

"Thank you, Senhora," said JP as he shook hands. "What you say is true, and I can appreciate the great agony that you and your family are going through. I am so sorry."

Senhora Monterroso managed a slight smile in acknowledgement, then sat on a couch next to her daughter, signalling for the men to sit too.

"So, Major, what have you found out so far?" asked Mrs Monterroso, who clearly had no qualms about her own directness.

"We know that your husband was unconscious, or dead, when he fell," said Savedra. "The forensic team has told me just two hours ago… and an autopsy will reveal which it was." Mrs Monterroso closed her eyes briefly at the mention of an autopsy, which the Major noticed. "I am sorry, Senhora, but we have to do…"

She interrupted. "Yes, of course you do, and you will hear no objection from me, Major. You must use all the resources at your disposal to find out who did this, and bring them to justice."

"Thank you, Senhora. I know that my other police colleagues have asked you many questions already, but I have a few of my own and, if you don't mind, Mr Peregrine has some too that he would like to ask?"

"Yes, that is fine, gentlemen, I will answer what I can. Please go ahead."

The Major smiled.

"We think it may be the case that your husband discovered something somewhere that was unexpected and considered a danger to other parties. They wanted to silence him because of it. Can you tell me, did you notice that your husband was behaving any differently from normal, more worried… stressed…?"

Senhora Monterroso stared at the Major, and said, "Actually, Major, now that you mention it, I think I can say that he was. He seemed a little nervous, a little distant. I asked him about it, what was worrying him, and he said it was nothing, some trouble at work. I asked again, and he brushed it off, said there were some promotion difficulties for a couple of other people and they were arguing about it. Not my husband; the other two people."

"Senhora," said JP, "excuse my asking this, but did you believe your husband? Or did you feel he didn't want to talk about it?"

"Mr Peregrine, my husband and I were very close, and he never lied to me."

JP smiled at her. "Of course not, Senhora."

"On the other hand, there were times when Jorge preferred not to worry me with things. After so many years of marriage, he learned not to upset me and I learned not to pry. To him, he was protecting me. It was a kind of code that couples have sometimes." She paused, then asked suddenly, "Are you married, Mr Peregrine?"

"Er, no, Senhora."

"Ah. Then you have all this to come."

"Indeed I do." The Falcon smiled, and Carla helped his isolation by adding, "And so do I, Mama!"

"Yes, dear, I know." She continued to JP. "And so, Mr Peregrine, when I say to you that I do think that Jorge was acting a little strangely, and that he avoided giving me a straight answer when I asked him about it, he was not lying to me. But I knew something was not quite right, and that he was… concerned. Of course I had no idea it was to lead to his being killed, and I'm sure he had no idea either, because he most certainly would have told me more about it in that event, obviously. I think what happened to him must have come completely out of the blue. Whatever he found or discovered was, I believe, more serious than he realised…" She suddenly stopped speaking as her eyes filled with tears, and brought out a handkerchief from a small pocket in her dress. Carla put her arms around her again, and tears were in her eyes too.

"Thank you, Senhora Monterroso," said JP. "I am sorry to have had to ask. But I think what you have said may prove to be really very helpful to us."

Mrs Monterroso blew her nose gently and pulled herself upright again.

"Not at all, Mr Peregrine. I hope it is of some use."

"And Senhora," said the Major, "yesterday, when the awful

deed occurred, how did this come about… you were out, of course?"

"Yes. I usually go out at around 11am for a little shopping, for the freshness of the vegetables, meat, fish; you know. I was gone maybe two hours. When I came back there were masses of people around at the base of the building, I walked over, and that's when I saw…"

"Yes, quite," said Savedra, "I understand, thank you." He turned to the Falcon. "Do you have anything else, JP?"

"Just a couple more questions. Senhora, what kind of work did your husband do?"

"He was a computer specialist - a programmer and designer. Actually an engineer by profession."

"Why was he home yesterday?"

"Oh, he had a day off. Nothing unusual, he had them midweek every now and again. He worked away from Rio, closer to São Paulo actually, the company provided a small but comfortable flat for him as part of the job for overnights, although he was able to work often at home. He loved his work, but he loved to be here with us at every opportunity. He was a good family man. He was back most weekends, and usually there was one day off midweek every other week."

"And, where did he work?"

"He was Head of Design and Research at the Advanced Development Facility at the Taubaté Science and Technology Centre."

"Sorry, Senhora, I meant, for whom did he work?"

"Oh, yes, of course. He was an aviation engineer, for the Rovalle Aircraft Corporation."

19

THRÓISMA TOU ANÉMOU

STEPHANIE AND ANNA were quickly in complete darkness save for the light from a gibbous moon, and had to rely on the headlights of the car. They drove past row after row of olive trees, broken up every now and then with a field of planted crop. They passed the two forks that Stylianos had referred to, then a few minutes later reached the farm buildings, where the road split with a ninety degree turn to the left. They drove past the buildings, and soon could make out the house.

The farmhouse was a small L-shaped stone cottage and had long since fallen into disrepair. The walls were no more a white render but a dirty grey, peeling and cracking badly. The roof consisted of the semi-circular Roman roof tiles that are typical all over Cyprus, but many had fallen off exposing beams and opening the inside to the sky. Of the four windows that could be seen from the front, only one had any glass intact. There was a short open drive, guarded by a large oak tree at the entrance. Anna pulled off the road and they got out, closing the doors quietly.

A man stepped from the darkness at the entrance doorway.

"Come, this way," said Stylianos in a low voice, beckoning them in.

The two women joined him, and closed the rickety front door. Inside, a Gaz lantern was set on a low table and there were two chairs. Stylianos pulled out a lighter and lit the lantern, which hissed out its strong light; he adjusted it to a low glow. He pointed the girls to the chairs, and took an old beer crate from the corner of the room and flipped it upside down, for his own seat.

"So." He looked at the girls. "You are reporters."

The women looked quickly at each other, then Stephanie spoke.

"Not exactly. But we *are* looking for a story."

"Good," said Stylianos, "because honesty will get you much further with me than lying."

Stephanie smiled and looked at the man kindly. She opened her mouth to speak, but Stylianos had more to say.

"Because I know who you are."

"What do you mean," said Stephanie, crossing her arms on the table, so that her right hand could rest nonchalantly inside her jacket on the Shield[7] tucked close behind her left breast in the holster stitched onto her undershirt tank top.

"You look older. You have done something to your hair, and your eyes. But beauty such as yours is very hard to hide. You are Stella, aren't you? Mr Malekka's woman. Or, rather, forced woman."

Stephanie was taken aback. For a brief moment all the emotions and fears of her ordeal flooded back. Her time as Stella, her kidnapping from St Lucia, the forced physical abuse by Malekka subsequently on his yacht, the *Excelsior*, and then at Cuttle Cove on Cyprus… It was an integral part of JP's plan in defeating Malekka in Spider 2-3 as a sting operation, and she went into it voluntarily, knowing what could happen; but, the ordeal had left its scars. She opened her mouth to speak, but nothing came out. Stylianos switched his eyes to Anna.

"But you, I do not know." He smiled with no humour.

Stephanie recovered her composure.

"Yes," she said, "I am Stella. I'm astonished that you can recognise me; I thought my disguise was good enough, but

---

[7] *Smith & Wesson M&P (Military and Police) Shield, a lightweight thin but powerful handgun. The magazine is 8+1 x 9mm rounds.*

obviously I was wrong."

"Oh, it's good," said Stylianos, "but I and the other men - and some of the women - were able to study you and look at you during your time with Mr Malekka. As I said, it would be hard not to recognise you."

"I think I will try to take that as a compliment."

"Yes, you should."

"And you, Mr Agne," said Anna, "who are you? And what did you do for Mr Malekka?"

"Ok. I will tell you what I know, what I can. I was one of five personal aides, manservants you would probably call them," said Stylianos. "My wife was a domestic. We were both on board the *Excelsior* and also working at the estate here on Cyprus. And we had been with him in Iran at the Palace. Eight years in all. You think in that time you would get to know someone you admired and respected as an employer."

Stylianos took out a cigarette, offered one to the girls, lit one, breathed in deeply. He sat back in the chair and puffed the smoke into the air in a long column.

"But you don't. We had little knowledge of Mr Malekka's business affairs, or his purpose and goals. We served. We were happy. You get a feeling that you were part of a big family and being looked after, respected. But then, what do we learn? Suddenly we are given instructions to prepare to leave in twenty-four hours, a 12.30am departure the next morning. We are told to pack. I and my friend Yusuf, one of the other aides, after packing clothes and taking them to the plane, were told to shred papers. I was sent on an errand to Morfou, to deliver money, to a supplier of food, the last payment to him. As I return at midnight, half a mile away, I see the explosion. Soldiers everywhere, gunfights... The estate is closed off, nobody is allowed in or out.

"Finally Yusuf is released. He has been questioned for four days by British Intelligence. And I get to hear what has happened… that Mr Malekka was planning on bombing people but was discovered.

"We were doing Allah's work, we were told. We would be safe. The world would be a better place, we were told. And what happens? He runs and leaves us all to die. We learn he was trying to kill a country. A whole country. He tried to destroy the estate, all of us, as he made his getaway. And my lovely wife, she is killed. To him, we were nothing. Just so that he can make his escape. He was a murderer, a killer of men and women and children."

His eyes had filled with tears. He took out a dirty rag as a handkerchief and wiped them.

"This Malekka is a madman," said Anna, shaking her head.

"How would you know, unless you experience it."

"I have experienced it," replied Anna, staring at Stylianos. "You said you do not know me. It's true, you don't. So I will tell you. Malekka killed my father. And then he killed my fiancé. So, I have some experience."

Stylianos looked across at Anna in astonishment. His face softened.

"I am sorry. I did not know."

Anna shook her head.

"Stylianos," continued Stephanie, "I too was hurt by Malekka. Now I work for the British Intelligence. And we need your help. And your friend's help too, Yusuf. We need some information."

"Me, you have. Yusuf, no, he cannot help you."

"Why not?"

"Because he is dead. He was murdered. Three days ago. He was found by a roadside. His throat had been cut."

"Oh no," said Stephanie, "my God. I'm sorry."

Stylianos looked at the women slowly, in turn, to register the expressions on their faces. "You see… Malekka's power is still here. You must be careful. I must be careful. That is why we are talking here… and not in a bar.

"Yusuf told me he had been as helpful as he could when he was interviewed. That is why he was killed. A couple of others, too, just dead, suddenly. Disappeared. As a warning, to others. But for me, I no longer care. If there is anything I can do to hurt Malekka, to get back at him, I will do it."

He reached for another cigarette.

"Stylianos, let me tell you something," said Stephanie. "The explosion that you talk about, that killed your wife. That was not Malekka's main effort. He was planning another explosion, much bigger, that had it gone off would have killed thousands on Cyprus. Luckily, we were able to stop it. But as you said, Malekka made his escape. When the security forces came in and took over, they discovered other information, about something else that he was working on, and we believe that, if this other operation is successful, thousands of other lives, perhaps hundreds of thousands, may be lost also. We need any information you can give us that might help us stop him."

Stylianos nodded.

"We were never near anything to do with Malekka's business affairs. I cleaned shoes, pressed suits, helped dress him, laid out new shirts, carried his trays of food… With one exception. When we were told to shred things. That was the only time I came across papers and so on."

He paused to draw on the cigarette.

"Yusuf told me that he had read a name and address several times, which stuck with him. It was in Panama in Central America. And there was also something in Brazil. I don't know the details of anything more there. But he was shredding more than I. I was told to help him for a while."

"Does the term 'Decoy 17' mean anything to you?" asked Anna.

"Decoy 17? No I am afraid not. I have not heard that

before."

"What about the term 'Stingray'?" asked Stephanie.

"Stingray? Setingerai! Yes, Stingray I know."

The girls looked sharply at each other, and waited with baited breath.

"So what do you know about it?"

"Five boxes for shredding each had that title on them, and it appeared on many sheets inside, I could see when I put them in the shredding machine, but I only did one box. The small writing seemed to be in a code, or a different language. And there was an address."

"Can you remember what it is?" said Anna

"Do you have a pen?"

Stephanie handed one over, and a small notebook. He started to write, speaking at the same time.

"Zamenhofstraat 178, Amsterdam 1022 AG, Netherlands." He handed the notebook and pen back. "That's all I can remember. And Setingerai - what you call Stingray - was on several of the same sheets too. I hope it helps."

Stephanie looked down at the notebook. "Amsterdam," she reiterated. "Holland. I wonder how that fits in."

"Yusuf would have known much more. He may have known about the Decoy you mention. And I am sure he would have told this to the man who asked the questions, your people. But he said this was done quietly, privately, to one man. Even then he was worried about repercussions, that Malekka might somehow hit back."

"Malekka did hit back," said Stephanie. "He killed the man who would have been the one asking the questions. He had him murdered, in London."

Stylianos shook his head.

"This is evil."

"Yes," continued Stephanie. "Of course, Malekka doesn't do these things himself, personally. He's too clever and powerful for that. He has his people do them. But people die. Families suffer. People have pain. So it was for this man, in London. Our friend. He, too, died."

"And my friend, Yusuf, also. Someone loyal to Malekka must have mentioned something to one of his people still here on the Island. And Yusuf died too."

Stylianos let out a deep sigh.

"And you two women need to be careful. As do I. But as I say… I don't care any more."

"We'll be careful," said Anna, and she put her hand on his arm. "And you must be too, Stylianos. One day you might care again. As, one day, I hope I might care again."

Stylianos moved his lips into a small smile.

"Maybe. We will see."

He reached for the knob on the Gaz lantern.

"That is all I have for you," he said as the flame died. The room was in darkness once more.

"Thank you," said Stephanie, and held out her hand. Stylianos took it and said, "I am glad to have helped, if it actually has helped."

"I am sure you have helped," added Stephanie. "We don't know what it means yet, but we'll find out."

The moon in a dark clear sky lit up the inside of the open-roofed room and cast eerie shadows of the broken beams onto the stone floor. The three stood and made their way to the door. He gave it a yank and pulled it open, and held it for the women. "Please," he said.

Stephanie went out and Anna followed. It was a strong moonbeam glinting on a metal barrel and throwing a small reflection that caught Anna's eye. In an instant she could make out the weapon and arm of the shooter, aiming at Stephanie. She shouted, "Look out!" as she shoved Stephanie aside. A white flash spewed from the gun. Stephanie fell to the ground on her left but was already reaching for her Shield. She fired twice as the bullet from the man's gun hit Anna in the chest. She let out a scream and collapsed. The man was hit by both shots from Stephanie, and dropped to the ground dead.

"Anna," screamed Stephanie, back on her feet, still aiming in the direction of the shooter, but glancing quickly at her friend. She ran to the man first, checking that he was incapacitated, and alone. Then she was back on the ground holding Anna's head in her lap. Stylianos had vanished. There was a bright red patch of blood spreading fast on Anna's T-shirt just under her left breast and she was panting, choking, as she breathed quickly.

"Stephie," said Anna, then drew her breath, and repeated, "Stephie." Her eyes stared, wide with shock, into Stephanie's, who desperately looked around, then down again to Anna. She pressed on the wound, trying to stem the flow of blood.

"Stephie…" said Anna once more, and then her breathing stopped.

Stephanie's eyes filled with tears.

There was the rustling of the wind as it rippled gently through the branches of the olive trees.

But only Stephanie could hear it.

For Anna Kepling was dead.

20
RIO LEARNING

IN THE MORNING of that same day, six and a half thousand miles southwest of Cyprus and six hours behind in local time, the Falcon and Brazil's Police Commissioner & Head of the Anti-Terrorist Squad had thanked Senhora Monterroso and Senhorita Carla for their time, and left.

"I didn't know Rovalle had any base in Brazil," said JP, thinking about what the significance of the dead man's work could be.

"Yes, they opened over ten years ago," said Savedra. "It's a research and technology centre arrangement set up to work with leading Brazilian scientists and universities. It's quite a big place they have."

"Everything Rovalle has is big," joked JP.

"Yes, I guess so," said the Major, smiling at the remark.

They were back at the car and quickly inside. "The Centro Ciência et de Tecnológico de Taubaté - sorry, the Taubaté Science and Technology Centre - itself is big and impressive too. The modern Brazil. We don't just produce sugarcane, you know."

Savedra started the car and pulled out.

"Well I think that has to be my next port of call," said JP. "Can you get me an appointment to see the top guy there, this afternoon?"

"I'm Head of Police. I don't do appointments, I just walk in. Unless you'd prefer to go on your own?"

JP smiled. "Of course, I was forgetting. No, I don't need to go on my own, I'd prefer we go together."

At the top of the road Savedra turned left into Rua Bulhões de Carvalho and then left again into Rua Francisco Sá to take them down to the water.

"I think I'll drop you at your hotel, go into the Station and we'll do a little research on who the people are at Rovalle," said Savedra, manoeuvring the car into Avenida Atlântica across the first three lanes of traffic and through the gap in the central reservation, to turn left. "As soon as I have a name I'll come out and pick you up. It's a bit of a drive there from Rio."

As the car sped along, JP stared out of the window at what was one of the most expensive and desirable pieces of real estate anywhere in the world. The grey and white geometric wave design of the mosaic paving of the walkway, that divided the glorious sandy beach off on the right from the traffic, was full of revellers and businessmen and -women alike, and it was as common for a business meeting to be held on the beach as much as it was for a game of volley ball. The road followed the ocean in a gentle northeast curve, with the Hotel Othon Palace one of the tallest of the building skyline, beaten in height only by the Hilton at the other end of the shore. Beyond were the green hills of which Sugar Loaf Mountain and its cable car was the most famous and perhaps the most beautiful. The beachfront walkway was busy with refreshment stalls and seating set under wide low-rising conical roofing, matched by smaller bright-coloured beach umbrellas that together made for an appealing and fun-filled view as they passed by. The sun was high in the sky, and despite the cloudless blue a strong wind was blowing in from the ocean that caught the numerous multinational flags on their tall poles scattered along the sand's edge and made them flap crazily. The Major went past the Hotel, heading for the next break in the reservation, then turned into the south lanes and reached the Othon Palace.

"Thanks," said JP as he opened the door.

"Give me an hour. I'll find out what I can, and I'll be back to get you."

The Major drove off. JP reached his room, closed the doors

firmly, used the bathroom and then collapsed onto the bed, staring up at the ceiling.

That was two deaths that Malekka was responsible for in almost as many days, he said to himself. How does Monterroso fit into all of this? He seems to have been a decent hardworking man, with a good family, a wife that clearly adored him, a caring protective daughter and a well-paid job at which he apparently excelled. He had a comfortable flat, the mortgage was up-to-date, so Savedra had said, there were no excessive debts and he was climbing socially. Whatever it was that he had discovered - either by searching for or, more likely thought JP, by accident - could only have happened recently, and it was something that someone else knew he had uncovered, otherwise there would not have been a killing.

JP reached for his phone. He did a quick internet search for Rovalle in Brazil. There wasn't much online for him to read, and he had to dig around hard to find that. The links seemed to lead back to Rovalle's headquarters and its enormous centre at Portland, Oregon, in the USA. JP knew that Fabian Rovalle had been born in the same year as the first flight by the Wright brothers, in 1903, and was one of the early great aviation enthusiasts. Wiki filled him in on the rest. An engineer by trade… designed his first aircraft in 1928… cargo planes and light aircraft… first passenger design in 1947. Formed Rovalle Corporation Inc in 1949 just after the war... first jet in 1953, rivalling the British Comet and Boeing 707… many military contracts… huge growth and success followed especially in wide-bodied jets… most carrying the prefix letters 'FAB' taken from the founder's first name. Rovalle now one of the top three aircraft manufacturers in the world. Current value around $200 billion today.

JP put in a quick call to Charles Melton, and got straight through to him on the scrambled line.

"Oh good, JP, we were about to contact you," said Melton.

The tense excitement was obvious in his voice. "We have a bit of news, well, two pieces actually."

"Hi Charlie, great, what have you got?" said JP.

"First, we've been able to recover some images from the cameras of those two private investigators who were hired to take photographs outside Tilsen's flat. And guess what - there's one image that's particularly interesting."

"That's a bit of good news I could do with," replied JP, pleased to have something positive and helpful from London at last. "How did the techies manage to do that?"

"It's what we thought. The formatting by the cameras was not low level so the cards were not wiped properly, although it damaged some files, and also as they were later overwritten by subsequent pictures. However, they've been able to recover some."

"Ok, so what do you have?"

"There's a clear picture of you as you exited Tilsen's flat. Also of me, for that matter. But, more importantly, there are two of a suspicious looking character who we think may have been Tilsen's murderer."

"Good work, Charlie."

"Thanks, we'll pass that along. I'm going to send you those two pictures now…"

A few seconds later, JP's phone pinged, signalling receipt. He opened the images. He cursed as he saw the one of himself. He flicked it across and the picture of Dave Tilsen's killer appeared. A man in a full-length lightweight coat, a cap on his head, his collar turned up. The Falcon went to the third and last image, which was a head and shoulders take. The man was almost looking directly at the camera. A squarish head. Very dark eyes - a visible feature even on the covertly-taken picture. And a scar down his left cheek.

"Any idea who that nasty looking guy is?"

"No, none," said Charlie Melton. "We've started to look at

all the general surveillance cameras in the area, to see if we might get lucky and pick him up, so that we can trace him and get a name. There's nothing yet. But ten to one he's the killer. We've got the local boys to check with the other residents to see if anyone recognises the man. I'll have that back in a couple of hours, and I reckon he'll be a stranger to everyone. Which means he's probably the killer. It's another lead, and we'll work it. I'll let you know."

"Good, Charlie, very good. What's the other bit of news?"

"Tilsen had a tracker on the heel of his right shoe."

"What?"

"Yes, it was so small it was missed in the flat by the CSE folks, but they were dealing with the blood and the killing. When the body was moved to the morgue at Vauxhall the first automatic electronic surveillance sweep picked it up - they're done every five minutes all over the building and it caused an immediate alert. In fact the security boys rushed in ready to pounce."

"Christ, how did they get that onto him?" asked JP, amazed.

"We don't know for sure, but we think it was done at the airport; it would be logical to assume, that they would get to him once he'd landed at Gatwick. They wouldn't have been able to get the tracker through the security at Cyprus on the flight; it would have set off all sorts of alarms. As you know, shoes are examined very carefully these days at airport security. So we think they had people at the airport in the international arrivals hall. And we're looking at all the surveillance cameras there too."

"So this was a pretty determined effort to get Tilsen."

"Yes, but it doesn't make sense to wait to hit him in London if they were at Gatwick when he arrived back. What would have been the point. We think they were following and waiting for the right moment, when they could search him as well as kill him."

"The SD card?"

"Yes. So if he had it on him, the chances are that they took it. And there's something else."

"What's that."

"The little gizmo was a tracker with a range of about two miles the techies reckon. But it doubled as a bug, it had a microphone that could be remotely set to transmit sounds from the immediate area."

"Oh no," said JP, "does that mean that they heard our conversation, when we looked at the note Dave had left? And that they'll know that we know about Decoy 17?"

"It could have done. Though I doubt the assassin and any accomplices would have hung around for long. We had a bit of luck there, though. When Tilsen was shot he fell onto the desk and rolled off and down hard onto the wooden floor. It seems that the heel of his right foot smashed onto the wooden floor, and the gizmo was damaged. We know it now, because an essential bit was broken off the bug and it was found in the vacuumed dust items that the CSEs lifted from the floor when they went through the apartment. So, luckily for us, there could not have been any transmission."

"It goes to show what an adversary Malekka is, Charlie," said JP, his concern making him begin to think again through all of his other movements so far, and those he had yet to undertake as well as plan.

"That's for sure, JP. He's a very smart, very dangerous killer. So watch out."

"Yes." He was about to end the call, but thought of something else, and spoke again to Melton.

"Charlie, I have a question."

"Yes?"

"I don't understand something. Surely Dave would have written some of this stuff down, somewhere; what he had found out, what his conclusions were. He wouldn't keep it all in his head, would he?"

"No, not necessarily, JP. Dave Tilsen had a photographic memory, that apparently rivalled even Sir Alastair's. He would have had no need to write anything down, until coming in to see me and making his report, and probably not even until after that. Also, he had a deep-rooted mistrust of electronic files, while paper files were to him as good as putting things in newspapers, they could so easily be mishandled. Now, he *would* have filed a report in due course, and I think had he come in to see me the day he was killed instead of aiming to take the plane out to Panama, we would have had everything from him - if not in writing we would at least have known all the details - of course, ultimately, it would be on paper, locked away here for the records. But not necessarily yet."

"Yes, you're right, I'd overlooked his memory. It was part of what made him a great spook. He was a bright lad, Dave Tilsen."

"He was. But there are a couple of other things. You already know he had made a note on his Firm calendar about the plane trip and the person he was to meet, Jon Lano, as well as the details of the flight. I'm pretty sure Dave Tilsen *did* have one electronic file, something like a Folder Lock file. They're heavily encrypted, almost impossible to break. But where it is, if it does actually exist, we have no idea. We're searching; and Jenny is being helpful too, poor girl. Even if we find it, it could take weeks for us to break into, if we ever can. And when we do, it might be empty."

The two men spent a minute reminiscing about how good Tilsen had been; and then they spoke about the demise of Monterroso.

"We're doing something right if it has already produced ripples to cause another killing," said Melton.

"I'm not sure that's a direct result of what we've done," said JP. "How would they know we were coming to Brazil, we only found the address to Monterroso when Coco and I entered Lano's office two nights ago, and we were careful to ensure that anything that was touched was put back in the same place."

"Yes, that's true," said Melton. "Which means they needed Monterroso out of the way for reasons of their own and you've come across his demise as a coincidence."

"Yes, I think that's probably more the case."

"We've put out an updated story about Spider, like Jane suggested. I'll send it through to you. It says the authorities believe that a wealthy Iranian has been behind the cell and the entire plot and that we are making further enquiries. Malekka will have to assume that we have his picture, although he won't know it for sure as we haven't said it or released it, and he will have to be careful with any travel plans."

"That's good, Charlie, that should help keep him pinned down in Iran and make it more difficult to get hold of any new codes or details that he needs to bring Stingray forwards." He then switched the subject. "What about the girls, have you heard anything from them?"

"Yes. They met with Gaunchon. Everything is in place and to schedule. They started work last night, and it's carried through to today. No developments yet. By the way the lab folks are going through the files that you lifted from Lano's computer, much is heavily password protected and secured by good software. But they'll crack it. And the two PCB boards should be with us shortly. As soon as we have something I'll let you know."

As the conversation ended his phone sounded to announce the arrival of a text message, saying Major Savedra was downstairs. JP, who had already packed, quickly checked out using the hotel's internal room system, grabbed his jacket and bags and left.

JP exited the hotel and looked for the same car in which he

had previously been ferried around by Savedra, but it was nowhere to be seen. However JP soon spotted its replacement - a rather large and shiny Mercedes S Class. A rear door opened and Savedra stood out, beckoning him over. The driver exited the vehicle too, and held open the other rear door.

"I think I've done enough driving today," said Savedra to the approaching JP, porter and bags in tow. "It's time to sit back and we can talk and concentrate more easily."

"No complaints from me," said JP as he settled into the back seat.

"Ok, Pedro, let's go," said the Major.

Pedro returned to the driver's seat and steered the car out of the forecourt of the Othon Palace Hotel. The car, which was the long wheel base version, had been altered so that there was a glass divide between the passengers in the back and the driver. Savedra pressed a button on his door and the glass partition closed up.

The car headed southwest on Avenida Atlântica but then swung round across the central reservation and headed in the opposite direction.

"Isn't Taubaté southwest of here?" asked JP.

"Yes," said Savedra, "but it's also almost three hundred and fifty kilometres from Rio, much farther than I realised. And I have no intention of driving that distance, no matter how comfortable a car. No, we have the helicopter standing by at the airport, and that's where we're going."

With blue police lights flashing in the unmarked official limousine, the car sped along the roads and reached Rio's Antonio Carlos Jobim International Airport, which everyone still called the Galeão International Airport, some twenty minutes later. They quickly gained admittance to the tarmac area and pulled up alongside the Eurocopter EC145 in its strong red and blue flashes. Savedra dismissed Pedro, they boarded the aircraft and the pilots were powering up before the door was closed.

The helicopter was fast and sleek, with a twin-engine system that comfortably pulled the aircraft to its chosen altitude of five thousand feet in a little under four minutes. The French Turbomeca Arriel gas turbine turboshafts each pushed out seven hundred and thirty-eight shaft horsepower and the aircraft surged forwards at a hundred and thirty knots, or one hundred and fifty miles an hour. Because of the integrated headset speaker system that meant that the pilot and co-pilot could hear everything they said, JP and the Major kept conversation to a minimum. There was an option to switch the intercom off but the pilots controlled it, and the two men felt it best they should guard their conversation for the journey.

The aircraft routed south away from the busy airspace of Galeão Airport and then turned west, quickly leaving the beaches of Copacabana and Ipanema behind but following the coast to be clear of the mountains to the north and their turbulence, dropping to a height of five hundred feet. They traversed the waters of Saco do Piaí south of Santa Cruz, made land again at Conceição de Jacareí with its sandy beach reflecting the sunlight and then were over the water once again at Jacuacanga Bay. They crossed the shoreline south of Taquari, where the topography rose steeply and the helicopter pushed its altitude to six thousand feet to clear the hills a thousand feet below as they flew from the State of Rio into that of São Paulo. The land became rolling hills with heavy vegetation and trees, but gradually declined in height as their journey continued. Suddenly the speed of the Eurocopter began to lessen and the aircraft started a slow descent. As it levelled off at three hundred feet it was clear that the pilot was tracking a highway, which was the SP-060, off on its right beam.

The pilot spoke.

"That's it, Major, down on the right."

Between the helicopter and the SP-060 sprawled an enormous commercial development of six main hangar-like buildings and several smaller ones separated in the middle by a long silver tubular walkway. The road entrance was on the south side away from the highway and was served by a separate and wide road which ran parallel to the highway and around the perimeter of the Science and Technology Centre. They could see Taubaté behind them off to the northeast, and the smaller town of Caçapava ahead and to the southwest.

The helicopter hovered and after a minute or so moved forwards slowly, as the pilot had earlier been instructed, to give his VIP passengers a clear view of the centre from the air.

"Ok," said the Major, "we've seen enough. Go on to land."

"Yes sir," replied the pilot, and the engine sound increased slightly as the aircraft gathered forward speed once more. A couple of minutes later and the helicopter was making its landing approach to the airport; it was soon in, taxied a little way and finally touched down. The captain closed the engines and his passengers disembarked.

"This is the Aeroporto Internacional de São José dos Campos Professor Urbano Ernesto Stumpf," said Savedra, as the two men walked a few steps from the aircraft stretching their legs.

"You folks do like to go in for long names, don't you," said the Falcon, smiling.

"Yes," the Major laughed, "but it's referred to affectionately as Stumpf Airport. Do you know who he was?"

"Professor Urbano Ernesto Stumpf? Of course," said JP. "He was the one who invented the first practical motor engine that runs on ethanol, and on which just about all modern motorcar engines are based, or they at least incorporate his technology."

It was clear that the Major was impressed. "Very good, Falcon. Brazil found a good use for all of that sugarcane. We supply fifty per cent of the world's sugarcane, which as a by-product of sugar production produces ethanol. Because of Professor Stumpf we have over fourteen million cars running on neat ethanol; and just about all petrol around the world has a percentage of ethanol in it, usually between ten and twenty-five percent. His technology altered the world. It's cleaner, saves the petrol and earns Brazil lots of money."

The little history and economics lesson from Savedra was given with a considerable amount of pride. Stumpf Airport was not large, it had one runway and a couple of modern-looking terminals, and it seemed the main business was cargo rather than people. Savedra told the flight crew they would be a couple of hours, and the two men walked over to the waiting car, a duplicate of the one they had left behind in Rio.

They were quickly out of the airport along a few simple slip roads that were not well tarmacked. They joined the SP-060 highway and headed northeast. Some fifteen minutes later they broke away from the highway onto a single lane but wide road leading to the Science and Technology Centre, the entrance to which was marked by a large archway covering the access and controlled by a checkpoint. The guard moved rapidly once he saw the flashing blue lights; the Major lowered the rear window and spoke firmly in Portuguese while flashing his official badge. The barrier was raised.

They drove along on the road to the far side of the Park, where there was another checkpoint. The same procedure produced the quick raising of the gate, and the car swiftly moved in to park outside the Rovalle building, which was the largest of the principal six rectangular constructions that JP and Savedra had seen from the air.

Large double glass doors opened into a grand reception hall. Major Savedra marched up to the desk located at the centre of the far wall, spoke to one of two women behind and again showed his credentials. She immediately made a phone call upstairs and left the desk to escort Major Savedra and JP to an elevator that took them to the second floor. The girl walked them along a wide hallway to a door that carried the legend *'Edson Ramos, Presidente'*. She knocked and they entered; the internal office was occupied by a couple of PAs and secretaries. One of them took charge and led the two men to the large office at the end of the anteroom. She knocked, and the men walked in.

"Mr Ramos?" said the Major, once again ready with his badge.

Edson Ramos was a tall elegant man of about forty, in a light grey suit with waistcoat. His face was clean-shaven, his hair dark and brushed back on the sides and held in place with gel, leaving the bald head to fend for itself. His eyes were sharp and busy, he exuded confidence and authority with a stylish charm. There was a short conversation in Portuguese with the Major and then the talk switched to English.

"Mr Peregrine?" said Ramos, extending his hand and waving both men to the two comfortable black leather Chesterfields that faced each other, and then continued to Savedra, "Please, tell me what I can do to help. What is all this about?"

"Mr Ramos, I am sorry to drop in on you unannounced but we believe you may be able to help us with our enquiries. Your colleague Jorge Monterroso..."

"Yes, you mean our Head of Design and Research, that Jorge Monterroso? Do you want me to fetch him so you can speak with him?"

"I'm afraid he isn't in today," said Savedra, "and won't be again. Somebody threw him off his balcony at his home yesterday. I am sorry to tell you that he is dead."

"What?" said Ramos. JP noticed a little colour drain from his tanned face.

"I'm afraid so…" The Major filled in the background, as

far as he could, to Edson Ramos about the sad demise of Monterroso, and then JP added an explanation, albeit superficial, as to why he was in Brazil. When they had finished, Ramos was clearly shocked and even upset. It was obvious he had liked Monterroso.

"...and so because he worked for you we thought that the next step should be a conversation with you to see what you can tell us about him and what he was working on," said Savedra.

Ramos raised his hand.

"Yes, of course, Major Savedra, but wait a moment please. I need some coffee."

He picked up the telephone on the glass-topped small table to his left, and ordered his refreshments, and added, "Gentlemen, will you have something?" and both his guests also asked for coffee.

"It's not every day here at Rovalle that the Chief of Police and Counter Terrorism walks into my office and says an employee has been murdered and might have been involved in terrorism." He regained his composure, and continued. "Very well, now, how can I be of assistance?"

≈

Downstairs, in the reception hall, the woman who had taken Major Savedra and the Falcon up in the lift to Ramos's office excused herself from her colleague and walked to the ladies' restroom. Midway across the reception hall she opened her handbag, pulled out her small cell phone and made a call.

≈

"Mr Ramos," said the Falcon, "the first thing I'd like to ask is, what do you do here? I was surprised to learn that Rovalle has a presence of this kind in Brazil, what is the work at this facility?"

"That's an easy one," said Ramos, settling back into the Chesterfield. He had come to terms with the news quickly and was once again in control. "Rovalle is the world's third largest aerospace company and leading manufacturer of commercial jetliners and defence, space and security systems. Brazil has always had an active and vibrant aviation industry. Our history in Brazil dates back to 1961, when we delivered our first commercial airplane to Brazil. Vadob, which was an acronym for Vias Aéreas Do Brasil, or Brazil Airways, was the first airline founded in Brazil, in 1929, and was the country's national airline. Through the years, the airline purchased numerous Rovalle aircraft - in fact our *FAB Conquest* in its various formats was the organisation's workhorse - and Vadob was a very good friend. Sadly, it got into difficulties even before the global economic crisis was upon the industry and had to be restructured, into an 'Old' Vadob and a 'New' Vadob. The former was eventually closed; the latter was sold to Ponto Linhas Aéreas in 2006 for a total of $311 million. Presently Ponto operates one hundred and thirty Rovalle *Conquests* of various specification and variants, and has orders with us for a further one hundred and twenty nine aircraft. We are happy they continue to choose our venerable *FAB Conquest* instead of the comparable Boeing 737 or Airbus 320," he added with some pride.

There was a knock at the door; a smartly dressed young man walked in with a tray and the coffee.

"Ah, thank you, Vicente," said Ramos, "please just put it down here."

"Yes, sir," replied the lad, and walked out.

Ramos picked up the coffee pot and poured first for his guests and then for himself. JP had noticed that Ramos was speaking English with an American accent that was almost entirely clear of any Portuguese influence. Their host settled into the sofa, held the saucer up and took the cup to his lips, taking a couple of sips. He sighed, put the saucer on the mat on the table and said, "I'm sorry, gentlemen, I needed that." The other two nodded and smiled without humour.

"As for the other airlines," continued Ramos, "CASA Airlines Brasil, or in Portuguese, Companhia Aérea Sul Americana do Brasil, is sadly primarily an Airbus and Boeing customer, with the former's 330 and the Boeing 777, but they still have twelve *FAB Conquerors* and even eleven *Jupiters*. We hope to change the numbers," he smiled. "As I'm sure you both know, the *FAB Jupiter* is Rovalle's equivalent to Boeing's Jumbo Jet and the Airbus 380, and still holds many global flight records including the longest non-stop flight for a passenger aircraft. Neither Boeing's 787 Dreamliner nor our own *FAB Whisperer* has beaten that. There are various other operators in Brazil, several of which have several of our aircraft. So you can see, gentlemen, that Brazil as a country is a very important territory for Rovalle. Add to that, the enormous size of Brazil and her extraordinary rate of growth, we believe that partnering with various common aviation interests will further Rovalle's interests here."

"And this facility?" said JP, "What is its importance and purpose?"

"Our title is Rovalle Pesquisa e Desenvolvimento Brasil - Rovalle Research & Development Brazil - better known as RPD Brazil. As the name suggests, we're primarily a Research & Development centre, but with a sizeable manufacturing arm. We work with Brazil's leading scientists from both the public and private sectors, including universities, to advance R&D and evolve innovative aviation technologies. Our activity focuses on advanced air traffic management and supersonic and hypersonic flight boundaries, including new metals and compound materials. For example, we were heavily involved in the development of the new composite materials used in the Rovalle *FAB Whisperer*. And you must have heard recently of the reducing of the sonic boom to no more than the sound of a slamming door? That was our pioneering development, led again by Jorge Monterroso; an essential breakthrough in eventually bringing back supersonic passenger flight in the next decade. We work closely with companies like Embraer, the Brazilian aerospace conglomerate, which as you may know is the world's fourth largest producer of civil aviation aircraft after ourselves, Boeing and Airbus, and with Brazil's Department of Aerospace Science and Technology, and their National Institute for Space Research. It's part of our continuing and evolving collaboration with Brazil. We also have offices in São Paulo and seven retail travel outlets in other Brazilian cities. Our co-operative shared R&D will benefit Rovalle and the people of Brazil, as well as other communities around the world. Brazil has some of the world's brightest scientists and engineers, you know, and this centre functions as a vehicle for these minds to join forces with others, and create."

"Isn't it unusual for you to have facilities like this outside the United States?" asked JP, who was listening intently.

"You might think so," replied Ramos, who was enjoying the opportunity to talk about his company, especially after receiving such ghastly news. "But in fact this is Rovalle's seventh advanced research centre outside of the United States. There are similar centres in South Africa, Europe, Russia, Australia, Mexico and even China."

"Really," said JP. "I didn't know that."

"The world has become a much smaller place in the last couple of decades, Mr Peregrine," said Ramos. "RPD Brazil will link with our other centres around the world, to enhance Rovalle's overall global commercial and business interests."

He sipped at his coffee one more time.

"I suppose you could translate all of that crassly, gentlemen, into meaning that it helps us sell Rovalle aircraft."

"And what about Jorge Monterroso," said Major Savedra. "Where does he fit in?"

"Jorge was an immensely gifted and intelligent engineer who headed up one of the R&D sections. He was responsible for the development of various work lines in bio-materials, progressive flight speeds and in advanced air traffic management that I referred to earlier. He joined RPD Brazil when we first came into being, although the official opening of this Taubaté Science and Technology Centre, or STC as we call it, did not take place until a couple of years later. He was a fine leader of the people in his department, extremely bright and very hard working. He lived in Rio de Janeiro, as you of course know, and because of the distances involved, and because we wanted him here, we put him up first at a local hotel and then in an apartment for the days he was here, which generally were Monday through Thursday. Friday he went home, spent the weekend with his family, and was back here early Monday mornings. Sometimes he had an extra day off mid-week. He was much liked. I don't know how I'm going to tell the others here. They are going to be very shocked."

"Was there a particular priority area of work that he was focusing on?" asked JP.

"Yes. Advanced air traffic management systems. He headed up Rovalle's NextGen ATC capabilities developed for the US and global systems."

"What does that mean," asked Savedra, "exactly?"

"Well," said Ramos, taking a deep breath. "It's the latest requirement for all aircraft around the world and is going to enhance greatly - revolutionise, in fact - the way aircraft function and are controlled in flight. Are you familiar with the concept of NextGen Air Traffic Control gentlemen - are either of you pilots?"

"No," said Savedra.

JP didn't want to correct him. Instead he let the conversation flow. The hairs on the back of his head had suddenly begun to tingle. He knew that was always bad news.

"Very well, then let me explain briefly. When the skies weren't so busy, identifying aircraft wasn't particularly important. With the advent of civil aviation and the carrying of passengers, and the establishment of air routes, it began to become necessary to know on the ground where aircraft were in the skies. This was important in time of war too for military aircraft - which was a friendly aircraft and which was not. With the advent of radar - where a radio signal from the ground hits an airplane and is reflected back - it became possible for people on the ground to see and track aircraft in the air. That's what's called Primary Radar. But it was not very accurate, especially with regard to the aircraft's height, and it did not identify one aircraft from another. So a different type of radar identification process evolved, called secondary surveillance radar. This relied on a simple bit of electronics - well, simple by our standards today - whereby a box in each aircraft would be interrogated by a signal sent out from the ground. When this signal hits the aircraft, the box, called a transponder, activates and sends back various data - the aircraft's distance and height or rather altitude. What is now known as Air Traffic Control, or ATC, on the ground allocates a different four-digit code to each aircraft, called a squawk code, which the pilot or flight crew enters into the transponder. The ATC can then identify each aircraft individually and fairly accurately, to within a hundred feet. This makes the required height separation of one thousand feet between commercial aircraft easy to achieve and maintain, and similarly for the standard horizontal separation of five nautical miles. The system has worked very well for many years, for military, civil and general aviation aircraft alike. It went through various stages of refinement, and nearly every aircraft in the skies today, including small general aviation aircraft, has a transponder.

"However, our skies have become very busy and are getting clogged. It was reasoned that if a more accurate system could be developed, more aircraft could operate in existing airspace, especially in the congested areas above major cities around the world. Enter ADS-B, or the Automatic Dependent Surveillance - Broadcast system."

"So what's that?" said Savedra.

"It's the new system that's been developed and is being phased in all around the world, and known colloquially as the Next Generation of air traffic control, or NextGen, to which I referred earlier. The new ADS-B transponder is being fitted to all aircraft - either in addition to the earlier transponder or as a straight replacement - and is based on the Global Positioning System, or GPS, which as we all know relies on the signals from satellites in orbit around the earth, and which pinpoints our position to within a few feet. Everyone already uses or at least has access to GPS in our cars as sat nav, through Google Maps or other brands like TomTom or Garmin. ADS-B is basically sat nav for aircraft. Stick sat nav in a plane so it knows exactly where it is, then transmit the data and Air Traffic Control knows where each aircraft is to within a few feet in all three dimensions of height, distance and geographic location, as well as its speed. It consists of two interlinked avionics functions, ADS-B 'Out', and ADS-B 'In'. The ADS-B box transmits or *broadcasts* - that's the ADS-B 'Out' bit - the aircraft's positional and other data twice a second. The signal is collected by dedicated ground stations that in turn relay the information to air traffic control, either by a ground based link or satellite connection, or both, for precise tracking of the aircraft. But it's not just the ground stations that can collect the 'Out' signal. Each aircraft in the local vicinity within a hundred nautical miles can also receive it - that's the ADS-B

'In' bit. So, every broadcast signal from an aircraft is picked up by every other aircraft in the area; the ADS-B transponders can all 'talk' to each other. Pilots will have the ability to see, on their in-flight display, other traffic operating in their airspace. So, in addition to giving ATC much more accurate positional data about aircraft in the skies, the system provides pilots with improved situational awareness and so makes flying significantly safer for everyone. This means ATC can with absolute safety reduce the horizontal separation of aircraft from five miles to three, meaning more aircraft in the same airspace. It's a huge leap forward but has involved enormous investment in technology, infrastructure and of course money."

"When does all that start," asked Savedra.

"It already has, in some places. But the important deadline is the end of this year. All aircraft operating in US airspace that currently require a transponder must be equipped with ADS-B by 31st December. After that, as of 1st January next year, if they don't have one, they're grounded. Those from outside the US will simply be refused entry into US airspace. There are around ten thousand Rovalle aircraft carrying over two million people in the air around the world at any one time; that's a lot of updating. Of course, new aircraft leave the production line already ADS-B capable."

"It's a big change, for sure," said JP.

"That's putting it mildly," said Ramos. "It's the largest single change to aviation since the invention of the jet engine. There are actually other advantages to the system; ADS-B 'In' can also receive automatic weather updates, for example. But that, in essence, is what the big change is all about. And this is what we at RPD Brazil are handling, first the design and then the integration of the system into all Rovalle aircraft. And Jorge Monterroso was leading the work."

"What exactly is involved?" asked the Falcon.

"There are two elements. First, the ADS-B boxes or

transponders themselves - that's relatively straightforward. The box goes into the cockpit as part of the standard updated electronics. Second, the ADS-B system has to be integrated into the computer system of each aircraft. That involves a more complicated procedure in the main electronics section of the aircraft, which is usually located below the flight deck or further back towards the tail of the aircraft, depending on its design. Newer aircraft have more computers, and integrating new avionics and the appropriate software can make installing ADS-B in them more expensive; it's much easier and cheaper to upgrade older aircraft. The time for conversion can range from a few days to as long as three weeks. As for cost, well that can run between $50,000 to $400,000 depending on what avionics are currently installed and what work has been done in the past. All standards for certification and operational approvals have been in place since 2011; we started our own work on this then. But like everyone else, the airline industry has had the global monetary collapse and recovery to deal with for years, and many aircraft of other manufacturers and airline operators have yet to be converted. Rovalle will be ok though, our work is virtually complete for all Rovalle aircraft around the world save for the last few and so we'll get there comfortably before the deadline. Jorge Monterroso was responsible for the software that integrated ADS-B into all of our onboard computer systems. Obviously he worked closely with Rovalle colleagues in the States but essentially it was his baby."

"So Monterroso designed the software, and then what happens?" asked JP.

"We make up the individual electronics here, specific to each aircraft. The physical dimensions of the equipment vary obviously - aircraft series such as the *FAB Jupiter*, the *Whisperer*, their type and so on - but the software is essentially the same. Brand new aircraft coming off the production line have theirs fitted at the outset, as I say, as part of the new build. For existing aircraft needing the upgrade, once some maintenance time for the work is scheduled and the equipment requested, which we know of here well in advance of course, the systems are made specifically to order and sent to Portland in Oregon to Rovalle's Head Office for distribution. Either the upgrade is carried out by Rovalle in Oregon, or it's sent on to the individual Rovalle aircraft operators, whether in the States or worldwide, who placed the order, for the airline to do the fitting themselves. We make them, but everything goes to Oregon and then they take over."

"You mean you manufacture the electronics here?"

"Yes, of course. That's the manufacturing arm that I mentioned earlier. It's cheaper for the work to be done here than in the USA, although physically in terms of size it's a rather small output."

There was silence as this wealth of information was being digested by Savedra and the Falcon. Edson Ramos took the moment.

"Major Savedra, may I ask a couple of questions?"

"Yes, although I cannot promise an answer."

"I would like to know… what happened? Jorge Monterroso was a brilliant engineer and also, I'm proud to say, a friend. Over the years, we developed a good working relationship, his children knew my children… it was like that. So, what happened, do you have any idea why he was killed? Or who did it?"

The Major sighed. "I'm sorry, Mr Ramos, I have to give the standard professional answer at the moment, and that is I cannot comment on an open investigation. I would like to, but I am not permitted."

"Oh yes of course, I see," said Ramos.

"As soon as we do find out anything, and I am able to discuss it, I will be in touch with you personally, that I can promise."

"Thank you, Major." Ramos paused, and added, "On a practical level, trying to put aside the emotional and personal feelings and looking at the business, this is going to make things a little difficult for us. Especially as his right hand man left rather suddenly too."

His two guests sat up with renewed attention.

"What do you mean, Mr Ramos?" asked JP. "Who left?"

"Well it was a woman, actually. Denise Oliveira. She had been working alongside Monterroso as Deputy Director for years, almost as long as the centre has been established. She was very bright; more an administrator than creative engineer, but someone that was important to the department. She suddenly decided to leave, and didn't return to work any more."

"When did this happen?"

"Er, about four days ago; no, longer than that, about eight days. Yes, eight. She just left us."

"Could I have a copy of her personnel file, please?" asked Savedra. "And, while I'm about it, perhaps I should have Monterroso's also."

"Of course," said Ramos. He picked up the telephone and spoke briefly into it.

"Well, Mr Ramos, thank you for all of your help," said JP, "it's been very much appreciated."

"Not at all, Mr Peregrine, I don't know that I've actually helped at all, but anything I can do to assist you in your efforts to track down who killed poor Jorge, I will do."

There was another knock at the door. The same young man who had brought the coffee walked the files of Monterroso and Oliveira over to the Rovalle President, who nodded his thanks.

"Actually, there is one more thing," said JP, as Savedra quickly studied the personnel files.

"Yes?"

"Could we see Monterroso's office please, where he worked?"

"Certainly." Ramos rose, and the other two men followed suit. "Please, come this way."

He walked them out of his office and down a series of long corridors. The last set of double doors opened to a small hall off which there were a number of rooms. Ramos pushed open the door to one of them.

The room was large and comfortable, with a sizeable desk facing inwards and set in the corner alongside windows that overlooked the forecourts and were shaded from the sun with drop blinds. A filing cabinet lay close by. A small conference table with six chairs rested at the corner alongside the same wall as the entrance door. Set in the wall opposite were adjoining double glass doors, that opened into a large busy factory-like workspace where around thirty men and women of various ages dressed in white coats were busy at desks, computers or drawing design tables, and beyond them towards the end, separated by wall to wall protective glass and a double doorway, were the welding and sealing machines that finally output the micro circuitry and other electronics.

"This was Monterroso's office. And through those doors," he pointed opposite, "is the research and manufacturing assembly area of the electronics."

JP and Savedra quickly went through the papers in his desk. There was very little; Monterroso had clearly been a tidy and organised individual.

"I'd like this boxed up please, and any of his private correspondence files in that cabinet," said Savedra, pointing to the single four-drawer cabinet. "The same for this other person, the woman."

"Very well," said Ramos. He was once again on the phone. Some staff appeared and the contents from both offices were quickly copied and boxed.

JP stared through the double glass doors.

"Can I go in?"

"Well, you can, but it's a sanitized area. That's why everyone is wearing the white coats and hats, and shoe covers. But we can get you prepared."

"No, that's ok," said JP. "What I would really like, is to have a look at one of your ADS-B systems that you send out for aircraft upgrade. Would that be possible?"

"Certainly," replied Ramos, "I'll have one brought out here immediately."

Another phone call, and five minutes later a technician appeared through the doors carrying a large aluminium box, with its lid resting loosely on the top. He placed it down on Monterroso's desk.

"Please, use the gloves, senhores," said the man, who handed over some nitrile examination gloves. JP put a pair on, as did Ramos.

"This is the ADS-B transponder box itself that sits in the cockpit," said Ramos, gently taking out a unit from its foam bedding. It had a front panel twenty centimetres wide by ten and was twenty-five deep. He carefully removed it from its plastic covering. The panel had a small display screen, numbers and various function keys. Ramos took out a plethora of cables and small electronic chips and boards. "These are the various sub-units and wiring that go with it." JP picked them up one by one. Finally Ramos took out a larger board. "… and this is the Primary Board that fits into the electronics control system and integrates everything into the aircraft's onboard computer." He handed it to JP, who carefully took it out of its wrapping. It was about twenty by twelve centimetres and maybe three centimetres thick at one end, from the centre of which the board and circuitry, no more than eight millimetres thick, protruded.

The Falcon had seen one before. Actually, he had seen two

before. One had been in Max Schroeder's safe. And the other had been in the Bicsa building in Panama City on Avenida Balboa across from Avenida Aquilino de la Guardia, in Jon Lano's office, in his safe.

Still looking at the various bits of wiring and other elements of the system, he said casually to Ramos, "How do you get these to your Rovalle HQ, Mr Ramos? I presume you fly them there?"

"Oh no," replied Ramos, "It's much cheaper for us to send various consignments to the States by ship. We always watch cost as much as we can. There's so much ethanol and sugarcane going that way anyway, and we're very close here to the commercial centres of São Paulo and the ports. So we put the crates on the tankers or cargo ships going that way anyway. Provided it's not an emergency of course. The system is well organised, with timings worked out to the day."

"Yes, I'm sure," said the Falcon. "So is that to Miami or New York?"

"No, it goes straight up to San Francisco, which is the single largest port of intake in the USA, especially for ethanol. From there, the consignments are put on an internal flight for the last hop to Portland."

"San Francisco? So that would mean routing through the Panama Canal then?"

Ramos looked a little surprised, and gave a slight shrug of his shoulders.

"Well of course, Mr Peregrine. Nobody goes round the Horn any more. The ships all pass through Panama. In fact the latest consignment should be docking in Panama tonight."

21
AFTER RAMOS

IT HAD BEEN a shame that the computers used by Jorge Monterroso and Denise Oliveira had been part of the main Brazilian Rovalle computer system. Otherwise Major Savedra could have asked to commandeer them. But, it was linked into the network and so impossible to separate out instantly; and Savedra couldn't get tough as he didn't have any kind of warrant or legal standing at that moment, although he didn't think he would need it with Edson Ramos, who had bent over backwards to help JP and him as much as possible. It had been left that Ramos would lock and freeze out of the system the computer access codes and files used by Monterroso and Oliveira, and the Major would arrange for some of his computer people from São Paulo to attend the offices of RPD Brazil tomorrow and, working with one or two of Rovalle's top IT staff, to go through the files and copy out what they would like to have. As far as things were at that moment, that was the best they could hope for.

Some Rovalle staff carried out the ten boxes or so of files to the police car. Major Savedra and JP thanked Ramos for his assistance, and they parted, Savedra and the Falcon keen to get back to the helicopter and Rio with the information they had gathered, and Ramos left with the unenviable job of gathering his staff and telling them of events connected with Monterroso.

The car set off smoothly, its boot laden with archive files packed away neatly in the storage boxes. They were quickly out of the Taubaté Science and Technology Centre onto the slip road, and then joined the SP-060 highway to route back to the Stumpf Airport. Traffic was light, the driver hugged the slow lane yet maintained a steady eighty kilometres per hour.

Savedra closed the partition from the driver.

"That's quite an impressive setup they have there," said Major Savedra. "What do you think? Did you get anything useful out of it?"

"It certainly is impressive; a very slick operation. Everything you'd expect Rovalle to be, actually. I thought Ramos was sincere, helpful and genuinely upset about the loss of his colleague. Mind you, I didn't get that he had the same feeling about the woman, Denise Oliveira, did you?"

"No. We need to find out about her. She lives in São Paulo - or used to, anyway. Ramos said he hadn't been able to get in touch with her since she walked out. I think we'll find that she's disappeared."

"I bet you're right, Major. I think she will have vanished. The question is, why."

"Yes." Savedra paused, thinking, then continued. "What about those components, why did you want to have a look at them? Did they mean anything to you?"

"Actually, they did. I've seen the Primary Board twice before, and both times in Panama, once in the office of Jon Lano that I mentioned to you when we first met, in the same safe that had Monterroso's name and details. A member of Panama's security forces and I broke in overnight and raided the safe. And, the second one was also in Panama; one of Lano's sidekicks had one, at another location. But I have no idea why. At least, they looked the same; of course I don't actually know for sure that they were the same."

"Well assuming they were the same," said the Major, "what could it…"

Just then a large Range Rover that had been matching the car for speed on the adjoining lane suddenly veered over and slammed violently into the Mercedes, pushing the car towards the edge of the road and then off it. The Range Rover had timed the move to perfection; a road sign spanning the three lanes of the highway from the central reservation to the side of the road was supported by heavy concrete pillars each side set deep in the ground, and at that particular point there were no edge barriers on the road - they had vanished as though the post had been designed for this purpose. The driver of the Mercedes had a fraction of a second to react and his foot was on the brake far too late. The men screamed for him to lookout, the car smashed into the concrete post hitting it squarely in front of the driver with such force that all airbags inflated. The car rotated round anticlockwise and its momentum carried it past the post and into the slight ditch beyond with enough leverage to flip the car upside down. It crashed back down onto its roof, scraped further forwards and finally came to a rest thirty yards distant. The vehicle was already on fire. All three men were unconscious. Then JP came to, blood dripping from a wound to his head. He pulled the handle to the door to unlock it, then tried to open it; it wouldn't move, the hinges were bent. He kicked it open, forcing it ajar, then looked over at Savedra. The man was in a bad shape, with glass cuts all over his face, but he was still breathing and beginning to open his eyes.

The Falcon grabbed Savedra's seat belt and pulled it out, pushing the airbags out of the way. His head was hurting badly, throbbing as though a train had run over it, but he knew he had to get out, and fast. The flames were already making the inside very hot. He yanked Savedra across his side and pulled him out after he crawled out himself, and kept going for a few feet. The flames were getting higher. He went round to the other side, trying to get the driver's door open. The man was seriously injured, with blood everywhere, some teeth hanging out and doubtless some broken bones, maybe internal bleeding. Then suddenly Savedra was there too, helping to yank on the door, and finally they got it open. The seat belt wouldn't undo. JP reached for his knife sheathed on the belt at the left side of his hip. He sliced once forcefully at the seat belt, splitting it easily. The man was free and they yanked him out and away.

The petrol tank exploded as they staggered off, destroying the vehicle and its contents and sending burning and twisted debris high into the air. Its shock wave hit Savedra and the Falcon hard in the back, flung them ten feet forwards and smashed them onto the ground. The driver rolled like a football that had been kicked. JP wasn't sure the man was still breathing.

There was a row of houses fifty feet away across a small slip road, and people were already coming out to see if they could help. Savedra and JP crawled over to the driver, put him on his back and loosened his collar and tie, what was left of them. Somebody must have called the emergency services; in a couple of minutes, or so it seemed anyway, some police were there and so were two ambulances. The fire engine appeared soon after, and what was left of the car was quickly foamed down.

Savedra sat on the ground, breathing hard, and looked over at JP, who had managed to find a small tree and was propped up against it. Savedra nodded his thanks. JP nodded back.

"Shit," he panted to Savedra, with a caustic smile. "This is getting bloody dangerous."

The ambulances got the three men on board and transported them to the Hospital Municipal Dr. José de Carvalho Florence, which as luck would have it was less than three miles away. They were seen at once in the emergency department. The doctors and nurses cleaned them up, stitched wounds, sent them for x-rays, Savedra had an MRI scan, but mercifully there were no broken bones or internal injuries. They were both going to ache considerably for a couple of weeks, but otherwise they were fine.

The driver had not been so lucky. He had a punctured lung,

some broken ribs, his right arm was broken above the elbow, his wrist smashed and his left shoulder dislocated. He was admitted to hospital and was going to be there a good few days. They were operating within forty-five minutes; it was close, but he was going to be ok.

Major Savedra was in control again quickly. Once the local police realised whom they had in their care they sharpened up considerably and listened intently to what Savedra had to say, ready to follow his instructions. The military police arrived and a two man guard was placed at the hospital for the driver; another four were provided for himself and the Falcon. More civil police were there quickly too, and enquiries put out and made about the vehicle that had deliberately rammed the Mercedes.

After their treatment, Savedra and JP were offered some coffee and sandwiches, which they both took with relish, although putting food and drink to their mouths was a painful movement. But the refreshments helped enormously. They sat quietly in a corner, with the four armed police officers sitting a few feet away.

"I think we've stirred up a real hornet's nest," said the Falcon.

"Yes. And I'm going to do all I can to get the bastards," said Savedra, who grimaced as he sat upright a little more, stretching his back.

The Falcon leant forwards, rested his elbows on his knees and put his head in his hands, staring for a while at the floor. He ran his hands through his hair, pushing it back, then stopped sharply as one of his fingers caught at some stitches. He grimaced and sat back up.

"Ernesto, I need to get back to Rio," said JP. "I think it's pretty obvious that there is some kind of link with Panama, there must be. I've been thinking - seeing as how those electronics go through Panama when they get shipped, maybe they are used as Decoys somehow, and that's what Tilsen meant when he wrote Decoy 17 before he died. And if the latest consignment gets to Panama tonight, I want to be there too and find out what I can. That's the next lead."

Savedra was nodding.

"How are you feeling?" asked JP, with a slight smile.

"Everything aches," said Savedra. "But we're in better shape than Henrique. They almost killed him. As it is the poor lad's going to be laid up for weeks."

"Does he have a family?"

"He got married last year, apparently. One child, a baby daughter. Four months old." He shook his head. "These are not nice people, JP."

"No. What I don't understand is who tipped off Malekka's cronies that we were at the Rovalle centre. Oh, and make no mistake, Ernesto, all of these people, the ones in Panama, the killers of Tilsen in London, Monterroso in Rio, and nearly of us here; they all are Malekka's people. He might be a long way away, physically, and in terms of links in the chain. But you can be certain that he's pulling the strings on all of this, and foots the bill for these scumbags."

"I think I will stay here, and go back to Rovalle tomorrow with a few more of my lads, and we'll case the joint properly. I'll see if I can track down how the news about us got out, and who arranged that little assassination attempt. Are you sure you want to go back tonight? It's just gone 7pm. Would you rather rest here? There are some nice hotels close by, and we would be secure? You could rest up a few hours till morning, and then go back up."

"It's a nice thought," said JP. "But there's no time to spare, I should get back and find out what I can. But do something for me tomorrow - that woman that was helping Monterroso..."

"Denise Oliveira."

"Yes. Ten to one she was the person who booked the ships

that carried the consignments. Find out if that's the case, and see if there's a link with the ships. I've a feeling they're all going to be from the same shipping line. And if so, see if you can trace the ownership."

"What are you looking for?"

"We know Malekka owns shipping lines. That's part of how he was able to get the weapon out of Russia[8]. If they're fiddling with the consignments, it would be much easier for them to do that if they were being loaded on board ships that Malekka owns."

"Ok I'll check it out. What do you think he's up to?"

"I don't know yet. But I'm beginning to get an idea of it. Supposing, when the deadline for NextGen arrives, all of a sudden the new electronics in the Rovalle fleet become faulty and don't work. As I understand it from Ramos, the entire fleet would be grounded. Ten thousand-plus aircraft around the world. Or what if the ADS-B transmission signal is interfered with somehow and gives false readings or becomes unreliable. That would cost Rovalle millions of dollars, maybe billions, in repair or replacement costs and lost seat revenues for months, it could rock the US Stock Market, damage the economy... International espionage or sabotage can be a very effective weapon."

"Yes I see what you mean. Ok, well I'll find out tomorrow morning when I go back. We'll check the remnants of the files that were in the car of course but I'm sure it's all destroyed. Very clever. It's a good job they were copies. But that wasn't the target, was it. We were. They were trying to kill us."

"Yes, Ernesto, I'm afraid so. We were the target, without doubt."

"Then we both have to be extremely careful from now on."

---

[8] *See Spider 2-3.*

JP nodded sombrely. His phone rang. With surprise on his face the Falcon reached into his inside left jacket pocket, and pulled it out.

"Wow, after that spill I didn't think this would still be working."

He looked at it thoughtfully. It was a call from the SIS in Panama, Colonel Alessandro, or at least so the Falcon assumed.

"Excuse me, Ernesto, I'd better take this," said JP and stood and walked away a few feet to talk on the scrambled line.

"Colonel? Is that you?"

"No, Mr Peregrine. It's Alberto - Alberto Mendes. I need to speak with you."

"Oh yes of course, Alberto, go ahead, is there something new?"

"Yes. I am sorry to have to tell you this, but the Colonel thought you should be informed at once."

"What is it?" asked JP, a heavy frown already lying across his forehead. "What's happened?"

"It's about Coco. She didn't report in yesterday, not at lunchtime nor at the six o'clock evening check-in. If she missed the first, which happened often because of the other people that were around her at work, she was required as standard procedure to check in at six in the evening. We didn't hear from her. So we had people go round to her apartment."

"Oh no…" JP let out the words quietly, as much to himself as to the voice on the other end of the phone. He was dreading where the story was heading.

"It had been ransacked… thoroughly and carefully," continued Alberto, his voice shaking slightly. "So we put out our normal urgency alerts and searches. There was nothing overnight nor through the day today. It was as though she had vanished into thin air..." Mendes paused for breath, or perhaps it was for the strength to carry on. "Until for about an hour ago, or an hour and a half. We had news of a naked female body found in the Bay by a local fisherman. And I regret to say…" Mendes stammered, "I very much regret to say, Mr Peregrine, that it was the body of Coco Chavarez. Our people took her in to the medical centre. She had been raped and sodomised and tortured quite brutally. She died at her own hands, though, somehow she got to the poison. It would appear she held out and took as much from her captors as she could, until she could take no more."

"Alberto, I'm so sorry," said the Falcon. He sat down on a chair against the wall, his head in one hand and the phone at his ear, and looked over at Savedra. The Major was staring at him, his mouth slightly ajar, gauging the severity of the call by the expression on JP's face. "She was a great operative," said JP. "And a lovely person too."

"Thank you, Mr Peregrine."

"JP, please, Alberto, for Heaven's sake."

"Yes, thank you, JP," Alberto said again. "The Colonel wanted you to know, of course, but also because it would seem highly likely that your entry into the ISTRAS Building was somehow discovered. We must assume that they know of your involvement. And, they may now be seeking to kill you. You must be careful, JP."

"They've just tried. A car ran us off the freeway into a concrete pillar."

"Oh my God!"

"Nearly killed us all. Me, the driver and Major Savedra, the Head guy here."

"Are you ok though?"

"Yes, just about. We're in a hospital getting checked out and treated. The worst of us is the driver. But anyway, Alberto, thank you. And far more importantly, please let Colonel Alessandro know how very sorry I am to hear about Coco. I will continue to do everything I can to bring these people down. Tell him that too, please."

"Yes, I will, of course. He wanted to call you himself but is not able to speak easily at this time."

"I understand."

"No, JP, I don't think you do. You see, Coco was Colonel Alessandro's daughter."

Ernesto Savedra was still looking over at the Falcon. He thought that the young man had seemed crushed a few moments ago, deflated, and then watched as the Falcon's face had momentarily shown a light flush of red. Not the red of embarrassment. The slight rouge mottling of the upper cheek. Anger. Fury. Danger.

The Falcon ended the phone call with Alberto Mendes, looked up at Savedra and moved back over to him, sitting again at the adjacent chair.

"It did not seem to be a good phone call, my friend," said Savedra.

"No," said JP. "It was from Panama. The operative I worked with there, who helped me break into Jon Lano's office at ISTRAS. She'd as good as saved my life a few hours before. She's dead. Tortured and dumped in the bay. But she revealed nothing; she took a pill to end it. Shellfish poison. I've no idea where they hide it - tooth, fingernail - but she got to it. She would have died in seconds, mercifully. Bloody bastards."

"I'm sorry, JP."

Jim Peregrine shook his head, looked up and pushed his shoulders back. He took a deep breath.

"Ernesto, we have to be careful. Your man here in the hospital, guard him well. And I think maybe we should take care of the Rovalle people too. Who knows what Malekka is going to try now, who's next on the list to be executed. I will be on it for sure. You too, probably."

Savedra nodded. "I'll pull in some more men, and you

must have two to accompany you back to Rio." He went to speak to one of the armed officers, who strolled aside into a corner and began to radio for more support.

Savedra walked back to JP.

"That's done," he said. "The time is going by; I think you should be on your way. The extra manpower will be here in another twenty minutes, and you should go then."

"Yes, I'll be ready. Do you have the…" The sound of his phone ringing again cut him off. He pulled it out once more, staring down at the name of the caller. He froze, a feeling of cold dread reappearing in his stomach.

It was Stephanie. But it wasn't supposed to be. They were not to talk directly, because of possible insecure lines phone to phone. So why was she calling him? He looked at the phone again, said to Savedra, "I think I should take this too."

The Falcon stood and took a few paces away once more, and tapped the answer button.

"Hello?"

JP listened silently. Then he slumped in a chair.

The call ended. JP folded the leather cover on his phone and slipped it into his pocket.

The Falcon looked straight ahead, bent down, put his head in his hands and stared at the floor. Major Savedra watched him shake his head slowly, and heard Jim Peregrine mutter one word.

"Christ," was all he said.

22
LEAVING BRAZIL

IT WAS A dejected JP who got into the back of the unmarked police limousine after he had shaken Major Savedra's hand in parting.

They sped along the road heading back to the airport, a police car in front and one behind, a small convoy, lights flashing. They were quickly at Stumpf Airport and through the security gates, arriving at the steps of the EC145 helicopter as the sun was beginning to get low in the sky. They were airborne in ten minutes, routing fast back to Rio's Galeão International.

The Falcon stared out of the window, but wasn't seeing the view. The phone call from Panama had been bad enough, to learn that such a fiery, talented operative as Coco Chavarez had been murdered by these monsters. She had been such a positive force; clever, professional, dedicated, and good company to boot. He thought of how she must have felt, being snatched, and then alone in a ghastly room somewhere, with a couple of men who were getting to work on her. He knew that she would have been brave, defiant; she would have tried a cover story, and then another, always hoping that there was a way out. He was distraught that he hadn't been able to help her, that he hadn't been there to rescue her. When she couldn't take any more, when she knew there was to be no rescue, she took the brave way out so as not to prejudice or compromise her colleagues, family, friends. She fought to the end.

JP let out a heavy sigh and slumped further into his seat. What a loss. How her father was feeling right now he could only imagine.

And there was the other phone call, coming a few minutes

on the heels of the first. He could still hear the distressed sounds of Stephanie's voice as she told him that Anna was dead, how she had pushed Stephanie out of the way of a bullet and saved her life but lost her own. At that moment he cursed Malekka again, cursed the madness of his evil, cursed the whole world for still being such a dangerous and primitive place. He had lost comrades before, usually in battle, but never a woman, and despite all of society's equality rules and modern new practices, whether imposed or voluntary, he couldn't get rid of that natural instinct inherent from the millennia of human existence, for a man to protect a woman - a feeling still shared by many men in the forces. Somehow he felt guilty and responsible that Anna and Coco were both now gone.

His mind wandered back in time about Anna, to when he had first met Dr Keppof's daughter over ten years before. Closer to fifteen, he thought. She had been young, pretty even then and very bright. She could already speak English beautifully. He thought of his time at Cambridge, when Dr Keppof had visited as a guest lecturer, of the fascination he and the other students had felt for their new professor as he kept his audience spellbound with his special talent for imparting knowledge. He thought of the laughs they had all had together off campus as they had gathered around Keppof while he held court. Somehow a special bond between Keppof and JP had developed, and they had remained friends after JP had graduated, through his time first in the army and then in the SAS.

And now Anna was dead. Like her father. Killed by Malekka and his henchmen.

Yet, how would he be feeling if the bullet that had taken Anna's life a few hours ago had found its way to its intended target and killed Stephanie? He closed his eyes and rubbed his forehead in contemplation of that chilling thought. He knew he had found someone special in Stephanie Raughton, and he knew that he couldn't bear to lose her. Yet they were both involved in a dangerous enterprise… although they had believed it was over. But they had been wrong. Now, once again, they were risking their lives. And for what? For their job; for Queen and Country? He laughed out loud to himself at that last one. It sounded such an odd, old-fashioned thing to say. For Queen and Country. But, the simple fact was, that was the reality.

Suddenly Jim Peregrine wasn't so sure he wanted to be in a game that in an instant could take the life of the girl he loved. Maybe something a little safer, that didn't involve guns or knives or bombs, something slightly more traditional for a man and a woman as they set out on the path to share their lives together, would be more appealing. But he smiled. No, that was not for Stephie, nor for him. They were what they were. Maybe it would change one day. But that wasn't going to happen any time soon.

Ninety minutes after departing Stumpf Airport the Eurocopter touched down at Galeão International. It taxied at two feet above the ground along to the location of the private jets, finally settling on the tarmac a few metres from the Gulfstream G650. The plane had been guarded throughout its wait at the airport and especially when Savedra had called through to the local military police. The pilots had remained close to the aircraft, one on board at all time, and had personally overseen the refuelling and restocking of supplies which had also been thoroughly checked.

The Falcon thanked the two pilots in the helicopter's cockpit and he and the armed officers that Major Savedra had sent along as added safety for JP disembarked. They walked briskly over to the waiting G650, JP shook hands with both of them in thanks and took the airstair two steps at a time. The captain was already powering up as he got to the top. He entered the cockpit and gave the destination to the pilots: New York JFK. The crew filed the flight plan as they taxied, and the Gulfstream was airborne in less than fifteen minutes.

JP stared sullenly out of the window again as the twinkling lights of Rio de Janeiro fell away beneath him and then disappeared under a thin layer of cumulous cloud. A few minutes later the plane reached its cruising altitude of forty-one thousand feet, where there would be little or no turbulence en route.

JP turned his mind to considering what had happened at the Rovalle centre and, more importantly, afterwards. He was convinced that Jorge Monterroso had stumbled across something inadvertently that was extremely problematic, perhaps catastrophic, and had paid for it with his life before he had been able to tell anyone what he had discovered. Then at around the same time his sidekick, the woman Denise Oliveira, the Deputy Director of Design and Research, suddenly leaves. As her body hasn't been found at the bottom of an apartment building or half eaten by sharks and deposited onto a beach at the Atlantic Ocean, JP felt it was safe to assume that she was the one who was active behind the scenes, and the plant within the company working for Malekka. Or one of them anyway. What she had been doing and organising had cleverly been going on for years, a long extended plan that Dave Tilsen had learned was called Stingray, and which was obviously shortly to come to fruition, perhaps any day now. And the link with Panama and the Canal suddenly was obvious too; whatever Malekka's people were doing they made sure all of the output - he assumed for this new air traffic control NextGen system, that is critical for aircraft navigation around the world and a legal requirement within the USA as of 1st January - had been passing through Panama, and presumably that's where Jon Lano came in. Somebody was doing something with the computer PCB boards. Switching them? Were they Decoys?

Is that the Decoy 17 that Tilsen wrote about with the last strength in his body as he lay dying on the floor of his apartment? Was it an enormous blackmail operation against Rovalle that was about to be perpetrated? No, it would be far worse than that. Sixteen Decoys had gone… and Decoy 17 was left. One chance left to save the world? Was that it? From what? A global biological gas attack? The murder of millions in the West?

Should they say something to Rovalle, he thought. He smiled ruefully and shrugged his shoulders. Say what, exactly? That he thinks somebody in Panama may have been fiddling with the new air traffic control system of the Rovalle Aircraft Corporation? Edson Ramos and the Rovalle bosses in Portland would laugh at him. And what action could they take? Have all their aircraft inspected, all ten thousand of them - and more - operated by umpteen airlines around the world? Ground them now? The thought was ludicrous. There was no proof, no evidence, nothing concrete and no real indication that anything was likely to happen to Rovalle now or in the coming weeks and months. And if any such rumour got out into the open and was seen to be taken seriously, the Rovalle stock would plummet. No. No rumours could be made, and no aircraft could be grounded. It would cost Rovalle an absolute fortune, and they could end up bankrupt, or ruined, or an international laughing stock.

He would have to unravel more of what was going on first; get some evidence, find some proof. The trouble was, he and MI6 were certain that there was a threat of some kind and it could go live at any moment... And they knew that time was running out.

The one-person cabin crew, an attractive girl of about twenty-six, seeing that her care had settled down after takeoff, left her seat farther back in the cabin, walked to JP and enquired if he would like to place an order for dinner. It took him a second or two to take in the girl's question, but he realised he was hungry and decided to eat.

As she wandered off with his food selection, he thought briefly how easy it would be to poison him, but he knew the food was safe, especially as the meals had been loaded at Panama and Colonel Alessandro had ensured that all edibles had been checked by his people.

The Falcon ate sombrely, deep in thought.

Another thing was troubling him. Someone had tried to kill him, or Major Ernesto Savedra, or both, as they were driving away from the Rovalle meeting back to Stumpf Airport. It had been cleverly executed, and had nearly succeeded. But, how on earth had the enemy learned they were in town and who they were? The flight to Rovalle and the Taubaté Science and Technology Centre had only been decided on earlier that same morning; so from the time of the departure from Rio in the helicopter to that of the attempted murder had been, maybe, four hours, five tops, thought JP. Could the advance warning information have come from Rio? If not, then it had come from someone at Rovalle, which meant that they had had even less time; perhaps two hours, to arrange their attempted assassination. Either way it was a short period of time to organise the hit. And, whether the instruction had come from Rio, or Rovalle at the Science and Technology Centre, it seemed clear that both locations were rife with Malekka's people.

There wasn't time to take things slowly. Something had to be done fast to flush people out, or at least to worry the other side, to try to slow them down.

When he had finished his meal and the tray had been cleared away, the Falcon put his head back and closed his eyes.

But Jim Peregrine wasn't sleeping. He wasn't even resting. His mind was flashing through a multitude of images and ideas, of possibilities, of actions to take and their results, of conceivable countermeasures and redress. He was the chess Grand Master again, but operating in the perilous world of terrorism, murder, subterfuge and violence in which the Falcon always seemed to excel, and which was the reason why he was the bearer of the Fifth Rubric. He was not part of the security forces of his country; he was more maverick than that. They needed him to be that way, to operate outside the law, yet be loyal to it. And the Falcon was never more dangerous than when the enemy had lashed out. Which they had done, to Coco Chavarez, to Anna Kepling, and to Stephanie Raughton. For that matter, to him too, and Ernesto Savedra.

Under an hour later, as the hands on Jim Peregrine's watch approached midnight and were about to herald in the start of a new day, his eyes opened. The period of self-reflection and detailed planning was over. It was time for action.

And the Falcon knew exactly what he was going to do.

PART FIVE

THE FIFTH DAY

23
RECOVERY

STEPHANIE RAUGHTON LOOKED up to the skies through her tears after Anna had exhaled for the last time.

There was no point in trying any CPR. There was already a massive amount of blood on Anna's clothing and the shot had clearly gone through an artery close to Anna's heart. Nevertheless, Stephanie pushed a hand hard against the neck to check for any signs of a pulse, and there was nothing - just soft flesh that would soon start to turn cold. She gently laid Anna's head onto the ground.

For the third time, Stephanie wiped away some tears. She looked across the road to the olive trees that had given the shooter cover. Her eyes had adjusted well to the moonlight and she stood, about to walk over to the dead man, but instead moved back into the derelict farmhouse, wiped her bloodied hands on her clothes, took out her phone and placed a call to Sir Donald Gaunchon. She knew she had woken him up but she didn't care. Neither did he. Gaunchon would be on his way in minutes. She decided to put a call through to JP. She knew she wasn't supposed to, but she would risk it. She suddenly wanted desperately to have contact with him, to hear his voice. She spent thirty seconds on the call; she felt a surge of strength and comfort when she heard him say "Hello" and as she shared the awful news with him she could hear him let out a heavy sigh and a moan. She said she was ok, help was on its way, and then she hung up.

She pulled her gun from its holster, ran out from the farmhouse to the car and opened the passenger door, switching off the internal lights that had automatically turned on. She rummaged in her shoulder bag and removed a small torch and some gloves. She ran to the man lying dead amongst the olive trees. She listened intently and looked around.

She turned on the torch using its green filter and looked at the man. She recognised him as one of those who had hit on Anna and her in the bar. He had actually been charming and quite attractive. Fucking pig, she called him to herself. She took out her phone and clicked a picture. She pulled on the nitrile gloves and rummaged through his pockets. Car keys and some money - notes folded in one pocket, change in another. A cell phone. Nothing else on him. No wallet; no ID. She put the phone and keys into her pocket.

Stephie moved slowly through the olive trees that lined the edge of the road, away from the farmhouse. It wasn't long before she found it. A hybrid car, that had approached using its electrical setting so that there was little sound. Even so, she was surprised that they hadn't been able to hear the car at all; the evening air had been quiet and the conversation with Stylianos at a low level, almost whispered, and the road was rural - almost a dirt track, not tarmacked. But, the distance must have been sufficient. She searched inside the car thoroughly and could find nothing. She used the keys to open the boot. She saw the drone and stared at it coldly. Now she understood how they had been traced; the drone had been high in the sky tracking them automatically, sending their location and images to the man's cell phone. He had stayed well back as he drove following so that there was little sound to reach them, nor could the car's lights be seen. Once their motion had stopped, the man had recovered the drone, driven farther along and walked the rest of the way. He waited amongst the olive trees and took his shot as they exited the farmhouse.

Stephanie made her way back to the farmhouse, still walking amongst the cover offered by the olive trees.

As she arrived, she heard the whirring blades of helicopters that quickly became louder, until she could see the three Bell 412 aircraft, from 84 Squadron based at Akrotiri, hovering above the farmhouse. Suddenly their three strong searchlights flicked on and the area was instantly as bright as day. The aircraft landed in a clearing to the east, and then the place was swarming with around twenty burly men armed to the teeth who secured the area. Gaunchon appeared, in dark battle fatigues, a bullet proof vest and a baseball cap, and with two soldiers standing either side of him.

He held out a rock-hardened hand and Stephie shook it, and then he put both arms around her and embraced.

"Christ, Stephanie, are you ok?" he asked, keeping his arm round her as they walked from the landing zone over to the farmhouse.

"Yes, Sir Donald, I'm ok now, thank you for coming so quickly."

They reached Anna's body.

"Oh, dear," said Gaunchon, getting down on to one knee, looking at the lifeless corpse. "Oh dear, oh dear," he said again. He picked up one of the girl's hands and held it in both of his, squeezing gently, shaking his head. "Bloody buggers," he muttered. He stood.

"Stephanie, this is Major Harding, Captain Nielsen," he said of the two men, adding "Stephanie Raughton, MI6." They nodded in greeting to each other. "So, continued Gaunchon to Stephanie, "fill me in?"

"We were talking in the farmhouse with the man, our contact. We'd just finished, we came out and Anna saw the gun that was being levelled at me. She pushed me out of the way, the bullet hit her. I shot back. He's over there."

She walked them across the road to the dead man.

"Do you know who he is?" asked Gaunchon.

"No. Only that he tried to chat us up in the last bar we visited, where we met the man we arranged to see here. We left the bar about half an hour afterwards and drove to this farmhouse. He has a car farther down the road, I found a drone in it. That's what relayed the location so he was able to find us. The car's a hybrid, so virtually silent, but he parked far enough away and covered the rest on foot. And waited, until we came out. I don't know how much he heard, if any; I don't know if he relayed any of that to anyone."

"Did you search him?"

"Yes," replied Stephanie. She pulled out the cell phone. "There was this, which doubtless received the drone signals tracking us, and the car keys," she said, handing them over.

Gaunchon pocketed the phone.

"What happened to the man you were talking with?"

"I've no idea. He wasn't there after the shooting started, I haven't seen him since. He must have bolted. He was pretty wary about talking to us, so it's not surprising he vanished."

A third man approached them and saluted.

"Sir, we've picked up two blips, helicopters for sure, they'll be here in seven minutes."

"Right, thank you." He turned to one of his two companions. "Captain, get the dead girl's body bagged and onto the aircraft. And Ms Raughton's car driven over to the aircraft. Get it chained and ready to go." Stephie handed over the keys.

"Yes, sir." The Captain saluted and walked off smartly. Gaunchon turned to the other man.

"Major, lock this place down tight, impound the man's car. Our Turkish friends can take it when you've finished with it. And him too," he added, looking at the dead body on the ground with disgust. "Let them see if they know who he is, or can find out. Take some pictures first, fingerprints, some hair for DNA. You know. Ms Raughton will come back with me now."

"Yes, sir." The Major headed off, calling to a couple of

other men.

"We must get you away from here, right away. We let our Turkish colleagues know of this event just before we crossed into the Demilitarised Zone. Those are their helicopters on the way."

Stephie nodded. They walked quickly over to the car that Gaunchon had provided them with less than forty-eight hours ago and that was now adjacent to one of the helicopters. Three soldiers were busy around it, throwing lift chains over and under. Stephanie said, "Excuse me, boys," and she opened a door to remove her bags and Anna's. Captain Nielsen was back accompanied by another man, saw the three cases, pointed and said, "Corporal." The soldier grabbed the luggage. They walked over to one of the other aircraft and the luggage was loaded.

Thirty seconds later the lift helicopter took off with the Daihatsu Charade dangling beneath.

"There's no need to give our Turkish friends your details left in the car, fingerprints and so on," said Gaunchon as Stephanie and he climbed aboard their transport. She nodded her agreement.

They were airborne in another thirty seconds, a full four minutes clear of the arriving helicopters. As the pilot sped them at tree-top height south across the Demilitarised Zone and into the Republic of Cyprus, Stephanie stared at the black bag on the floor of the aircraft containing the dead body of her friend.

They landed at RAF Akrotiri in under half an hour and were met by several of Gaunchon's men. Stephanie was escorted by Sir Donald and two others to the domestic quarters of the base, where she was shown to her room for the night, which was comfortable if not very large, but which came with a welcome soft double bed. A female RAF officer was standing by to assist.

"You'll be safe here," said Gaunchon, "You've had a hell of a night, and it's almost 4am. You must be exhausted."

Stephanie gave a wry smile. "Thank you."

"Corporal Jennings - Michelle, is that right?" he asked of the young woman.

"Yes, sir," replied the girl.

"Corporal Jennings is here to assist you in any way, Stephanie; eat, drink, whatever you need. And there's a shower or bath in there, or go straight to bed. Relax, as best you can."

"Thank you, Donald, for everything once again," said Stephanie, sitting down on the edge of the bed. "I should call London first, to update Charlie Melton. Then I think I'll just turn in. And, probably aim to return home sometime tomorrow; or, rather, later today."

"Whatever you want. There'll be two men outside this door, through the night. Michelle will be through there," he pointed to another door, "in the adjoining suite."

Gaunchon left. Stephanie didn't want any food and there was bottled water on the coffee table, so she let Corporal Jennings go too. She pulled out her cell phone, put a call through to London and spoke at some length to Charles Melton on the scrambled line. Then she locked both doors, pulled the curtains across the window that overlooked the internal forecourt of the domestic quarters of the base and took a long drink of water. She used the bathroom, took off her top layer of clothes, placed her gun under her pillow and climbed into bed. She leant across to switch off the side light, but stopped herself.

She slid out from under the covers and knelt down at the side of the bed. She made the sign of the cross, closed her eyes and said a few prayers for Anna Kepling. Minutes later she was back in bed.

She would grab a few hours' sleep, she thought. Then she

would leave for London, meet with Charlie Melton; and JP would be back soon too, maybe…

Despite the events that had happened in the last few hours, exhaustion took over. She laid her head on the pillow and pulled the duvet over her shoulders.

She was soundly asleep within five minutes. She hadn't switched out the light after all.

≈

In London, Charlie Melton slumped back in the chair at his desk and stared at the phone he had replaced onto its base following the conversation with Stephanie. He drew in a deep breath, and shook his head as he exhaled. He hadn't been home yet and probably wouldn't that night.

He picked up the phone again and tapped some numbers to get through to Jim Peregrine. The Falcon answered in the G650, about five hundred kilometres southwest of the mouth of the Amazon River, forty thousand feet above the State of Pará, northern Brazil.

24
SENDING A MESSAGE

JIM PEREGRINE LEFT his seat, went to the cockpit and gave the new destination to the pilots. He put a scrambled call through to Panama to Colonel Alessandro, taken instead as he expected by Alberto, who was surprised to hear JP's query.

"Do you have some?"

"Yes, Mr Peregrine, I mean JP, we have it somewhere, well, I can get it, but I'm not sure what you want it for. I think I should check with the Colonel, but he is not available, the family are in deep shock."

"There's no need to check with him," said JP. "This is on my responsibility. I'll fill you in when I'm there. Can you meet me when I land?"

He spoke to Alberto for another minute, then hung up.

JP thought it was time to call Charlie Melton in London. As he stared at the screen it lit up and began to ring. It was the call from Melton.

"Hello, Charlie," said JP, the concerned tone clear in his speech. "I had my phone in my hand about to call you."

"Hi, JP. Great minds, eh?" said Melton with no humour. It was good to hear his voice, thought JP. At least it brought some cheer.

"I've just spoken to Stephanie at length. Jimmy, I was so sorry to hear about Anna, and I wanted to tell you personally. I didn't know her well, but what was obvious was that she was a brave and fine young woman."

"Thank you," said JP back. "She was all of that. And Keppof was so proud of her."

"I'm sure he was, and rightly so."

JP took a deep breath and made a conscious effort to move on.

"Did you get all the details of what happened?"

"I did. I gather that, if it hadn't been for Anna, we'd now be talking about a dead Stephie instead."

"Yes. I haven't spoken to her again yet, I haven't been able to, how is she?"

"She's ok, as much as she can be. Gaunchon got his people over there fast and helicoptered her out back to Akrotiri. She'll be leaving for London later today. But they had discovered something, did you hear it yet?"

"No, nothing, Stephie called to tell me about Anna. It had just happened and obviously she was distraught. She said she'd got the bastard, was isolated and waiting for Gaunchon, she said she was ok and not to worry. Then she hung up as the line wasn't secure. Thirty seconds; I didn't have a chance to say or ask anything."

"You'll get to hear all of the details later, but there's one important thing she found out - it's an address. It's in the Netherlands and it's definitely linked to Stingray. I'm sending it to you securely now."

"Well, that is some much-needed good news," said JP. "Well done them, at least they had that success." He paused, "Did you hear about what's happened in Panama?"

"No?" said Melton.

JP's phone let out a ping, indicating the incoming message, as he began to fill his friend in about Coco Chavarez.

"Oh my God," said Charlie Melton after hearing the story. "These people are devils."

"Yes. I got the phone call from Panama first. Then the one from Stephie came in a few minutes later. And at the time I was sitting in a hospital…" and he continued to give his report of what had happened to him and Ernesto Savedra after leaving Rovalle.

"That all ties in with the other reason why I was calling, JP," said Melton grimly. "You remember those pictures I sent, taken by those two private investigators outside Dave Tilsen's flat?"

"Yes?"

"One was of a man we now believe to be Tilsen's assassin. And one was of you, as you were leaving the flat?"

"Yes."

"Get this - that same picture of you was on Jon Lano's computer."

"Well, well," said JP, with some irony in his voice. "Now why doesn't that surprise me?"

"Quite. We'd been able to make a bit of progress getting into the data you had copied from his computer in Panama and that Coco and her people sent over to us the same evening. Looking at the received date of the JPG file, it would seem that Jon Lano had your picture on his PC as you were landing in Panama. He knew you weren't Dave Tilsen even before you walked into his office."

"So no wonder they tried to get to me."

"No wonder."

"That confirms it then, doesn't it. Jon Lano is definitely Malekka's crony."

"Without doubt. And given that they tried to silence you in Brazil, I would say that your picture has also made its way down there too." He paused for a moment, and added, "You know what else it means."

"Yes. It means we're definitely on the right track."

JP and Charlie Melton spoke for a few more minutes. The PCB boards had arrived in London and the lab was getting to work dissecting them. JP told Melton about his plan. Then the call ended.

It was a little before 2am local time that the Falcon landed once more in Panama City. Alberto Mendes was waiting in the executive forecourt and drove the car close to the Gulfstream as its brakes went on and the ground crew pushed the chocks under the wheels. The door opened, the airstair descended and JP was running down the steps before they were firmly settled on the ground. He was dressed entirely in black, with a thin jacket that concealed the gun in his shoulder holster, and was quickly at the car's passenger side.

"Hi, Alberto, ok let's go."

"Where?" he asked, as he put the car into drive and sped towards the airport exit.

"To Jon Lano's International Shipping Transport Services building close to the Canal."

"What are we going to do there?"

"We're not going to do anything. I am."

"I think I'd better come with you, whatever it is I want to help."

"Nope. This meeting is unofficial for you, you aren't here. You just drive. I don't want you involved."

"I think I'm already involved."

JP smiled in the darkness, and gave a quick glance over at the driver, who added, "What are you going to do?"

"I'm going to send Lano a message, and Malekka. And I'm going to strike one back for Coco."

It was Alberto's turn to glance at JP.

"Whatever it is you're going to do, I'm with you."

"As well as for another friend of mine," continued JP, and told Alberto what had happened to Anna.

"I'm sorry, JP," said Alberto, "this is not good. So how are we striking back?"

"Like I said, we're not. I am. Do you have it?"

"I have it. But it's my unofficial present, given as I'm not officially here. So I'm in too." The Falcon let out a short laugh and smiled.

They continued in silence for a while. Alberto steered the

car swiftly amongst the occasional night traffic, turning into the Puente de las Americas and picking up more speed. JP had another question to ask.

"Alberto, what's happened to the ISTRAS block at the Business Park, since Schroeder tried to kill me there and I had my little encounter with his two cronies?"

"The police went in straight away, I think they were there by the time you came in to see us for the first time at the Teatro. The two men that you laid out were arrested and have been charged with attempted murder. Schroeder was killed in self-defence of course, there will be no trouble over him. The two men will stand trial, be convicted on the evidence of Coco's report and your own statement, and go to prison for a long time."

"Good. And the building?"

"After two days it was vacated by police and handed back to ISTRAS for its continuing business. We have brought nothing yet against the company itself, you understand. All this will change soon though, because of everything that's happened and the new information we have. But for now, they have said that Schroeder was acting on his own and they deny any association."

"That's what I thought. So, it's business as usual again there."

"I don't know about as usual, because they know that they are being watched, but we think they believe they cannot be touched."

Alberto turned the car into the Boulevard Panamá Pacífico.

"But they stop at around 11pm. It should be deserted."

"Who's running the Canal office now for them?"

"I don't know." Alberto shrugged his shoulders. "Oh, but I can tell you, Jon Lano has disappeared."

"What do you mean," asked a surprised JP.

"What I say. He's gone. Vanished. He left on a business

trip overseas. His private jet departed for Toronto, but the plane didn't arrive. Wherever he's gone, it's not Canada. But we'll find out where it routed to."

The Falcon smiled to himself that Lano had used the same trick he himself had done and switched destinations in mid-flight. He couldn't worry about Lano now. He'll have to deal with him later.

Alberto turned the car into the industrial estate. The large steel buildings glinted eerily in the soft light thrown by a waxing gibbous moon that peered out from behind a layer of thin low cloud. The street lighting had been switched off for the night, and save for the car's headlights the roads were all but in darkness.

"Park up a couple of blocks before the ISTRAS offices and let me have a look."

Alberto did as he was asked, and switched the engine and lights off. JP had pulled some binoculars from his rucksack and was already surveilling the building.

"I thought it was supposed to be empty," said JP in a low voice.

"At this time, it is," whispered Alberto.

"There's a dim light on at the ground floor, no actually it's a light coming from a basement window, above the lawn on the right."

He handed the binoculars to Alberto. While his companion looked, JP reached to the back seat of the car and emptied the contents of a small carry case into his own rucksack. Alberto handed the glasses back.

"Perhaps it's been left on by mistake."

"Maybe. Maybe not."

"Ok, so what are you going to do?"

"First, I'm going to go and see what's going on." JP took his Sauer from his shoulder holster, pulled the slide to put a round into the chamber and pushed the weapon firmly back into the holster. The gun already had its silencer attached. He thought for a moment. "Alberto, I wasn't going to involve you but as you're in anyway… Look, it may be that there are some people down there and if so I have no way of knowing how many. Do you have a gun?"

"Yes," and Alberto pulled out a Beretta from the pocket of his jacket.

"Ok, good. Now listen. We go in quietly, and let me lead. If we find anyone, I'll do the talking. If I have to fire, I will do so alone and you do nothing, unless it's absolutely necessary or unless I tell you. Don't be shocked at anything I do or say."

Alberto smiled. "Ok, Falcon. I'm ready, let's go." JP was impressed with the young man. His business was electronics and not field work; but he was here, ready to help. JP knew it was for Coco. For a split second the thought flashed across his mind that Alberto and Coco had been much closer than he had realised.

The two men slipped silently out of the car and pushed the doors closed with the minimum of sound. In darkness except for the moonlight they crossed the street and ran against the shadows of other buildings, past the couple of blocks and up to the ISTRAS entrance. They made their way round the side of the building to the low basement window from which glowed a dim light, but the window was heavily curtained and nothing could be seen of the other side, nor were there any sounds to be heard. They moved quickly back to the front of the building.

JP pushed against the heavy entrance door. Although the *Please Enter* sign was still on display, there was to be no easy access this time. He pulled out a small flat leather wallet from a jacket pocket and selected two of the lock-picking tools. He jiggled them in the cylinder lock and a few seconds later felt the barrel turn and the door move inwards. The dead bolt hadn't been turned, that's made it easier, he thought. He returned the kit to his pocket and pulled out his gun as he stepped silently into the large hallway beyond. Alberto followed and closed the door behind him without a sound. JP had half expected to have tripped some kind of alarm system and was ready to respond, but nothing seemed to have been set off.

The door to Schroeder's office on the other side of the hallway was wide open, but there were no lights on and it appeared empty. A few feet to the left was another door which was bordered by light stabbing through between its edges and the frame. They crossed the hall and as they got closer could see that the door was slightly ajar. JP crouched, put his face close to the opening and listened. He heard the sounds of banging followed by scraping as though something was being dragged or pushed along the floor or a table.

Then a man said, "Ok, let's do the next one."

The Falcon pushed open the door slightly and peered inside. Wide steps with a simple handrail on one side led down against the wall to a tiled floor that had a large table in the centre. A long work surface bordered the wall opposite. The table had six low wooden crates on it and a couple of backpacks, and two heavy boxes with their tops open sat on the work surface behind. Two men were rummaging around the contents of one of the crates on the table. The older one was about forty, dark-haired, heavy-set with a bit of a paunch and dressed in jeans and a T-shirt. The other was mid-thirties and thinner; his open-necked shirt was hanging out over dark trousers and he was wearing spectacles. A notepad rested on the centre table in front of him. Together they lifted a silver-coloured box out of the crate. A cold shiver went down JP's spine as he recognised the Rovalle *FAB* logo on the front. They began to open it up.

The younger man took out an electronic board from the box, turned it over and read out, "Six two nine eight three dash eighty-two." His companion went to one of the boxes on the worktable behind them, leafed through a number of items and pulled out what appeared also to be an electronic motherboard. He read back, "Six two nine eight three dash eighty-two, got it." He held it out and the two men exchanged items. The replacement was put into the aluminium box, the cover went on and the box was put back into the crate. The original board joined the second box on the worktable.

The Falcon had heard enough. He stood, pushed open the door and began to walk slowly down the stairs, at the same time saying pleasantly, "Good evening, gentlemen." The two shocked men looked up, staring first at JP and then at the gun that was being levelled at them, silencer attached. With surprising speed the older man veered to his right grabbing a gun from the nearer backpack but before he even had a chance to bring the weapon round to aim, the Falcon had fired. The bullet hit the man in the centre of his forehead an inch above his eye line. His upper torso was bent backwards violently and he dropped to the floor dead. The younger man raised his hands quickly above his head stretching them high and stepping away, a look of terror on his face, almost screaming, "Don't shoot, don't shoot!"

"I won't shoot, unless you give me reason to," said JP, who had reached the floor at the bottom of the stairs. "Those reasons would include any quick movement from you, and any failure to answer my questions immediately." The Falcon was now four feet from him, the gun pointing at the man's heart. "Do I make myself clear?" he suddenly snarled.

The man nodded, "Yes, yes," and added again, "please don't shoot."

Alberto had joined JP now and was staring at the dead man on the floor. He hadn't quite expected such a fast turn of events. But then he thought about Coco again and what JP had said to him in the car. He clenched his jaw and any remorse or shock vanished. JP spoke quietly to the man.

"I want you to tell me exactly - and I mean *exactly* - what you are doing here, with these boxes. If I like your answer, you will not die tonight. If I don't, the next bullet will enter your heart and you can join your friend on the floor."

The man spoke quickly, his voice shaking. The Falcon listened grimly, asking a question every now and then. In ten minutes he had it all. He understood.

"I want you to give me the last board you put in that case. And the one you removed from it." The man obliged. JP checked the serial numbers; they were a match. He took out his combat knife from its sheath on his belt, and marked the original with a scratch on its edge. He turned to Alberto.

"Do you have any handcuffs on you?"

"Yes."

"Ok, put them on this guy. And truss him up like a chicken using some of that." He nodded towards some strong nylon cord that he had spotted in the corner at the end of the worktable. "Join his feet but leave him able to walk." JP kept his gun pointed at the man - whose name they discovered was Paulo Rodrigues - while Alberto did as he had been instructed and restrained their prisoner, who offered no resistance; his hands were cuffed behind him and his ankles joined by half a metre of the tough nylon cord, making anything but short paces impossible. JP cut off a further length, made a noose at one end and slipped it round Rodrigues' neck, then pulled him to the floor. He tied the other end to one of the legs of the work surface, which was bolted to the floor.

"Right, that will do for now," said JP.

"What's next?"

"Go and get the car, and bring it to the front. This guy says there's no-one else around but be careful just the same."

Alberto disappeared. He walked swiftly to the car, started it up and repositioned it at the front of the building. He was quickly back inside.

The Falcon and Alberto carried out the six crates from the centre table and the other two boxes that contained the replacement and some original boards, stacking them into the boot of the car and onto the back seat. They returned again to the basement of the building. The removals had taken less than a quarter of an hour.

JP took off the end of the tether around the man's neck from the leg of the work surface and handed the cord to Alberto.

"Put him in the back seat of the car. I'll join you in five minutes. If he gives you any trouble, put a bullet in his head."

Alberto nodded and grabbed the man by his hair, pushing him to the steps.

Once Alberto had left the basement JP took off his backpack and removed its contents, placing the six items onto the table. He carefully wrapped the two electronic PCBs he'd selected in some protective packaging from one of the crates. He placed them into an empty smaller box lying on the work surface and packed the box into his backpack.

The Falcon set the timers of the six charges for four minutes, left one in the basement, moved upstairs to the ground floor and placed one at the extremities of the building, going into three or four other rooms to do so. He left the last one in the hall.

He closed the front door behind him, walked quickly to the car and joined Alberto in the front.

"Done?" asked his companion.

"Done," replied the Falcon. "Let's go."

They had turned onto the Puente de las Americas when the C4 went off. The ISTRAS building ignited in a ball of flame that in less than a second reached a hundred feet above the top floor, and kept rising. The quantity of explosive had been carefully selected and skilfully positioned. The sound of the explosion shattered the windows in a few buildings close by but most of its force was contained and directed to act on the structure of the building itself. The foundations fractured, the walls dropped and collapsed inwards and in under twelve seconds what was left of the roof settled on top, reducing Jon Lano's entire Canal operation to a spectacular orange and crimson beacon in the night sky, fuelled by a fiercely-burning pile of rubble less than thirty feet high.

25
MALEKKA

AT THE SAME time that the Panama Canal operation of his company was being blown to pieces by the Falcon some eight thousand miles to the southwest, although he didn't yet know it, Sheikh Barakah Malekka bin Kabiri bin Ali Saleh Al Falahi, or more simply known as Mr Barakah Malekka, was finishing a light lunch in his Palace close to Tehran. He had been listening to the lengthy update given him by his two chief aids and bodyguards, Latif Yameen and Esam Duha.

He had viewed the picture of JP as he left Tilsen's flat soon after its upload. He knew he had seen the man somewhere before. It had taken him a little time but it had come to him. He was Stella's boyfriend, who had inadvertently - or so Malekka had thought - played a part in Spider 2-3.

However, it was becoming clearer that this person was hardly just 'a boyfriend'. What was he doing outside Tilsen's flat? What connection could this man possibly have had with Tilsen? What was he doing in Panama in Lano's office? And then in Brazil?

The answer was simple. The man must have been a covert operative, a plant, right from the start. This was a shocking realisation to Malekka. And, did it mean that somehow Stella had been used unwittingly by him, or even involved directly? Surely not…

He had no idea how this infiltration could have occurred. He had gone over everything in his mind repeatedly during the last four days, and was doing so with Yameen and Duha once more now, and he could not see how he had been tricked. He was convinced his side had been watertight.

However, he had been wrong. Now he had evidence that the failure of Spider 2-3 lay at the hands of this man, this so-called boyfriend, who wasn't just a boyfriend at all. Therefore Malekka had already instigated a major investigation into the man. His various UK resident operatives, which included Tilsen's assassin Riad Al Solh, as well as those in the USA, which numbered many more, were under instructions to find out about this person, his name, where he lived, his background, training, work…

The operatives knew about the earlier media story, that an Englishman had been involved in the destruction of Malekka's previous effort at his base at Cuttle Cove, and that although the man's name and true identity were not known, he had a nickname which had leaked out: *The Falcon*. That was a good start for their enquiries. This person must be part of the British or American intelligence communities, and, as he was supposed to be English, it must be MI6.

Malekka was convinced he was the person in the picture seen exiting Tilsen's flat that he had recognised as the boyfriend. He must be this Falcon person. And, along with the instructions Malekka had issued, came another. Kill him.

It had been a shame that Jon Lano's first efforts in Panama to do just that had failed. It was also frustrating that the female presumed to be a Panama security forces agent, Coco Chavarez, had revealed nothing about him under torture before she died, not even his real name. Malekka's forces in Brazil had made a good effort to kill him, but the Falcon had survived that attempt too.

Malekka was also informed by the two men sitting with him that there had been two female so-called journalists sniffing around in Northern Cyprus asking a lot of questions about him, and that one of his people had been killed after killing one of those women. He didn't understand if there was any significance to that. But one less nosey journalist, if they had actually been journalists, or one less opposing agent, could only be a good thing for him.

In Rio, that nuisance of a man Jorge Monterroso had been silenced. Malekka didn't know how he had found out about Stingray, especially when it had been going on under Monterroso's nose for several years successfully without any interruption; but the right action had been taken. His operative Denise Oliveira had been extracted from Rovalle after her last service - arranging for Monterroso's demise. The work in Brazil and at Panama was virtually complete anyway, so there was no harm done; everything was almost ready for the instigation of Stingray.

Except, he did not have the micro SD card. That, and the initiators it contained, had been lost. He had issued instructions for the codes to be recovered and reconstructed as soon as possible. That work was under way.

However there was one bit of information that had not been reported to Malekka or anyone else, nor was it likely to be. Jon Lano, not wishing to lose face with his employer, had not passed on to Malekka that this Falcon person had infiltrated his offices and removed two electronic circuit boards from his safe and Schroeder's, and that these were therefore now in the Falcon's possession - *as was the entire copied contents of his computer*. The boards, Lano reasoned, wouldn't matter as they were genuine Rovalle boards and although they linked him to Rovalle they could reveal little; while he shouldn't have had them in his safe, in a few days none of it would matter anyway. As for the computer, much of the contents were heavily encrypted and it would take time for the enemy to interpret it. Assuming the Falcon was foreign intelligence, Lano had no intention of telling Malekka that the security forces of probably several countries now had copies of the information contained on his computer which they might be able to decipher. And he certainly wasn't going to admit that the picture of the Falcon outside Tilsen's flat had not been stored in the heavily encrypted part of his computer; and that it would thus be among the first items to be revealed. Anyone in possession of that picture would be considered by the enemy to be linked to Tilsen's murder and to Malekka himself. The discovery of the picture on his computer would therefore firmly incriminate Lano. However, Lano reasoned, there was ample time for Stingray to be actioned and for him to receive the balance of his enormous fee from Malekka. This was Jon Lano's sole concern. He preferred to be paid by a grateful employer for a job well done rather than executed for botched security.

Understandably, Lano decided to stay quiet.

However, today, Malekka was delighted with the report and updated intel information.

"Thank you, Latif, Esam; all this is good work," said Malekka, dabbing his lips with the silk napkin as he finished his dessert. Coupe Denmark - vanilla ice cream served with hot chocolate sauce, a creation that had originated from the Copenhagen Tivoli. The West has some strange yet wonderful inventions, Malekka often said, and this is one he loved. "However, you are saying to me that this Falcon person is still very much alive and interfering in our work. So where are we on finding out who he is and where he is?"

"Frankly, sir, we haven't got very far," said Yameen. "The efforts in Washington have produced nothing. Our person at the CIA does not have high security clearance, as you know, and has discovered nothing. In London, although we don't have anyone in MI6 our loose discussions socially with several contacts who do work there have produced nothing. We have made enquiries through our agents to the British army, navy and the RAF and similarly have no information."

"Sir… Latif…," ventured the more junior Esam Duha, "I have an idea, if I may?" he suggested nervously. He was delighted to have been selected for his new role and was keen to impress his Master.

"Yes, Esam, what is it?" said Malekka.

"Well, sir," began Esam, "the Western media knows there was a man involved at Cuttle Cove who has the nickname of the Falcon."

"Yes?"

"But, they don't have a picture of him. Nothing has been released to the media, they don't know who he is either, nor what he looks like."

"No, unfortunately that's true," said Latif. "So what are you suggesting?"

"We have a picture of someone we believe is this Falcon person. So… why don't we give the picture to the media? That will ignite the story again. The media of the West will go crazy about it, if we release it cleverly to the right people, and they will want to know who he is. Give them the picture, and they will do our work for us and find out. Once they know, we'll know."

Malekka and Yameen looked at each other. They nodded, and smiled.

"That's wonderful!" said Malekka. "Very good, Esam."

"Yes, that's an excellent idea," said Latif. "Very clever."

"I like it," said Malekka, exuding more enthusiasm. "Then there will be hundreds of people in London, the UK, Europe, the United States, who will be trying to find out who the Falcon is. And once we have a name…"

"Yes, once we have a name," Latif Yameen took over, "we will find out about this person, where he is."

Malekka was delighted. He smiled at Esam.

"Well done, Esam."

"Thank you, sir. I hope the idea will work."

"Very well," said Malekka. "Do it immediately, choose our best media contacts in London and get the picture and the story out. We will soon have a name, and you can track him down." Malekka dabbed his lips again, and replaced his napkin onto the table. "And then, we will kill him."

Malekka smiled at the pleasure, and pondered for a few seconds. "You know, I think I'm going to have some more of that," he said looking at his finished dessert plate. "Gentlemen, would you care to have some dessert with me?"

The two men beamed at such a rare invitation.

Forty-five minutes later, the three men stood after coffee. A delighted Yameen and Duha, who had much enjoyed their special moments with their Master, were about the leave when there was a knock at the door.

"Come," said Malekka.

A man approached with an envelope on a silver tray.

Malekka opened it. His eyes widened as he read the note and looked at the pictures on the second page, which showed the burning pile of rubble resting where his building in Panama used to be. His cheeks reddened in fury and he scrunched the papers in his hand.

"It seems, gentlemen," said Malekka, shaking with anger, "that our building… at the Panama Canal… has been demolished. Destroyed. Blown up."

Latif and Esam looked at each other, their mouths ajar. Malekka was strolling back and forth, waving the papers in the air.

"It's this man, I know it," said Malekka. "This Falcon. I know it."

"But they would never be allowed to do that," said Yameen, "They have their laws, they can't do that."

"Well they have," spurted Malekka. "*He* has. Here," and he thrust the papers over. Yameen and Duha stared at them.

"We have two days to go to Stingray. Two days. I want you to find this man," said Malekka, almost screaming the words.

"I want you to find this man. And I want you to kill him."

26

ALBERTO TAKE CARE

AFTER THE DESTRUCTION of Malekka's building, Alberto had driven the car to the headquarters of SENAN or Servicio Nacional Aeronaval, the senior organisation of the Panamanian security forces, where he entrusted the shaken and terrified Paulo Rodrigues to colleagues with instructions that he be placed in one of the secure lockup cells in the basement. The lower floor of the premises had seen much unpleasant activity during Panama's last military dictatorship of Manuel Antonio Noriega, and was still held in dread by the people of Panama.

"We'll let him stew for a while and see what else he might tell us," said Alberto.

"How long can you hold him?" asked JP as Alberto moved the car away and headed for the airport.

"Oh we'll keep him locked away for a week or so," he replied.

"Really?" The surprise in JP's voice was noticeable. "I thought you'd say a couple of days. That's good."

"Panama is different in that way from your country," smiled Alberto. "We have a border with Columbia. Drug trafficking is rife in Panama and not tolerated. When we want to, we can invite certain people to stay as our guest for a considerable period of time. A week is nothing."

"That cuts out the possibility of any news leaking back to Malekka from him then."

The two men sat in silence. JP looked at his hotel as the car drove swiftly past and he thought briefly of the last time he had seen Coco Chavarez, when she had dropped him off after their midnight visit to Jon Lano's offices, an excursion that had somehow been discovered and that had resulted in her torture and death. Alberto noticed JP's concern.

"Are you thinking of her?" he asked. "I know she dropped you off there."

"Yes, I am actually," replied the Falcon. "If I hadn't come to Panama, she would still be alive."

"Yes, that may be true," said Alberto, "but let me tell you something, Falcon. It's also true that if you hadn't come to Panama, we wouldn't know about Jon Lano and his operation, and of what's been going on with Rovalle cargo right under our noses. As a consequence, we're going to be able to break Lano now; his operation here has been highly illegal and he's going to get closed down. He's finished. And, what's more, you're uncovering something that's deadly and could kill hundreds maybe thousands of people, and now you've got a good chance of stopping it. You might not know how yet, or even what it is, but I reckon you'll do it one way or another. And I can tell you, if Coco knew all this she wouldn't have minded not being around now. She was that kind of girl. A total professional. Dedicated to serving and saving the lives of others."

JP looked across at the young man sitting next to him, driving effortlessly as he spoke about his dead colleague. He saw him swallow as he uttered the last sentence, and thought he could see some welling of tears as the street lights flashed by; Alberto had choked up a bit on his last words.

"So don't you worry about that, JP," he continued. "Coco knew what she was doing. So does the Colonel. So do I."

JP felt a surge of admiration and respect for the young man next to him. And pride; pride to know him and his boss; pride to have known Coco.

"You make sure you get these people, JP," said Alberto, steering the car onto the start of the South Corridor. "Stop them in whatever they're doing. Then it will all have been worthwhile. It will all be ok. And Coco will rest easy."

"I'll do my best, Alberto," said the Falcon quietly. "I promise you can be sure of that."

The conversation fell away for a while. The Falcon thought, then said, "Alberto, whatever this Stingray thing is, I think what we have on the back seat and in the boot is the key to it. I'm going to take the one genuine board I marked up and its replacement with me to London. I'm going to leave the rest with you."

"Ok," said Alberto, "what do you want me to do with them? We don't have a very big tech lab, remember."

"I know, and that's fine. I want you to keep them with you at all times. Don't let them out of your sight. These are the only things we have that I think can explain what Malekka is up to, and what Stingray is about. I have a pair of them; you have the rest. Take them to your HQ and wait. Then I want you to get them to Rio de Janeiro, to Major Savedra. He'll get them to the Rovalle people, and then they can examine them in detail and try to find out what's been going on with them. That will be two groups of technicians, in Brazil and in London, trying to decipher what's happening. Can you fly out later today so they go down as soon as possible?"

"I guess so," he said with hesitation. "But you know, I'm not a field agent, JP, it's not really what I do."

"I know," replied the Falcon, "but you're doing fine. All you have to do is take a plane ride and hand them to Savedra's people at Rio. Then you can come straight back. Tell your department to lay on a plane for you - the commercial flights are too late in the day. Keep the crates inside the cabin as luggage or on the other seats, there'll be plenty of room. Take another person with you, it will be easier. Savedra is staying overnight at a hotel close to Stumpf Airport down at the Taubaté Science and Technology Centre where Rovalle is based. As long as he feels well enough after being bashed around in the car crash he's going back in later today with some tech guys to examine more of Rovalle's computer files and find out what he can. I'll call him and have you met at Rio; you hand the crates over to his people at the airport and they can take it by helicopter to him at Stumpf. That ok with you?"

"Sure," said Alberto, secretly enjoying the excuse for an excursion to Brazil. He would have loved to be able to stay and spend some days in one of the world's most beautiful and exciting cities; but with Coco gone he didn't much feel like it, and anyway her family needed him around. He wanted to be around too.

"If you leave at the same time I did, 10.30am or 11am, you'll be there at about 8pm - time enough to hand the crates over and they can helicopter them to Savedra straight away. He'll have them by about 9.30pm. You can fly back immediately, or stay in Rio for the night. I'll call the Major and set it up when I'm airborne."

They were at the Tocumen International Airport in another couple of minutes. Alberto slowed the car to a crawl as he approached the private security access road and flashed his ID to the guard. The gate was raised. He drove to the VIP forecourt and up to the G650 aircraft, coming to a rest at the foot of the airstair. The men exited.

"Hang on a minute," said JP and went up the steps and inside the aircraft. He had sent a text to the captain thirty minutes earlier and both pilots and the stewardess were on board and ready. He gave the destination and was back outside in less than a minute. The aircraft was powering up as he stepped onto the forecourt again.

"Alberto, I want to thank you," said the Falcon, holding out his hand. Alberto took it and smiled, giving a silent nod, as JP continued. "Listen, my friend. You must be extremely careful. You are probably a target now, if they can get at you they will. I don't want another phone call from somebody else like the one you placed to me a few hours ago. I suggest you keep that Beretta loaded and with you at all times. Get a shoulder holster and wear it. Put a bulletproof vest on and keep it on. And make sure someone is with you all the time, someone you can trust. At least until we're through this thing."

"Thanks for the advice, JP. I will. And… well… you take care too. And go get these people. For all of us."

Then the Falcon was gone. The airstair raised as he stepped into the cabin and its door closed neatly onto the fuselage behind him. Alberto returned to the car, got behind the wheel and drove a few metres away from the aircraft. He glanced at the clock on the dashboard; it was almost 4am. The sun wouldn't begin to break the darkness of the night sky for another two hours.

The G650 began to taxi and was quickly out of Alberto's view behind the terminal building as it headed for the runway threshold.

In another two minutes he saw the plane surge down the tarmac and lift gracefully into the sky.

27
RECRUITING

JIM PEREGRINE THOUGHT long and hard about his next phone call. He had a clear idea of what he wanted to do, but this time it would need the co-operation of Charlie's crew at MI6 and the last thing he wanted was to upset anyone at his friend's place of work. Even in times of stress and crisis, let alone a national emergency, which JP thought this was fast becoming, people are always individuals and he usually found that the brighter the person the more of an ego they had. Especially scientists. He would step carefully.

He decided to wait until the plane had cleared Panama airspace and was above the Atlantic Ocean. As with most long-haul flights, the aircraft was following the arc of a great circle as the shortest route from Panama to England, and this would take the G650 over the Caribbean Sea, clipping the airspace of Haiti and directly over the Dominican Republic. He had two hours.

When the stewardess came up to him offering a meal, he ordered one. He settled back and ate calmly, although his mind was racing. His decision to return to Panama from Brazil, to be there when the latest consignment of electronics arrived to upgrade designated Rovalle aircraft to ADS-B compliance, had proved to be shrewd. He had decided to ransack the ISTRAS centre at the Canal to find out what he could about the consignment, and then blow up the building. It was sheer good luck that he arrived at the same time two of Malekka's cronies - he now knew for certain – were switching the key Primary Boards for exact look-alikes. He had proof at last, Rovalle could be warned and they would know for sure that their electronics had been tampered with and that this had been going on for some time. JP felt a slight sigh of relief; at least he had been able to establish what the essence of Stingray was.

As with Spider 2-3, this was a masterly plot from Malekka, intricately planned, international in scope and with a foundation laid and built up over a number of years. JP was certain that Rovalle would be able to see that something was wrong and take steps to neutralise the replacement boards. He didn't know how long that would take. But, it was significant progress.

While the captured Paulo Rodrigues willingly explained his job of replacing the aircraft electronic PCBs, he had no idea of its point nor of its effect. He was merely required to do various jobs, as had his now-deceased colleague, and he was paid well for his services and for his silence. The crates were delivered earlier that evening and were to be collected the following morning, to go back to the same ship before it transited the Canal. Alberto and his team would be making some cogent enquiries of the Captain of the container vessel, to see what could be uncovered and hopefully find the collaborators, even if one of them was the Captain himself. The ship's transit permit would be revoked and the vessel held in Panama until the authority's enquiries had been completed.

It seemed pretty obvious to JP that the aim of the replacement Primary Board was to interfere with the ADS-B system of navigation and communication. Sabotage of this kind could lead to garbled connections and broadcasts, misinformation from the aircraft of its position, incorrect aircraft separation in the skies, possible mid-air collisions, serious loss of life, damage to Rovalle as one of the USA's foremost corporations as well as to all airlines operating Rovalle aircraft around the world, and the possible wiping out of billions of US dollars on all international stock markets. The airline industry would be in chaos. Although he presumed Malekka could somehow avoid damaging the airlines and economies of friendly countries, especially Iran itself.

He felt that he had largely been able to uncover what Dave Tilsen had been trying to tell his colleagues before he died. The decoys were the replacement boards, which appeared to be the genuine article but had a separate, concealed purpose.

Although, reflected JP, Tilsen had written 'DECOY 17' on the envelope on the floor... Why seventeen, or seventeenth?

There was another part to the puzzle that he had yet to unravel and which would have to be dealt with, and fast. How was Stingray going to be implemented? Was there an internal piece of timekeeping within the software of the boards, that kicked in at a specified moment, like an alarm clock ringing in the morning to wake a person up? That seemed unlikely; as the preparations for Stingray had been going on for several years, there would have to be some flexibility in the timing, since what might have suited Malekka originally for an initiation date might have to be altered later. If the plan was to initiate Stingray everywhere at the same time, which would presumably have maximum effect since doing it piecemeal would allow Rovalle and the intelligence services the opportunity to understand Stingray and annul it, how could ten thousand plus Rovalle aircraft in the air at any one time around the world receive a coordinated signal to activate the Stingray software?

The Falcon hated to admit it, but he couldn't help but acknowledge Malekka's genius and the scope and boldness of his plan. The Falcon sipped at his coffee, thinking coldly about his enemy. This might not be a war played out on a battlefield; but a war it was, with hundreds, maybe thousands, of lives at risk, as well as the economic security and stability of the West.

JP looked at his watch. The two hours had passed. He took out his cell phone, and placed the call to Charlie Melton in London, where it was 12 noon. He got hold of Melton immediately and gave his report.

"... so I have two of the PCBs with me, and Edson Ramos's team at Rovalle should have the rest this evening," said JP. "They can see the proof for themselves, and take action to deal with their aircraft and protect lives."

"That's really good work, JP."

"But we can't rest yet," said JP. "All we know now is what Malekka has infiltrated, and how he did it. We don't know what Stingray does, although we can make a pretty good guess."

"Yes, agreed. And Stingray could be implemented at any time. So we have to do two things. Find out what it does and find a way of stopping it if it gets actioned; and, preferably, find a way of stopping it from getting implemented at all."

"Exactly. How are the lab techies getting on with Lano's computer download, and the boards that you were sent?"

"Frankly, we're struggling. The data that you copied from his computer is heavily encrypted, well most of it is anyway, and is proving difficult to break. The PCBs we've only had for a little over twenty-four hours, and they're not so easy either. We have a team of eight, but we were thinking of calling in outside help because this is so time-critical."

"Really?" said JP with some relief. "That makes what I was going to suggest much easier then."

"What do you mean?"

"I know your folks are good, Charlie, but there's one guy I think we should get in."

"Steve Montague?"

"How the hell did you know that?!" said JP, who could hardly hide the amazement in his voice. "Yes, Steve Montague."

"This is MI6, JP, we're in intelligence, remember?!" he joked, rather enjoying that he'd impressed his friend so much. "If you really want to know, his was the first name suggested by the techies for additional help. You know him, don't you?"

"Yes, we've been friends for years. He's brilliant, Charlie. He owns Stemont, the electronics computer firm, he deals with loads of sensitive military systems contracts all over the world. If anyone can compare the two PCBs quickly and find out what the difference is between the boards, and identify any rogue coding, he's the one."

"I know Steve Montague," said Charlie Melton. "I've met him a couple of times. We know his work here, and we've tried to recruit him for the firm on two or three occasions. But he says we'd never be able to pay him enough to make him leave the private sector. And that he wouldn't want to work for anyone else any more. Says he's too old for that."

JP laughed. "Yes, that's probably true, he makes loads of bucks. And he's only about thirty-five or so, hardly too old, but he is very much an independent. Could you get him in later today? Tell him what we need?"

"What time are you back in London?"

"We should be on the ground at around 7pm."

"Ok. I'll do that. We'll get you collected and brought in here. By the way, we think you should get out to that Amsterdam address as soon as possible afterwards. So we're making arrangements."

"Very well. Though I've no idea what Amsterdam has to do with Panama and Rio. But obviously there's a connection and it's the next lead. Is Stephanie back yet?"

"No, but she's due in a couple of hours."

"I'd like her to come to Amsterdam with me. She was the one who dug out the connection and Anna died for it. It might do her some good to see first-hand what the two of them produced. Might do me some good too. What do you think?"

"Good idea, as long as she's up for it of course."

The two men ended the call.

The Falcon was pleased that Steve Montague was going to

get involved on this. He had played a small but vital role in Spider 2-3 by providing a little electronic gizmo that had wreaked havoc on a computer system in Moscow. His participation had been critical to Malekka's defeat and had, as a coincidence, produced an additional result that would have enormous positive consequences for years to come. The Falcon had held back that piece of information in his debriefing by Charlie Melton after Spider 2-3 had ended; at the time, JP had seen no reason to involve Steve, who had said he didn't really want anyone to know.

JP hadn't been happy about keeping Steve's involvement from Charlie Melton, but had deemed it was for the best. Though, somehow, he reckoned Charlie knew about it anyway…

After all, his best friend was Deputy Head of MI6. That means he's a real smart cookie, smiled JP to himself.

28
ARRIVING HOME

JIM PEREGRINE WAS, for once, able to catch up on some sleep during his flight back to the UK. However, before he settled down for the shuteye, he placed the call through to Major Savedra in Brazil, after his conversation with Charlie Melton. He reached Savedra just before 9am, told him what he had discovered in Panama and that there were going to be a few crates of Rovalle items along with the duplicate replacement PCBs brought to Rio by Alberto Mendes of the Panama SIS. Savedra was excited to hear the news. He was about to head back into Rovalle at the Science and Technology Centre - Edson Ramos was expecting him - and he would be taking in a crew of eight; four techies to tackle the computers, and four other personnel to aid with the research as well as interview several of the staff and general administration men and women in the centre. He would arrange for two of his team to meet Alberto at the Rio Galeão International Airport, get the items onto one of their helicopters straight away and fly it to Stumpf Airport, where Savedra would meet it and take charge.

Good, thought JP. That was under control, as much as it could be anyway. He had the other two boards; Charlie Melton had been fine about Steve Montague's joining them; Stephanie would be heading back home from Cyprus and would probably be there before he was. There would be an update and brainstorming discussion that evening with Melton at MI6, and then he and Stephie would head to Amsterdam to follow the next lead. There was nothing more he could do just now.

He asked the stewardess to make up the stateroom at the rear of the aircraft and in five minutes JP left his seat and headed for the bed. As he closed the door to the suite and changed into the luxurious sleepsuit provided, he had a glance around and thought he would have to look at getting one of these for himself. He had the benefit of coming from a family that was fairly wealthy, but his escapade over Spider 2-3 had allowed him to become extremely rich. Having his own aircraft, so he could fly at short notice to any part of the globe, had been part of his plan he had put in motion in St Lucia with the two women. They were to be his new colleagues, his partners, each of whom, he had made sure, was to receive $200m as a share in his Spider 2-3 gains. His London flat was being sold, which was why he had been staying at a hotel; he'd handed everything to agents before Spider. They had found a buyer and he needed to pack to get ready for Completion and the move; the sort of thing that normal people do in a normal life, he laughed to himself. Now he would buy much larger premises in the heart of London, to be his headquarters in his campaign to fight international terrorism. And then there was the jet. Maybe a Gulfstream G650 would be the right one.

At least, that had been the plan. Anna Kepling had been shot less than fifteen hours ago and was dead. Now he would have just the one partner, Stephanie Raughton. He sat down onto the edge of the bed. Christ, Anna's dead, he thought again, placing his elbows onto his legs and holding his head in his hands. He was staring glumly at the floor. He thought about her for another few minutes, but then stopped himself. There was no point in dwelling on it . He forced his mind off what had happened. He had to stay positive; too much depended on it, depended on him, and he needed to rest. And, who knew what Amsterdam would bring?

The Falcon slipped under the duvet and switched out the light. The gentle purr of the engines was comforting, relaxing… He tossed and turned for a while, but fell asleep in less than thirty minutes.

By the time the aircraft touched down at London's Heathrow Airport a little before 7pm, JP had showered, shaved and was dressed in a business suit with a sharp blue tie, tiepin and a handkerchief popping up from his breast pocket. As soon as the plane came to a halt in the private executive forecourt he moved to the cockpit and thanked the pilots, then the stewardess, grabbed his bags and was standing by the exit as the door and its airstair lowered. At once he felt the chill of the early May evening, groaned quietly at the pouring rain and grey clouds in the dimming light that was fast approaching sunset and smelt the familiar aviation fumes and dampness. Still, this was London, and he was glad to be home.

He started down the steps heading for the waiting transport, but then the car's rear door opened and to his surprise and delight the woman he loved slid gracefully out. He stopped halfway down, not caring about the rain pelting onto his suit; he stared at her. She was beautiful, and all the more so because they had been forced apart again for a few days and he hadn't rested his eyes on her for all that time. Her blonde hair blew wildly in the wind, her light pink coat flapped around her and then behind, letting her curves come briefly into view until she took a couple of manoeuvring steps in her high heels and grabbed it round her again. How could anyone so gorgeous also be a competent, fearless, ruthless agent? For a crazy second, one of the early thriller books he had read as a young teenager flashed into his mind, about Bulldog Drummond, by Sapper[9]: *The Female of the Species*. Deadlier than the male.

She waved and smiled, beckoning him to stop staring and come to the car. He ran the rest of the way, plonked his bags onto the soaked tarmac and grabbed her round the waist, kissing her hard. They held one another and kissed again and

---

[9] *A military engineer, and the nom de plume of HC McNeile.*

again, not caring that they were both getting drenched, just happy to have their arms around each other once more. He felt the firmness of her breasts pushing against him, the slimness of her waist, the softness of her lips, the smell of her hair; she felt the passion in his arms as they held her, the desire in his kiss, the power of his chest, the seductive height of his frame as her hands reached up around the back of his neck, drawing him in towards her.

JP pulled away, looked into her sparkling emerald eyes and said, "Hey, I think we're getting wet."

"Are we?" she smiled back. "I hadn't noticed."

JP grinned, kissed her quickly again and moved to pick up his bags. The driver was there now and collected the suitcases, placing them into the boot as his two passengers got into the car.

They held hands all the way into central London, sometimes kissing too, and once Stephanie slid her arms around his chest and kept them there, her head resting at the base of his neck. JP stroked her hair gently, comfortingly, then his hand moved down to settle at her waist. He was content; glad to be home and with her again. The streetlights flickered on, the M4 gave way to the Great West Road and Cromwell Road, the familiar buildings and hotels sped by. Past the Victoria and Albert Museum and the Brompton Oratory the driver turned southeast to bypass Knightsbridge, instead weaving his way through some of the smaller streets of Belgravia until turning into Vauxhall Bridge Road. They crossed over the Thames, turned left into the Albert Embankment and the car drove straight to the covered protected entrance to the headquarters of MI6.

The Falcon and Stephanie Raughton were greeted by Lieutenant Jane Chapman. She escorted them to an elevator at the end of a short corridor, JP wheeling his suitcases along as Stephanie's hand rested loosely around his left arm. In the elevator Jane pressed the fourth button below 'G'. After they had descended there was another corridor, and then finally they reached the main conference room.

It seemed strange to be back here so soon again; calm, secure… it was almost surreal. Like the safe house on Hanover Street, the room's centrepiece was a big mahogany table with twelve high-backed chairs, the walls were decorated with a deep red damask paper and a crystal chandelier hung from the ceiling. Large interlinked viewing screens rested on each wall and three computers on tables set to one side provided the electronic information and data support for the room. A picture of The Queen hung between a pair of wall lights, kept company by one of Margaret Thatcher an appropriate distance away on one side and a large print of the famous 1943 Arthur Pan painting of Winston Churchill on the other, the original of which had its home, somewhat ironically thought JP, on a wall in the US Embassy a few hundred yards down the road.

Charlie Melton was the first to reach JP. The friends shook hands and smiled soberly, then embraced in a bear hug with a slap on the back. Melton's thick wavy hair was a little uncombed; he hadn't been outside the building for two days and had worked, slept, shaved and showered in his office suite throughout. Steve Montague was close behind and the two of them greeted each other warmly. Montague was just under six foot, with close-cropped curly brown hair and sharp hazel eyes that darted everywhere, the window to a frontal lobe of a brain that was constantly working in overdrive. He was in a dark suit with an open-necked shirt. As her flight had landed a few hours earlier Stephanie had already spent some time debriefing with Melton in the same conference room, but Montague had arrived after she had left for the airport so JP did the introductions.

The last person was Vaani Chakrabarti, a slim woman of

Indian descent dressed impeccably in a bright red skirt suit and white blouse with pleated frills over the button line which contrasted beautifully with her brown skin and dark wavy hair curling to the front over one shoulder. The jacket was drawn together tightly at the waist and the skirt short above the knee. One of the key personnel in the tech lab with an official title of Director, Electronics and Cypher Section, she looked about twenty years old but JP learned she was actually a young twenty-nine, with a reputation of outstanding brilliance matched with long daily hours of dedicated professional work. It was she who had requested external help for her team due to the sudden and urgent workload and had suggested they bring in Steve Montague.

Charlie Melton, taking his seat at the head of the table and gesturing to the others to sit, began with a quick résumé of the circumstances. He then said, "Steve Montague is here, coincidentally, at both Vaani's and JP's suggestion. Mr Montague runs an international conglomerate called Stemont, which is a computer firm responsible for various government contracts of military systems all over the world. We have given him temporary top-level security clearance, and he has been brought fully up to date with the unfortunate circumstances in which we find ourselves." He turned to JP. "Would you like to give us the latest?"

The Falcon did so. He outlined his return to Panama from Brazil, his visit to the ISTRAS building at the Canal, that he had found two men with the latest consignment of Rovalle PCBs relating to ADS-B compliance ready to go into new aircraft or those being upgraded, and that these men were switching the boards with ones that appeared identical but which were undoubtedly not.

"One of the men became very co-operative. He told us that this switching had been going on for a number of years, since the conversion work began. He didn't know what the purpose of the switch was or what the other boards did."

"Excuse me, JP," said Steve Montague, a little gingerly, as it was his first question at the meeting, and indeed his first time at MI6. JP and Stephanie were sitting opposite Montague and Vaani Chakrabarti. "I don't yet know how these things are done, so forgive my asking, but when you say he didn't know, how can you be sure? I mean, couldn't he know and just not want to say? And the other one too?"

"Well, by then the other man was dead. He'd pulled a gun on me, so I shot him."

"Ah," said Montague, slightly taken aback.

"And I believe the other man because my gun was a few inches from his chest, and I told him that if he didn't give me straight answers I would put a bullet through his heart."

"Ah," said Montague again. "Yes, well I can see that might make someone decide to be truthful." He glanced at Melton, whose face was expressionless, and then at Vaani beside him. She seemed relaxed, reaching calmly for her glass of water. "Sorry. Now I understand better."

JP smiled. "Don't worry. Panama SIS are sweating him anyway," he continued, "and if he knows anything else I'm sure we'll get to hear of it. But I believed him and there was nothing more to come from him. They were hired staff of low level but well paid, so that they kept their mouths shut. Oh, let me give you these…" The Falcon stood and walked over to his suitcases to retrieve the box. He brought it to the table, opened it and handed the two electronic circuit boards to Montague, who passed one to Vaani.

"The one with the knife etch on the edge is the original. I saw them open the Rovalle case, remove it and replace it with the other, before they realised I was there."

Montague stared at the PCB in his hand. He had the replacement. He held it up to the light, and turned it over a couple of times.

"On first inspection," he said, "I would say this has been made in Europe. Western European. By which I mean in the EU."

"How can you know that?" asked Stephanie, somewhat in awe of an immediate diagnosis.

"Well, the substrate - the card on which the circuits are laid down - is definitely European." Montague handed the board to Vaani. "Wouldn't you agree?" he asked, taking the original back from her in exchange.

She looked at the board carefully, but then said, "I'm afraid I have to say, I'm not sure."

Montague continued regardless.

"As we already believe that one of the identical UL marks that appear on each of these - that means Underwriters Laboratory, a kind of unique coding on every printed circuit board in the world that together with various other numbers make up the identifier of a specific board or group of boards, rather like a book's ISBN number - cannot be genuine, we must look for something else. The card or substrate that holds the circuit is, in the briefest outline, made from glass fibre coated with an epoxy resin which are pressed together at around fifteen hundred psi and then baked at a hundred and seventy degrees Celsius. Their thickness, colour and the amount of light that can pass through them, if any, can be marginally different depending on the type of materials, their mix, their concentration, even the country of origin of the chemicals used to make them. The EU specifies certain categories, concentrations, and so on. These are different from those in the Americas."

He looked at the original, then tore off the top page of the writing pad in front of him, discarding it, and tore off two more, laying the pages down on the table next to each other in a landscape position. He put the board on one of them, then politely took the other board back from Vaani and put it onto the other page so they were side by side.

"This is an exceptionally fine copy," said Montague of the replacement board. "They are virtually identical. In fact, only a highly trained and experienced eye - and I don't mean to be pompous - can see any difference, and even that would be more difficult without the original lying side by side for direct comparison. There are probably only two or three other people in the world who could notice the difference straight off. It's a superb imitation."

"But Steve," said Charlie Melton, "if someone wanted to create an identical PCB to match one made in the States or, in this case, Brazil, wouldn't they make sure that they had got hold of the exact same raw materials that are used in the manufacture in the other country, namely Brazil, so that they end up truly identical?"

Steve Montague carefully picked up the imitation one. He laughed slightly.

"They have," he said, almost in admiration. "But it's not quite as simple as that. Let me give you a comparison… a different area but with an exact parallel. Take… say… pianos. Steinway Concert Grand Pianos. Beautiful instruments. Now, there are actually two types; one is made in Hamburg, Germany, one in New York in Queens. The same material; the heart of each of them is the soundboard, made of aged North American Sitka spruce. Yet when they're made, differences of atmospheric pressure, humidity, individual workmanship all play a part. Most people can't tell the difference; the outside basically looks the same. Except the lid or fallboard over the keys - the American lid often has a hinged lip at the top, the German one does not. Leaving that aside, the top concert pianists can tell; the Hamburg piano has a more mellow tone, the New York is brighter, and the touch can be slightly different. Ultimately it boils down to personal choice. It's the same for the boards. You can put the same material into them, and make them the same way, but there are always going to be slight variations."

There was silence as Steve Montague paused and his words were digested by his audience. He resumed.

"However, we all already know that they're different, don't we," he said looking to JP. "You've already established that, Jimmy. What we need to find out, why I'm here, is what the replacement does that the original does not. And that," he said turning to Vaani, "isn't going to be nearly so easy, is it?"

"No, I don't think so," she said. "I have to say, Steve, I can't tell the difference that you can just by looking at the boards…"

"That's ok," he said with blatantly false humility, "like I say, not many can..."

Vaani smiled and continued, "…but what we have found is that the material you copied from Jon Lano's computer and had sent over, JP, is heavily encrypted and is proving difficult to break. Some of it is not so intense; the pictures of you and Major Melton, and the other man believed to be the murderer, coming out from Dave Tilsen's flat, they weren't so deeply protected. We've been able to unravel bits of other enterprises that Lano, or probably Malekka, seem to be involved with. But we haven't started on the PCBs, we needed more people. Top experts. Hence the call, Steve…"

Montague smiled. "Thanks." He added, "What's this about a micro SD card you mentioned that's missing, Charlie? If there's anything like that around, it could be helpful, if it's a key or code like you told me earlier?"

"We're not sure it is," replied Melton, "but even if it is, we haven't got it, we can't locate it and it would appear that Malekka doesn't have it either. We think that's the reason why Stingray hasn't started yet. But we're still looking. If we find it, you'll be the first to know." He looked at JP. "Anything else?"

The Falcon shook his head.

"No, not really. Other than Jon Lano has disappeared. He left Panama thirty-six hours ago, before I landed first thing this morning. Panama SIS have learned he changed his flight plan mid-air, to Vienna. They've asked Interpol to try to find him, though it's doubtless a cold trail now. Presumably he decided to go on the run and get away before Panama SIS learned of the events there and picked him up. As for the other Rovalle crates, they and their intended replacements are on their way to Rio, where they'll be helicoptered to Major Savedra at Stumpf Airport ready to take to Edson Ramos at Rovalle first thing tomorrow, so they can start examining the boards as well. But if we're right and there is an SD card that's needed to interpret or unlock what's on the replacement board, they're going to have a problem finding out what's been going on too. But at least they will have physical evidence in their hands that the boards have been getting switched, they can see the imitations and I presume they will take the matter seriously and talk to Rovalle in Portland and some safety steps globally can be taken."

"Ok, JP thank you," said Melton. He turned to Stephanie Raughton. "Stephie, you want to fill in your side?"

Stephanie did so. She explained how she and Anna had gone to Cyprus to see what they could find out about Stingray and Malekka, hopefully what Tilsen had discovered and for which he was murdered. She mentioned how they tracked down Stylianos Agne in a bar one evening, arranged to meet him later in a quiet place, how they had been followed and how Anna had been killed. However, Stylianos knew details about Stingray and had provided an address, Zamenhofstraat 178, Amsterdam 1022 AG, Netherlands. This had to be the next port of call.

"Thank you Stephie," said Melton. "And I'm sure we would all like to say how sorry we are about Anna, and how much we appreciate what you and she have done."

Stephanie nodded her appreciation. She could hardly believe it happened less than twenty-four hours ago.

"So," continued Melton, "Jane - what do we know about this place in Amsterdam?"

Lieutenant Jane Chapman pressed the buttons on the remote that worked the wall monitors, and opened her notepad. The screens lit up.

"A standard satellite picture of the area taken within the last twelve hours. As you can see, it seems to be a large office block set on two floors, with three joined sections extending out into the back at right angles by some four hundred metres or so, which we believe to be a manufacturing or engineering plant of some kind. We don't have any more information on it as yet and there is little detail on firms that occupy the building. The premises are located at the northern side of the Dutch North Sea Canal that allows ships access to the Port of Amsterdam directly from the North Sea through the town of IJmuiden at the western end of the Canal. The main part of Amsterdam, including the large railway station and many of the principal ports themselves, are situated on the other, south, side of the Canal. Entrance to the premises is via the road at the north of the building; the other end of the block is very close to the waterway and has its own access. Nothing has been flagged by our friends at AIVD[10], the Dutch General Intelligence and Security Service; they have no records of any concerns about the building or its occupants. The main airport, Schiphol, is fifteen kilometres to the southwest." She paused for a moment. "Other than that, sir, that's about it so far."

Melton nodded. "Thank you, Lieutenant." He looked across the table at no-one in particular and said, "Well, what do

---

[10] *Algemene Inlichtingen- en VeiligheidsDienst.*

you think?"

"We should be there first thing in the morning when it opens," said Stephanie.

"I agree," said JP. "We should fly tonight, kip there and be ready to move in early."

"Yes, ok," said Melton. He looked at Montague. "This may be the source of the PCBs that you referred to as coming from Europe."

He nodded. "Indeed it may," he said looking again at the electronic boards on the sheets in front of him.

"I have a question," said JP. He was about to continue but the intercom on the switchboard telephone by Melton buzzed. "Hang on, JP." He picked it up, listened, said, "I'll be right out," and put it back onto the base unit.

"Take 5, everyone," said Melton, standing, "I have to go out for something," and he left the room. The others took the opportunity to make use of the coffee, tea and water refreshments along with some sandwiches that were on the tables against the walls. Melton was back in just over fifteen minutes, a puzzled look on his face. The discussion resumed.

"That was Scotland Yard, the Police Commissioner. Apparently Dave Tilsen's mother is dead. It seems she committed suicide, four days ago, or to be specific five evenings ago."

"Really?" said JP amongst the murmurs of sadness and regret that came from everyone. "Doesn't that make it the same night Dave was killed?"

"It does."

"How did she die?" asked Vaani.

"They believe she threw herself off Beachy Head."

"Oh my God. Because Dave had been murdered?" asked Stephanie.

"No. They reckon she did it three hours *before* he was killed."

"Before?" said JP. "The mother commits suicide in Sussex and three hours later her son is murdered in London? That can't be a coincidence, surely."

"I wouldn't think so," said Melton, his mind racing. "I don't know what it means but we need to find out. The Police Commissioner said Mrs Tilsen's house had been ransacked, like in a thorough burglary. The local police had been trying to locate any contacts for her next of kin but couldn't find anything; they assumed they must have been on her mobile phone but it had been smashed. The house was sealed after the preliminary discovery of the ransacking and death; the theory was that Mrs Tilsen had decided to destroy her house herself and then commit suicide. So the local forensics didn't go in until Monday morning. However, they soon realised that some other people had been there. On Tuesday afternoon the house was upgraded to a crime scene and the CID got involved first thing Wednesday. They eventually got hold of her mobile phone number from a neighbour, got the court order and went into the voicemail in the Vodafone system this morning. They discovered two messages left by Jenny - that's David Tilsen's wife," he said for Montague and Chakrabarti, "- asking Mrs Tilsen to call. There were also two from Sir Alastair. They looked them up, saw Sir Alastair is the Head of MI6, contacted the Met, filled them in on what had happened and so the Commissioner came round here. Someone has gone to visit Jenny this evening too."

"Mrs Tilsen knew Sir Alastair?" asked JP.

"Apparently," said Melton. "He's on a flight coming back overnight from Los Angeles, he gets into London tomorrow morning."

"I hope he's on a Boeing or an Airbus," said JP with a little sardonic humour.

Melton smiled. "I made sure of that. He switched yesterday."

"Charlie, have they recovered Mrs Tilsen's body yet?" asked Stephanie. "I know those tides in the Channel can be really strong."

"No. The Coastguard is still searching. It could be days, apparently."

"Gosh, how awful," Stephie said again. "I wonder why she took her own life."

"If she did," said JP.

"Yes, if she did," said Melton. He turned to Jane Chapman. "Lieutenant, when we're finished here, I want you to find out how the review of the surveillance cameras at Gatwick is coming along. Tell them to widen their search, to include the trains going north or south, and Eastbourne Station. Get them to crosscheck images of the people who were at Gatwick when Tilsen arrived with people on the trains heading in either direction, and at Eastbourne station - if they have any cameras there that is."

"Yes, sir."

"This doesn't smell right," said Melton. "Not at all. We'll find out about it." He sighed. "Ok, let's get back to where we were. JP - you had a question?"

"Yes. It's about the boards. I've been wondering for a while. Given that Malekka has successfully replaced genuine Rovalle electronic circuit boards with the alternative PCBs, it seems a pretty good assessment that Malekka's plan is to impair or destroy the new ADS-B NextGen navigation systems of these aircraft and cause confusion, damage to the West, to Rovalle, cause collisions in the air and loss of life."

"God, what a thought," said Melton grimly.

"Indeed."

"And presumably this is the DECOY 17 that Dave Tilsen was trying to tell us about when he died, that the switched boards are the decoys?" said Jane Chapman.

"And the seventeen… could there be seventeen thousand of

them and he didn't live long enough to write the zeros?" put in Stephanie, pondering on the image of disasters in the air.

"I don't know," said the Falcon. "Maybe. Probably. It's impossible to know what Tilsen meant for sure. In fact, we may never know."

"Anyway, carry on JP, please," said Melton.

"Ok. So, given these things, I'm wondering how the boards in the aircraft get activated. I think it's highly unlikely - and you'll have to correct me if I'm wrong, Steve and Vaani - that the software in these boards can have an internal timing device. This replacing activity has been going on for some years. Malekka is too smart not to be able to control exactly when Stingray starts. If there had been a pre-set clock in the software for automatic initiation, Malekka would have no way of changing the start time in the event of rescheduling his plans for whatever reason. And the other part of this is, I believe Malekka would want to start Stingray all at once, for maximum damage and effect. Otherwise the plan would be flawed since, if it was initiated bit by bit, we would learn what Stingray is and be able to introduce countermeasures to stop it. Therefore, my question is: how the devil does he start it? How does Malekka turn Stingray on at the same time in ten thousand Rovalle aircraft flying in the skies around the globe?"

"That's a good question," said Melton thoughtfully. "I don't think it can be through the ADS-B system," he continued, looking at JP and Stephanie. "Yesterday, before you two came back, I was researching about how this new system works and I don't see how it would be possible to use the ADS-B to reach scattered aircraft linked in with various unconnected air traffic control units in numerous countries."

"I agree," said JP. "It can't be done. He must have something else planned."

Vaani had been sitting quietly. She interrupted.

"Excuse me," she said, glancing round the table. "Excuse me."

Melton said, "Yes, Vaani, what do you have?"

"I know how he's going to do it, Mr Melton," said Vaani excitedly, then looked at the Falcon. "The copy of all the files on Jon Lano's computer that you sent back from Panama..."

"Yes?" said JP.

"I mentioned it was heavily encrypted, but that we were making some progress in deciphering and reading it. One of the things we have been able to find is some other companies or groups of businesses that Jon Lano interacts with, and that these are owned by someone or a group in the Middle East. I presume that's Malekka. Anyway - one of those companies is AstroGem TV."

"AstroGem!" exclaimed Jane Chapman. "My God, they're huge."

"Yes, I've heard of them too," said Steve Montague, looking with admiration at the code cracker Vaani sitting at his left. Deciphering high security computer systems and their data was not easy.

"Oh my God," said JP. "Do they own their own satellites? Does Malekka have the resources to put satellites into orbit as part of Stingray?"

"Jane?" said Melton.

"Give me a couple of minutes," said the Lieutenant, leaving her seat to shift over to one of the computers.

"If they have that," continued JP, "they can put out a signal instantly worldwide, just broadcast it around the globe." He looked at Stephanie beside him, who shook her head, and muttered quietly, "Shit."

"That's how he's going to do it," said JP. "Of course. Christ."

The Lieutenant was back a minute later.

"It's as we feared. AstroGem transmits globally, all five

continents, including the United States and the Middle East. They make their own programmes, and design and build their own satellites. They have several in orbit around the globe. And their primary offices and studios are headquartered in Dubai."

"And who launched the satellites I wonder?" asked Melton.

"I've found that too. They have had a number launched by the US, Russia, France - and, guess who… Iran."

"Oh no..." murmured JP.

"I'm afraid so," said Chapman. "Tehran established the Iran Space Agency in 2004. The ISA has had Satellite Launch Vehicle, or SLV, capability since 2009 and have been launching orbital satellites regularly ever since."

"That's it, then," said Melton. "That's how they're going to do it."

"Sometimes it seems like this guy owns or controls half the world," said JP, as much to himself as to the others around the table.

The phone at the head of the table by Melton rang. He picked it up, snapped, "Ok," and put it down. He turned to Jane. "Lieutenant, turn the television on, quickly, Sky News."

Everyone looked at Melton, then at the screens. The picture came into view, the image stabilised, the sound of the voiceover kicked in half a second later:

> *"...is the person believed to be largely responsible for discovering the terrorist cell. Luckily, before they could do any harm to others, the terrorists blew themselves up accidentally in what was a huge explosion, as we reported two weeks ago. The details of what this man, known as the Falcon, did for the*

> *intelligence forces are not yet clear. But whoever he is, we'll continue to follow the story and bring you any further developments as they happen."*

The voiceover announced they'd be back after the commercial break, so Jane quickly froze the screens before the fade-out, capturing the image.

The group round the table stared at the monitors in stunned silence.

The picture was of Jim Peregrine as he exited Tilsen's flat following his friend's murder four days ago.

29
AMSTERDAM

IT WAS STEPHANIE Raughton who broke the shocked atmosphere, by saying, "Not your best side though, darling, is it."

"It's full on frontal," said JP.

"Yes. That's what I mean."

The laughter burst out all round, then vanished as quickly as it had come, replaced by silence.

"Assuming nobody on our side released that," said JP, taking a deep breath, "I think there can be only one purpose."

"Yes," said Melton. "They're trying to track you down, Jimmy. They haven't been able to do it themselves. So they're throwing that out there because they know sooner or later someone will come up with your name. And everything else that goes with it. You'll have to be very careful now."

JP nodded.

"Steve, Vaani," said Melton, "I think you should make a move. We've been through everything we needed to, you have the boards. You should get to work. And I don't have to say it's vital that you find out all you can as quickly as you can."

"Ok," said Steve. He and Vaani stood and made ready to leave.

"You're taking them back to your London place then?" confirmed Melton.

"Yes, I think we should," said Montague. "We have excellent equipment there, it's one of the best facilities in the world. Vaani and I can work with a couple of others that I have laid on. But you'll send some people with us, right?"

"We have three of our best men who will accompany you to your firm, they'll stay with you both and protect you and the four boards. We can't afford to take any chances now, and if you want to work at your place, for reasons which I totally accept, then we have to take care of them, and you."

"Ok, let's get started," said Vaani.

"You know what to do?" asked Melton. "What we're after?"

"Yes," replied Montague. "We'll concentrate on these two, I think. That makes the most sense, as we know they're a swap pair. Check the authentic Rovalle board. Find out what the replacement board has and does that the original doesn't. Find out how it gets activated." He moved behind his chair and pushed it back under the table. "We'll be at the lab at Stemont by 10pm. We're going to work through the night and just keep going."

"Steve," said JP, "when you…"

"Yes, JP, don't worry. When we have something, you and Charlie will know it as soon as we do. Oh, I'd better take these," he muttered, making out that he'd almost forgotten the boards.

"Thanks," said JP. He added quietly with a smile, "and you're a lousy actor."

Montague grinned.

The Lieutenant walked Vaani and Steve out.

Melton turned to JP and Stephanie. "I can say this now those two have gone; I didn't want to scare them too much." Melton's lines of worry across his forehead had deepened. "I'm not kidding, Jimmy, you have to watch your back. Watch each other's back," he added. "I think it's clear that Malekka has recognised you from Spider 2-3 and realises you weren't a casual boyfriend. He's probably figured out you were a major player and he's out for revenge - not to mention trying to stop you from preventing Stingray. He's out to kill you. Not only does releasing that picture help him find out all about you, because the media will do that, but it's a blatant message to you, as bright as day. He's saying I'm coming after you."

JP nodded. "We'll be careful, Charlie."

"Stephie, I don't know if Malekka's figured out about you yet. But for God's sake be careful too."

The Lieutenant was back.

"Sir, I was wondering if we should release the picture we have of Malekka," said Jane Chapman as she took her seat again. "Putting JP's picture out sends a warning and message to us. Why don't we send them one back?"

"We could. But we're not going to." Melton was decisive. "If we put Malekka's picture out, Malekka and his lot will know it's a response, and that will confirm that he's correct about JP. And, it does nothing to make JP and probably Stephanie any less of a target."

"Ah yes, of course," said the Lieutenant.

"So we'll keep it back, until a time when it can help us."

JP nodded. "Ok, Charlie. Good plan."

"Jane," said Melton, "what have we got lined up in Amsterdam?"

Thirty minutes later JP and Stephanie were standing at the enclosed forecourt of MI6, heading with luggage to the car. Ben Alton got out from behind the wheel.

"Hello, sir," he said, holding open the back door.

"Ah, Ben!" said JP, shaking hands warmly but briefly. "Stephie, this is Ben Alton. He's the guy with two pairs of eyes..." Alton smiled. "…who spotted the photographers outside Dave's flat."

At JP's request, Ben drove first to Claridge's. JP went upstairs to his suite, collected a few things and put them into a small suitcase. He was walking through the lobby again and back in the car within twenty minutes.

The passengers settled in the back seat, Stephie's arm in JP's and hand in hand. They said very little as they drove to Heathrow. Within the hour, the car had reached the Gulfstream

G650, which by agreement MI6 had borrowed, along with the same pilots and crew, from Panama SIS. JP removed a Beaulieu tweed cap from an outside pocket of his raincoat, pulled it over his head as he exited the car and followed Stephie up the airstair. He still couldn't help but look at her legs as she went up.

The plane was airborne in twenty minutes. Its two passengers spent the first half of the flight in the private room at the back of the aircraft, where the Falcon attached the dark-haired goatee beard and moustache that he had brought from his rooms. He rearranged his hair, so that instead of being brushed back it was parted on the left and pushed flat to the right over his head, with a fringe dangling across his forehead and almost obscuring one eye. He popped on the dark-framed, zero-prescription, clear-lensed glasses. He turned from the stool at the mirrored dressing table to look at Stephanie, who was sitting on the bed. She smiled and nodded. It was a remarkable transformation, and the best he could come up with in the time available. A navy-coloured Fedora completed the job, and a stoop of the shoulders, to lessen the appearance of his height, would complement it.

They ate sandwiches and coffee, and in another thirty minutes landed at Amsterdam's Schiphol Airport. A transfer car took Stephanie and JP to a door at the side of the main international terminal; the driver knocked and opened it for them.

"Here they are sir," he said standing to one side to let his passengers pass through.

"Ah, come in, come in," said a voice from behind a small desk in the centre of the room, followed by, "thank you, Aernout," to the driver, who left.

"Welcome to the Netherlands. I am Hendrikus Vandevoort," said the owner of the voice, rising to walk round to the front to greet his visitors. "Deputy Director-General of

AIVD. Hennie to my friends."

"Jim Peregrine," he said as they shook hands.

"Stephanie Raughton," said Stephie extending her own to their guest.

Hennie Vandevoort was black and a man who emanated authority. He had a strong physique, a face that was serious and rugged with a full head of dark short-cropped hair divided on the left and sideburns on an otherwise shaved skin of a length that seemed to belong rather more to the '70s than the present. He was about forty, dressed in a three-piece suit with no tie and had steady dark eyes that were reassuring and friendly.

"I'm very pleased to meet you both," he said smiling, looking for a half second longer at Stephanie than JP, giving away he was perhaps especially pleased to meet her. JP was used to it. No man could look at Stephanie and not want to keep on looking.

Hennie gestured his guests to the two chairs in front of the desk and went back to his own on the other side. The excellent English was interjected with a guttural rasp every now and then. "I've heard at length from Charlie Melton. I am aware of what is happening. We've had the place under surveillance from 6pm and there is nothing out of the ordinary going on so far as we can tell. The building seems to have shut down at 7pm; nobody has been in or out since. Nor have we had reports of anything untoward connected with it."

"Do you have a list of companies based there?" asked JP. "Or names of anyone associated with the building?"

"There is only one: Teulen Holdings BV. They have shadow directors, three of them - two are lawyers, one is a firm of lawyers. All are also stockholders in trust. Who runs and owns it we can't yet say." Vandevoort's left eyebrow rose slightly and intermittently when he spoke. "It's a manufacturing and production company, established in 2008, good turnover, very successful. They make a variety of items, but their main output speciality is glamourous and very pricey bespoke mid- and full-sized oceangoing superyachts, together with all the internals and peripherals that go with them. The back of the building opens onto the water and they launch their latest creation there every now and again, perhaps two a year. In addition, they manufacture computer games, sound systems for computers and televisions as well as their own monitors." Hennie looked up from the sheet from which he had been reading. "However, more importantly," Vandevoort paused for effect, continuing with a broad smile, "…is that they also manufacture the computer and GPS navigation systems for the yachts."

Stephanie and JP looked at each other, then back to Vandevoort.

"Well, well. This must be the source of the boards. It seems we are perhaps in the right place," said the Falcon.

"When do you want to get in?"

"There's nobody there at the moment, you say?"

"No. It's in black-out, entirely dead."

"If we raid it now, it will alert people who turn up in the morning and before they enter the building, and so could send out alarms when we don't want anything of the kind," said JP.

"We should wait," said Stephanie. "Go in first thing and lock it down."

JP nodded. "Yes, exactly." He looked at Vandevoort again. "Can we do that? Raid it with a team, kill the phones, communications, internet… lock it out completely? Cell phones too?"

"Yes. We'll apply for the court order, we'll have the clearance in a couple of hours."

"Ok," said JP. "I presume companies start at, what, 8am?"

"Normally 8.30am but it could just as easily be 8am, or 9am."

"Right. Let's give them a chance to get in first. Tap all the lines overnight as soon as you can. Stephanie and I will go in just after nine forty-five to give it a quick once-over... We'll say we've had an idea on a whim, we're thinking of buying our own yacht and ask them about a general brochure for inspiration and design concepts. You guys come in at ten, cut everything off and keep everyone. We'll see where that leads us."

"Ok," said Vandevoort. He smiled. "That will give us something to do for the next twenty-four hours! The boys and girls will love it."

"It also means that Stephanie and I can grab some shuteye," said JP, smiling. "Can we get a lift to the station?"

"The station? Don't you mean to your hotel?"

"No," said JP. "We're going to arrive as tourists this evening. Just in case. The less attention we draw to ourselves the better."

"That's probably a good idea, now that your face has been on every TV screen in Europe."

"You saw it too?" asked Stephanie, horrified at the thought. Secretly she was desperately worried about JP's safety, in spite of his disguise. She knew how ruthless and crazed-driven Malekka was.

"Yes, and it's probably going around the world now. Although I must say you've covered it well - you hardly look like the picture at all. In fact, I don't think I would recognise you."

"Good," said JP. "It's the best we could do in the time."

"The TV picture is from the man you call Malekka?"

Stephanie nodded. "It's one that his hired help took outside Dave Tilsen's flat. Releasing it means the media will dig and dig until they have a name. It's a clever move."

"It's really irresponsible of the media to run the picture."

"It would have been impossible to stop them, Hennie," said

JP. "You know that. Even if we'd been asked about it first in the UK, which we weren't. And anyway, it would quickly have appeared somewhere else - *Der Spiegel* in Germany loves that sort of thing, or South America, Russia, anywhere; Malekka has enough contacts globally to make certain the picture got out and the story was re-ignited."

Vandevoort nodded. "I have arranged for some people to tail you. And there are four at your hotel." JP began his objections, but the Deputy D-G raised his hand. "Falcon, if I may refer to you that way, as half the world will be doing by tomorrow; you are a guest in my country, and you are the bearer of the Fifth Rubric for yours. Stephanie is a guest here too; and a very beautiful one, if I may say so." Stephanie smiled graciously. "There is no way I am going to let the two of you wander around Amsterdam without some good, very discreet, well-armed colleagues from my office." JP stopped his objections. "That's just how it's going to be."

The Falcon nodded and smiled. "Ok, Hennie. And thank you. I guess we'll see you tomorrow at the building, just before 10am."

JP and Stephanie left the small interview room and got back into the waiting car. It swept away from the airport and travelled the few miles into the city centre. The late evening traffic was light. At Central Station they exited the vehicle and stepped onto the forecourt set beneath great archways of steel girders and glass, at the apex of a horseshoe road along one side of which the cars and taxis slowly approached, made their drop or collection at the top, and then drove away on the other.

The temperature had dipped and they were glad of their coats. They wheeled their luggage along and crossed the road, the biggest danger being the large number of cyclists that were still out even at the late hour of the evening. They could hear the lapping of the water of the North Sea Canal, colloquially known as the IJ, against the harbour walls and moored boats, most of which had tied up for the night with the exception of the ferries. One was about to leave and JP and Stephanie were quickly on board. They moved forwards along the open section of the boat into the enclosed area that contained the more comfortable seats and windows offering protection against the wind. They went through the door the other end into the forward open area and rested their luggage against the left side of the boat, next to a large bench. Stephanie slipped her arm into JP's as they stood and waited.

The ferry was symmetrical with sleek lines, blue markings and sloping wall edges curving down either end to the bow and stern, with the rectangular bridge set above the central enclosed passenger area. It was double-ended with propellers and a drawbridge apron ramp at both its bow and stern, titles which were therefore interchangeable and would become switched on its return journey because of the reversed direction.

A bell sounded, the stern apron ramp raised and the propellers began to turn. The boat gathered speed and bobbed along gently in the calm waters of the IJ, heading towards Buiksloterweg, three hundred metres opposite at Overhoeks, in Amsterdam-Noord.

"Is that it?" asked Stephanie, pointing to a tall rectangular building opposite with a distinctive separate square structure on top set forty-five degrees from the rest of the tower, still visible in the city lights.

"Yes," said JP. "It's not the whole building but a number of floors, I guess it's a boutique hotel. It's nice though, I've stayed there before. That thing on top gives a good view of the city."

"It would be fun to go up there… some other time."

"Yes. Shame that's not why we're here. There's a revolving restaurant up there, pretty amazing. It would be closed now. Hey, are you hungry?"

"No, not really. The food on the plane was enough for me. Are you?" she asked, turning to look up at him.

"No. I'd just like to get to bed." He looked into her eyes and raised an eyebrow.

"Why, are you tired?" she teased.

"Not that tired..."

She smiled, and tilted her head as he kissed her softly.

The ferry ride was short and half a minute later the boat began to slow, preparing to dock. The captain navigated the ferry towards the berth, and it came to a halt with a gentle bump. Two men tied up the ferry cleats securely, the ramp came down and Stephanie and JP walked off along with the other few passengers. They turned left and walked on the cobbled pavement, which wasn't much help to the wheels of the suitcases and made them rattle uncomfortably, so they stepped onto the Buiksloterweg road, which was devoid of cars. They walked past the Café du Pont, onto the IJpromenade, and up the incline of a small pedestrian bridge spanning the narrow Buiksloterkanaal. The walkway on the other side led them to the entrance to the Sir Adam Hotel at the base of the A'Dam Tower with its four V-shaped supporting legs stretching down from each corner.

The check-in process was smoothly handled by the staff. The matter had been carefully discussed in London - JP used the David Tilsen ID. Even his alter ego ID of Julian Pilkington, as it carried the same initials, was ruled out for the hotel. There was no option for another identity; no time available.

So David Tilsen checked into the Sir Adam, along with Clara Johnson, the identity that had been quickly prepared for Stephanie by her boss, Charlie Melton, as she and Anna had passed through London three days ago on their way to Cyprus.

Declining any help for their luggage, the couple wheeled their cases to the small elevator, that was already on the ground floor. They were the only passengers. As soon as the doors closed and the elevator began its journey, they kissed, passionately, again and again, touching and caressing.

Still breathing quickly Stephanie pushed JP away for a moment, smiled and whispered teasingly, "So what do you want to do, then, boy?"

JP looked at her, his blood on fire.

"I want to grab you, pick you up and throw you onto the bed… and then ravage you."

She smiled. "So… why don't you, then."

The elevator pinged, interrupting, and the twin doors parted. They followed the signs to their suite, JP opened it and they wheeled the suitcases in.

He took the Do Not Disturb sign off the handle, hung it outside and closed the door, locking it firmly.

≈

Five thousand nine hundred miles away to the southwest, another Gulfstream G650 flying Alberto Mendes, the Rovalle crates with the Printed Circuit Boards, the boxes of the replacement primary boards and Alberto's colleague, Flávio Veloso, from Panama to Brazil, touched down at Rio's Galeão International Airport, and came to rest in the VIP forecourt a few metres from where JP had departed some twenty-four hours ago. The Eurocopter EC145 was close by; the pilots were already on board and two men stood beside it, ready to help with the transfer of the cargo from the Gulfstream.

Alberto was first down the airstair of the plane. He met Major Savedra's men, they ID checked each other and then they all climbed aboard the G650. After the first crates had been moved to the helicopter Alberto stayed by it, waiting for the return of the men with the remaining crates and boxes. The transfer took less than ten minutes.

Savedra's men boarded the helicopter and Alberto and Flávio moved to the tarmac at the foot of the stairs to their plane, waiting. The EC145 powered up, taxied at a few feet above the ground and then departed, gaining height away to the southwest.

Alberto and his colleague, Flávio, had decided not to stay in Rio overnight, so they re-boarded their aircraft. In twenty minutes it was airborne, climbing to forty thousand feet, heading back to Panama City.

The helicopter pilots, who were the same crew that had taken Savedra and JP to Stumpf Airport the previous day, followed the route they had flown before - south, then west along the coast. They cruised at five hundred feet, and the four men chatted to each other in the headsets, with the pilot interrupting every so often to communicate with Air Traffic Control en route. Major Savedra was already at Stumpf Airport, awaiting their arrival.

As the aircraft approached Ilha Grande, or the Big Island, two men on a speedboat lurking in the dark in the Bay looked at their iPad again. One of them said, "Get ready."

The other picked up the Russian 9K333 Verba, better known to NATO and the western forces as the SA-25. Several had found their way from Syria into Iran, and Malekka had a few placed at centres around the globe. The fourth-generation infrared homing surface-to-air MANPADS[11] missile, which had evolved from the 9K38 Igla, was the equivalent of the American FIM-92 Stinger missile, and now boasted a multispectral optical device that searched in the mid-infrared, infrared and ultraviolet ranges. Three other pairs of men, also armed with a Verba, had been strategically positioned along a line north into the mountains that reached up to four thousand

---

[11] *Man-Portable Air-Defence System.*

feet, giving an area of attack and range that covered any possible alternative helicopter routing.

The man on the boat with the iPad was tracking the signal from the small magnetic box that had been placed onto the helicopter by a refuelling technician, in exchange for a considerable number of Brazilian Reais. It was working perfectly.

At around the same time that JP and Stephanie left the check-in and stepped into the lift at their hotel in Amsterdam in the far northeast, the other man on the boat put the Verba, which was about one and a half metres in length, onto his shoulder. As the Eurocopter came into view less than two kilometres away, its lights blinking in the dark night sky, he fired.

A small hollow metallic 'phut' sounded as the ejection motor pushed the missile out of the tube and clear of the man, then its solid-fuel rocket motor immediately ignited. The missile surged into the sky with a loud 'whoosh', a bright orange exhaust burning from its rear and a long plume of smoke trailing in its wake. The missile had instantly acquired its target, and headed towards it at fifteen hundred miles as hour.

Five seconds later the missile slammed into the Eurocopter. Its three pound annular blast fragmentation warhead detonated and blew the vehicle apart in a loud explosion that lit up the night sky. The four men on board were killed instantly, the vehicle and everything in it was cut to pieces and the precious cargo of computer circuit boards was vaporised.

What was left of the EC145 helicopter, contents and passengers dropped from the sky in widely-dispersed pieces and hit the water five hundred feet below. They sank into the depths of the Baia da Ilha Grande, settling on the murky sand at the bottom of one hundred metres of water.

PART SIX

THE LAST DAY

30
THE RAID

THE DAY DAWNED bright and sunny. The car collected Jim Peregrine and Stephanie Raughton from their hotel promptly at 9.30am. It drove along Buiksloterweg and Van der Pekstraat, and turned right onto Johan van Hasseltweg to cross the small Noordhollandsch Kanaal, depositing them on Zamenhofstraat a few blocks from their destination. The couple strolled arm in arm along the wide sidewalk, like two lovers enjoying a lazy morning. It was a fairly quiet road; a park ran parallel on the left, and only a few people passed them by, some in business clothes going to or from meetings, some in jogging attire making use of the open space. A woman with two young children crossed the road, heading to the playground in the park.

JP and Stephanie could see the front of the building now, a plush pair of double glass doors set beneath the company name *Teulen* and a classy logo that embraced the outline shape of a yacht set on capri-azure blue waves. With only sixty metres or so to go, JP's phone rang.

They stopped walking as JP saw who was calling. "Oh," he said. "I'd better take this, hang on."

He answered the phone, listened intently and lowered his head to look at the ground. He replied briefly; then hung up.

"What is it?" said Stephanie. "What's happened?"

"That was Savedra, in Brazil. The other boards, the ones for Rovalle, never arrived. They left Rio ok on the helicopter, but disappeared. They've found out why."

"What's happened," asked Stephanie, her heart skipping a beat.

"Malekka. He's got at it. God knows how. But the

helicopter was blown out of the sky half way along the journey to Stumpf Airport, hit with a MANPAD missile. Both pilots are dead, and the cargo is either in pieces or has been vaporised. Either way, what's left is at the bottom of the sea."

"Oh my God," said Stephanie. "So what's in London is the only proof of anything then?"

"Yes. Savedra's going to call London now and fill them in. He wanted to tell us first."

"It goes to show what a spider's web Malekka has. Nobody's safe. We've got to get him, Jimmy."

"Yes." He took Stephie's hand and put it through his arm once more. "Come on. Let's get to work."

With feigned smiles and laughter, they walked up to the front door of the building, pushed the large glass entrance ajar and walked in.

The reception hall was lavish and brightly lit by overhead and wall lighting, with expensive tiling, an ornate large palm tree that somehow grew out from the floor against the middle of one wall, three pairs of comfortable armchairs around tables that were perfect for impromptu discussions with potential clients, and various large pictures on walls together with models in glass cases that proudly displayed the company's past creations - luxurious classy upper-end bespoke yachts. On the right were four small conference offices, two of which were occupied by one man and a woman, each busy on their respective computers. A girl looked up from the reception desk a few feet away towards the back of the hall, but JP and Stephanie ignored her for the moment, and walked slowly along the left wall admiring the designs and lines of the ships in the pictures. They crossed to stop at two of the models on display. JP took Stephie's hand, smiled broadly and said, "Come on then!", leading her over to the desk.

The girl looked up. She was used to seeing wealthy people walk in to talk about yachts and these two, she thought, judging by their impeccable clothes and style, had money to burn. She smiled broadly at them.

"Good morning," said JP. "Do you speak English?"

"Good morning," said the girl back, "yes of course. How can I help you?"

"Well," said JP, smiling with bashful enthusiasm. Stephanie giggled, partly for show and partly genuine. "This lovely lady and I are getting married next month. And I thought it would be rather nice to mark such a wonderful occasion..." he looked over adoringly at Stephanie - there was no acting there - "...with something really special."

"And so here we are," said Stephanie, smiling, raising her eyebrows in excitement.

"Yes, here we are," continued JP, "because we thought we would like to have our own yacht. To commission one, design it, create it... And as we're in Amsterdam we thought we'd visit a few companies who can do this and well, as I said, here we are!"

The girl at the reception looked as though this was entirely normal behaviour. Some people buy a fur coat; some buy a car; some buy yachts. "What an absolutely wonderful idea!" she said, with genuine appreciation. "We'd love to help you, we'd be privileged to help make a dream come true. How exciting!"

"Yes, isn't it," beamed Stephanie.

"We're sorry to drop in like this, but one has to start somewhere," said JP, sitting down on the corner of the girl's desk.

"Not at all, sir, I'm delighted you came in. Let me call one of our executives and ask them to come down to meet you.

"Oh no," said JP. "We're not ready to see anyone yet, it's much too early. What I was rather hoping," he said, as his eyes rested on a pile of brochures on a cabinet behind the girl's chair, "was that you might have some material that we could have about your firm, designs of yachts you've built, you know, that sort of thing. Then we can look through and call you to make an appointment."

"So we can do the thing properly," said Stephanie, "especially as I haven't a clue about yachts. Except that I'd like to have one," she giggled again.

"Oh yes, I see, of course," said the girl.

"But maybe we could come back tomorrow or the day after to see someone?" continued JP. "Whom would we be best seeing, do you think?"

"I would always say to meet the President first," she replied confidently, "but unfortunately Pierre's away just now; but the Managing Director, Mr Ambroos Bakker is here, I think you should see him." She reached behind and brought out two thick glossy brochures. "You could begin by having a look at these, it will give an idea of what you could have, the style, the range, the number of berths, and so on; it depends what you want."

"Oh, that's wonderful," said Stephanie, taking one.

"Thank you so very much," said JP, flicking through briefly, making ready to go.

"Er, could I take your names, perhaps, sir, and a contact telephone number, so I can pass your interest on to Mr Bakker?"

"Of course," said JP. "I'll leave mine. Mr Julian Pilkington. And you can contact me on this number…" He took out his cell phone, and gave the number that Hennie had provided him with less than an hour ago as a point of contact.

"Thank you, sir… madam," said the girl, "please, let us know when you'd like to come in again."

"We will," smiled JP. They began to walk towards the door, seemingly engrossed in the brochures. JP wasn't looking at the yachts, but for the company information. He flicked to the last page, where the names of key personnel were listed. He read the top line once, then looked over at Stephanie in amazement, stopping them dead in their tracks. She looked at him.

"On the last page. Key personnel. You won't believe it."

"Believe what," she said. "What is it?"

He read it again, out loud.

"It says, *'President: Mr Pierre DeCoy'*."

They stared at each other. Stephanie's mouth opened slightly in astonishment. "DeCoy," she said.

"It's not DECOY. It's *DeCoy*. A name."

"Zamenhofstraat 178, Amsterdam," said Stephanie. "Dave was writing it the English way, with the number first."

"And died before he got past the one seven. DECOY 17."

"Christ," said Stephanie. They stared at each other, thoughts flashing through their minds. He spoke again.

"Just a minute," said JP, "wait here. Keep busy, keep looking at the book."

He turned, taking his cell phone out of his inside breast pocket. He walked back to the girl, flicking nonchalantly through some pages on the phone. He found the one he wanted.

The girl looked up again, delighted to see JP return with another query.

"Yes, Mr Pilkington? How can I help?"

"I just wondered," said JP. "Your President, the one you said is away?"

"Yes, sir?"

"By any chance…" he lowered his phone down in front of her eyes, "…is this he?"

"Why, yes!" said the girl, surprised, "do you know him?!"

"As it happens," said the Falcon, "I do. Where has he gone, will he be away for long?"

"About four days, I think. He left for Dubai this morning."

JP took back his phone, looked grimly at the picture of Jon Lano, closed the flap and put the phone back into his pocket.

Just then, at exactly 10am, the lighting went out, the computers turned off, the phones went dead, mobiles lost signal and several armed police officers burst through the front door, followed by Hennie Vandevoort.

31

BILKO

THE SEVENTY-FOUR men and women who raided the *Teulen* premises were a select group made up of armed police, KMar military police, Korps Commandotroepen - the special forces of the Royal Netherlands Army - and members of AIVD. In an expertly planned and executed operation, they closed down and sealed off the entire premises in less than thirty seconds. Teams not only entered through the front of the building on Zamenhofstraat but also secured two separate doors on the west and south sides of the building, while on the east, which opened into the IJ Canal and so to the sea, the sliding doors of a hangered quayside were quickly breached and locked down. A bewildered Mr Ambroos Bakker, as the senior company officer at the building, was presented with full due court papers and warrants endorsing their action to detain all personnel and seize all corporate files, records, and electronic equipment, under the Dutch Counter-Terrorism legislation.

As the lockdown proceeded Hennie Vandevoort went over to JP and Stephanie and escorted them out of the building.

"Good job, Hennie," said JP.

"Thank you," he replied with a slight smile playing on his lips. He clearly enjoyed his work and believed in its value. He had no respect or tolerance for terrorists. "We'll tear this place apart and by the end of the day should have a pretty good handle on what's been going on. Those that don't want to talk will be tougher of course but a lot of these people will not be directly involved and may know a great deal of value and be happy to tell us about it all quickly."

"How long do you think before the news people turn up?"

asked Stephanie.

"A couple of hours maybe. Sooner or later some member of the public will phone it in, and mentions will doubtless start appearing on social media soon, but we've already prepared a story for release - that a possible terrorist bomb is suspected of being placed inside this building, or in three surrounding cars, and so we'll be escorting everyone away to safety in buses. In fact they'll go off to various detention centres in the city and outside, for interrogation."

"What's that lot doing?" said JP, looking at some police who were just entering the adjoining company building.

"We're clearing the other local buildings too. And there are three other places in the city under investigation, with armed police activity at each, as a further cover. So that it looks as though Amsterdam is under a possible terrorist attack. That will take the focus away from this building, and confuse people for a couple of days."

"That's clever, good," said Stephanie.

"Yes," agreed JP, "Hennie, we've discovered something critical…" and he quickly filled in the Deputy Head of AIVD with what they had learned.

"So that's what the DECOY is then?" said Vandevoort, with an incredulous shake of the head.

"Yes. Pierre DeCoy, the President of this place. Whom we know better as Jon Lano, from Panama City, who's had a direct hand in switching the Rovalle PCB boards, who tried to have his henchmen kill me and who tortured a female operative of the Panama Security Forces that resulted in her death. He's the key to this whole thing now. He's gone to Dubai."

"Which is where AstroGem has its headquarters," said Stephanie.

"I think you're going to find that *Teulen* is where the substitute PCB boards have been manufactured," continued the Falcon, "probably in a separate high-security plant here.

Or maybe even done in the open under everyone's noses - they can't all be involved. We know Lano fled Panama City over forty-eight hours ago and went to Vienna. He must have travelled by train from there, or maybe flown, to cover his tracks, to get to Amsterdam and become Pierre DeCoy again. Can you find out when he got back here, and for how long? And any other details you can, where he's staying in Dubai, anything at all."

"Yes, will do," said Hennie. "What are you going to do?"

"I think we have to go to Dubai, right now, as fast as we can, and get Lano. If we're right and the boards are made at *Teulen*, then Malekka may have told Lano to recover the information that was on the micro SD card that Malekka left behind on Cyprus. I believe that's why Lano came back here. So now, he may have that information, which is why he's gone to Dubai and AstroGem's base, perhaps to synchronise with something there, and probably to start it."

"You mean… DeCoy, or Lano, has the initiator of what you call Stingray?" said Hennie.

"Yes. And the clock is ticking."

≈

Sir Alastair Crewe's plane touched down on time at 8am at Heathrow Airport. He was met and escorted swiftly through the private immigration and customs hall, and to the waiting car. Fortunately the traffic into London was surprisingly light and he was at the MI6 Headquarters at the Albert Embankment within an hour.

"Welcome back, Sir Alastair," said Charlie Melton to his boss, as he walked into Melton's office. Crewe's own was one floor above, but he had decided his bags could go up there and he would visit Melton at once to get the latest update. "Good flight?"

Sir Alastair was not a tall man but he exuded an air of authority. A retired colonel, he was sharp, intelligent, used to being in control, did not like to waste time and nor would he tolerate fools. He was fifty-nine years of age and sported a jovial face which diverted one's attention from the dark steady eyes that absorbed and analysed everything, and which placed all he saw into his famous photographic memory. His thick white hair was brushed straight back across his head, above a forehead that carried deep lines.

"Yes, thank you Charles, just long." Melton smiled to himself. His boss never called him Charlie. They sat opposite each other in the dark-brown buttoned leather chairs at the small table set at one side of the room. "So what's the latest?"

Charlie Melton filled Crewe in with all the developments over the last five days. Sir Alastair listened intently, sipping at the black coffee that someone had brought in half way through the briefing. His face became dejected and he shook his head when he heard of the death of Anna Kepling and the torture and killing of Coco Chavarez.

"And they went for Peregrine in Brazil too?" said Sir Alastair.

"Yes," said Melton, "and they almost got him. He was in the hospital being patched up when the news came in about the two women."

"Your friend Mr Peregrine certainly has a way of shaking things up and digging things out."

"He does that," said Melton. "He's sent the PCB boards to Rovalle in Brazil to be examined; and he brought one and it's substitute back here for us to dissect. I've called in Montague, and the team is looking at it at Montague's HQ…" he picked up the story and continued relaying events to Sir Alastair. A couple of minutes later Sir Alastair spoke again.

"So they'll be going into the building in Amsterdam round about now?"

"Yes. But sir," said Melton, "there is something I have to tell you, sadly. Close to the end of the discussion here, the Metropolitan Police Commissioner turned up and asked to see me, as you were away. I regret to have to say that apparently Dave Tilsen's mother is dead, she committed suicide."

"What?!" said Sir Alastair, incredulously.

"Yes, I'm afraid so. I gather you knew her. I'm so sorry to have to give you the bad news."

"What happened?"

"Well, it's rather strange. It seems she committed suicide, the same night that Tilsen himself died, three or four hours earlier. The Police believe she threw herself off Beachy Head."

"The mother commits suicide in Sussex and three hours later her son is murdered in London? That doesn't make any sense."

"That's what we all said," and Melton relayed the details of her death, of the ransacking of her house, the subsequent involvement of the CID as a crime scene, and the tracing of Sir Alastair's name because of voicemail messages that he had left her.

"Have they recovered the body yet?"

"No. The Coastguard is still searching."

"Then how do they know she went off the cliff and that she's actually dead?"

"Apparently the dog was tied up at the bench she used to sit on looking out to sea, and it suddenly started going berserk. The noise brought some people out. When they undid its lead from the bench it pulled straight towards the edge of the cliff. They're sure she went over."

The conversation was interrupted by the ringing of Melton's phone at his desk. He excused himself and walked to take the call.

Sir Alastair sat mulling things over. He stood and paced

slowly to one of the three large windows set in the wall behind Melton's desk. He looked out thoughtfully, hands joined behind his back. He could see Vauxhall bridge to the left, carrying its traffic and pedestrians across the Thames. The waters looked brown and cold in that crisp May morning. Sir Alastair heard Melton put the phone back on its base, but then almost immediately it rang again, and Melton picked it up once more. Crewe carried on gazing at the London vista. How I love this city, this country, he thought. Millbank was on the other side, also busy with traffic now. He could see the beginnings of the Grosvenor Railway Bridge further to the left around the curve of the river, with two trains on their way into Victoria Station, and the tops of Chelsea Bridge beyond.

No, Sir Alastair said to himself. It's just not possible. It doesn't make any sense.

He turned to face the room.

Melton came off the phone. "Sir, the first call was Peregrine…" and he relayed JP's brief update about the raid.

"So: DeCoy. Now we know what Tilsen was trying to tell us," said Sir Alastair. "Brave man, right to the end."

"Yes. At last there's some real progress. JP and Stephanie are on their way to Dubai. I hope to hell they get to Lano."

"Quite."

"And the second call was from Ernesto Savedra in Brazil, telling me what I had also learned from JP just now, that the helicopter was blown up and the boards destroyed on their way to Rovalle."

Melton was standing once more, and the two men walked slowly back towards the table in silence. Then Melton spoke.

"We must tell the CIA again, and get them to take this threat seriously."

"Yes, you must keep them appraised. But they won't do much, if anything. They can't. Not without proof."

"No, I know. But at least we will have done all we can."

"Yes." Sir Alastair seemed almost dismissive of the morning's discoveries from JP. "Major, I want you to do something."

"Yes, sir?"

"Get the helicopter ready. Get a car ready. In twenty minutes, I want to leave for the Heliport."

Melton immediately headed to his desk.

"We're going to Eastbourne."

Melton picked up the phone, pressed a button and said, "Jane, could you come in please."

"Make your call quickly to Slim Wilkins in Virginia." Wilkins was Melton's opposite number at the CIA in the United States. Sir Alastair looked at his watch. "It's early there, but serve him right if he's not awake." Melton smiled. "I'll go up to my office for a few minutes to freshen up and change my shirt. I'll join you again downstairs."

There was a knock at the door and Lieutenant Jane Chapman walked in.

"Good morning, Sir Alastair," said Jane, "welcome back."

"Good morning, Lieutenant. Thank you."

"Jane, we want a car for the Heliport in twenty minutes, and scramble the helicopter. We want to go to Eastbourne."

"Very good, sir," said the Lieutenant calmly. There was very little that could faze Jane Chapman.

"We can land on the green area opposite Mary Tilsen's house, it's fairly flat there," said Crewe. "Get the local police to cordon off the area. And I want the lead investigator to meet us there. Not the head dignitary; I want the person leading the investigation that knows the details."

"Yes, sir," and Jane Chapman turned to walk to the door to carry out her instructions. She was stopped at the exit.

"Oh, and Lieutenant," said Sir Alastair.

"Yes, sir?"

"Er, do you happen to have a, er, safety pin?

"A safety pin, sir?"

"Yes. A safety pin. A little personal matter… I seem to have damaged the chain on my tiepin. I do so hate ties that are flapping around."

"I'm sure I do, Sir Alastair. Now, sir?"

"Yes, please. Now."

The Lieutenant left the room.

"Charles, there's something you should know about Mary Tilsen," said Sir Alastair, walking over to the window again, looking out briefly once more. "It's not widely known. She always wanted it kept quiet, no fuss. That's how she was…"

There was a knock and the door opened once more.

"One safety pin," said the Lieutenant, as she walked across the room. "It's rather on the small size, sir, I hope it will do?"

Sir Alastair took the pin from her.

"It's perfect, Lieutenant, thank you."

The woman left to make the arrangements.

≈

Hennie Vandevoort organised a car for JP and Stephanie. "You'd better have an escort as well." He issued some orders and two of the many police cars on site rolled up at the kerbside thirty seconds later.

"Thanks for the help, Hennie, and well done again, it's a thorough job."

He smiled. "You're welcome, my friend. I'm not having these evil creatures in this town. We'll get on with dissecting the place. Whatever we find we'll pass it straight over."

Vandevoort held open the door to the second car. They said their goodbyes and Stephanie and JP got in.

"They'll use the blues and twos on the way, the traffic could be heavy."

JP nodded as Hennie closed the door.

The cars departed with lights flashing and sirens belting out their double-tone sound, but these were turned off as they approached the hotel. The cars parked around the corner, out of site of the reception area. JP and Stephanie went quickly up to their room and grabbed their things, checking out using the in-room system. Then they were back at the vehicles, their luggage was loaded and the cars set off again, screaming their way through the city out to Schiphol Airport. They were there in twenty minutes.

JP had considered the idea of getting a supersonic military flight to Dubai, to catch up some time on Jon Lano, and Stephanie and he had discussed it briefly with Vandevoort. It would have meant that the Netherlands Authorities would have had to obtain approval for an overflight across Europe, some of the most densely populated territories on the planet. Sonic booms do not sit well with dense built-up areas. In fact they would have to obtain clearance to fly through the airspace of around nine countries in all, some of them not particularly friendly to the UK, the EU, or the USA. Trying to secure this would have taken time, and some countries may have refused. It was judged that the fastest way of getting to Dubai was to get a move on and fly there subsonic. And the Gulfstream G650ER could manage and maintain Mach 0.925, some seven hundred miles an hour.

In another fifteen minutes, the Gulfstream was airborne, on its way to Dubai. It was a little after 11.30am, on 7th May.

The flight would take around six and a half hours, maybe less, depending on the prevailing winds.

≈

"I'll tell you more on the way," Sir Alastair had said, and disappeared up to his own office. Melton spoke briefly to Slim Wilkins and in fact did wake him up at home. Melton asked if it was time for the CIA to talk directly with Rovalle. Although taking the matter seriously, Wilkins said there was no firm evidence of anything, since the PCB boards in Brazil didn't reach the Rovalle offices there and had been destroyed, and the remaining two known to have been in a switch were already being examined in London. And, while one was obviously an authentic board, Rovalle presently wouldn't be able to verify it. MI6 could send them to the CIA in the States, and so on to Rovalle, but if the threat was real, as both respective SIS forces believed, the matter was time-critical and it was best that the examination continued in London. However, Wilkins would talk to his own boss, and maybe a discreet chat with the head of Rovalle in Portland, Oregon, could be undertaken, and a warning given about a possible breach of integrity of the ADS-B NextGen system - although not even that as the target was certain. He said he could also slip it in for discussion at the regular briefing at the White House.

Charlie Melton felt some relief at that. He could appreciate the CIA - as indeed MI6 - couldn't call alarm for every threat they came across, as their credibility would be damaged if proved false - they would be accused of crying wolf. It was a nice balance that had to be weighed up.

Melton gathered a few things, told Chapman to hold the fort, took the elevator downstairs and waited for his boss to arrive. Two minutes later they were in the car, blue lights at the front flashing, driving southwest along Wandsworth Road, turning right onto Nine Elms Lane and the A3205. Sir Alastair pushed the button to close the partition with the driver.

"Dave Tilsen probably never told you about his mother and her professional career," said Sir Alastair.

"Well, actually, no, now I come to think of it," replied Charlie Melton. "Nothing at all."

"She wouldn't have allowed her son to do so; and I doubt even he knew all of her exploits."

"Exploits? What do you mean, exploits? Who was she?"

"Mary Tilsen isn't - or wasn't - just Mrs Mary Tilsen. She was actually Dame Mary Tilsen, GCB, CBE. She spent most of her working career at MI6."

"Really?!" said Melton. He hadn't known that. "I haven't seen her name on any of the accreditation boards or in fact on anything at all."

"No. She had always asked that her name was never shown. The Firm respected that. The truth is, she was one of our most successful operatives in East Germany and East Berlin in the Cold War and eventually became Head of Section. She could speak German, French and Russian fluently, like a native. And when I joined the Firm, she was my boss for a number of years, when I took over her former post in Europe."

"You were there during the time of the fall of the Berlin Wall, and the end of the USSR, isn't that right, sir?"

"Yes. Dangerous times. The Russians had left their nuclear weapons and machines all over the place when the Soviet Union collapsed. But that's a different story. The point is, Mary and I were good friends and remained so through the years after her retirement. She sadly fell ill and in fact had terminal cancer, with only a few months to live."

He paused, and sighed, perhaps at the thought of losing a close friend with whom over the years he had travelled down many long roads. His companion said nothing; he waited patiently for his boss to continue. The car moved along against the backdrop of apartment buildings, some older council houses, construction sites, then under four railway bridges and past Battersea Park.

"And she was only eighty-six," he suddenly continued, "which isn't exactly ancient in today's age, but nevertheless, that was the status. However, she was still very active, her mind was as sharp as ever and I can tell you now, without any doubt whatsoever, that she would not commit suicide because of depression, her terminal illness, resentment… Not in one hundred years. She simply wasn't like that."

"So what do you think happened?" asked Melton.

"I don't know. But we're going to find out."

They were almost at the London Heliport. The driver turned the car off right to leave the A3205, which at that location was York Road, onto Lombard Road and then left to Bridges Court Road. A sharp left again brought them to the Heliport entrance. The two men were met by the senior executive staff of the Heliport and taken to the tarmac. The smart Eurocopter EC155, or H155 as Airbus liked to call it, had arrived from its base thirteen miles away at Biggin Hill after a seven-minute flight, and rested on Pad 3, its rotors still running. The men boarded, the aircraft taxied the few metres to the short takeoff runway, positioned on two-zero and then lifted off. It rose to five hundred feet over the river, the wheels came up smartly and the aircraft headed southwest, climbing initially to two thousand feet.

The EC155 routed over Croydon, then east of the busy London Gatwick Airport and to East Grinstead, maintaining a direct course of one seven eight degrees and its top speed of a hundred and seventy-five knots, or two hundred miles an hour, and was descending over Eastbourne twenty minutes later. The local police had cordoned off a perimeter on the open grass area on the other side of the road from Mary Tilsen's house some fifty or sixty yards away farther down west. One of the officers was in contact with the aircraft by two-way radio as it approached, the wheels came out again and the helicopter landed smoothly. A small crowd of onlookers had gathered and others were peering out of the windows of houses.

The two passengers were disembarking before the rotors stopped and Detective Chief Inspector Sandy Eastham was beneath the still-rotating blades too, extending a welcome. It was not every day that a helicopter flew in from London and landed on public ground at Eastbourne, nor that the two top executives from the country's spy organisation MI6 visited, either. Eastham was in his fifties, a little under six feet tall and had a round face with rather mottled tanned skin and a nose that was slightly to one side of straight. It was a lasting souvenir from his amateur boxing days and a championship bout of which he often remarked that he might have been made prettier but he wasn't the one who needed carrying out half way through the next round. His hair was brown with some grey and considerably thicker at the sides than on top. He wore a suit, a long raincoat and a Trilby.

"Sir Alastair?" said Eastham in greeting and extending his hand. "DCI Sandy Eastham."

"Yes, how do you do," said Crewe, "this is Major Charles Melton."

The two smiled and also shook hands.

"This way, gentlemen." Together with two constables, he escorted his guests through the gathering crowds, across the road and through the line of police tape that cordoned off Mary Tilsen's house from the general public as a crime scene. They stepped into an enclosed canvas tunnel covering the pathway to the house.

The front door was unlocked and Eastham took them inside, closed the door and spoke. "Sir Alastair, Major Melton, I'm afraid it's going to be difficult for you to see much inside the house. Presently this is very much a crime scene under investigation and we're heavily into it, so I must ask you to stay in position here. As you're doubtless aware, the SOCOs[12] or CSEs - CSIs, if you like the American TV series," he said

[12] *Scenes of Crime Officers.*

with a rather humourless grin, "- must take precedence over everything just now, I'm afraid."

"Yes, of course," said Crewe, looking around.

"God, what a mess," said Melton. Various items of furniture were strewn on the floor, the telephone to the landline lay smashed on the ground, the small bookcase had been pulled down and the books and their spines leafed through. It was obvious the disruption extended into the other rooms of the house, since the doorway to the kitchen was open and two people dressed in examination coveralls were working away at items that seemed to have been pulled out or thrown down onto the floor.

"Yes it is, and I'm afraid it's the same upstairs. The team did an initial visual examination of the scene, to establish what warranted closer inspection, and decided they should tackle the entire house. However, the entrance area - door, hallway, walls, carpet, furniture - has been examined, fingerprinted and anything of interest for DNA sampling has already been removed. So we're ok here. They have also done the outside porch, the gate, the paving slabs, and the grass verges and garden beds."

The DCI paused for breath, then continued.

"Everything was photographed and videoed, both inside and out, including all the possible exits, entrances and routes between. Now they're moving on to every footprint, partial footprint, trace of footprint, which will be diagrammed, measured and photographed with scales. And of course they'll look for any blood, the tiniest of droplets, even if wiped. Hairs, skin residues, anything that could leave DNA… The usual thorough stuff. We already know some other person, or persons, were here and caused some of the trouble."

"How do you know that so quickly?" asked Melton.

"That's an easy one," said Eastham. "Footprints, mainly, or traces of them. Some on top of the disruption; some beneath.

So the mess occurred while they - we think two - were here.

"Oh yes, of course."

"The footprint sizes were much too big for Mrs Tilsen. We believe they wore gloves; however, there's an interesting latent fingerprint on the number plate on the front gate, that's nowhere inside, not so far anyway. It may mean something; but it could just be the postman's. We have yet to establish firmly Mrs Tilsen's prints, but they'll figure that out." He paused, and then said to Crewe, "Although, perhaps you could help there, sir… I presume she was one of yours?"

Sir Alastair looked hard at the Chief Inspector, summing him up. He decided he would trust him.

He nodded slowly and said quietly, "Yes. She was one of ours, Chief Inspector. And an old personal friend. We'll get them to you."

"Thank you. That will help."

"But keep that very quiet. I don't want it out in the media. That's critical. Especially for the next few days."

"Of course. Just send them to me personally."

"I presume you know about her son?"

"Yes," said the wily policeman, who had not referred to that. "We understand he was murdered in London a little later the same evening." He paused, then added with a slight smile back, "We do have his prints."

"What about neighbours, witnesses, her routine?" asked Melton.

"We've already gone door to door, and are continuing with local enquiries. Because of her age and health condition - er, you know she had terminal cancer, sir?"

"Yes," said Crewe sadly.

"Because of these factors Mrs Tilsen was on our list as a vulnerable person. So far, nobody knows anything about visitors to the house that evening. We're talking to the local shops too of course, and pubs, restaurants. And we've asked for any CCTV recordings anyone might have of the evening. That could throw something up. In fact, there's a pub of interest round the corner, apparently one of the barmaids working that evening recalled seeing someone unusual come in. She says about thirty, dark skinned, possibly eastern, possibly Turkish, or Arabic. He rather stood out, she felt. We'll let you know what's on the disks and if we get anywhere."

"Thank you, Chief Inspector. And, we're looking for something. A micro SD card. Anything like that turn up yet?"

"No, sir, not at all."

"If it does, we need to know at once, and we need it immediately, it is not to be examined by anyone other than our lot. Is that clear?

"Yes, sir."

"But, you mustn't let it be generally known that we're looking for the card. You must keep that to yourself, it must not get out, even to your colleagues."

"Very well, sir."

"Thank you, Chief Inspector. We think that's why they were here. I can't tell you the reasons at the moment, but I can say that it is vital that we get as much information that you can provide over the next twenty-four or forty-eight hours. It could be critical. The man in the pub. The card, if it turns up. Anything at all. The lives of many could depend on it."

"Yes, I understand, sir. The Commissioner made that clear to my Governor. We'll pass anything we find along at once. And I gather you'd like me to call in every two hours with an update."

"Yes please, to Major Melton here."

"Very good, sir."

"Now," said Sir Alastair, relaxing slightly. "Where's Bilko?"

"Bilko?" said Eastham. "Who's Bilko?"

"Bilko," said the Head of MI6, "is Mrs Tilsen's dog. While I'm here I should see him, find out if he's ok and what's going to happen to him. She would have expected that of me."

"Oh, right, yes of course. He's up the road. A Mr Higgins a few doors up took him in for now. We'll walk you up."

As they exited the house and turned left to walk along the pavement, they could see on the other side that the open pathway had been cordoned off all the way up, including around the bench some way off in the distance at the top. Several police officers lined the route, keeping the public at bay. A few CSEs were examining the walkway.

"Oh, we thought we would close off the pathway too and see what we can find. There are a few areas of light mud. We might find a footprint; Mrs Tilsen may have dropped something. Or thrown something. And if the card's up there, we'll find it too."

"Very good, Chief Inspector," said Melton.

A few minutes later the group reached their destination. One of the constables knocked on the door, Sandy Eastham did the introductions, using only the first names of his guests and saying they'd come down from London to help with their enquiries. Mr Higgins was a kindly gentleman, recently retired, and clearly upset to learn about the events surrounding his friend Mary Tilsen. Eastham explained they'd come to look at the dog.

"I'm sure he'll like the attention," said Higgins. "He's been very poorly. He hardly moves or makes a sound; he just sits in the corner where we've put down a blanket for him. He's a good dog, never barks, I've taken him out for a short walk twice a day, he gets fed once. But he never wags his tail either. He seems terribly sad. If I didn't know better, I'd say he was heartbroken."

He led them down the small hallway.

"He's in the sitting room."

He opened the door and they filed in, except one constable who waited by the front door. The room was small, with a table and two chairs at the bay window overlooking the road, from which Mr Higgins had waved to Mary Tilsen, and a small three piece suite with a coffee table in front. There was a modest television beyond and some family pictures hanging on the walls.

The little Scottie dog was lying in the corner on the floor on a brown blanket, his paws out to the front and his face resting between them. He raised his eyes and looked mournfully at the men that filed in. Then all of a sudden, he raised his head. He sat up. The tail started to wag, and he let out a little bark.

He could see Sir Alastair now. The head of MI6 smiled, and the dog got more and more excited. "Hello, Bilko," he said, animatedly. And the dog charged over, wagging his tail furiously, running around and around Crewe's legs. The men were smiling; Higgins had a look of amazement on his face.

"Come on then, boy!" said Crewe, clapping his hands, "Come on!" and the little dog jumped up in the air. Sir Alastair caught him, and then the dog was licking his face, making him laugh. "Stop it, stop it," he giggled. He put him down, and got to his haunches to pat him some more.

"Well, blow me down," said Higgins. "He certainly knows you!"

"Yes, Bilko and I are old friends." He gave a few more pats, then he stood.

"Mr Higgins, I wonder if I might borrow this room for a few minutes, I need to talk to Charles here about the investigation… and Bilko. Would that be alright?"

"Yes, of course, of course," said Higgins, "you go right ahead. He certainly seems to know you and if you want to take him with you that's fine with me, he'll be much happier with you! I was only ever going to be the caretaker!"

"Thank you. Would you mind, gentlemen?" said Sir

Alastair to the others. With consenting murmurs, they left the room. Sir Alastair closed the door. He walked to the sofa and the coffee table.

"Charles, come and sit down. I want to tell you something."

Melton obeyed. Bilko was sitting next to Crewe, so close that the dog was leaning up against his leg.

"Let me have this for a minute, old fellow," said Crewe and he unbuckled the dog's collar. Bilko didn't seem to mind at all; he was delighted to be with a friend again. "You see, Charles, I don't believe Mary Tilsen just committed suicide." He turned the collar round in his hands, and read the metal nameplate engraved with the Scottie's name and address, riveted into the leather of the collar. "Oh, I'm sure she jumped off the cliff, to take her own life. She was ill and knew she didn't have long." He removed his breast pocket handkerchief and laid it open on the table; then took out his wallet from inside his jacket. "It still took enormous courage, of course; but that was Mary all over." He opened the wallet and pulled one of the partitions ajar, looking for something. "But… the real purpose of her jumping was to send a message…" he found what he wanted, "…to me." He slid out the safety pin that Lieutenant Jane Chapman had given him earlier, and opened it. It was true, the chain on one of his tiepins had been damaged. But fastening his tie to his shirt wasn't the only reason he had asked for the safety pin. Especially as the second tiepin he was wearing was doing the job perfectly. "The message was in two parts." He levered the edge of the dog collar down, with some difficulty, to reveal a little depth of the left edge of the nameplate. "The first part said, come down to my place." He picked up the safety pin, put the point in the tiny hole that was now exposed, and pushed. "And the second part…" he continued, as the minute catch inside popped and raised the top surface up, "…said, I want to give you…" and Crewe withdrew the safety pin and used it carefully to lift the cover of the plate, which turned stiffly on its internal hinge the opposite side, "…this."

Sir Alastair Crewe turned over the collar, and shook it. Onto the handkerchief a couple of inches below gently plopped a small rectangular item that had been concealed inside the tiny secret compartment of the nameplate. Its dimensions were fifteen millimetres, by eleven, by one.

Sir Alastair looked at Melton beside him, one eyebrow raised, a slight smile playing on his lips.

"Good Lord," said Melton. "The SD card."

32
DUBAI

WITH FULL SPEED but all due courtesy, Sir Alastair Crewe and Charles Melton expressed their thanks and left the home of Mr Higgins, who was only too happy to relinquish his guardianship of Bilko. Once in the street, led by Sir Alastair, the group of men virtually ran down the hill towards the helicopter, with Melton explaining to Sandy Eastham that they had to get back to London urgently and thanking him and his officers for their assistance.

The pilot was standing by the aircraft talking with his co-pilot with a plastic cup of coffee in one hand and a sandwich in the other midway up to his mouth, when he spotted the men charging down the hill. Melton raised a hand above his head and moved his wrist in circles. The pilot muttered something under his breath, tipped the liquid onto the ground and handed the cup and sandwich to one of the police officers nearby, and told them to get everyone back again. They were powering up the aircraft and the rotors had started to spin as the two men and the dog boarded. It was airborne within a few seconds, leaving a bemused DCI Sandy Eastham looking up at the departing aircraft as it gained height and disappeared to the north. He scratched his head, wondering what the sudden excitement had been about, and walked away, ignoring the questions from the local press. His PR people would put out some kind of anodyne cover statement shortly.

Sir Alastair sat thoughtfully in the soundproofed VIP passenger section of the helicopter, fondling Bilko's ears. The dog was between his legs sitting upright looking up at him, his tail wagging. He seemed pleased to be with someone he knew.

Melton shifted in his seat on the other side of the cabin and looked over at his boss with admiration.

"Well done, Chief. That was impressive."

"Thank you, Charles," said Sir Alastair with a rare, broad grin.

"There's something I don't follow, though. So... Mrs Tilsen sent you her message, which you understood. Only you could have done that. But, what on earth was the micro SD card doing there in the first place?"

"That, Charles, is a very good question. I think it was like this. Tilsen was going abroad in a few hours the following day, excited about what he had found out from his informant in Cyprus. The meeting with the contact in Panama was all set. He had separated the SD card from the phone as standard procedure. But he had already sent a great deal of Malekka's material back to London, including several computers, phones, iPads and boxes of paper files, which he believed would hold the intelligence data to come from Cuttle Cove. To him, the SD card was an insignificant item that he brought back simply because, that day, he was heading home to the UK. I was abroad; you were going to see the PM in my stead for the regular weekly meeting. As Tilsen couldn't see either of us that morning prior to his departure abroad, he thought he would leave the card with his mother for safe keeping. It was harmless enough, he probably thought. And, it was her birthday - her last - and I believe he thought she would get a little kick out of being asked to take care of something associated with work one more time. Perhaps he even knew about the dog collar. So, believing the item would be safe, he left it with his mother and set off for home and Panama, planning to collect it on his return three or four days later."

"... but, he didn't realise the card was, in fact, vitally important to Malekka," said Melton, "nor that he was being followed or tracked..."

"That's it exactly. The card would have come back in the

usual small plastic container. I also think he'd originally planned to leave the card at home with Jenny but decided on his mother; and for some reason put his own SD card in the container, as it wasn't in his phone and the container had gone. And this one," he said patting his wallet, "definitely isn't Tilsen's, it doesn't have the Firm's tiny dot mark on it."

"So you think when they killed him, they found a card, took it but it was his?

"Actually, yes, I do. And Malekka must have been - how shall I put it - seriously displeased when he examined the SD card and saw what looked like holiday snaps of Cyprus. As you know, all business items are stored internally on our phones, not on external cards."

"Yes."

"Strictly speaking, Tilsen messed up. It was out of order. Yet, it's one of those strange random moments on which, down through history, important events can often hang and mighty battles are won or lost. I believe that, had Tilsen not left the card, Stingray, whatever it is, would have been activated by now. Or, at least, we wouldn't have the slightest chance to stop it."

The two men sat with their thoughts for a few minutes, looking out of the windows. The aircraft was already over Croydon again and had started a gradual powered descent, with no reduction of forward speed.

"Where did the dog collar thing come from?" asked Melton. "That's a little gizmo I haven't come across before."

"No, I'm not surprised," said Sir Alastair. "It's something that Mary Tilsen created herself years ago. She had the backroom boys make the first one for her in Germany. She's had a canine companion with her for as long as I can remember. She managed to walk many a microdot and even small film negatives across from East to West Berlin. She was never suspected; never once discovered. She simply had the nameplate changed when one pet sadly left her and was replaced by another."

Bilko was curled up comfortably on the floor. Sir Alastair fondled his ears again. The dog raised an eye sleepily but didn't move. The tail gave it away though.

"Presumably in the search the intruders used metal detectors of some kind. The aluminium-iron oxide coating on the inside of the top flap would have disseminated any radio scan, and the layer of composite metal foam would protect from X-rays or gamma rays. A detector would have picked up the metal on the collar for sure but it would have appeared as merely a dog's nametag. Mary may have been eighty-six, but she always had this little thing updated as the years went by. We were happy to do it. I guess she was still very proud of it."

Melton smiled and shook his head in admiration.

"I wish I'd known her," he said. "But, to throw herself off a cliff… I suppose the fact she was being raided made her realise that what Dave had left was actually of vital importance, and so… what, she wanted them to think she had it on her when she jumped… to gain more time for Dave, and us?"

"Yes, I think so. And send the message to me. Though I've no idea how she managed to persuade her captors to let her out with the dog for a walk. But then, Mary always could invent and spin a good yarn…"

The helicopter touched down at the London Heliport. The two men and one dog were quickly at the waiting car, which sped off with its double police escort towards the headquarters of Stemont Inc and the frenzied work of Steve Montague and co.

≈

The routing for the G650 flight to Dubai had been carefully

planned. A direct line had to be avoided, as that would involve an overflight of Iran. People in Iran were trying to kill Stephanie Raughton and Jim Peregrine. And, Malekka had already managed to use a missile to shoot down a helicopter containing vital evidence of Stingray that was en route to Rovalle in Brazil. Iraq was supposed to be safe for commercial traffic, Syria too; but JP wasn't going to take any risks. The decision was made to route direct to Rhodes, avoiding Muslim Turkey, then through Israeli airspace, across Jordan, with which the UK and USA had close ties, overhead the northern part of Saudi Arabia and into the United Arab Emirates.

JP and Stephie heard from Charlie Melton that the micro SD card had been found, and Steve Montague and his team were trying to decipher it. That was tremendous news! Perhaps, having been behind for so long they were now catching up with Malekka, to level the play. At about four hours into the flight, JP received a call from Hennie Vandevoort. They had learned four important facts from the raid so far. First, Pierre DeCoy did have an association with AstroGem, though nobody knew what it was, or if they did, they weren't saying. Second, AstroGem's main physical transmission station in Dubai, as with a number of other networks, was located at the top of the Burj Khalifa, the tallest building in the world, which rented out two dedicated communications floors above the residential and public viewing levels. Third, Pierre DeCoy planned to visit that section. And, fourth, DeCoy had arrived back at *Teulen* yesterday morning, spent the day in the office, then left for Dubai in the evening. His staff did not have an address for him and thought he may have his own apartment, but one person remembered that he had stayed at the Burj Al Arab Hotel before. JP and Stephanie had discussed whether to request that the Dubai security forces apprehend DeCoy ahead of their arrival, but decided against it lest the information reached the wrong people and Lano was tipped off. They had called Melton and he had agreed. Play safe. Too much was at stake.

The sun had already set as the G650 approached Dubai over the dark waters of the Persian Gulf. The glittering lights of the Palm Jumeirah, the iconic and stunningly beautiful man-made island shaped as a flattened palm tree within a circle, were visible off to starboard, and the sail of the Burj Al Arab Hotel, the proud bearer of a seven-star rating, stood a little further along the shoreline, with the white, yellow and blue carpet of the City's lights stretching for miles around. As the aircraft continued its descent, the Burj Khalifa twinkled into view, towering above the surrounding matchsticks of glass and steel, graceful, resplendent; yet concealing a deadly trigger for an unknown function, that one man was about to pull.

The bordering houses and headlight beams from the cars and trucks below were left behind as the aircraft crossed the boundary of the seven thousand two hundred acres that comprised Dubai International Airport, identifier DBX, to touch down on Runway 12R. It taxied to the end, vacated right and rolled onto H Apron, then followed the air marshaller's instructions for parking. It was a discreet area, at the southeast tip of the airport, away from the exposure of the main terminal buildings.

The two passengers were ready to leave before the aircraft had stopped. JP was in a light grey suit with a white shirt and blue tie; Stephanie had dressed down, to meet the customs of the land, and wore a white business suit, low shoes, an opaque cream lace blouse that went up almost to the neck. Her hair was tied in a bun. The jackets were essential attire to conceal their firearms.

The stewardess opened the door. The heat assaulted them like an atmospheric tsunami, a rolling thirty-three degrees Celsius force that collided with the comfortable air-conditioned environment of the cabin. The airstair touched the tarmac and JP was about to lead the way down with bags in hand when four men walked up towards him. He stepped back inside.

The first man in flipped open an ID wallet and held it out to JP.

"Tyle Brannigan, Mr Peregrine, British Embassy," he said, the perspiration on the brow something he had never been able to prevent in the two years he had been stationed in Dubai. "Welcome to Dubai. It's really hot here, are you anxious to get to a pool?"

"No, dinner first. Then a shower."

"Hello," said Brannigan with a smile.

"How do you do," replied JP, pleased to have completed the additional security phrases that Melton had set up. He held out his arm. "Stephanie Raughton."

"Hello, Ms Raughton, so pleased to meet you," said Brannigan. He was just over thirty, blond hair, had a brown face with heavy facial growth from the day and brown eyes that tried to smile but somehow failed. Tiredness.

She shook his extended hand. The group moved further back into the cabin. JP and Stephanie sat down again and invited the others to do the same. Brannigan continued.

"This is Mr Badour, of Airport Customs and Immigration, who's here to take care of the formalities."

"Hello, Mr Peregrine, Ms Raughton," he said in good English, "may I see your passports please."

It was more of a command than a request, as is often the way of immigration personnel, and the two visitors handed them over. He brought out a little leather case that was bulging in his jacket pocket, placed it on the table where JP was sitting and brought out the stampers. JP's passport was authorised first, then Stephanie's. He handed each of them back, smiled, then said to them, "Thank you, and welcome to Dubai."

They nodded their thanks, and Mr Badour was on his way. That was that. The power of the Bearer of the Fifth Rubric, and of Governments of course, thought JP. He smiled at Stephanie, and with a fleeting press of his left arm against his chest felt the comfort and security of the Sig Sauer P226 with its attached silencer tucked away neatly in its shoulder holster under his left armpit.

"Mr Peregrine, this..."

JP interrupted Brannigan politely with, "JP, please".

"Er, yes, thank you," smiled Brannigan, "this is General Dahek Elamin, who is head of the Dubai Police Special Unit."

JP was standing again now, wanting to get on.

"General," said JP, shaking hands, as did Stephanie.

General Elamin was forty, fit, muscular and looked as tough as nails. His face was rough like sandpaper and a thick black moustache leant out over large lips and a flat jaw, beneath dark and foreboding eyes. His grey suit was tight fitting, and looked expensive. I'm glad he's on our side, thought JP.

"My colleague, Lieutenant Makki Zakaria," said General Elamin in beautiful English. They nodded to the Lieutenant. He was also in a suit, ten years younger than Elamin, with a tall, wiry frame and a face that was rather square-set beneath short dark hair. The eyes were cold and grey.

"My Government tells me that you are here on a critical mission, continued the General, "and I am under instructions to assist you fully. I know that this is a serious matter, since I do not get a call from Saif bin Zayed Al Nahyan, our Minister of the Interior, with instructions like that every day. I do not know any details and have been told you will tell me. I am here to help. What do you need?"

"We're looking for a man. We have to find him, and fast." He took out his phone and showed the two policemen a photograph. "Do you know him?"

They said they didn't.

He showed the picture to Brannigan.

"No, I don't know him either. And like the General, I've been told nothing other than merely to assist all I can. Who is he?"

"Pierre DeCoy. From Amsterdam, with links to AstroGem here in Dubai. Also known as Jon Lano, from Panama in Central America, and Hong Kong. We believe he is about to initiate a plan that will damage the navigation system of thousands of aircraft in the air around the world, leading to massive confusion and considerable loss of life. We have to stop him. We understand he arrived in Dubai earlier today. We don't know how, or which entry point into the UAE he used. He may be at the Burj Al Arab Hotel; he may have an apartment; and if he isn't at those we believe he will be at the communications platform of the Burj Khalifa. We need your help in access and apprehending this person. But, we mustn't scare him off. He has to be caught. Or stopped anyway."

"Very well, JP," said General Elamin. "The Police Special Unit is only forty or fifty strong, a small force overall, but we are well trained. Lieutenant Zakaria and I are at your disposal. If more personnel are needed, we can get them easily enough."

"Thank you, General." The Falcon looked at Brannigan. "Tyle, is the helicopter here?"

"Yes, JP, all ready."

"Ok, let's go."

He grabbed his bags, nodded again to the flight crew and followed Brannigan down the airstair. The heat was sweltering and the slight breeze was a welcome relief, even if it carried the smell of warm tarmac and the inevitable aviation fumes along with it. Brannigan walked to the waiting helicopter, signalling to the onboard crew to power up as he went, and opened the door to the passenger section. The aircraft was an Agusta 109e, an Italian aircraft perfect for the short hop they were about to take, powerful and comfortable, and well kitted out for its VIP clients. JP stepped aside for Stephanie and followed her in. The other three joined the club seats opposite. The marshaller was back and closed the door, and the helicopter departed one minute later.

The machine routed south, to be clear of all the busy airways, and then west out over the water. They could have flown direct, over the city, but that would have been unusual and could have alerted watching eyes. At five hundred feet and one mile out from land it turned southwest, flying parallel to the shoreline. For a couple of minutes the passengers could admire the Dubai skyline.

There was another development similar to the Palm Jumeirah, JP knew, named the Palm Jebel Ali, a little farther along the coast, but not so easy to see; most of the land had been reclaimed but the development had been put on hold since the global financial crash of 2008 - even the vast wealth of the United Arab Emirates and its thirty-plus resident billionaires had been touched. But now the country's mixed free-market economy was booming, and although still largely based on oil and natural gas production, the manufacturing, commerce, hotels and real estate sectors accounted for thirty per cent of the UAE's GDP. The UAE was a proud, great country, offering a high standard of living for its people. The Falcon shook his head. How he loathed that such enormous wealth had been bequeathed people for no reason other than simply because some black gold lay beneath their sandy Bedouin topsoil. How much misery and loss of life had that wealth caused in the hands of the wrong few, such as Barakah Malekka. Was it the old clash again, the old war that had arisen once more, of Islam against Christianity? Was it the re-igniting of the Crusades after eight hundred years from the death of Richard the Lionheart? And merely the continuing of all those subsequent campaigns?

Stephanie had seen the little shake of the head and was looking at JP inquisitively. He shook his head again, dismissively. It mattered not. JP's job now was to deal with this nightmare.

The helicopter turned again, southeast towards the shore, and then there it was. The Burj Al Arab stood in all its glory, a magnificent representation of the sail of a ship, of exploration, of nation meeting nation, for friendship, and not for war. The aircraft climbed another two hundred and fifty feet, approaching the helipad on the landward side of the sail, where Roger Federer and Andre Agassi had once played some spectacular knock-about tennis. The aircraft came in and settled onto the tarmac, six hundred and eighty-nine feet above the waters below.

As the rotors slowed the Hotel staff were quickly outside the aircraft, ready to welcome their guests and deal with luggage. The group exited, walked down the metal access stairway to the level below and onto the red carpet that directed them through double doors into the hotel. They were escorted into a private registration area, where JP and Stephanie checked in. The two newest guests of the Al Arab excused themselves from the others while they were taken to their suite to deposit their bags. While they were gone General Elamin, as planned, discreetly produced his Police ID and without mentioning any names requested to view a screen of those who had checked into the hotel that day.

"Nothing," said Elamin when JP and Stephanie returned two minutes later.

"Ok. So, let's go to the other place."

They started to walk towards the lift to go down when JP's phone rang. It was Charlie Melton.

"It's London, I must take this," he said, and walked away with Stephanie.

"Hello?" said JP. "Charlie?" To Stephanie, he added,

"Let's go outside again."

"Hello, JP, yes, can you hear me?"

"Yes, go ahead, we're just going outside to hear you better."

"Ok, JP, listen, I've got Steve Montague on the line here as well. Steve, can you hear?"

An excited and desperate-sounding Steve Montague started to speak. "JP, we've cracked it, we know what the boards do… Hello?"

"Hello, Steve, yes, I can hear, go ahead?" They were through the doors again and outside.

"Hi, ok, JP, listen and listen good. We know what's going on. The SD card contains a series of numbers. These pair up with similar number strings on the computers brought from Malekka's base at Cuttle Cove. When they're joined together each number becomes a cipher sequence that includes the serial number of a PCB board that went into a specific aircraft. There are thousands of them, one for every transponder PCB that they've swapped and put into each Rovalle aircraft for the new ADS-B navigation system. And, at the start of each string, is the same group of numbers. That's clearly an activation sequence."

"Oh God," said JP, "so what does it do?"

"Hang on, that's the first part. The second part is this. On the PCB board here that you brought back we've found some covert computer programming, and we believe this is on all the other replacement PCBs, which is why they were switched. The ADS-B 'In' part of the system is a radio receiver, right? It can pick up transmissions from other local aircraft. But that means it can also receive other transmissions as long as they're on the right frequency. When it receives a broadcast that includes its specific cipher, each replacement PCB will release and inject that programming code into its plane's computer. It just takes a typical TV or radio transmission via satellite worldwide on a slight frequency moderation, which is where

AstroGem comes in. Malekka's not trying to mess up aircraft navigation around the world, it's got nothing to do with that. It's worse."

"I don't get it, Steve," said JP, loudly. It was a bad line. "So what does it do then?"

"Ok, listen. We think that the computer half of the numbers is already in the system at AstroGem. The SD card, with its group of numbers, is the primer - that's why it was so important to Malekka to get back. As they couldn't get the card, we reckon they sent DeCoy back to where the PCBs were made, Amsterdam, to recreate the numbers. And all DeCoy has to do now is input the new data into AstroGem to live the system, like they presumably planned to do before. Then push one button, or place one phone call to a master box, and the entire transmission will go out worldwide in less than ten minutes. And Rovalle aircraft around the globe will receive that as an activation sequence."

Steve Montague paused for breath.

"And?" said JP, as his heart skipped another beat.

"And, we now know what it does. Commercial aircraft use an autopilot, from almost immediately after takeoff and for virtually the entire flight. The rogue coding infiltrates the main computer and the autopilot, and the fly-by-wire system if the aircraft has one. It gives a command; then corrupts the system; then locks it. It can't be overridden, or disengaged. And the command is, to adjust the angle of its horizontal stabilizer in the tail."

"What?" said JP, incredulously. "Oh my God."

"Yes. It makes each stabilizer deflect to the maximum down angle. If the system receives the initiator signal, the rogue programming is activated, it passes to the computers and the stabilizer in the tailplane will dip. Every Rovalle aircraft in the sky, ten thousand of them and over two million people, will lock into a nosedive and crash."

"Bloody hell," said JP, staring at Stephanie, who was looking at him open-mouthed. She couldn't hear it, but could tell it was bad.

"You've got to stop him, Jimmy. You've got to stop DeCoy. He'll kill hundreds of thousands of people. You must find him."

"Ok," said a shocked JP, amazed at the turn of events. "Well, he's not at the Hotel. I'm going to the Khalifa. Great work, Steve."

The Falcon hung up the phone, grabbed Stephanie's hand and they ran together back to the door of the hotel. He told her of the conversation.

They took the elevator down to the lobby and JP filled in the other three as it descended.

"…and we need a car, and we need to get to the Burj Khalifa fast," ended JP.

"We have two," said Elamin, "I had them sent here for us."

"Good, General. Let's go."

As soon as the elevator doors opened they charged across the luxurious upper lobby, set beneath the world's largest atrium that soared upwards from its gold-coloured foundation of giant baseball-bat pillars. They had reached halfway when JP's phone rang again. He stopped.

"Hello, Charlie?" said JP, as General Elamin showed his Police ID to the hotel security officers that had approached amidst the screams and gasps from the other guests, to calm the disturbance and to reassure everyone.

"There's more, JP," said Melton on the other end of the scrambled line. "Something's happening. The CIA called me as Steve was talking to you - Slim Wilkins said that ten minutes ago Iran closed their entire airspace."

"Christ," said JP, thinking furiously. "What the hell does that mean..."

"And so as of ten minutes ago," continued Melton, "any

approaching aircraft will be denied entry on first contact with Iranian Air Traffic Control and will not be admitted. All aircraft inbound to Iran must turn round and go elsewhere. And - Iran has just issued a directive via their ATC for all of the aircraft currently in their airspace to land immediately at the nearest Iranian airport and to ensure that they are on the ground tonight by 10.30pm latest their time. That's 10pm your time in the UAE."

"It's going live, isn't it," said JP. "Christ…"

"Yes. It's going live, it has to be."

JP's eyes were caught by a television screen...

"Iran doesn't want any crashes in its own backyard to have to clean up," continued Melton. "So they're grounding all aircraft. I reckon you have until 10pm. That's fifty minutes from now."

"Shit," said JP.

His eyes were still glued to the TV screen. He took a deep breath.

"Just a minute, Charlie, there's something else…"

"What?"

"Hang on."

The Falcon walked over to the large television screen playing in the corner. It was showing the news, and on the screen was a famous Rovalle aircraft. He could hear the sound now…

> *"…departed two hours ago from Hawaii bound for Cairns, Australia, to be present at the celebrations tomorrow, May 8th, of the anniversary of the Battle of the Coral Sea - the great Battle in World War II when the Allies stopped the Japanese expansion in the Pacific*

and so prevented the invasion of Port Moresby in New Guinea and ultimately the invasion of Australia herself..."

The picture showed a beautiful white, red and royal blue jet surging down a runway, tilting up gracefully and lifting away into the sky. The most famous Rovalle aircraft in the world. A Rovalle *FAB Jupiter-300B*. Tail number 41000.

"...Air Force One departed from Honolulu at 6am this morning on its eight-hour journey, carrying the President - whose grandfather took part in the battle - and her husband over some of the most open stretch of ocean on the planet, to greet and stand shoulder to shoulder again, this time in remembrance, with a good friend and an old ally..."

JP had lowered the phone to his waist as he looked on in horror.

"He couldn't have done that," said JP to himself. "He couldn't possibly."

"What," said Stephanie, by his side now and overhearing him. "Done what?"

But JP knew that was exactly what Malekka had done. In that instant he realised what the prize target was, and why the activation was happening now.

"Oh my God," said the Falcon.

33

AT THE BURJ KHALIFA

JIM PEREGRINE RAISED the phone to his ear again and almost shouted, "Charlie are you still there?" at the same time as holding out his hand to grab Stephanie's and pull her to run with him.

"Yes, JP, what's going on?"

They ran through the upper lobby again as JP yelled, "Come on," to Brannigan, Elamin and Zakaria. They dashed round the magnificent Lobby Fountain that was in the midst of its display of choreographed clapping water spouts rising and falling as a rhythmic bateria, then over to the right escalator to race down, ignoring the stupendous Cascade Waterfall that stretched all the way across to the ascending escalator opposite.

"It's Air Force One, Charlie. It took off two hours ago, from Hawaii."

"Oh Christ," said Melton, at once knowing what JP meant.

They were at the top of the stunning aquaria of fish that complemented each escalator's lower journey.

"The President's on her way to Australia, with her husband and children. I saw it on the TV in the lobby here, purely by chance."

They were through the internal glass doors and running over the red carpet to reach the outside doors, and were met by the onslaught of the heat that bounced off the black marble panelling of the hotel entrance.

"Where are the cars?" said JP to Elamin, pausing by one of the huge decorative globes at the kerbside. The row of white Phantom Rolls-Royces of the Hotel were lined up impeccably in the bays left; the General saw his men on the opposite side and beckoned.

JP had his phone at his ear again.

"You've got to convince the CIA now, Charlie. Remember that stretch of water?"

"I remember it," said Melton. "If Malekka gets Air Force One two hours into the flight, they'll be a thousand miles from anywhere."

JP and he had taken a flight from Hawaii to Sydney some years back. The ocean route is remarkable in that for the first two hours there is no island with any landing strip to accommodate an aircraft in an emergency for over a thousand miles in any direction. The Marshall Islands were twenty-two hundred miles away; the Johnston Atoll would be hundreds of miles from the aircraft and, apart from intermittent visits, remained closed and deserted.

The General's drivers had started their sumptuous Bentley Continental GT four-litre twin-turbocharged V8 five hundred and forty-two horsepower engines, and the two sleek white unmarked police supercars pulled forwards.

"Jeepers!" said Stephanie in admiration.

"This is Dubai, Ms Raughton," said the General with the hint of a smile along with some pride. "We have the best for our police. Money is no object."

The fantasy-like moment was fleeting, replaced by desperate cold reality.

"General, Stephanie and I will ride with you," said JP. "Tyle, you're with the Lieutenant in the second."

They piled in, and the General's car shot out across the Hotel Bridgeway to the mainland, its blue lights flashing front and rear, with the second Bentley following.

JP was at the phone again.

"Charlie?"

"Yes, I'm still here."

"We're going to hit the Khalifa and AstroGem. It's all we

have. If he's there, I'll get him; if he isn't we've had it."

"Right," said Melton. "I'm going to call the CIA and try to convince them to take action, at least over Air Force One. They'll have to rip the bloody thing out, if they can. I'm not sure turning the transponder off will be enough. Who knows what else Malekka's done to the system."

"Yes, I agree, Charlie. They must do something. If they down Air Force One and kill the President and her family, there will be a war."

"Good luck, Falcon."

"You too, Charlie."

The Bentley had joined the D94 right and was surging down it, then glided left onto the D63 heading away from the coast towards the prime highway in the city, the E11. Known locally as the Sheikh Zayed Road, it was the main artery of Dubai, though hardly a road in the traditional sense since it boasted sixteen lanes. Superhighway was a better description.

JP glanced at his watch. It was 9.15pm. Forty-five minutes left. He was trying to formulate a plan. If DeCoy was at the Khalifa, what floor? The place was huge; at least the Communications and Broadcast floors were somewhere at the top, which, as the building's design was tapered, meant that their floor space was reduced.

JP was behind the driver in the back of the Bentley with Stephanie beside him.

"General?" said JP.

He turned round from the front right to face JP.

"Do you know what floors the Communications section is on? A broad idea of the layout would help."

"Yes, of course," he replied. "I visited the Khalifa many times at various stages in its construction, and also we advised on security. The Burj Khalifa has one hundred and sixty-three floors, and the Communications and Broadcast floors are on one-five-six to one-five-nine. The two lower floors are rented to various smaller companies. AstroGem, which is by far the largest media company in Dubai - in fact one of the largest in the world, certainly in our country - has both of the upper floors, one-five-eight and one-five-nine. The floors are entirely automated and should be deserted at this time."

"Ok. How do we get up there?"

"I've been thinking about that. The public entrance to the Khalifa is through the Dubai Mall but there will be hundreds of people around at this time and it's a distance from the Burj Khalifa itself, so we'll skip that. We'll go into the tower from the VIP and Private Residents entry on the other side. From there we can cross to get the service elevators and avoid the tourists. We'll have to change elevators on the one hundred and twenty-fourth floor, the *At The Top* observatory - which actually incorporates floor one-two-five as well - just like the tourists have to, although we won't see any; the next elevator will take us to the *At The Top Sky* observatory on one-forty-eight. There's no public access after that level. So, another change, and then we get the ride to the remaining floors from there. You want to go above or below?"

"We'll go one below and walk up," said JP, "it'll save a little time."

He paused, thinking, then carried on.

"I really want this man myself." He turned to Stephanie. "But, we'll have to split up. There's no option."

She nodded.

"You take the top floor…" JP looked at Elamin again, "…which was what again?"

"One-five-nine."

The cars were roaring along the E11 at over a hundred miles an hour, their flashing blue lights helping to clear the way.

"Ok, Stephie. We'll get the elevator to the hundredth and fifty-seventh floor. Then we're on the stairs. You go with

Lieutenant Zakaria and take one-five-nine. I'll go with the General here and do one-five-eight."

"JP, I suggest we reverse that," said the General. "The higher floor contains the larger international satellite dishes. If he is going to broadcast a signal that is to go around the planet then I think this man DeCoy is more likely to be on the higher level where that equipment is located."

The Falcon thought for a second.

"Very well, General, thanks." He paused again, then added, "Of course, we could all go for the one floor but we can't waste any time, we must hit them both in case he's not on the upper one. So Stephie you and the Lieutenant take the lower floor, one-five-eight. I'll go up with the General to one-five-nine."

"Ok," said Stephanie calmly.

He spoke to the General again. "Is Zakaria good?"

The General nodded. "He's very good."

"Does he have any trouble working with a woman?"

"Not at all."

"Ok, that's fixed then. Stephie, DeCoy has to be taken down. He won't hesitate to kill you if he gets a chance, so shoot to kill if you have to."

She nodded confidently.

JP glanced at his watch again. 9.27pm. Thirty-three minutes.

"General, how many elevators up from one-four-eight?" asked JP.

"Only two, as far as I can remember."

"Are they close by each other?!"

"Yes, in a single corridor."

"What about stairs?"

"Same level, adjacent."

JP glanced at the driver. He was a regular police officer, carrying a firearm.

"Ok. Let's get your driver to come up to the corridor and

apprehend DeCoy or anyone for that matter that comes down to that floor."

"Yes, very well," the General nodded.

"JP, what about a command centre for the Khalifa, or a control centre?" said Stephanie. "There must be some kind of hub that monitors the building and controls all the switches. Shouldn't we get to that too? Get them to kill the power on those floors?"

"Good idea." JP looked over at Elamin. "How about it, General?"

He shook his head. "It can't be done. There is a control centre located in the basement and it's state of the art. But the power to the broadcast section of those floors is external and comes straight from the grid, to ensure continuity and stability for their transmissions and operations. That way there could be no fluctuation caused by other usage or surge from the building, or a possible malfunction. There is no switch here; it's at the electricity substation itself. In theory it should be possible to kill the power. But I doubt they'll want to do it. There would be massive consequences legally and financially for the Khalifa and they'd probably want an order in writing from the owners of the building and an instruction from someone in the Government. The power comes from the Hassyan power plant fifty kilometres to the south, but the switch is at the DEWA Substation - DEWA means the Dubai Electric and Water Authority - about four kilometres to the north of the Burj Khalifa. I could go there and bully them into it, maybe; but even if I drop you at the Khalifa and drive on, I think we'll be well past the deadline of 10pm."

JP looked at his watch. "Nine twenty-nine. No time. We'll stick to the plan. You send the other driver and I'll send Brannigan with him down to the control centre. They can get on to the power station and at least try to talk them into it. And they can look at the cameras here, right? They'll have surveillance on every floor? That might help, especially if DeCoy makes a bolt for it."

"Yes. All the public areas; not privately owned floors of course, nor those that are rented commercially. So they'll have them in the hallways on those floors, but not inside them."

The talking fell silent. JP's mind was racing. What else do we need to do, he thought. He's there, I know he is. I can feel it. What if he's loaded the data early and he's finished? No, that doesn't matter, he won't set it off until 10pm or after, as that would make things messy inside Iran. They have until 10pm. But not later. He looked at his watch again. 9.30pm. Thirty minutes.

The Burj Khalifa was close by now, reaching for the stars twinkling above, the tallest building in the world, eight hundred and twenty-eight metres high, with a base shaped like a desk tidy of tubes of varying diameters and height for pencils and pens, joined together at the ground but then stretched high, and getting ever thinner as it climbed skywards... It looked such a beautiful building, thought JP, if it wasn't at that moment so deadly. Within sixty minutes, over two million people around the world could be dead because of its dark secret, which JP and Stephanie and Melton and others knew about, yet wouldn't be able to expose in time, before the deadline of 10pm - which was 7pm in London, 2pm in Washington, 8am Hawaiian time on Air Force One - was upon them.

The Bentleys had left the E11 and were running parallel to the D71, heading southeast; in another minute they turned again, inwards towards the Burj Khalifa, first on Al Mustaqbal Street, then Sheikh Mohammed bin Rashid Boulevard. Their flashing blue lights were turned off as a precaution. Less than half a kilometre to go, and they'll be out of the car, off to stop Malekka's henchman that Jim Peregrine knew as Jon Lano, that Dubai and AstroGem, and Amsterdam, knew as Pierre

DeCoy. He would stop him somehow; he had to. Even if he had to trade his own life for DeCoy, to stop the impending disaster that Malekka was once again trying to cast upon the world.

The cars pulled into the Burj Khalifa Park and onto the slip road that led to the private entrance to the huge building. There was a security gate; the bar was promptly raised once the guard spotted the vehicle was a police car, backed up by General Elamin's ID. The cars purred quickly forwards along the smooth grey block paving, a darker shade every tenth row giving a welcoming line enhancing the curve of the large roundabout, and pulled into the arrivals bay that was lined with half-metre black pillars sunk into the walkway, ensuring vehicles went no further. The occupants of both Bentleys were out, running towards the Residence Entrance, with the uniformed officers well in view. They dismissed the two porters that had come out to greet them and ran to the glass entrance, set beneath a graceful tiara of ribbed steel. They were through the revolving glass doors, heading over the elegant low bridge that spanned a small lagoon rippling quietly with water flow, beneath another cavernous atrium propped up with angled chrome knitting-needle tubes climbing like an angle of swords to an apex, each bearing intermittent cymbal-like disks resembling huge petal wind chimes.

They were at the Reception. Elamin had his ID out again and the male Reception staff were soon attended by two burly uniformed security guards, each of whom knew General Elamin. They were instantly alert and ready to help as the General spoke urgently to them.

JP turned to Tyle. "I want you to go with one of the police drivers to the Control Centre in the basement. One of these guys will take you both down. Tell them to get power to the Communications floors switched off. It can't be done here, they'll have to call the power station."

"Ok," replied Brannigan, listening intently.

"If the power's cut, then the signal can't be transmitted. They'll probably refuse, or hesitate and ask for more details or authority, but it's worth a try. Do what you can. And, monitor the CCTV cameras, watch out for DeCoy in case he bolts."

Brannigan, a police officer and one of the security guards disappeared through a panel door to head downstairs.

"Which way to the service lifts, to the top?" said JP to the remaining security guard. "Quickly!"

It jolted the man into action. He led the way through the double glass doors and began running along the start of a myriad of corridors. They came to an opening hallway of four elevators. They were quickly in one. As the door closed, JP glanced at his watch. 9.41pm. Nineteen minutes.

The elevator was fast. The numbers flashed by on the displays set in the three sides as the elevator climbed the shaft at ten metres, or two and a half floors, per second. It reached the one hundred and twenty-fourth floor in exactly one minute. They ran out, down another series of corridors that opened to a second almost identical hallway, with a further set of four elevator doors. The group was quickly in another car that lifted them a further twenty-four floors; then they were out and running down more corridors. Finally they reached a hallway that this time was slightly smaller, and had only two elevators.

Seventeen minutes.

"These are the only elevators that go up higher?" asked JP of the guard.

"Yes, sir, these are the only ones. There is no public access any higher, strictly staff only and authorised corporate officers and personnel."

"Ok. General Elamin, stake your man here."

The General issued the order to the other driver. He was to remain with the security guard and ensure that anyone who came down the two elevators or adjacent stairwells was apprehended. The policeman drew his firearm, and had it at standby. The General looked over at Lieutenant Zakaria, and said, "Are you ready, Makki?" The man nodded.

"Ok, JP" said the General. "We're all set."

"Stephie?" said the Falcon to the woman he loved. She nodded.

They entered the last elevator. It took them up the remaining nine floors, to one-five-seven. JP led the way as the door opened, his gun drawn. The hallway, which was identical to the one below, was empty; the corridor spawned a labyrinth of doors. The three men and one woman slipped silently through the door leading to the stairwell, and began up the stairs. At the next floor, Stephanie drew her firearm and led the way through the door to the floor, followed by Zakaria.

Fifteen minutes.

JP and General Elamin climbed the remaining stairs silently, and reached the one hundred and fifty-ninth floor. They peered through the stairwell door, and slipped silently inside. JP started to walk down the corridor, hugging the right wall. On either side twenty feet down were double doors with the legend 'ASTROGEM' in large letters set in an adjacent plaque, with smaller lettering below saying 'TRANSMISSIONS'. JP was wondering which one to try first, when General Elamin spoke, in a low voice.

"The one on the right. It has the larger satellite dishes. If he's here, Lano will be setting Stingray in there."

It was the tiniest of slips. But it was enough to ring a warning sound in the Falcon's head as loud as a klaxon horn on a ship. Elamin had not been fully briefed and only knew about a plot and a man. How did he know the name Stingray? In the split second of assimilation, JP started to turn, and the arm that came round his neck from behind pushed the six inch blade of knife up and in but it was now off-target and didn't penetrate through to his heart or lung. The bullet-proof vest helped stop the blade too, but it was ballistic armour, not stab-resistant armour. The blade sank into JP's lower left back, and he began to bleed profusely. He let out a yell and dropped his gun in reflex. He spun round to confront the traitor, who realised his mistake, whose eyes were now wide from adrenalin, whose right hand was holding the bloodied blade back ready for a second strike and moved forward. Elamin thrust viciously, JP put his left hand onto Elamin's right arm and pushed away; he tried again and JP was in quickly with both hands on the arm to block the slash, then again; the fourth time the Falcon moved in and deflected the arm round the side of his chest and held it, wrapped in closely against him so the knife was neutralised, then pulled Elamin to the wall, stepped across him and threw him over his leg. In the same fast movement JP slid his hands down the man's arm as he went and grabbed on to his wrist. The man crashed onto the floor and with a vicious twist upwards JP broke Elamin's wrist, the knife flying onto the floor. The man was screaming but somehow he was up, his face distorted in agony, the eyes deep black pools. He tried to reach for the gun with his good hand but it was on his other side, he was in pain from his useless wrist and disoriented. JP smashed his right fist into Elamin's face with all his strength. The force flung the man against the wall again, dazing him more, then JP followed with a left hook, then a right, then a left, each one harder than the other, oblivious of the grave wound to his side and the damage it was doing internally. His opponent went down, but he was still conscious and somehow scrambling to rise. The Falcon flung himself on top of his would-be murderer and chopped his throat viciously with his right hand. The General's arms came up and flayed in feeble protection. The Falcon chopped again, the arms fell away and the traitor's eyes began to bulge. He chopped again with all his might. And once more.

Breathing heavily, JP crawled over to retrieve his gun. He

was sweating, he could see his own blood on the floor and knew he didn't have long. He thought of Stephanie, who had obviously been met by Lano. A clever trap. Lano must have been warned too. He hoped Brannigan in the control centre had seen the fight and they'd get someone up here... No, Lano's too smart, the corridor cameras would suddenly have failed on several floors to hide his own visit. JP glanced at the dead man on the floor, then saw the clock on the wall by the elevators.

Eight minutes.

Jim Peregrine pushed through the door to the stairwell, and as quietly as he could went down the steps, leaning against the wall for support. A line of blood smudged along the marble as he went, and drops of red plopped on the ground. He was at the entrance to the other floor. He pushed aside the pain, forced himself to concentrate. He breathed deeply, grabbing for oxygen to clear his head. He didn't know why the words came to him. But they did... *force your heart and nerve and sinew to serve your turn long after they are gone*... Yes, that's about it. He shook his head, wiped the sweat from above his right eye. Force it... *hold on when there is nothing in you...* The Falcon slipped through the door into the corridor.

He passed the elevators and glanced at the clock.

Six minutes left, to 10pm.

He saw the doors and the signs that mirrored those on the floor above. He quietly reached the pair on the right. He'd try those first. Elamin might have been telling the truth as to which side. He pushed the door open slowly. He had the right door ok.

The room was a mass of white painted steel and fibreglass, aluminium and ebony boxes, awash with huge satellite dishes and their smaller siblings. On the floor by the entrance lay Lieutenant Makki Zakaria on his right side in a pool of blood, his lifeless eyes staring blandly ahead. And in the centre of the room stood Stephanie Raughton, her blouse torn, her jacket ripped, her hair dishevelled, and blood running from her nose, dripping onto her white lapel. Jon Lano stood behind her, shielded, with a cocked revolver against her head.

"Ah, there you are, Mr Tilsen. Or whatever your real name is," said Lano. "Do come in. Elamin messaged me you'd both be visiting. And lower your gun. Or I'll blow this young woman's head off right now."

JP walked slowly in, and lowered his Sauer to his side.

"That's better. As you can tell, the young lady and I had a little confrontation, after I killed her companion there. She's good. Very good. But then, Mr Tilsen, or whoever you are, I've been a Ninth Dan for many years longer than she's been fighting."

Stephanie looked up at JP. She saw the blood on his left sleeve, and the drops falling to the ground. She saw the sweat on his brow, and thought she saw him sway a little. How could she help, she thought? The man behind her has all the cards at the moment…

"And I assume, as you're here, my good friend the General will not be joining us."

"I'm afraid not," panted JP. "He's on his way elsewhere."

"How resilient you are, Mr Tilsen."

"I try."

"No matter," said Lano. There was no compassion. No regret. "In a few minutes, I am going to send the signal to implement this transmission and my business here will be finished."

"You don't have to do that, Lano," said JP. "Don't do it."

"Oh, but I do have to do it, Mr Tilsen. You see, I'm getting paid a considerable amount of money for this, with a rather large chunk still to come, and it's taken some years to get to this point. So I am not going to have any more delays now. Just a few more minutes."

He glanced away fleetingly to a phone in his left hand. He held it out at a slight distance, to read it. Why did he do that, thought JP? He flashed through his thoughts… the meeting… the glasses... Lano had put them down onto the desk...

JP realised. He's long sighted. He can't see it close up…

"And then once this is done, I will take care of you and your female companion here. I should have killed you in Panama."

"Well you did try," said JP. "But they bungled it."

"Yes. We got that girl though. You didn't realise, when you went into my office, that there were two sets of cameras. There you were, as plain as day, going through my office. Tisk, tisk."

Lano held the phone out again and briefly looked at it. Clear of Stephanie's head. Dare he try? He looked straight at Stephie. She saw him. He winked at her. She knew what it meant. It was the same as her wink to him a couple of weeks back. She was ready.

Lano was looking at JP again. Still holding the gun against Stephanie's head, ready to shoot in an instant. At that range it would be impossible for him to miss her.

"And in another minute there will be a little bleep and the programming will be complete, and at 10pm I will send the signal."

Lano looked across at the Falcon with disgust on his face.

"You look pathetic. You're almost dead anyway. It's time for you to drop your gun, Mr Tilsen. Now please."

JP made as though to discard the gun as ordered. Then a bleep sounded.

"Ah." Lano smiled, and extended the phone again to glance at it. His thumb was poised over the screen, ready to press it.

It would have to be the shot of his life. An impossible shot.

And the Falcon took it.

In one lightning move JP brought up his gun and fired as it

was still rising. There was a 'phut', the bullet left the Sauer and whizzed by Stephanie's temple so close her hair moved. It hit Lano's left hand, severing the thumb from its base and sending the phone backwards clear into the air. Stephanie was already dropping and turning for it. As Lano screamed he pulled the trigger of his gun, but Stephanie was away. The Falcon fired again.

The last thing he remembered was seeing the top of Jon Lano's head come clean off, and Stephanie Raughton in a horizontal leap behind trying to catch the phone.

Then there was darkness, and the Falcon collapsed onto the ground.

PART SEVEN

AFTERWARDS

34

ALL THE TIME IN THE WORLD

JIM PEREGRINE WOKE up two days later in the American Hospital on 19th Street, a few miles northeast of the Burj Khalifa. Stephanie Raughton was sitting in a chair by his bed. He said later that it had been the best view he had seen for a long time. In fact Stephanie had been by his side for almost the entire time he had been unconscious, save for when she used the bathroom amenities in the adjacent room, which the hospital staff had made available for her along with some basic clothes for her own stay.

Charlie Melton had been in to see him too, unbeknown to JP of course, as had Sir Alastair Crewe, Steve Montague and Vaani Chakrabarti. After he had collapsed, Stephanie recovered her firearm, picked up JP's, removed the spare magazines he always carried in his pocket, locked the doors to the large room and barricaded herself in. She realised that General Elamin had in fact been one of Malekka's people and so decided she couldn't trust anyone. She called Melton, said that Stingray had been primed but not initiated and that she had the phone that Lano was going to use to activate Stingray safe and secure. She said that Lano was dead, and that JP had sustained a knife wound and had collapsed. She did not know if Malekka had the number to initiate Stingray, but to be absolutely sure the best thing was to cut the power to the Communications and Broadcast floors immediately. There was evidence of a major event and there should surely be no problem in shutting off the power as an international emergency safeguard. Melton spoke to Sir Alastair who called the Prime Minister; he immediately placed a call to the Emir of Dubai, Sheikh Mohammed bin Rashid Al Maktoum, and the power was cut within fifteen minutes. Stephanie sat in the darkened room for a further fifteen minutes, tending JP as best she could, using the light from their cell phones, until some American forces arrived from their station at the Port of Jebel Ali twenty miles away, accompanied by personnel from their hosts, in the guise of a top military squad and the Head of the Dubai Police himself, together with emergency ambulances and medics.

It was mutually agreed that the UK should send a crew to disable and remove the Stingray data and software from the AstroGem equipment, which is why the others had arrived from London. The two senior MI6 personnel brought the UAE Government up to date, and enhanced the two countries' good relations still further, while Steve Montague and Vaani Chakrabarti, along with a security-cleared senior officer from AstroGem, ripped all the Stingray information out of the media giant's equipment, after which power was restored to the floors and AstroGem resumed its usual programming, having been off air globally for forty-eight hours. The official explanation was "technical issues". The Company was now under investigation by the Government and Police, as were other elements of Dubai and the UAE, to ensure any connection with Malekka was thoroughly purged.

Once JP was awake and feeling better, on the third day after he was injured, the Emir of Dubai (and ruler of the UAE) visited to thank him and Stephanie in person for their efforts. He stayed a full hour, and a good friendship was born. On the fourth day, JP was discharged from hospital, although his lower back and abdomen were enveloped in bandages tight like a corset and he was still in some discomfort. Stephanie and he returned to their suite in the Burj Al Arab Hotel to discover that they had been upgraded to the Royal suite and that their bill, for however long they chose to stay, had already been taken care of, as indeed had the accounts of the other members of the British contingency. Sadly, though, in view of other work outstanding and JP's own commitments, they decided they should return in the G650, which was still parked at Dubai International Airport, the day after tomorrow.

Stephanie and JP enjoyed a half day in the sun at the Burj Al Arab, a wonderful dinner, a glorious night's sleep, and one whole day again in the sun by the pool. It was what JP needed; his batteries were being recharged and he was recovering well. However, as he was in the middle of selling his apartment in London, he needed to move his last things out and find a new home; and the death of Anna was weighing heavily on him, and of Coco Chavarez. So, after returning to London to wrap things up, they would at last take that holiday. But, rather than St Lucia, they would come back to Dubai to have their long vacation and allow JP time for his full recovery - in spite of what had transpired they both felt confident they would be well looked after and protected, and be very safe in the Emir's city. They had had little time together since Spider and were looking forward to being with each other, especially when nobody was trying to shoot them or blow them up.

On their second and last night, prior to the group's departure back to London, Stephanie and JP decided to have dinner at the Al Muntaha Restaurant on the twenty-seventh floor of the Hotel. They both dressed up for the occasion. Stephanie was dazzling in a full-length off-shoulder sumptuous red brocade dress and overskirt with a lapel and bow at the neckline, embellished below the knee with beaded-sequins. JP was dashing in a black Dolce & Gabbana dinner-jacket and dress shirt with black pearl studs, luxurious deep silk satin bow tie and black Italian dress shoes. They were seated at a private table for two away from other diners, at the farthest corner of the Restaurant, which JP had requested earlier in the day. The meal was exquisite, the champagne and wines magnificent and the view from the restaurant superb.

It seemed that the nightmare Stephanie had endured during Spider had been overcome, and she was once again a beautiful young woman enjoying life. Yet, they were both aware the bad days would continue to return but with the passage of time they would lessen.

JP knew that he had fallen in love with Stephanie, as she had with him, and during the meal each, finally, confessed their feelings to the other. It was at last the happy time they had both wanted. They held hands discreetly from time to time, were lost in each other's eyes frequently, and felt the passion, beauty and desire of their love constantly.

But there was something that had been playing at the back of Stephanie's mind for a while.

"You know, Jimmy," she said with a hint of conspiracy and a teasing smile dancing yet again around her soft vermilion lips, "there is one question I want to ask you, but it's to do with business, and the last thing I want to do is spoil this evening but I must know the answer."

"You mean, after all I've gone through to create this dinner, the planning, the discussion…" she started to giggle… "the dressing up, not to mention the vast expense…"

She giggled more. "What vast expense!" she said, "this is all on the Emir!"

"Well, ok, yes, apart from the vast expense then, after everything else, you want to talk about *business*?!"

"Only one question, I promise."

"Ok," he said with a sigh, resplendent in his false indignation, "but only one question."

She smiled and nodded.

"And I get to ask one question back, ok?"

"Of course, darling, anything. What is it, are you worried about when I said your full frontal picture on television wasn't your best side?!"

"I must say, that was very hurtful indeed, and I have been

shattered for days thinking that you only ever want to see me from the side."

She laughed again.

"Or the back, I suppose."

"Stop, Jimmy!" She shook her head, giggling again. "I can't take any more! Ok, you get to ask me one question. And listen to me, I want to ask mine now."

He sat upright, put on a solemn face and leant in towards her. She moved in too, then spoke, lowering her voice.

"Ok, I want to know. Seriously now. In that room, at the Burj Khalifa, when you fired the first shot…"

"Yes," said JP, his eyes inquisitive.

"Were you aiming at the phone? Or, ummm…" and Stephanie briefly put her elbows on the table, her hands together and tapped her left thumb with the fingers of her other hand.

"Ah," said JP. He thought for a second. "Honestly?"

"Honestly."

"He had a gun touching your pretty head, darling. If I had shot the phone, there wouldn't have been much pain for him and he might still pull his trigger. I thought if he had some pain it would interrupt that process and gain us half a second. So that's what I did. Was it intentional? Yes. Was it lucky? Well…"

"I want to thank you, Falcon. You saved my life. Again."

He smiled.

"Do you know what I learned?"

"No, what?"

"You'd make a great goalkeeper."

She sat back, her mouth open.

"What?!"

"I mean, the way you went for that phone, sweetie! The last thing I remember is seeing you horizontal, off the ground, arms ahead of you, trying to catch that phone."

"Oh I see!" She had recovered her composure. "Yes, I suppose it was rather a good catch, wasn't it?"

"Sure was, my darling," said JP, looking lovingly into her eyes.

She smiled again, then said, "So what was your question?"

"Pardon? Oh, yes. Well, I've been thinking too. We're in a dangerous game. And I don't see how we're ever going to stop it. I mean, you're not going to quit, like you've said to me before, and I'm not going to. It's kind of how we are, isn't it?"

"I guess so," she said with a sigh. "So, yes, I suppose that's just who we are. But we're a pretty good team, aren't we?!"

"We sure are. However, I feel that if we're going to be running around getting into scrapes like this all the time, well, you'd better look after me, and I guess I need to look after you, and we should stick closely together… So my question is…"

And Jim Peregrine brought out a little box from his left jacket pocket, placed it on the table and slid it over to her. Stephanie opened her mouth and let out a little gasp. She smiled, her eyes widened then welled up with tears of joy, and her fingers trembled a little as she opened it.

"…will you marry me, darling?"

≈

The flight back to London in the G650 was uneventful. There followed a couple of days spent on debriefing, on examining and understanding the other elements of the events of the last few days, and in tying up loose ends. The unknown man who had exited Dave Tilsen's flat and who had been photographed by the two private investigators had not been known by anyone else in the building or surrounding area; as Charles Melton had earlier surmised, the man was without doubt Tilsen's killer. CCTV outside the apartment block was not good, they had been unsuccessful in tracking him and the man had disappeared. But, they had his picture and he was now a person of interest to the Police.

A great amount of the effort focused on the surveillance cameras at Gatwick airport as well as some imagery that MI6 had been able to obtain from a couple of cameras in Eastbourne. The latter had picked up images of three persons arriving at the station at the same time as Tilsen, two on his train and one by car. The two were traced back and found to have arrived at Gatwick and been in the arrival's hall at the same time as Tilsen. MI6 also established that one had been behind Tilsen in the queue for tickets and even saw the 'accidental' kick from him at Tilsen's heel, which was deduced as the moment when the tracker was placed on Tilsen's person. Eastbourne caught images of the two men entering a car, the number of which was traced to a hire company at Gatwick, and images were collected not only as the driver hired the car at the counter but also as he entered it in the parking lot. That same person was on the CCTV camera at the pub round the corner from Mary Tilsen's house, and it was established that the team was three-strong. They saw the car arrive back at Eastbourne station later that evening, and one of them get out, buy a ticket behind Tilsen and travel on the same train as Tilsen to London. There, the cameras picked up Tilsen entering a cab and the same man from Eastbourne catching a cab behind him. Then the trail evaporated. However, the method of tailing Tilsen had been established, and once again the Police now had images of three men in whom they were interested, as did MI6.

Detective Chief Inspector Sandy Eastham later confirmed that the latent finger print on the gate to Mrs Tilsen's house belonged to the postman. However, suspect DNA evidence was recovered from Mrs Tilsen's home, which it had been clear was generally kept impeccably clean. Enquiries to establish and locate any other visitors to Mrs Tilsen's house did not produce anyone except a female cleaner, who last cleaned the house the day before her son's visit. Four strands of male head hair were collected. One was identified as belonging to Dave Tilsen; but two were from one other individual (one found upstairs) and the third from another man. The DNA of these men was now, therefore, known.

The surveillance cameras tried to track the men further and did see two return to Gatwick train station and head separately to London, but once again the surveillance faltered and they disappeared.

Various personnel in Brazil, some at Rovalle, some in the police, some at the airport, suddenly disappeared or turned up with their throat cut or a bullet in their head. One was the receptionist at RPD Brazil at Taubaté. As a result of aggressive tracking, Major Ernesto Savedra finally caught Denise Oliveira, in Brasilia, the capital of the country, as she was preparing to board a flight - an Airbus - to Argentina. In return for a reduction of what was going to be a long prison sentence, Ms Oliveira began to sing like the proverbial canary. She identified the two men whom she had instructed to murder Jorge Monterroso and they were caught. She identified two men, already found dead, who had been in the car which forced Savedra and JP off the road in an attempt to kill them following their meeting at Rovalle with Edson Ramos. Oliveira admitted what Savedra already knew, that it was she who booked the transport of consignments to San Francisco, always through the same Iranian-owned shipping line. It was also she who covertly had been sending the specifications for each ADS-B board to Amsterdam for a replica to be made, with the additional coding, then transported to Panama ready for the switch. It was this that Monterroso had accidentally discovered, and for which he had been silenced. All were awaiting trial.

In Panama, various persons working at ISTRAS suffered the same fate and were killed by unknown third parties, presumed to be executioners hired by Malekka to close any open loops. Backed firmly and publicly by the Government the security forces moved in, the company was impounded, its assets frozen and its Canal licence revoked, ensuring ISTRAS met a swift conclusive demise.

Eight hundred and fifty miles and one and a half hours into its flight, Air Force One had received the critical warning from the CIA of imminent attack at 9.30pm Dubai time, which was fifteen minutes or so after JP had spoken to Charlie Melton from the Upper Lobby of the Burj Al Arab. The Captain and co-Pilot immediately switched off the ADS-B transponder, pulled its breaker and one of the crew entered the computer area of the *Jupiter 300B*, found the PCB board and yanked it out of the aircraft system. In the meantime, the Captain decided to divert at once to the Johnston Atoll which at that time was one hundred and eighty miles to the north. The President was surprised neither her sanction nor opinion had been sought over this action but was politely told by her Chief-of-Staff that the Captain of the aircraft outranked her in this instance even though she was Commander-in-Chief, and he had therefore proceeded regardless. The Atoll was deserted at the time; Air Force One overflew the runway at low speed and minimum altitude, the Captain decided the landing could be made and that no alternative area was needed, and the *Jupiter* made a safe emergency landing. The aircraft was on the ground within thirty minutes of its diversion. POTUS's military escort circled the Atoll on high alert. Once the action at the Burj Khalifa had concluded and the power to the Communications and Broadcast floors cut, it was deemed safe for Air Force One to resume its journey. The Captain took off, the cruise speed was increased considerably, though kept within its (classified) maximum to make up for the lost one hour and a half of diversion, and the President arrived at Cairns on time, eight hours after departure from Honolulu, at 10am

Australian Eastern Standard Time on the morning of 8th May, the date in the year on which the Battle of the Coral Sea had ended in 1942.

The body of Anna Kepling was returned to Russia to be laid to rest beside her father. At the invitation of General Alexander Bortnikov, the Director of the FSB, Sir Alastair Crewe - the two SIS heads, although on opposing sides, had known each other for almost thirty years - led the British contingency of MI6 personnel who had participated at Dubai, along with Jim Peregrine and Steve Montague, in attending her funeral. General Bortnikov announced in the service that Anna had posthumously been promoted to the rank of Major, and furthermore that the President had made her father a Hero of Russia, the highest honorary title that can be bestowed on an individual in the Russian Federation.

In England, Mary Tilsen's body was finally recovered from the English Channel. They attended first David Tilsen's funeral service, at which Charles Melton spoke of Dave's quality of work and devotion to duty, but added a number of anecdotes of their time together in the military, all couched in general and vague terms as security was an ongoing concern. Then there was Mary Tilsen's funeral which everyone also attended, including Bilko, who although very happy with his new master and life, somehow understood the event and displayed a sadness during the ceremony. Sir Alastair Crewe spoke eloquently, recounting in particular Dame Mary's extraordinary courage and service to her country. She was buried next to her husband and adjacent to her son on the other side. At the end of the burial, Bilko resisted Sir Alastair's tug on the lead to go; instead, the dog pulled forwards and took him to the foot of his mistress's grave, and lay down. So Sir Alastair stood quietly again with him. It took thirty minutes and would have been longer had Sir Alastair not lifted Bilko up and carried him away. If a dog was ever able to cry and express grief, said Sir Alastair later, they had all just witnessed it.

The Stingray incident wound down. It was officially codenamed *Decoy 17* by MI6, in quiet deference to Dave and Mary Tilsen.

Finally, JP and Stephanie were able to leave everything behind and make their escape for their holiday and plan their futures. Stephanie joined JP at his suite at Claridge's, but for one final morning, before departing to Dubai later that day, they returned to JP's flat off Fulham Road in Chelsea, which he had now sold and from which he was due to vacate within hours. The media had discovered the Falcon's name; the story had broken five days ago and for a while JP became an unwilling celebrity in absence, as he was abroad in Russia and couldn't be found for comment. The story fizzled out. Nevertheless as a precaution the police had been posted at JP's flat ever since as a security measure. The property was almost empty; everything had already been removed to storage save for a few boxes that Stephanie and JP were loading themselves in the car downstairs in the garage, and JP's old desk and leather chair that had belonged to his father. That would be the last thing to go in about an hour, when the final van arrived to take it.

He sat thoughtfully for a while. Then he opened the desk drawer, took his cheque book out and his fountain pen, and a sheet of writing paper. He wrote an address on an envelope. It began, 'Colonel Hector Alessandro', and from his phone he copied the address that Charlie Melton had given him a day or so ago. On the sheet of paper, he wrote:

For your dream
And, for Coco

He opened his bank book, filled out a cheque, tore it off and used a paperclip to attach it to the top of the page. He took one of his business cards from his wallet and slipped it under the paperclip, on top of the cheque.

One side of the card was blank. On the other side, was a picture. It was of a bird. Of a falcon. The fastest falcon. A Peregrine Falcon.

He folded the paper, put it in the envelope, ripped the strip off and pressed the flap down; then he reached for his stamp book and stuck some on, together with a blue airmail label.

He placed the remaining contents of the desk into the small packing box on the top and sealed it. As he finished, Stephanie came upstairs and walked into the front room.

"All set?" said JP.

"Yes, those other boxes are in the car. I'll go and freshen up before we leave."

"Well as I know that can take another twenty minutes," he teased, going over to her, "I guess you're not ready at all then are you!"

"I'd like to look my best for when we go, Mr Peregrine. You have a problem with that?"

"Nope, not at all, future Mrs Peregrine."

He was close by her now, and they kissed.

"Ok," he smiled, "I'll get the car and park it on the other side of the road. Then I'm going to post a letter, I'll be back in a few minutes, will you lock up?"

"Ok, do I get to drive your Jag?"

"Sure, if you like, I'll leave the keys in the car. Just don't hit anything as we go!" he said cheekily and smiled at the comment that came back.

He went down to the garage, yanked the door up and walked out onto the pavement to talk to one of the two armed policemen from the Specialist Operations directorate of the Metropolitan Police, on protective security for them at the building. They stood either side of the steps leading up to the two large white pillars and the front door.

"We're about ready, Giles. I'm going to pull the car out and park on the other side, seeing as how there's no room here. Then we'll be off."

"Very good, sir," came the reply.

JP got in the driver's seat and started the engine. He backed the Jag over the pavement, reversed it up the road a few yards, then forwards and right onto the other side, where there was a convenient space between cars in the bays opposite. He stepped out of the car onto the pavement, tighter that side of the road, that ran alongside the low white walls sprouting short cast iron Victorian Fleur-de-Lis railings bordering the houses.

The post box was round the corner and left at the top on the main road. He followed the bend in the road, and could see the busy traffic crossing each way at right angles at the end. He walked up thoughtfully, with the flaps of his jacket held back, hands stuffed in his pockets. Two million dollars should do it, he thought; the Colonel had said it would need one point two, so there would be a little over just in case. He hoped Alessandro would like it; and the theatre was beautiful, for sure. As Coco had been, he thought sadly. She would have liked it too.

He turned the corner at the top, reached the red Royal Mail pillar box and took out his letter. He looked down at it reflectively, flapping it against the other hand, then dropped it in.

That was one good thing done.

JP started to walk back. He turned right at the corner into his road, his thoughts already again on Stephanie, the plane flight, the hotel… Time together for themselves at last. He reached the bend in the road, and passed the small boutique hotel on the other side.

An elderly man sitting in the bay window watched him go. The man put down the newspaper that he hadn't been reading.

From his vantage point he had a clear view down the length of the road. He had seen the Jag reverse out and pull onto the other side; he had watched the Falcon make his errand. The elderly man rose, put on his coat and shuffled out of the hotel, a walking stick in his hand. He turned left, towards the Falcon's flat.

He saw the girl exit, walk across the road and get into the driver's seat of the car, then watched discreetly as the Falcon, whose name he now knew was Jim Peregrine, climb into the passenger side and close the door. He made a mental note of the registration number. The car's engine gunned and it drove slowly away.

Once the car was out of sight, the elderly man stopped walking. He could go to his room now and check out. He would dispose of his disguise on the way home. As he turned to shuffle back the way he had come, the sunlight caught the side of his face. A heavy scar trickled down from the left eye across the cheek to the corner of his mouth. The eyes were cold, dark; almost black.

He had been successful. He knew the final information. Now he only had to choose where, and when. He already knew how.

The man smirked.

He had time.

All the time in the world.

*** THE END ***

AUTHOR'S NOTE

I had the idea of *Decoy 17* as the sequel to *Spider 2-3* in 2016, and started to develop it. The action of deflecting the horizontal stabilizer had already become part of the story and was being worked on long before the two tragic crashes of the Boeing 737 Max aircraft on October 29, 2018, and March 10, 2019, which were caused as a result, apparently, of the MCAS system and the computer's downward deflection of the horizontal stabilizer. This book in no way imitates or is derived from any parts of those horrendous events, and in fact is published later than intended as a result.

The ADS-B NextGen system is real, and the reader will be pleased to know that it has been safely implemented and is now operational. The concept of its receiving a standard radio signal or transmission as portrayed in this book comes from my pilot training days many years ago. From time to time one of my flight instructors would tune in the aircraft's ADF/NDB navigation system to a local radio station and play its music into my headphones, leaving this student a slightly more challenging environment in which to concentrate and function. I remembered that experience and applied it to the NextGen ADS-B navigation system in *Decoy 17*.

I look forward to seeing you again with the next adventure for the Falcon, *The Fifth Rubric*.

Robert Vallier

www.robertvallier.com

The Falcon will return

in

The Fifth Rubric

The *Teatro Nacional de Panamá,* prior to its restoration.
Photographed from the stage by the Author.